CASH MARTIN

Cash Martin

CONVICTED

D1462030

American Publishing

Copyright © 2000 by Cash Martin

All rights reserved. No part of this book may be
reproduced in any form or by any electronic or mechanical
means including information storage and retrieval systems
without permission in writing from the publisher, except by
a reviewer, who may quote brief passages in a review.

This work is a fiction. Any reference to historical events, to
real people or to real locales are intended only to give the
fiction a sense of reality and authenticity. Names,
characters, places and incidents either are the product of the
author's imagination or used fictitiously, and their
resemblance, if any, to real life counterparts is entirely
coincidental.

Library of Congress Catalog Card Number: 99-97001

ISBN 0-967720-90-7

Published by
American Publishing
761 Blue Hollow Road
Mount Airy, North Carolina 27030

Printed in the United States of America

In CONVICTED, Ben Down is a lawyer whose world comes crumbling down around him. He must fight to save his client who has been charged with a murder she did not commit. Moreover, as he becomes entangled with the powerful forces who have assassinated the Vice President of the United States, he must wage a war of his own. He must confront the demons in his own life that threaten to destroy him. Finally his efforts to save his client become a battle to save himself.

Author's Note

For as long as I can remember, I wanted to be a lawyer. The seed for this great desire was planted long ago by my father and nurtured throughout the years by my family. One of my earliest memories is of my grandmother and me as we played Perry Mason, one of the early television lawyers. I was Perry Mason and she was the judge. I have pursued this dream all of my life and I have not been disappointed.

After I became a lawyer, I went into the private practice of law for a brief stint then became a prosecuting attorney for several years. For over twenty years I have been a trial judge. From this vantage point I have had the best seat in the courthouse to watch lawyers. We tend to think that the great lawyers are the ones we see on television but I have learned that there are great lawyers in every courthouse.

The great lawyers have several things in common. This is true whether they are courtroom lawyers or office lawyers. All of them have highly developed skills. The best skill, and without a doubt the most entertaining to watch, involves taking a truly adverse factual situation and turning it into a positive force for the lawyer's client. Many times I have watched as one side developed a fact that appeared on its face to sink the other side then I watched in amazement as the opposing attorney crafted the nasty little fact, putting it in a different light, so that it helped the client.

Another thing that distinguishes the great lawyers is knowledge. They study hard, they work hard at mastering the basic and the esoteric in the law. They are just as vigorous at ferreting out the facts of their case. This part is drudgery for most but is exciting and invigorating for the great attorney. Knowledge is power in the office and the courtroom and they know it.

The dividing line between the mediocre and the best lawyers has to be persistence. The great lawyer will not give up. A loss is never a loss. It is merely a stumbling block on the way to victory. The force that drives that dedication and perseverance is the belief that the client has been done some injustice and only the attorney can right the perceived wrong. The great ones truly believe.

Just as I have enjoyed the professional side of the law, I have enjoyed the personal side. Each attorney brings a personality and a style to the practice of law that makes it always interesting and occasionally exciting. Courage by the yard and enthusiasm by the foot abound. Likewise the human element including all of its foibles, idiosyncrasies, peccadilloes and vices yields very interesting court sessions. The drama and the comedy have entertained me all of these years. Above all I always enjoyed the attorney rising to the occasion over personal adversity. I saw it numerous times and admired the effort.

This novel is a tribute to the attorneys. For my first offering I have written about one of those great lawyers who, shall we say, is somewhat down on his luck.

CHAPTER ONE

Earlier in the day the Vice President's plane had landed at New Hanover International Airport in Wilmington, North Carolina. The press had given little attention to the Vice President's plan to vacation with his family on Figure Eight Island. Except for one local newspaper reporter who had covered the Secret Service's preliminary investigation of security at the airport and the Island, no one had given it much thought. All of that would change dramatically within the next few hours.

Vice President William Keynard Anderson and his wife Marilyn had three children, two girls and one boy, all of whom were teenagers. Extensive arrangements had been made to spend the week with his old college friend, Bill Feinstein, his wife and their two daughters. As the family of the Vice President, they had received little publicity during his first term but as they approached the end of the second term and with the likeihood that he would be the nominee of the party for President within the next year, they found it increasingly difficult to do the most mundane things without media scrutiny. Both families had remained close over the years and with the knowledge that this was very likely the last vacation before the intense attention their lives would receive, everyone had looked forward with anticipation to seeing each other at Figure Eight again.

The flight and landing had been uneventful and except for several photographers who had slipped past airport security and made it to the reserved area of the tarmac, the arrival itself was hardly noticed. As they approached the waiting Lincoln Navigator for the drive to Feinstein's beach house, the Vice President had the Secret Service agent in charge to allow the photographers to approach. He hoped to satiate the media's desire for some coverage of the second family's last vacation before the election. By giving them access, he expected that they would honor his request, as they usually did, to give the family a little more breathing room to enjoy the beautiful Carolina coast and the hospitality of his old friend.

Figure Eight Island was a short drive from the airport. The entourage with the sleek black Navigator sandwiched between the government vehicles caught the attention of several motorists who blinked their lights and strained to get a view of the Vice President. When they drove past the guard station at the entrance to the Island, the security guard stood and saluted somewhat awkwardly. The agent driving the Navigator smiled and nodded his head as they passed.

When the vehicles pulled up in front of the huge pink stucco beach house, Bill Feinstein and his wife waited with several of the agents. At Feinstein's request and with the Vice President's acquiescence, the Feinsteins had arranged a brief reception. The gathering involved several of Feinstein's neighbors, many of whom had already met the Vice President when he had swung through North Carolina and South Carolina stumping for the President during his bid for reelection four years earlier.

While the vehicles were being unloaded, the two families exchanged pleasantries. Afterwards Bill Feinstein led them through the house out into the backyard where the guests had assembled. After recognizing several of the guests and shaking hands, the Vice President patiently waited through Feinstein's introduction which ended with " . . . and I give you the next President of the United States William Keynard Anderson."

"Thank you, Bill," he responded and assumed a position with the blue sky and the white-capped waves of the Atlantic Ocean behind him. "On behalf of Marilyn, Tari, Brittany and Mike, I want to let you know how much we appreciate your hospitality and your warm welcome here today."

He sucked in the salt air and obviously enjoyed the wind as it tossed his single shock of hair back and forth over his forehead. Not being able to resist the astute politician he was, he never missed an opportunity to spread the message that all was well and the future was bright.

"I know you didn't come to hear any speeches. In fact I was specifically informed by Bill to bring my golf clubs, which I have faithfully done, so that you may have a new victim and give Bill Feinstein some relief."

Several in the audience laughed. One called back, "Mr. Vice President, it will take more than the might of the United States government to get any relief for Bill Feinstein. He deserves everything he gets."

As the laughter died down, the Vice President continued, "I do want to share with you a few things. First, we are here for a vacation. I look forward to seeing each of you and enjoying the bounty of this great land and renewing our friendship. We live in an unprecedented period of peace and prosperity. And I promise you that I will do just as you know I will. I am taking all of the credit and none of the blame."

A little more laughter and a sprinkling of applause spread across the audience. The Vice President pushed the unruly shock of hair back and assumed his presidential pose with one hand out in front of him clinched in a light fist. "Secondly, I want you to know that I believe in working hard and playing hard. We are going to play hard this week. And next week we are going back to Washington to work hard for you."

He grinned sheepishly and said, "The fact that I will be taking a lot of your money with me from the golf course should be no reflection on the quality of our government. After all you can give it to me now or wait until we take it on April 15th."

Following several good-natured boos, he turned to a different subject. "Let me get serious for a moment. As many of you know, the Chinese premier will be arriving in this country from Beijing next week. It is important that we press the issue of human rights and the mistreatment of dissidents by the Chinese government."

He put his hand on Bill Feinstein's shoulder. "When Bill and I were in college together at the University of Virginia, one of our best friends was Doun Jae Bing who was at that time a student in the United States from Peking. Few people have moved me as much as Doun. He loved this country. He loved the liberty he had here. He loved the freedom to speak, to worship, to gather, to dissent. All of those things that we take for granted were denied to him when he returned home. He valiantly spoke out against the oppression and the restriction of personal freedom. His bravery . . . his voice died along with so many others on Tianemen Square. Unless we pick up the banner and carry it forward, unless we speak when others cannot, his death, indeed his very life, will have been in vain. As long as there is strength within me, I will not let his hopes perish, I will not let the efforts to obtain simple freedoms for the Chinese people be extinguished."

Extensive applause erupted. He spoke above the din of clapping hands and thundering waves, "Not now. Not ever. And I hope that you will support me and join me by doing all that you can to see that others enjoy the freedoms that we have."

The Vice President paused for a moment then halfheartedly apologized. "Well, I did not mean to get so serious but when I believe in something, as Marilyn will tell you, I am passionate about it."

He cleared his throat and smiled at Marilyn. As she put her arm around him, he called out, "Now let's have a party. Let's vacation."

*   *   *

That night two dark figures dressed like Ninja warriors waded across the inlet between Shell Island at Wrightsville Beach and Figure Eight Island. With its shifting course the inlet that had initially divided the two barrier islands off of the North Carolina coast had narrowed and moved so that only a small stream of water divided the two. Now Figure Eight, originally a secured and highly restricted private island, had become somehat of an adjunct of Wrightsville Beach which was open to the public. The walk at low tide could be accomplished in as little as five minutes.

After they reached the shoreline on the opposite side of the inlet, they immediately entered the line of sand dunes bearded with sea oats. The heavy growth that ran in a ring around the Island offered concealment. They slowly, surreptitiously manuevered along the base of the small dunes from the marsh toward the ocean side of the Island. They encountered little resistance as the growth was sparse in most places. After tearing through a protracted stretch of nettles that thrived in the brine that developed in the lower parts of the dune line, they stopped and unloaded one of their backpacks.

The larger of the two quietly ascended the dune and reconnoitered the area. During the breaks between the clouds, there was enough light so that he observed that he was within two hundred feet of a large beach house. Keeping his head just at the line of the dune, he waited and watched. All of the interior lights were off in the house except for the front porch and a hall light that shone through the upstairs window. He counted nine vehicles in the front parking area of the house.

Near the vehicles he spotted one man standing at the front entrance. At the rear of the house, he watched carefully. After a short time, he saw the fire in a lit cigarette moving in the shadows at the back of the house. Satisfied that he had seen all that he was going to see, he slowly slid down the dune and returned to the other man.

When he returned, he drew a square in the sand and marked nine lines in the front of the box. Then again without speaking, he pointed to the front of the box and raised one finger. Next he put a dot in the sand at the back of the box and raised one finger.

The shorter of the two dug into his backpack and withdrew a small canvas case. He crawled, GI Joe style, until he reached the back side of the crest of a larger dune. Upon reaching the top, he located the house then pulled night vision binoculars from the case. He slowly swept the front of the house with the binoculars. He made out a figure by the front door and another who appeared to be sleeping in the driver's seat of a van. Except for those two the front yard appeared to be clean.

By the side of the house nearest the dune, he observed movement. It was barely discernable but he stayed focused. As the irridescent figure became visible, he saw the outline of a man approximately one hundred and fifty feet away. He followed the figure up to the side of the house where it bacame stationary, then turned his attention to the house itself. Starting with the lower left window and working his way slowly across the house then repeating the same procedure on the second floor, he studied each window carefully for any movement. Observing none, he looked for the man at the back of the house. In the backyard he saw the outline of a man sitting near a small tree in the line between the yard and the undergrowth. He studied the figure carefully. The figure faced the ocean with his head down and except for a slight heaving up and down, did not move. He turned the binoculars back to the front of the house and repeated the same procedure. Finally he returned to the figure at the back of the house. It had not moved from the siting on the initial sweep.

After studying the tree line and its connection to the line of dunes, he memorized the backyard and the location of each thing. He made a mental note from point to point: tree, chair, table, wall, grill and back door. He compressed the binoculars, encased them and slipped down the sand back to his counterpart at the base of the dune.

When he approached, the larger one started to speak. Before he could say anything, the other one put his hand over his mouth and pointed to the box in the sand. While he put the binoculars in the backpack, he pointed to the nine lines in front of the box and held his finger up indicating one. Next he pointed to the front of the box and held up one. Then he pointed to the side of the box and held up one finger. Finally he pointed to the back of the box then moved out some distance and put his finger down making a dimple in the sand. He bumped the larger one on the arm and made a motion with his hands together beside of his head indicating "sleeping".

"Three more," the larger one whispered.

The shorter one put his hand over the larger one's mouth. "Shhhhh." He was quiet and emphatic. He pointed to the box and put three dimples in the sand inside the box.

The shorter one raised his sleeve and pressed his watch. As the face became luminescent, he held it so both of them could see. The time: 1:30.

The shorter one dug in his backpack again and removed night goggles. He slid them on and held them on his forehead. He pointed at the other man and indicated "stay". When he determined that he had been understood, he slipped the goggles down over his eyes and made several adjustments. He dropped to his knees and started crabbing along the edge of the dune. When he had worked his way to the tree line along the yard of the house, he positioned himself so that he could see the figure facing the beach at the back of the house. The figure had not moved. He looked for the figure at the side of the house. Locating him some forty feet out from the house, he slipped down to the ground and out into the open yard. He inched along to a wall about twenty-five feet from the house. When he reached the wall, he quietly checked both figures. No movement.

Concealed by the wall the dark clad figure lay quietly listening for any sounds and checking repeatedly between himself and the perimeter for any movement. Again satisfied that he had not been discovered, he crawled toward the house. Upon reaching the door he lay still and listened. Nothing. He reached up, checked the door and found it, as he expected, locked. His hand slid down the side of his leg and unzipped a small pocket. He removed the two-prong pick and raised up enough to work the lock. When it yielded, it clicked loudly enough to startle him. He dropped down and waited for a response. Nothing.

After a couple of minutes passed, he pocketed the pick. He reached up, turned the knob and opened the door about half of an inch. He again lay on the steps and with his hand moved the door slightly to determine if there would be any squeaking. Hearing none he moved the door wide enough for entry. He immediately slipped inside and closed the door gently behind him.

The door opened directly into the kitchen. He had memorized the layout of the house from the architect's drawing he had previously been given and knew that his destination, the bedrooms, was on the second floor. Again he waited and listened. Continuing to use night vision, he moved to the hall and slowly edged upward on the steps. He stopped before reaching the top of the steps. Hesitating he listened for any sounds and looked for a guard. Seeing and hearing no one, he moved onto the second floor hall and crept to the larger bedroom.

He assumed without knowing that the children would be in the smaller bedrooms and the adults would be in the larger bedrooms at either end of the hall. He opened the bedroom door and carefully scrutinized the two individuals on the bed. Even with night vision, it was clear that the two were not the ones he was looking for. Too short and too heavy.

Again he entered the hallway and moved silently to the large bedroom at the end of the hall. He opened the door, entered and watched the man and woman in the bed. He felt sure that this was the room and these were the two. Upon removing the goggles, he waited for his eyes to adjust to the darkness. While he waited, he listened intently to the sounds in the room. When the man's body turned over in the bed, he saw the outline of his silhouette. Confirmation. He had found his man.

He reached into his vest pockets and retrieved two large plastic containers. He found the small switch on the side of one of the containers, easily depressed once, and pulled the small antenna to its full length. He laid them directly under the bed beneath the man.

When he exited the room, he heard movement downstairs. He froze. The movement ceased then he heard muffled sounds that he believed to be a conversation. The voices ceased. Then he heard a few more steps. He strained to hear for several minutes; hearing only his heartbeats, he moved to the stairway and descended slowly. When he reached the first floor, he put on the night goggles and surveyed the hallway before entering it. He could see a man's leg extending from a chair through the doorway of the den at the other end of the hallway. With his eyes fixed on the den, he backed slowly down the hallway, turned through the kitchen and carefully worked the back door again.

When he went out, he invested another five minutes in traversing the yard. At the tree line, he stayed low and crab walked through the brush to the dunes. At the dunes he rested for thirty seconds then continued in the same manner until he joined the larger Ninja.

He gave a thumb's up indicating that he had accomplished his goal. They packed the backpacks and retraced their steps to the inlet. Squatting they checked for any sound or sign that they had been discovered before they left the dune line to walk to the swash. Nothing.

They walked to the stream and slowly waded across. After walking the short distance back to Shell Island, they hugged the shadows made by a series of condominiums. They worked their way down the beach toward the parking lot. They inspected the lot carefully before they came up into the street lights. Although there were several cars in the lot, no one could be seen. They approached the old Dodge they had parked there earlier, unloaded their gear into the back seat, and got in. Both of them pulled their black covers off and stuffed them under the front seats.

The larger one cranked the car and pulled toward the parking lot exit. The smaller one fumbled through the gear in the backseat until he pulled out a tiny transmitter.

"Pull up to point so we see Figure Eight," the smaller one said in broken English.

The larger one pulled out of the lot to the right and drove the short distance to the circle at the end of Shell Island. When he reached the point, he stopped. Both of them stared intently into the darkness across the inlet and marsh toward Figure Eight Island. They could see the outline of houses in the dim light and could tell generally where the house they had just left was located.

The smaller one lifted the antenna on the transmitter and turned the control knob to "On". He looked over at the driver and said, "You sure we be back 'cross bridge toward Wilmington in less than five minutes?"

The driver nodded his head and pointed toward the transmitter.

As he lifted the cap from the toggle switch and pressed it over once, a thunderous explosion erupted from the second floor of the house on Figure Eight Island. Fire billowed from the room and debris rained down around that end of the house.

The car backed up and turned toward the drive back to Wilmington. The driver laughed and said, "Hell to the Chief."

The smaller one pointed toward the house on Figure Eight Island and replied, " *Hao*!"

CHAPTER TWO

In Ogden, a small town near Wilmington, Wanda Stickley awoke from a deep sleep. Her eyes tried to focus but found everything blurry. After a while she partially rolled over and tried to get her eyes to adjust to the clock beside the bed. Finally she saw the hands: 2:37 a.m. She lay there listening. Something had awoken her she thought, something loud. She started to get up, could not and drifted back to sleep.

This time when she opened her eyes, she knew something was not right. She tried to see the shimmering hands on the clock. Finally the two blurs connected. It was quarter until three. She listened. There was something yet there was nothing. Then Wanda remembered the boom. It was loud but a long way off. A distant roar like a lion deep in a jungle or like a . . . . She fell asleep again.

It seemed as though a second had passed when she was jolted awake. Maybe it was Jeremy she thought. Still groggy she focused her attention in the direction of Jeremy's room. It was quiet. She listened again for several long seconds but nothing. The clock indicated 3:13. After a few moments she decided to get up and check on Jeremy. She lifted herself up onto her elbows. Maybe she would go to the bathroom on the way back and . . . . Her head nodded as she slid back into twilight.

Pizza, she thought. I have got to quit eating pizza so late. The last thing she remembered before she had drifted back into a deep sleep was the clock. She checked it again: 3:28. Her mind was flooded with a caleidiscope of images: the boom, Jeremy, pizza, the parade in Ogden.

She propped herself up in bed and rolled to her side. She listened again as she hugged her pillow with one arm and partially stretched the other. She was sure there was something but could not put her finger on it. No sound from Jeremy who was down the hall. No sound except her breathing. She squinted to make out the room in the darkness. Except a slight night light from the clock face that outlined the top of the night stand, the room was different shades of darkness.

This time she stayed awake. 3:30 Too early to get up and too awake to go back to sleep, she lay there in the darkness thinking about the previous day. The parade, the marching bands, the clowns. It seemed just as real as when it happened. Jeremy smiled at her as he walked past with the other Scouts. At thirteen he was somewhat large for his age and looked a little gangly in his uniform. He was all boy, she knew that. She smiled back as he pretended to trip over his own feet.

Jeremy was her only child and the only child she would ever have. He was a great kid. He was smart: A's and B's at Ogden Junior High. He was athletic. His interest in sports had made her the quintessential soccer mom. Every Saturday was planned with soccer, basketball and baseball as the seasons changed. Jeremy was good at each one and each year he visibly improved.

True, she thought, he was mischievous. High spirited and rambunctious. That was true too. She remembered the semi-urgent call to come to a meeting with his teacher during the parent-teacher conference week. It seems that, to use the teacher's term, he was most "devilish" when the substitute teacher was there. If he was not slipping out of class without permission or leaving crawling surprises in her seat, he was entertaining the class with his, to use the teacher's phrase again, "juvenile antics". Even with all of the nonsense though, he was easy enough to rein in. There was no harm in him and at most he was irritating. What thirteen year old wasn't, she thought.. A serious talk about what was expected of him had done the trick. Jeremy was mischief on two feet but he was not mean. He was nothing like his father. Thank God for that, she thought.

Wanda yawned and slid down in the bed. As she pulled her pillow into a bunch beneath her head, she tried to go back to sleep. Thoughts continued to rush through as though she were at a busy corner trying to cross through speeding traffic. She thought back to what had awakened her. She was sure it was a loud noise but a distant loud noise. Since it was not in or near the house, she felt there was no need to be immediately concerned. She would find out about it later.

The Ogden parade. She could not stop thinking about it. It should have been a great day and would have been a great day as usual if it were not for cruel people. The sun was shining on one of those glorious summer afternoons in Ogden. Occasionally a whiff of ocean salt could be picked up from the easy breeze. Jeremy had just completed the march down Main Street with his Scout troop and was coming back up the sidewalk to find her. The crowd was beginning to thin somewhat and people were walking in two's and three's as they made their way back to their cars and trucks. Jeremy was in front of his friends walking backwards and pretending to juggle his hat, billfold and a crumpled piece of paper. She was getting ready to call his name to get his attention when he bumped into three men who were coming out of the Longhorn Tavern.

"Hey, boy. Watch where you're goin'," one of three grumbled. He was redfaced and wobbly on his feet. "What's wrong with you anyway, boy?"

Jeremy backed up and started to pick up his hat and billfold. One of the two who was with redface beat Jeremy to the billfold and retrieved it from the sidewalk. Before he could say anything, the redface spoke again. "Well, what about it? You need a whoopen, you little yard ape."

"No, sir," Jeremy stammered. "I'm really sorry. I should have been watchin' where I was goin'. I, uh, I . . . ."

"Hey, don't I know you? Sure I do. You are Ralph Stickley's boy. You must be Little Stick. Are you Ralph's boy?"

Jeremy's eyes dropped toward the ground. He did not say anything.

"Sure you are," the redface blared. "Ralph was, hell, he is one of the meanest pieces of crap I ever knew. He tried to be all high and mighty and run around with all of those big shots but he was nothin'. Crap. He mighta hung a tie around his neck but he warn't nothin'. He was a sneakin' no good. He'd put a knife in ya' just to watch you die. I'm gonna kick his butt up to his neck. You tell him, boy."

"Sir, I can't . . . ."

Redface had worked himself into a lather. He was not taking "no" for an answer. He drew back to slap Jeremy.

"That's enough," Wanda yelled somewhat breathlessly as she approached. "Leave him alone."

Redface turned to see who was making all of the noise. As he did, Wanda stopped between Jeremy and him. She grabbed the billfold from the second drunk. "You ought to be ashamed of yourselves. Three of you picking on a kid. If I were a man, I would make you regret that you even thought about hitting my child. I may do it anyway."

She turned to look at Jeremy. He was trying to hold back his tears but he could not. When she reached for his hand, he bolted and ran away.

As she attempted to follow him down the street, redface yelled after her. "Now look what you've done. You've made the Little Stick cry." Redface burst out laughing followed by his two drinking buddies.

Jeremy might have been Ralph Stickley's child and might have looked a lot like Ralph, she thought, but he was nothing like his father. Ralph. How many times had she woke up thinking about Ralph? Most of the time she was wondering how she could have loved him so much and how he could have treated Jeremy and her so mean when both of them showed him they loved him so much. Evil. That is what it had to be.

She had adored Ralph when she first saw him. She was a freshman and he was a senior at New Hanover High. In fact he was the pride of New Hanover High. A double threat, he was good at football and basketball. All of the girls were crazy about him. Although she watched him whenever he was around, he had paid no attention to her. It was not until he dropped out of college that they became an item. He came back to Ogden and worked for his father in the tobacco warehouse business. He was good at it; he made money, a lot of money. Wanda half-smiled as she thought about the rides in his '57 Chevy. Ralph was wild even then but he was nice, really nice to her.

They married and it seemed the honeymoon would never end. His business flourished. He made friends and became very active in local politics. After a couple of years he financed the purchase of his own warehouse and engaged in some speculative beach property development. He talked of purchasing a warehouse in Florence, South Carolina to expand his operation. In this way he had hoped to get in the tobacco market earlier in the year since South Carolina typically ran a few weeks ahead of his North Carolina warehouse.

When he cut the ribbon celebrating the grand opening of the new warehouse, it was big news in Florence and Wilmington. He received a lot of publicity from his attempt to join the two markets and when he was successful, he was hot property.

As his stock in trade went up so did his political credibility. Politicians came knocking. When they did, Ralph made sure the press was there to mark the event with a front page photograph and an accompanying article. Speculation began to circulate that Ralph might run for office himself. Instead of becoming a candidate though, he raised a treasure chest of campaign contributions for various State and national offices. He reached the pinnacle of his business and political career when he was promoted as an ambassador to Costa Rica purportedly because of his knowledge of the international tobacco markets, but more realistically because of his contributions to various war chests.

Ralph was a lot like a shooting star, she thought. His rise was meteoric. It was a flash across the southeastern North Carolina sky. Those were the heydays for them. It seemed that the good luck would never end for Wilmington's golden boy but then things changed. His fall was just as unbelievable and just as fast.

He always drank a lot but it never got out of hand, at least, not until his father died. As his drinking worsened, his grip on his budding financial empire slipped. Farmers who had been faithful to the Stickleys went elsewhere. They could not tolerate Ralph's mood swings and his temper. The banks that had swung their doors open to the next generation of Stickleys began to put foreclosure pressure on due to late payment, then nonpayment.

Then Jeremy was born. Ralph began staying out late and coming in drunk. Feeling ignored and worse, feeling that Ralph was neglecting Jeremy, she demanded better treatment for both of them. That was the first time Ralph had hit her. It would not be the last. The violence and anger escalated over the next several months.

At the same time he began losing contracts at the warehouse. Buyers went elsewhere. He lost all control when they took the warehouse in Florence away. His next stop was cocaine. Then the cocaine never stopped. He raided the assets at the Wilmington warehouse. His business partners in the land development scheme sued him. He was barred from even going on the premises of the development. When he failed to show up for the trial, the courts entered a judgment against him in the amount of $375,000 for fraudulent conduct in enticing the plaintiffs to invest in wetlands that could not be developed. Then the bank that had financed the warehouse in Wilmington began making noises. When he threatened bankruptcy, the noise quietened a bit.

The ambassadorship slipped out the window. Politicians stayed away in droves. Although he still had contacts in high places, they were hard to find. Just as he had become hot property on the way up, he had become even hotter on the way down. He was a time bomb getting ready to go off and no one wanted to be involved in the fall out.

His cocaine use escalated. Underwritten by some of his inheritance from his father that he was able to secrete from his creditors and by surreptitious sales of assets of the warehouse business, he was always high. When she had had all she could take, she gave him an ultimatum: get treatment or get out. He beat her up in front of Jeremy. She charged him, they separated and he got probation. Two weeks later he came back to the house, kicked in the door and in a screaming rage, blacked both of her eyes. The judge continued him on probation but made him do four weekends in the county jail.

That seemed to work for a while. He stayed away for two months. Unfortunately he did not visit Jeremy who took it very hard. When he stopped paying child support, she waited as long as she could before pressing the issue. When she took him to court over nonpayment, the judge told him pay or go to jail. He paid. That night he was back at her house. In a drunken rage he drug her out into the yard and beat her until she almost lost consciousness. The judge gave him one hundred and twenty days in the North Carolina Department of Correction for assault on a female. Wanda still had some traces of the bruise marks on her back when he was released.

After hearing that the bank was beginning the paperwork to foreclose on his last asset, the Wilmington warehouse, he completely lost it. In the middle of the night he was found drenched in gasoline as he stood and watched the warehouse burn to the ground. While he was in custody, he sobered up enough to convince his mother and his brother to put up their homes as collateral for bail. The same night he was released on bond he showed up at Wanda's. He beat her again, ràped her and tried to kill her by choking her with a piece of cord.

Wanda thought of all of the horrible things he had done to her. The worst had to be when he was questioned in court during a pretrial hearing by the judge about his assets and connection to the community. The judge asked, "Do you have a child or children, and if so, how many?" Ralph responded, "I don't have no children."

Wanda's thoughts turned back to Jeremy. He was as good as Ralph was bad. He was Ralph's child. Although Ralph was his biological father, he had never been a father to him. Given the horror that they had had to endure from Ralph, maybe it was for the best. No, she thought, it was definitely for the best.

Her mind began to turn over the events of the day again. The drunks, Jeremy's reaction, the search to find Jeremy after the parade. She looked for Jeremy for half of an hour before she found him. He was down by the river where she had taken him fishing several times. Although he was not crying, he was still dejected.

"Catching any fish?" she remembered asking.

When he did not respond, she said, "We've had a lot of good times here. I used to come fishing on this very spot with my father. He used to bring all of us here, all of us. Mom, your uncle James, and me. Dad did it for us. He loved his family and we loved him. Now I know that . . . "

"I am not Little Stick. I'm not Ralph Stickley."

She took his hand. He did not pull it away this time. "I know you are not, Jeremy. You are a good young man and I am proud of you. You are not your father."

Still sullen, he blurted out, "I don't know why they had to say that. I am nothing like my father."

"Jeremy, there will always be hurtful people. Always. But that does not mean that you have to believe what they say or be hurt by what they say. Those three men were drunks: people who knew your father and knew the bad side of your father. They are just lashing out in anger and intoxication at some prior mistreatment. Who knows? Maybe a lot of prior injustices. But they don't know you."

Jeremy sat quietly and tossed a rock into the creek. He studied the ripples and watched the leaves float by. She picked up a rock and tossed it beside the place where Jeremy had tossed one. It made a new set of ripples that overlapped and erased the ripples from the first rock.

"They don't know you, Jeremy," she continued. "You are just like that rock. You will make your own ripples and your ripples will be good, good enough to wipe out the bad. When people do know you, they will like you and like you for who you are."

She remembered Jeremy smiling back at her and singing the line from Bob Seeger, "That's me. 'Like a rock'."

Suddenly her attention was drawn back to the present. She thought she had seen a movement in the darkness of her bedroom. She listened. All she could hear was her breathing. She stopped breathing. She listened again. She could still hear breathing. Horror set in as she realized someone was there. When she started to get out of bed, she could see the presence of something large before her in the darkness and then feel the weight of someone climbing onto the bed and onto her chest. She was terrified.

Pinned down she fought to break away. She could not move. In the dim light from the clock, she could see the glint of a knife in the attacker's right hand. Wanda started to scream but did not. She was fearful that if she called out, Jeremy would come and be killed or injured trying to defend her. She struggled but her efforts were futile. With his left hand he slapped her across the face.

With the taste of blood in her mouth, she clinched her jaw to avoid crying out. She studied her attacker. She had been raped once before and knew that identification was critical. Although the attacker was dressed in black and wore dark gloves which made recognition difficult, she felt certain it was a man. He was much bigger and stronger. The movements were much more masculine. The smell was more male.

His fist rammed into the side of her face. Once, twice, then again and again. As it continued, she began to lose consciousness. When she came to, his left hand was pulling at her clothing; his right hand held the blade of the knife against her neck. She was wearing panties and a long tee shirt. He had pulled the tee up and was leaning his weight to one side in order to slide her panties down. As his weight shifted, she pushed hard with the weight of her body to try to destabilize him. He leaned back in the direction of her push and as he did, she felt the knife slice into her neck.

She panicked. Before she could scream, he put his hand across her mouth to silence her. As she bucked and wiggled, the side of his hand slipped down into her mouth. She bit with all of the force she could muster.

"Arrrgh!" He groaned and jerked his hand back.

There was something about the groan and also something about the gesture. She recognized her attacker.

She made a muffled effort at screaming again. As she did, the attacker placed his left hand over her face and beat her repeatedly with the butt of the knife with his right hand. The last thing she remembered before she passed out was attempting to cry out: "Ralph".

CHAPTER THREE

Ben Down sat in the lawyers' lounge waiting for court to begin. He found himself at fifty-nine beyond his prime and still in the hunt for his peak. He had that distinguished look. At least that is what he had been told. Unsure what was intended by the phrase, he decided it meant: to be as old as he was, he still had all of his hair.

He winced somewhat as he thought about the gray in his hair. He had been quite athletic in his younger years. He played football for Wake Forest University and continued to play pick up touch football even into his forties but for the last fifteen years he had not seen a football. Except for the gray hair, Ben still had an athletic air about him and looked as though he could run the hundred. He had even thought about taking up running again but it seemed there was always something else, anything else that needed doing more.

Ben leaned forward on the couch. As he lit his cigar, he looked at his reflection in the window of the lounge door. He still did not look that old, he thought, but that gray hair gave him away. Maybe a little hair dye would do the trick but then, he thought, that is the epitome of vanity. He truly disliked anything that was not real, that pretended to be what it was not. Still, as he turned his face so the light reflected more of the gray, he felt a little touch on the sideburns would not hurt. He decided to think about it later.

He leaned back and picked up his newspaper. Before he started to read, he thought back to his days at Wake Forest. He had been an excellent debater and had been a star of the Debate Club during his junior and senior years. His success at oral argument had gotten him a recommendation for law school. He entered the School of Law directly after college and excelled in his studies. Although he enjoyed the study of law, his affinity for drinking with his buddies at the Tavern on the Green kept him a C student.

His strongest attribute was his oral presentation. On his feet the middling student became the formidable advocate. He spoke with clarity and fervor while other students muddled through a recitation on the cases assigned to them. Ben's recitations breathed life into the old cases. His talent brought him to the attention of Jeb Stuart, retired Dean of the School of Law, who had returned to teach criminal law and procedure. At the Dean's urging, Ben upon graduation became an assistant district attorney prosecuting criminal cases in the port town of Wilmington, North Carolina.

He quickly moved into felony prosecutions and by the end of two years, he was working the top five: murder, rape, robbery, burglary and arson. Two more years of felony trials and seventy hour weeks burned out his enthusiasm and toward the end of his fifth year, he delivered his resignation. Five years of felonies and a conviction rate better than any predecessor were all that followed Ben out of the DA's door on his last day.

Ben hung a shingle by the courthouse and took everything that came in. In the beginning his business thrived. Concentrating on his criminal practice, he had a lot of referrals from bondsmen, policemen and former clients at the old felony court. He tried to bring in an associate but each one found his temperament too cranky and crusty. His clients found him to be opinionated and sharp-tongued so his client base shrank over the years. The early flood of clients had been reduced to a trickle. His brilliant mind and strong voice languished because of a harshness, an inability to call a spade more than or less than a spade.

One of the few people who had a tolerance for his persimmon personality was Margaret. Margaret Goddard met Ben through the practice when she had filled in as a temporary secretary for him. Since her father who had been in law enforcement had been quite gruff himself, she was familiar with the trait and knew to look beyond the exterior. To Ben's surprise she stayed on when his regular secretary did not return. Margaret was as soft as he was hard; she was liked as much as he was disliked. When a client asked her how she could put up with it, she said, "His bark is worse than his bite. Ben's like a porcupine. Underneath all of that prickliness is a big old loveable tomcat."

They married and when their first daughter Sandy came, Margaret left the business and stayed home. Two years later Mary Lee was born. Ben eeked out an existence and from time to time, shared a secretary with other attorneys to reduce the overhead.

Occasionally he would represent a murderer who managed to warrant the attention of the local press. Each time Ben gave it his best and obtained good results. And each time he felt sure that the publicity and the victory would bring in a cadre of new clients. It did but somehow the practice never took off. It seemed that that old bruskness chilled the hormones that produce growth in small businesses. So Ben Down, Lawyer, never grew above a small concern that would feed his family and him and every now and then would provide a steak and a stiff drink of Jack Daniels, he called "Knock'em", down at Childrey's Grill and Bar.

Possibly Ben's love of Jack Daniels drinking whiskey may have played a part in the petrification that set into his business affairs. He could and did drink regularly. Of course he said he drank to celebrate although, to the untrained eye, one might not notice any cause for celebration. It was told around the courthouse that "if you don't mind a little hateful talk, the best lawyer to get was Ben Down, sober, and if you can't get him, get Ben Down, drunk." It was a joke that, like most, had some truth in it. It also had a great deal of exaggeration as well. Ben Down was never drunk. In fact that was part of the problem. He could drink and never show the effects. It was the hangover, that illness of spirit that takes the smile out of a beautiful day, that caused him the problem.

When he accepted a big case, he never touched the bottle until it was over. When it was finished, he tried to catch up. Then he hovered at about half hangover. Most of the time he had the smell of whiskey about him, that is, when you could smell anything other than the cigar smoke.

His reputation among the lawyers was one of misguided genuis. His knowledge of the law was legendary and his prowess in the courtroom was admired. Defense counsel often sought him out for a consult; after all it was free and better than a computer search. When it came time for light conversation about sports or the latest gossip though, they sought out gentler company. He was a fierce competitor in the courtroom but he always presented his opponent in a fair light. In fact if his clients had to be lawyers, his office would be "standing room only". His troubles were not with the law, the courtroom, and the lawyers; the troubles lay in his dealings with his fellow man.

Randy Bost, one of the two attorneys with whom he shared the secretarial services of Mrs. Janene Skittleran or "Skittle" as they called her, popped her head in the lawyer's lounge, saw Ben and came in. She sat down beside of him.

"Defending a dog on death row. So this is what it's come to." Randy smiled as she waited for Ben's reaction.

He kept reading his newspaper and did not acknowledge her. Randy put her hand on the paper and pulled it down. "Skittle told me all about it. She said . . . "

"Skittle talks too much," he growled.

"Agreed but she was right about this. She said, 'The great Ben Down has gone to the dogs.'" Randy laughed outloud and released his paper.

"Randy, you can think of more ways to irritate, aggravate and frustrate than any one human being I know of. It is a case. That's all. Not the case. Not the 'be all' or 'end all' of cases but one more case. And the way things have been going I am glad to have a case." Ben took a deep pull from his cigar and then moved it to the other side of his mouth.

"Yeah, but you've got to admit. It is a dog of a case." Randy grinned at her intended pun and waved at the smoke intentionally billowing in her direction. "And I can't believe your clients. They come into District Court without a lawyer and plead guilty to allowing their dog to run at large. The judge sentences them. Then they hire you to defend their dog. It's ludicrous."

"It pays the bills," Ben said offhandedly as he continued to chew on his cigar and stayed committed to the news.

Randy Bost was outspoken and direct. She loved to push the point until it demanded a response. It was that same propinquity that prompted her political science professor to encourage her to go to law school and it was that same stubborn, in-your-face personality that made her so effective as a lawyer and so obnoxious as a friend. Ben had liked her from the beginning when she had come to Wilmington to practice law. He liked her spunk and he found a fellow traveler when it came to dedication to the law practice. He encouraged her, helped her set up her own office, shared a secretary with her in the old Rice Building and put up with her uninvited opinions.

Randy stared directly at Ben hoping to provoke a more serious response. She waited.

Ben finally laid the newspaper between them on the couch. He fixed his eyes firmly on Randy and replied, "My young confused friend, it is time for a visit to the rules. Frequent recurrence to the rules is necessary to avoid the pitfalls of the legal profession. Rule One: This above all, the paying client is the beloved master to the servant. Or to put it in more apropos terms: never bite the hand that feeds you. Roy and Helen Kitner have paid, and I might add, have paid handsomely for the defense of their beloved Thor who, as we speak, is in a tight spot at the local animal shelter. By order of His Honor, Thor awaits execution in the gas chamber. The fact that his owners were convicted and have accepted their suspended sentences, all without the benefit of counsel, and have now spent a wad of the legal tender to have their beloved pet saved, as it were, jerked from the jaws of justice is no reflection on my clients. I know they are right and good. And why do I know that? They had the good sense to hire me. It is a case of canine injustice and I, friend to dogs everywhere, am the man for the job."

Randy growled, "Grrrrrr, sick'em, Ben."

As she picked up the paper and handed it back to him, she asked, "What's this really all about? Is the dog vicious?"

"No, but he is a canine criminal nonetheless. His crimes are these: One. He has violated the leash law by touring the neighborhood without benefit of attachment to his master's guiding hand. Two. He has growled at two people: a jogger and then the animal control officer. And three. His biggest crime. He is big, dumb and clumsy. He has had a Saint Bernard somewhere in his recent ancestry. He weighs about one hundred and fifty pounds. When you get all of that in motion and add sound effects, he might as well be 'Cujo', the killer attack dog."

"Skittle said he bit you."

Ben held up his hand and displayed a bandage covering the back of his hand. "Now there she goes again. My client did not bite me. I went out to see him and in his exuberance, he ran toward me. The big oaf was unable to stop and bumped into me almost knocking me down. His mouth was open so that his teeth raked across my hand as he slid into me. I did get a little scratch but nothing to worry about. He was not vicious. He was friendly. I wish my other clients were so enamored of me."

Ben rubbed his hand. "Too friendly," he opined.

Randy picked up his hand and studied the bandage. "Did you get any treatment for this?"

"No, well, I, uh, treated it myself. Don't tell Margaret."

"Ben, this needs to be looked at. I'm going to call Margaret. She'll make you go to the doctor."

Ben recoiled at the thought. "Why do you constantly nag me? God gave me a wife for that very purpose and she is excellent at it. No need for you to intermeddle. That job is being done, well done, thank you. Besides the only doctors in this town are witch doctors. They . . . "

"Don't change the subject. It won't work with me. I'm telling Margaret and I'm telling her for your own good."

Hoping to signal an end to the conversation, Ben held his newspaper up in front of him and shook it out. He started to read the sports section but found it dull. Randy sat and looked at him. Finally giving in, he gave her an "I surrender" look and said, "What now?"

"Which judge ordered the dog euthanized?"

"Judge Wolfe ordered Thor killed as part of the dispositional order in the case against the Kitners. He is here this morning and the DA said he could work me in."

"Which DA? I hope it's Rod Pemberton. You know he looks just like a young Mel Gibson. Every time I get around him, my knees get weak. He's a doll." Randy pretended to shiver.

"Good Lord, Randy. Why don't you get married so you can be miserable like the rest of us?"

"You're not miserable," Randy said defending Margaret. "If it weren't for Margaret, you would be pennyless, homeless and . . . and . . ."

"Come on. I know you can't think of another word ending in 'less'."

Randy smiled and retorted, "and less everything. Everything less."

"Better leave Rod alone. He's a good lawyer and a good DA. He doesn't need some woman screwing up his life. And to get back to the subject, if your knees are strong enough to take it, the DA is Jack."

"He's a Nazi but Judge Wolfe will treat you all right. He's a fair judge. Did you know they are calling him 'Judge Fudge'? He's been bringing in candy for everybody. He's a nice guy, you know. Wish we had more judges like him."

Ben grimaced. "Bet he wishes we had more lawyers like you. I bet you butter him up just like you do Rod."

"Huh. Not likely. Rod is the man. The man," she said emphasizing man.

Ben usually did not like the chit-chat but after he started, he would warm to the subject. It was not that he did not have anything to say; it was just that he did not like all of the courthouse gossip and rumors. He had heard it over the years and decided early on that he had more important things to do. He was not sure exactly what but anything besides idle chatter. This morning though he felt expansive and talkative.

"What are you doing this morning?" he inquired.

Randy was a little surprised. Typically she had to push and push until Ben finally gave in. Rather than answer the question, she responded, "You're in a good mood today. What gives?"

"Answer the question, counselor," he grumbled.

"I'm off to the land of irreconcilable differences and domestic turmoil. Judge Spivey has a one day session of civil court. Most of it is going to be uncontested divorces but he said there would be time to hear a few contested custody and child support cases. So I had them to add two of my domestic clients. One wants a divorce and child support; the other client does not want a divorce and does not want to pay child support."

"It's the lawyer's dilemma," Ben commiserated having been in the same situation numerous times. "You will argue in favor of a position and then in the next case you will argue against the same position. To the great mass of the unwashed, the unsophisticated in the world of the practicing lawyer, you appear to be talking out of both sides of your mouth. You appear to be a liar by supporting contradicting propostions when in fact you are advocating your client's postion not your own in each case."

"Exactly. You . . . "

Ben continued before Randy could pick up the banner. "It's an inglorious part of a glorious business."

His eyes sparkled for a moment thinking of old glories. He took his cigar into his hand and started to stand as he spoke,

"Members of the jury, I say to you, or better said, on behalf of my client, I argue and contend . . . ."

He walked toward the door tucking his paper under his arm, hoping to duck out on another lecture from Randy and gesticulating somewhat grandiosely with his arm pointed upward. His voice elevated, he postulated, "Or better yet. Judge Wolfe, your esteemed majesty and diviner of truth and justice, my client humbly beseeches you to spare the life of this poor beast, one of God's lowliest creatures. His error was a mere picadillo, a mere exuberance of spirit. Surely it does not merit a death sentence. Surely it . . . ."

Randy picked up the challenge arguing the prosecutor's rebuttal. "It's death, death to one of the hounds of the Baskervilles, that God awful creature who stalks the land at night and torments the meek. The tosser of trash, the baying howler that pierces the peaceful sleep. Let there be an end to it. I say death to the gnarling beast."

Judge Wolfe who had been walking by the lawyers lounge had heard the exchange. He opened the door and tucked his head in. He applauded lightly and grinned. "Bravo, bravo. Best save the theatrics for the courtroom though."

Ben bowed deeply. "Thank you, thank you, Your Honor," he replied in his best theatrical pose. "Indeed the best is yet to come. Two witnesses and one argument and you have seen all of me that you must today."

"Great. It's Friday and everyone has had a long week. I was hoping we wouldn't have too much today," the Judge said. "See you in the courtroom."

When he had left, Randy whispered, "Think he was bothered by our little morality play."

"No, not Bill Wolfe. He will do what he thinks is right regardless of what is done and said outside of the courtroom. Good judge. Hope he is good to us today." Ben stepped into the hallway. "I've got to do a nose count before court and see if my witnesses are in place. As for the horns of your dilemma, let me leave you with W.C. Fields. My dear, it's time you take the bull by the tail and face the situation."

The District Court was held in a small courtroom in the courthouse since there had been a shortage of space to cover all of the court services that had been developed over the years. The old courthouse was designed to resolve the disputes of an agrarian society and expansion efforts dragged woefully behind the demands engendered by the crush of humanity that needed the services of the court. Often the four to five hundred people who assembled for the sessions spilled out of the courtroom and down the hallway. It had happened so often that the linear mass of miscreants, victims, witnesses, family and friends had developed a name: the mumbling line. So named from the buzz of noise that emitted while those in the line waited.

The courtroom was well worn and even dirty. The lighting was taxing on the eyes with dark areas punctuated by the flicker of fluorescent bulbs. The acoustics were not conducive to a scholarly discussion of the facts and the law. One had to compete with the traffic on the streets outside of the courtroom, the pedestrian traffic in the courtroom from those hundreds who were ushered in and out over the nine to five schedule, and always, the hum of the mumbling line.

Somehow the business of the court carried on. Justice was delivered three or four hundred times per day dependent upon the numbers on the docket of cases scheduled. Somehow it all worked, not perfectly each time, but well enough, that there was a steady flow of ready, willing and able customers. This morning was no exception.

The District Court convened promptly at 9:00 a.m. Typically the church style pews were filled and the walls were lined with people. Today there was a sprinkling of people who had come to participate in what was billed as "The General Court of Justice". The lawyers called it "The Court of General Justice".

Ben walked in with snuffed-out cigar in hand, newspaper under his arm and brief case in his other hand. He checked each row of pews looking for his witnesses. When he saw them, he nodded at them and stepped over to tell them it would not be too long before the case would be called. After he had touched base with them, he took a seat behind the District Attorney and waited for his turn.

Jack Krait served as an assistant district attorney in the office of the elected District Attorney Butch Yeager. Butch started all of his assistants in District Court and usually the least experienced covered the Friday court. Friday court was a potpourri of odds and ends, things that had been started and needed concluding or things that were not quite important enough to be taken up on one of the larger dockets that covered Monday through Thursday. Frequently there were enough bar fights and neighborhood squabbles so that the court had been dubbed "the Friday fights". Jack had served as an assistant for three years, had not been promoted and moved upstairs to Superior Court for felony trials and, for some reason, had been punished by being assigned Friday court. He was not very happy about any of it.

"Your Honor, if the court please," he said without looking up from the stack of files in front of him, "this next case is at item twenty-three on your docket. Gutierrez, Ernesto Rojas." When no one answered, he called in a louder voice: "Ernesto Gutierrez".

A hispanic young man stood and approached slowly. Jack pointed to the table beside him to indicate where he needed to stand. He stood at the table and waited for a hispanic girl to come up beside him.

Jack asked him, "Do you speak English?"

Ernesto Gutierrez shook his head from side to side. The girl responded for him. "He speaks very little English. I am heez cousin and I can translate for him if you will let me."

Judge Wolfe indicated that she could translate and Jack said, "He is charged with operating a vehicle with no license, no insurance, no inspection, no registration and . . . "

He looked behind him at the three lawyers who were seated there and whispered somewhat loudly, "and no sense". One of the lawyers snickered at the comment then Jack turned his attention to the girl. "How does he plead? Guilty or not guilty?"

Without translating to her cousin, she said, "He pleads guilty, Your Honor, but he wants some time to pay the money.

Judge Wolfe was patient and much more tactful than the DA. He listened to both sides, ordered a fine and cost, and gave Senor Gutierrez time to comply. Jack went through several pleas in his lackluster way and finally called Ben's case.

"This next case," he announced with little interest, "is . . . . I'm not sure what it is but I believe Mr. Down wants you to reconsider a ruling you made earlier in the week concerning destroying the evidence in a case. A dog, I think."

Ben stood and, with an obvious dislike for the DA, objected. "Well, Your Honor, I'm going to have to object to this. He's trying to prejudice the case before we even get started. I don't want Your Honor to reconsider anything. This is not a review of an order. Your Honor has been in this business a long time and you know full well why you enter a judgment and you have good grounds for your ruling before you make it. I have filed a motion to modify a condition of probation in the cases of Roy and Helen Kitner."

"Objection, Your Honor. He's trying to run the courtroom." Jack had had about all he could stand.

"Overruled."

"As I was saying Your Honor, this is a motion to modify based on a showing of good cause. You will recall that the Kitners pled guilty earlier this week to allowing their dog, Thor, to run at large. They did this without the assistance of counsel. After consulting with an attorney, they would like the opportunity to present some evidence concerning the dog. Some evidence that Your Honor has not previously heard."

Ben motioned for Helen Kitner and the lady seated beside her to come up to the defense table. As they walked down the aisle to the table, Ben continued. "Your Honor ordered that the dog be destroyed as a part of the dispositional order in their cases. I will say on their behalf that they are not opposed to the probationary judgment that Your Honor imposed in the cases. Both of them felt the judgments were very reasonable. And as you know, they could appeal since we are still within the time period within which appeals are allowed. They have not asked me to appeal. They asked me to ask Your Honor to consider some additional evidence concerning their pet."

Jack was looking for a segway and looking for some way to avoid having to hear the motion. When Ben took a breath, Jack jumped in. "I think this is a matter that lies within the sound discretion of the court, Your Honor. I don't think you have to hear this. They will just have to live with it."

As Jack half smiled at Ben, he started to sit down. Before Ben could respond, Judge Wolfe interceded. "No, I think the law requires that the court hear the motion. Certainly fairness dictates it if nothing else. I'll hear the witnesses. Call your first witness, Mr. Down."

"Thank you, Your Honor. We call Sarah Morrison."

She stood and approached the witness stand. The bailiff directed her toward The Bible. When she was sworn and had taken the witness stand, Ben directed the examination: "State your name, ma'm, and state where you live, please."

"My name is Sarah Jean Morrison and I live at 3553 College Road in Wilmington."

"And where do you live in relation to Roy and Helen Kitner?"

"I live beside them."

"How long have ya'll been neighbors, Ms. Morrison?"

"For, well, eight years I think. And it's Mrs."

"Thank you, ma'm," Ben responded politely. "And are you familiar with their dog Thor?"

"Oh, yes."

"Do you know where they keep their dog?"

"Yes. They keep him in their back yard. They have a cable run between two trees and he is able to run back and forth along that cable. He is a big dog and needs a lot of exercise."

"Yes, well, have you known them to allow their dog to run at large, that is, to run loose in the community?"

"Objection. Your Honor, we've already tried that. They pled guilty to letting the dog run at large."

Not understanding the objection, she answered any way. "No."

"Objection overruled." Judge Wolfe looked over at Mrs. Morrison and asked, "Now what did you say?"

"No, I didn't know them to allow their dog to be loose. Well, except that one time when the animal control officer came out there and tried to catch him."

"How long have you been familiar with Thor?" Ben continued.

"Since he was a puppy."

"Do you think you are familiar enough with him to have an opinion as to whether he is aggressive, that is, whether he is a dangerous animal?"

"Objection," the DA stood. "That's not the issue here. The issue is whether the dog was evidence in the case and how the evidence should be disposed of."

Judge Wolfe intervened again before Ben could speak. "That's true but it is a narrow view of the situation. The court is interested in whether the dog is dangerous. Mrs. Morrison, you may answer the question."

"Thor is a good dog."

Ben picked up the examination again. "And why do you say that?"

"Thor is a good dog," she said emphasizing the "is". "He doesn't make a lot of noise and he is friendly. One time he was over at my house and when I walked out of my back door, he was standing there. He looked so big and serious. But I just said his name and his tail started wagging. Pretty soon he had his head in my lap and I was petting him. He's not mean at all."

"Do you have an opinion as to whether he should be euthanized, that is, put down?"

"That dog does not deserve to die. He hasn't done nothing."

Ben looked over at Jack and said, "Your witness."

By this time Jack was pretty bored with the matter and said, "No questions."

Judge Wolfe, who knew that he was going to have to rule on the matter and wanted more information, inquired on his own. "Mrs. Morrison, when we tried the case earlier this week, we learned that the dog had chased a lady who was jogging in your neighborhood. At the time he had his teeth bared and he was growling. Did you see any of that?"

"No, sir."

"And we also heard evidence that he had growled at another person who had come on the property. I believe the person may have been a telephone repairman. Did you see any of that? The man said he was terrified by the dog."

"No. I heard about that but I don't know anything about it," she replied.

"And finally, Mrs. Morrison, were you there when the animal control officer tried to apprehend him? The officer said he was trying to attack him. And let's see, looking back at my notes, he testified the dog came at him like he was angry and tried to bite him. Did you see any of that?"

"No, Your Honor."

"Any further questions, Mr. Down and Mr. Krait?"

Krait responded first. "No, sir."

Ben said, "Yes, sir. If Your Honor will indulge me for a moment?"

"Yes, go ahead," the judge replied.

"Mrs. Morrison," Ben asked, "You have lived beside Thor almost his entire life and you have known Thor almost his entire life, right?"

"Yes, sir."

"Have you ever, ever seen him be vicious, aggressive, angry, violent or act in any way that you would describe as inappropriate?"

"No, not at all."

"Thank you, Mrs. Morrison. That's all of the questions that I have. Would Your Honor have any additional questions?"

"No, sir. You may step down, Mrs. Morrison. Thank you."

Ben did not want to waste any time. He knew Judge Wolfe wanted to complete the docket as soon as he could and he did not want to give the DA any more opportunities than he had to to raise objections. He said, "Your Honor, I call Helen Kitner."

When she was sworn and had identified herself for the record, Ben asked her, "How long have you had Thor?"

"We've had him four years, Mr. Down."

"And how did you come to own Thor?"

"Well, Mr. Down, it's a long story. My dad was dying with cancer and wanted us to take care of Molly--that's Thor's mother--and Thor. Thor was just a little puppy. Dad kept thinking that he would get better and he would take them back but it never happened. Just before he died, he made Roy and me promise that we would always take care of them. Then shortly after Dad died, Molly died. I think she grieved herself to death. We just have Thor, well, we did just have Thor left."

Ben asked, "What kind of dog is Thor?"

"He is mostly Saint Bernard but he's not fullblooded."

"What is his approximate weight?"

"I don't know but Roy says he's over a hundred pounds. He's a big dog." As she spoke, tears started to well up in her eyes. "He's just a big ol' oaf. He's . . . he's all I have left of Dad. And . . . and we don't have any kids. He's like one of the family. He's . . . "

Krait looked over at Ben and said "Jesus Christ" just loudly enough for Ben to hear him. "Next we'll hear he saved their lives two or three times."

Ben did not acknowledge Krait's cynical remarks but kept his eyes on Helen Kitner. As she began to choke up, Judge Wolfe spoke softly. "Mrs. Kitner, do you need a brief recess? We can wait until you have had a chance to compose yourself."

She attempted to clear her throat. "No, I'm all right, Your Honor," Mrs. Kitner said as she searched her handbag for a tissue. When she found one and blotted beneath her eyes, she continued, "I know he's a big dog but we know there is a leash law and we have kept him confined on a run, that is, connected to a cable that allows him to run through the backyard."

"How did he happen to be loose on the day you were charged with allowing him to run at large?" asked Ben.

"I guess the cable broke."

"Well, if the cable broke and he was at large because of some failure of the equipment, why did you and Mr. Kitner plead guilty to willfully, that is, purposely allowing your dog to run at large?"

"Objection. Let's get back on track." Krait was obviously irritated and was ready to move on to some other matter.

Judge Wolfe retorted, "I'll decide whether we are on track or not, Mr. Krait. Mr. Down, I tend to agree. Let's hear about the dog."

"Yes, sir, Your Honor. Mrs. Kitner, would you describe Thor as aggressive?"

"No."

"Would you describe him as vicious or dangerous?"

"Absolutely not. He is a gentle giant."

"Now if Judge Wolfe decides to let you keep Thor, what can you say to assure him that Thor will be maintained within the leash law?"

"Well, we have a new, stronger cable and Roy is building a pen so that we can keep him in that when we have to be away for a while."

"Is there anything else you would like to tell Judge Wolfe as he decides this matter?"

"Yes, sir." She turned and looked directly at Judge Wolfe. She pleaded, "Your Honor, we will do anything you say but please let us have our dog back. He is a part of our family and we miss him."

"Thank you, Helen," Ben said. "Your witness."

"You didn't keep him on a leash before, did you?" Krait asked.

"I don't understand, Mr. Krait."

"Well, you pled guilty to letting him run at large, did you not?"

"Oh, yes, sir."

"And you weren't there when he attacked the lady who was jogging down your street, were you?"

"No, sir, but . . ."

"And he was growling and trying to bite the animal control officer who tried to capture him, was he not?"

"I don't know."

"The truth is, Mrs. Kitner, the dog is big and dangerous, isn't that right?"

"Well, objection, Your Honor. He is badgering the witness," Ben protested.

"Objection sustained."

Krait tried a different approach. "He is big, isn't he?"

"Yes, sir."

"And if he tried to attack a jogger and tried to bite another person, that is dangerous, isn't it?"

"Well, yes, but I don't know if . . ."

"That's all of the questions I have."

Ben asked several more questions on redirect examination to demonstrate that Thor had never attacked anyone before. Ben then presented a stack of letters from the friends and neighbors of the Kitners supporting their request that Thor be spared. When Ben indicated that that was all of the evidence for the Kitners, Judge Wolfe asked the District Attorney if he desired to present any evidence. Krait stated he would present evidence but needed a moment to prepare. While he was busy writing on something on the table in front of him, Ben rubbed his bandaged hand and whispered quietly to Mrs. Kitner. Finally Krait stood and addressed the court.

"Your Honor, the State has one item of evidence to present," he said. As he spoke he walked over to the desk where Ben was seated and placed a red State's evidence sticker on Ben's bandaged hand. "We have marked the exhibit with an exhibit sticker, Your Honor, and would now like to offer into evidence attorney Ben Down's hand as State's Exhibit Number One."

Ben was infuriated and stood up. "He can't do that, Your Honor. This is preposterous."

Judge Wolfe trying to keep things under control decided to try a little humor. He smiled sheepishly and said, "It looks like he's already done it. Mr. Krait, what's this all about?"

Krait smiled for the first time that day and pointed at Ben's hand. He stated emphatically, "The dog bit him. He can deny it if he wants to but the animal control officer said that the dog bit him when he came out there to see the dog." Looking over at Ben, he said, "Deny it if you can."

Ben rose pulling off the evidence sticker. His face reddened and his voice crackling with emotion started then stopped. He stood silently for a moment. When he had calmed himself down somewhat, he spoke evenly and slowly. "Your Honor, the gentleman's conduct is an affront. At worst it is an assault, both criminal and tortious, and at least, it is contemptuous. Your Honor conducts a court of justice and fairness. This son-of-a, this gentleman's poor manners demean your court and diminish the administration of justice. It deserves rebuke."

Judge Wolfe was clearly moved by the understated reaction. He looked directly at Krait and said, "Mr. Down's point is well taken and well said. Mr. District Attorney, don't ever do that again in my court."

Krait shrugged his shoulders as if to indicate that he did not realize that he had done anything wrong. Ben watched and extended the wait emphasizing the point that Krait had not apologized to him or to the court.

"Your Honor," Ben said, "obviously he is not going to apologize. I would accept it if it were tendered but it will not come from those lips. I would like to take a moment of personal privilege, if the court please."

Judge Wolfe nodded and allowed Ben to continue. Ben held up his bandaged hand. "I was not bitten by Thor. I visited the dog in the animal shelter and found him to be good natured even though I was a stranger. Indeed I found him friendly, overly friendly in fact. He came to me in his

excitement to see me and bumped me on my hand. No
aggression and no viciousness."

"All right then," Judge Wolfe stated as was his usual manner
to end a particular point. "Let's move on. Anything else for
the State?"

"No, Your Honor, but I would like to be heard."

"Proceed," the Judge stated cooly.

"I ask Your Honor to consider the evidence presented in the
hearing of the guilty pleas in this case. That evidence
convinced Your Honor that this dog should be destroyed.
Nothing has changed. That dog is big, he is bad, and he is
dangerous. To protect us, all of us," Krait argued as he looked
over at Ben, "he should be killed."

As Krait sat, Ben arose. "Your Honor, I ask Your Honor
to consider these things. Thor is big, but he is not bad and he
is not dangerous. He is not just an item of evidence, he is not
just property. He is a living breathing being and deserves every
reasonable consideration by Your Honor. He is loved and he is
needed by his family."

Ben put his hand on Mrs. Kitner's shoulder as she began
searching her pocketbook for her tissues. Tears started to slide
down her cheeks and she searched more feverishly for the
tissue. Ben kept talking as he reached in his pocket and
delivered a tissue to her. "Thor is the beloved last semblance
of a connection that Helen has with her father. He was
bequeathed to her conditioned on a promise, a promise that
Roy and she would take care of him. If he is killed, she will
feel that she has failed in her last words to her father. If he is
killed, it will break her heart."

Ben reached inside his coat pocket and pulled out his
handkerchief. Krait groaned audibly and Judge Wolfe,
recognizing this as a signal that Ben would take a while, leaned
back in his chair. Ben held the handkerchief in one hand and
put his glasses on. He picked up an old book from the table.
"I invite Your Honor's attention to these remarks from another
venerable judge. Harry C. Martin, quoting Senator Vest in
State of North Carolina versus Wallace, 49 N.C. App 475

(1980), considered the dog as a special creature on this earth and wrote the following: *"When all other friends desert, he remains. When riches take wings and reputation falls to pieces, he is as constant in his love as the sun in its journey through the heavens. If misfortune drives the master an outcast in the world, friendless and homeless, the faithful dog asks no higher privilege than that of accompanying him to guard against danger, to fight against his enemies. And when the last scene comes and death takes the master in its embrace and his body is laid in the ground, no matter if all other friends pursue their way, there by the graveside will be found . . . "*

Ben choked up a little, wiped his brow with the handkerchief and then continued, " . . . *the noble dog, his head between his paws, his eyes sad, but open in alert watchfulness, faithful and true in death."*

Ben looked up and pressed the argument. "He's a big old floppy dog. His act toward the jogger can be explained by his excitement at being free of the chain and a desire to run with the jogger. His actions toward the animal control officer can be explained by fear, the fear that the dog catcher, a stranger to him, was being aggressive toward him and trying to apprehend him. The evidence, the convincing evidence shows he's not aggressive but friendly; he's not mean, not mad, and not bad, but good to his owner and good to his neighbors."

Everything was quiet in the courtroom. This was a show and there were not too many shows in the District Courtroom. Usually it was noisy but a dull kind of noisy with one plea after another. This was good theater and the audience gave it its due. Even the clerk and bailiff stopped their muffled conversation to watch and listen.

Ben blotted his eyes with the big white handkerchief and raised his hand with index finger pointing toward the ceiling and pressing the old law book to his chest. "Your Honor, I implore you. Spare this faithful pet, let him be returned to his master, and let the word go forth that justice is tempered with mercy. Our courts are measured in the mind of the people by the way we rule. I say this is a matter that should be ruled by the heart. I ask you to find that justice is served by the conviction and punishment of the Kitners and that Thor should be spared from an ignominious death in some dark, damp death camp. We've had enough killing fields. Let Thor live. Your Honor, set him free."

Ben paused for effect and lowered his arm. He leaned over on the desk to accentuate the point. He let his voice drop as if one friend was talking to another friend. "Set him free, Your Honor. Set him free."

As Ben sat down, the Judge looked at the courtroom clock. He picked up the stack of letters Ben had presented. As he leafed through them, he announced, "The court will take a recess for about fifteen minutes. During the recess I will review the information provided to the court in these letters. All right then, Mr. Bailiff, announce a fifteen minute recess."

Everyone stood as the Judge left the bench. When the Judge had gone into chambers, Ben turned to Helen Kitner and asked, "Do you think we covered everything all right?"

She was still crying lightly and replied, "I don't know what else you could have done. Thank you, Mr. Down. What do you think he will do?"

"He's a fair judge but frankly I would not get my hopes up. It will be hard for him to change his earlier ruling but he might. As my father used to say to me, 'Hope for the best but expect the worst'."

Ben stepped over to the District Attorney's table. Jack was rifling through several of the files to determine which case would be called next. He said in a low voice, "Jack, you are a jerk. If you had shown a little mercy and let my clients get their dog back, they would have been your friends forever. Now they will probably join me in hoping that you rot in hell."

Jack laughed. "I must be doing a good job. I've got everybody mad at me this time."

Randy Bost came walking down the aisle between the rows of seats up to where Jack and Ben were glaring at each other. Randy sensed the tension and tried to divert their attention. "I can see that you two have been having a good time. It looks like another Friday fight."

Ben smiled a little. "Not this time," he said, "but one day." Ben turned his attention to Randy and asked, "How did your cases turn out?"

"They haven't yet. I am still in a holding pattern waiting to be called in. Oh, when I called Skittle to see what was going on at the office, she gave me a message for you. She said that Wanda Stickley needs to see you. Skittle said she was beaten black and blue and her face was swollen. Apparently she is pretty upset."

Ben led Randy back to the rail out of the earshot of Krait. "What's it all about?" Ben asked.

"I don't know the details but Wanda claims she was beaten and raped and the police won't do anything about it. She wants you to help her again."

"Was she able to identify her attacker?"

"You won't believe this. She says it was Ralph."

"Ralph Stickley?" Ben responded thinking outloud.

"Right. Isn't he in prison?"

Before Ben had a chance to answer, the bailiff walked over rather briskly. He had been listening to police communications on his hand held radio. He acted as if there was some urgency about the situation.

"Let me have your attention please. I have just been informed," he swallowed hard and spoke loudly enough so that everyone in the courtroom could hear him, "the Vice President of the United States, Vice President Anderson, was assassinated last night. Right here in Wilmington."

CHAPTER FOUR

"Did you see The Post this morning?" FBI Director Robert Fries held up the newspaper. In a banner headline the words covered most of the upper half of the page: "NATION MOURNS".

Assistant Director Michael Newman took the newspaper and scanned the articles. When he concluded his cursory review, he handed it back to the Director and leaned back in the chair. "The nation not only mourns but will be looking to us for the answers."

"This will be as big as JFK in Dallas and we can't drop the ball on this one. The public will demand to know what happened and we can't let the conjecture smolder as it has since the last presidential assassination." Fries responded.

"Well, this one will be different," Newman offered. "There was obviously a conspiracy this time. It is as clear as the two sets of footprints in the sand at Figure Eight."

"Yeah, but whose footprints and who is behind the ones who left the footprints? This cannot go down like the other assassination investigations. We've got to get the answers and we've got to get them first. Look. After Waco and Ruby Ridge, we need a win, a big win. Kansas City got us back on the right track but this is big." Fries hit the table with his fist. He almost shouted. "And it's on my watch."

"Yes, sir," Newman agreed. He sat up in his chair and pulled out a pocket pad. As he opened it, he said, "We are throwing everything we've got at this."

Fries, still somewhat emotionally elevated, tossed the newspaper to the end of his desk. "Right but what have we got? Two tracks in the sand? Come on. Surely they've come up with more than this."

"Well . . . "

Fries charged on through the thought without acknowledging the response. "I have a meeting with the President in a couple of hours. He has a press conference scheduled for this evening and he will want to know what to tell the public. His staff is receiving updates every three hours but he will want something, anything. He will want some answers. Do we have anything new?" Frustrated he decided to go back to the beginning. "What do we have at all?"

Newman referred to his note pad. "Sir, this is the latest information. Agents on the Island say the crime scene was kept in tact with little contamination. Secret Service, as shook up as those boys were, did a pretty good job of keeping everyone else out until we could get in. Except for the local firefighters with the fire department that responded shortly after the explosion, we knew pretty much who was there and who had access."

The Director looked at his watch. He thought out loud as he shuffled through the papers on his desk and pulled out two sheets.. "Let's see. We are almost nine hours off of the blast. How many Secret Service agents were with the Vice President that night? I have gotten conflicting reports. Donald said eight and the Service is saying seven."

""Seven is right. Donald is liaison interface with the Service but he is working here in Washington. I think Donald looked at the register at the main office. It always shows eight but they have a rotation and one is always rotated out of the line-up. Of the seven, all of them are accounted for. They were following procedure and had the perimeter properly protected, uh, according to their reports."

The Director looked up from the reports and picked up on the innuendo. "It's still difficult to see how anyone could have penetrated. A private island. One way in, one way out. Waterway on one side and Atlantic Ocean on the other side. One house and a large open area surrounding it. Somebody somewhere let something slip."

Newman nodded. "Agreed but all we have so far is the field reports from the agents who were there and they are tight. Nobody saw anything." He flipped through his pad and looked for a quote. "Here it is. 'Just another uneventful night until boom'. I seriously believe it totally caught them by surprise. We've run checks on each one of them and the credentials are impeccable. Patriots to the last one."

"What about the people who were there?"

"All family and friends. We're checking Feinstein and his wife but I am almost certain this will be a dead end."

"What is the latest status report on the Vice President's wife? Conscious yet?"

"No, it's a miracle she survived. She has extensive injuries and the doctors are saying she may very likely lose her leg, the right leg. They won't know for several days whether surgical procedures have been successful. She is still unconscious. The hospital is on the alert. As soon as she is able, we will have an agent there to see what she knows. She might be the only eye witness."

"Or the next homicide," Fries interrupted. "Have we done everything we can to see that she is protected?"

"Yes, sir. The hospital is pretty secure. And we have agents guarding her room."

"What about the children?" Fries continued.

"They are with the maternal grandparents in Silver Spring. All three have been debriefed by our office. They don't know anything. Understandably they are in shock. The grandparents are on notice to let us know if the children remember anything. And we have security there as well."

The Director intecomed his secretary. "Ms. DeReese, please bring me the reports from explosives."

Newman knew the drill and pushed forward with the overall. "As far as we can determine, there were two people involved at the site. Tracks indicate only two. Apparently they came from the Island just south of Figure Eight Island. It's called Shell Island and is a part of the area known as Wrightsville Beach. They parked in a parking lot and walked the short distance from there to Mason Inlet which separates the two islands. It is shallow and one doesn't need any special gear to cross over. They probably waded over under the cover of darkness. They hid themselves in a grove of small trees and sea oats, worked their way along to the rear of the Feinstein house. They appeared to establish a base a short distance from the house. Then one crawled to the back door. We can document that with physical observations and with canine."

"Right. I've seen the photographs. What does the lab make of the shoe prints?" Fries clicked the intercom. "Ms. Dereese, please get me an update from the lab re identification, shoe prints."

"Nothing so far," Newman pushed on. "They are nondescript. They do not have a known tread pattern. In fact they are theorizing, really just guessing at this point, that the tread was abraded to a flat surface and then a urethane glue was spread over the surface to prevent detection of the brand and type of shoe. A small glob of the glue was found in a track. It had apparently broken off. Chemists are analyzing it now. So far, zilch on the shoes though."

"Any other physical evidence? Fingerprints, hair, unaccounted for physical objects, anything?"

Newman looked somewhat dejected. "Nothing. Even the bomb itself appears to be somewhat generic. So far they have been able to assemble the larger pieces of it. Preliminary reports indicate that it was C4 attached to an incendiary activated by remote electronics. Simple, too simple. You could get the directions for it off of the Internet."

"No signature. Well, we'll get one out of the components. We have to." Fries looked off into space in deep thought. "Every bomb tells its own story. This one may not be distinctive as to type but the bomber put his name in there somewhere. A twist of wire, the components purchase, the combination of elements, the schematic. Somewhere. The puzzle will be solved somewhere within the thousands of pieces of that bomb."

Newman forged ahead with the report. "The agents there believe the bomb was planted then was activated from a remote sight. It looks like the bomb was planted during the night. Very likely underneath, probably under the Vice President's bed while he was sleeping. The house was clean after everyone left the reception for the Vice President. So it was planted sometime after 11:30 p.m., Thursday night. The explosion was at 2:36 a.m. We have a window of about three hours. Given the lack of sophistication in the electrical system and the short distance it would be operational, we are surmising that they waded across and planted the bomb, then waded back across the Inlet and detonated it. If that scenario is correct, then there is a good chance someone at Wrightsville Beach saw something unusual. The bomb made a lot of noise and a big fire ball. It very possibly would have awakened people about the time the bombers were leaving the area. We are going house to house now. So far, nothing but we will keep trying."

"Who's taking credit for it? Any group that we should take seriously?"

Newman blew out a stream of air showing his distaste for the subject. Every time a bombing or disaster took place, he thought, invariably the creeps came out of the wood work. "At last count, thirty-nine including individuals and groups." He flipped through his pad until he came to a list. "Citizens for a Peaceful World, Greener World, Aegus, the ICD, Save the Planet, a man who claims to be the rightful successor to Son of Sam, White and Right America and the list goes on. We aren't discounting any of these but frankly little has been developed through this 'wannabe' list. All of them appear to be nuts. None of them have a documented history of violence."

"Well, what about Khadafi, Sadam Hussein, mideast terrorists?"

"We haven't ruled them out but they don't fit the profile and the politics isn't right. In fact the Vice President, although he would not be considered a friend, certainly was not an enemy. He was the most moderate on peace initiatives with each of these pockets of terrorism. If he were elected President as many were predicting, all of them would have had a seat at the table so . . . "

"What about the backlash, extremists who would not want the U.S. too friendly with Iraq, Iran, Palestine or Libya?"

"Agents abroad are saying no. Our people in the field and CIA intelligence are telling us that they haven't picked up on anything, anything resembling any connection. True, the motive could be there but there is nothing concrete to tie any of them to the bombing."

Fries was getting a little perturbed with the lack of progress in the investigation. "Pursue them anyway. Anderson was outspoken on Chinese human rights. What about that angle?"

"Again we have sounded everybody. China, Vietnam, Korea, Latin America. Nothing."

"Who is top of the list on the local front?"

"No doubt about it," Newman looked somewhat relieved to be able to report something solid. "Antigovernment forces. Extreme right. The Vice President is, uh, was no friend to the fringe element, the so called Wackos over Waco. The militia groups are at the front of the line. Boulder has had a lot of talk of a political assassination although no names ever surfaced. Their skinheads are extremely violent. We are working them hard. Texas: the Free Militia of the Republic is at the top too. They march at Dealy Plaza in Dallas and claim Oswald was right. There are more but overall this seems the most fertile ground so far."

Fries slid his chair back and stood. He was in deep thought as he walked over to the window. He stared out. After a few long seconds he spoke. "You know you can walk out of this building, cross the street, go around the corner and walk right into Ford's Theater. I have walked up the steps and stood where John Wilkes Booth stood as he stared at the back of Lincoln's head. I can follow his footsteps through the seats and right off the balcony after he shot Lincoln. I can show you where he broke his leg. I can trace his retreat southward. I can name the ones we charged as conspirators."

He stopped talking and stared at the people down on Pennsylvania Avenue. Finally he turned and looked at the Assistant Director. "You know, there has never been an assassination in this country that has not been solved. That tradition will not be broken on my watch. In two weeks I want to be able to trace the footsteps of those two assassins through the Carolina sand all of the way into federal custody. All of the way."

*   *   *

In Wilmington the news had spread like wildfire. At first sketchy announcements were made in media reports then as word of mouth picked up the line, few people were unaware of the assassination. As the chatter spread, as is typical with gossip, the stories began to build upon themselves. Not only had the Vice President been murdered in his sleep but assassination attempts had been made on other members of the government. According to the scuttlebutt the President noticeably absent in the early hours of the reports had been whisked away and was secreted at Camp David or in some unknown military compound deep within the West Virginia mountains. By midday a rumor surfaced that martial law may be declared and that Wilmington might be cordoned off, quarantined and placed under military authority until the investigation was completed.

Of course none of it was true but enough anxiety had built so that the Governor of North Carolina and the Mayor of Wilmington scheduled an impromptu midafternoon press conference. Although they knew little in the way of details, they assured the public that an investigation was being conducted by numerous law enforcement agencies and there was absolutely no truth to any of the rumors that were circulating: no quarantine, no military force, no evidence of any local militia involvement, nothing to indicate there was any conspiracy, no mad bombers, and paraphrasing Roosevelt, fear only fear itself. Most of what they said was true; some of it was speculation but it was intended to calm. They asked everyone to let the investigation run its course and not be concerned with all of the wild reports that had "absolutely no foundation in fact".

Although the Mayor had privately expressed his concern that this would be a pariah for Wilmington such as the horror that had been visited on Dallas during JFK's assassination and his own fear that Wilmington, the beautiful port nesting by the Cape Fear River, would become a side show for the morbid gawkers who still stalk Dealy Plaza looking for conspirators, publicly he was saying that Wilmingtonians were strong and would rise above the adverse publicity. He asked the local citizenry to join with the Governor and him in praying that Marilyn Anderson, the Vice President's wife, would survive and their children would be comforted and protected during this time of loss.

Ben listened intently to the press conference on his radio as he drove back to his office from the courthouse. He wondered what they really knew: was there really a conspiracy? If so, who, how many and why? Was the Vice President the only target or were there more to come? Why Wilmington? He turned into the driveway and pulled into his parking space, gathered his briefcase and exited. As he walked over to the flagpole in the front of the Rice building where his office was located, he noticed that Randy's Jeep was not in the lot. After fumbling with the knot in the rope, he lowered the flag to half mast.

Mrs. Skittleran had watched him out of the front window by her desk. She turned her radio down and instinctively went to the back of the office to the coffee room. She heard him come in as she poured the water in the coffee pot and clicked it on. When she returned to the reception area, Ben was looking out of the window watching the flag. It barely moved.

Mrs. Skittleran went to her desk and started working through a form letter on her keyboard. Ben who had been lost in thought heard the noise and turned. "What do you think about all of this, Skittle?"

"It's a tragedy. I can't believe this. I thought when they killed John Kennedy, Martin Luther King and Robert Kennedy, it was over. I didn't think I would see it again in my life time."

Ben commiserated. "Me, too." Still somewhat distracted by his thoughts, he said, "The evil that lurks in the human mind can never be underestimated. It's hard to fathom the evil that would kill Vice President Anderson. Of all of the people who would be a target of an assassin, I would never have guessed him. He was a good man. Maybe that was the problem. He was too good. It's hard to imagine the evil that would kill a man in his sleep and have absolutely no regard for his wife lying right beside of him. It always amazes us, even stuns us when it happens but it shouldn't. Cain killed Abel. Brutus killed Caesar. It is the history of mankind."

"Is that what they say happened? He was blown up in bed?" Skittle had not heard the details since the on-air reports were mostly confined to the general announcement and government officials' comments.

"Right. I stopped at the Sheriff's office about a matter before coming back to the office. The detective I talked to said it happened in the middle of the night, well, really about two or three o'clock this morning. It was reported in the papers that he and his family were vacationing on Figure Eight with a Fein, uh, Fein something. He was an old family friend. Apparently investigators believe he was killed with a type of fire bomb."

"Do you know which house it was?"

"Not really. I've been out there several times over the years but I don't know the people he was staying with and from the description, I really can't tell which house it is. Supposedly you can see the house from Shell Island out at Wrightsville Beach. Bonnie in the Clerk's office lives on Wrightsville. She said she heard the blast this morning and said she saw the house this morning before she came in to work. Lot of damage, mostly to the second floor. She said the place was crawling with investigators." Ben felt around in his coat pocket for a cigar; finding none he began patting each pocket.

Having worked for Ben for seven years and having learned his proclivities, Skittle said, "They are on your desk."

Ben always hated it when she knew the answer before he asked the question. "I didn't want a cigar. I was just checking to see if I had any."

"Little testy, aren't we?" Skittle replied.

"No, not now, not ever," Ben returned the remark and continued to fumble through his pockets. "You know what galls me. Instead of being concerned about the Vice President and his family, people are more worried about themselves. I have heard more bull since the assassination announcement. A lot of people have worked themselves into a lather thinking the government is going to arrest the whole town of Wilmington. Have you ever heard of such?"

"Well, I heard that they might send in the National Guard . . . "

Ben fussed. "Now that's what I mean. People are so self-centered. Martial law. They are more worried about themselves. They ought to be concerned about his children and his poor wife rather than speculate about some nonsense."

"Boy, you are snippy today. I'll bet it was the dog case."

"Dog, nothing," he protested.

Skittle pushed on. "I talked to Randy and she said that the Judge wouldn't give you any relief or to put it as she said, 'Judge Fudge wouldn't budge'." Skittle stood up and started toward the coffee room. "All you need is a little ol' cup of coffee. Get you in a better mood."

"Skittle, if you don't cut out that mothering tone with me. I am a grown man and I can decide whether I need a cup of coffee."

Skittle continued on toward the coffee room and pretended not to hear Ben's argument. "I'll get it," she called back.

Ben kept on talking as she walked back. "For the life of me I can't see why Judge Wolfe didn't give us some relief on the dog." He started talking even louder so she could hear. "I mean, after all, they took the suspended sentence and we had plenty of evidence that releasing the dog to them wouldn't harm anyone. We had a stack of letters from neighbors who knew the Kitners and who knew Thor. All of them indicated he was no threat to anyone."

Skittle returned with the coffee cup and handed it to him. Ben continued oblivious to Skittle's return. "I mean that ol' dog is nothing but a butterball of fluff. It had to be Jack Krait. Any other DA would have backed up or at least stayed neutral but he had to fight it all of the way. No reason for it except . . . "

Ben took a sip of the coffee. "Except he's a son-of-a . . . "

"Now no need to be crude, Ben," she said continuing to mother him.

"Skittle, I tell you. This coffee needs something," he said as he looked at the coffee. He started walking back to his office.

Mrs. Skittleran started to work on the letter again but then thought out loud, "You think Jack Krait treated you badly; wait until you see Wanda Stickley."

While she was talking, Ben was in his office. He opened his lower right desk drawer and pulled out a bottle of Jack Daniels. He took a large drink of the coffee then poured a generous portion of the whiskey into his cup. As he walked back out of his office toward Mrs. Skittleran's desk, he said, "What did you say, Skittle? I, uh, I was busy and didn't hear it."

"Yeah, right," she replied aware of what he had done. "I said wait until you see Wanda Stickley. Both eyes are swollen and she has large blue marks under each one. She has scratch marks on her face and neck. She looks worse this time than she did last time," she said referring to the last time Ben had represented Wanda.

Ben sipped the coffee again. "Umm, just right," he remarked referring to the coffee. "Uh, when did you say she was coming in?"

"I didn't but she will be here," she paused as she checked her watch, "anytime. I told her three thirty and it's about that time now. Oh, I have some more news. You were appointed to a case: Noah Lyerly. Murder. He's in the local jail."

Ben rubbed his hands together and spoke in hushed tones. "A little case of murder, is it? I'm just the man for the job. Can't save a dog from the hangman but they think I might have a little luck with a man's life. I hope Mr. Lyerly is not allergic to a little rope burn."

"Quit being so negative."

Ben smiled and cradled his coffee in his hands. "Right. It is upward and onward for me. Down is up and Down is up to it." He walked back toward his office. "Come and get me when Wanda gets here and I'll go see Mr. Lucky Lyerly before I go home this evening."

Mrs. Skittleran had worked as a legal secretary for several lawyers over the years. She began as a typist in a large pool of secretaries for a large firm that specialized in tax and corporate law and she had learned much about the practice of law. Her training and experience got her in the door at Smith and Shelly where she immediately moved from receptionist to secretary to one of the attorneys. That office specialized in insurance defense work and was as she put it, "people short and paper heavy" referring to the few people who came into the office and the massive amount of paperwork that went out in the form of motions and discovery requests. After two years she grew tired of the routine and moved to the clerk of court's office. She excelled as a clerk but again found the lack of interaction with the public was very boring.

Ben, who was constantly in need of a secretary, recruited her out of the clerk's office. Everyone told her that she would detest his surly attitude and his gruff manner but she like Margaret had seen a sparkle of humanity underneath all of the gruffness that others had missed. She listened to his guff then gave it back to him with that mother hen approach. For some reason they clicked: he fussed about it then finally did whatever she said then he fussed some more. She had found all of the lawyers interesting but none as interesting as Ben Down.

At Ben Down, Lawyer, she liked the routine. In fact she liked the fact that there was very little routine. She told them at the clerk's office that "not too many came in but the ones that did made up for it". Ben's clientele were as varied as the cases. His practice was mostly criminal and consequently for the most part, criminals came to see him. While they waited to see Ben, they typically sought her opinion first: What do you think the judge will do? Do you think I can get probation for this? Do you think Ben can get my car back? How long will I lose my license? She listened to all of it and enjoyed hearing all of the hard luck stories. She was such a good listener Ben told her she should have been a judge instead of a secretary.

She received her nickname at the clerk's office. Not too many people could pronounce her last name after she got married, too many syllables, so they started calling her Mrs. Skittle. It finally shortened to Skittle. It carried over to Ben's office.

She liked Randy Bost and James Wilkes, the other two attorneys for whom she provided secretarial service. Randy was talented and outspoken, qualities she admired in a woman. Randy was also up and coming. It was easy to see that she would be successful no matter which direction she might take her practice. Presently it was fledgling and eclectic which kept Randy burning the midnight oil to stay abreast of all of the different areas her clients were taking her. James Wilkes on the other hand was a techno-nerd pushing the offices toward more computerization. He was also detail oriented and fact driven, excellent qualities for research and investigation. His practice drifted more toward real estate transactions, incorporations and estate practice. While Randy and Ben loved the courtroom and avoided their offices as much as possible, James lined his office with gadgets and rarely ventured out unless work mandated it.

The three of them barely kept Skittle busy. Randy and James were in the second year of their practice as sole practitioners. Randy's client base consisted of court appointments in indigent criminal and juvenile cases; Jim's work consisted mostly of bank referred real estate transactions for title searches and closings. He also represented a few small business concerns that needed occasional legal and tax advice. Ben was a criminal lawyer. Occasionally he would take a domestic case or a civil case but his heart was in the push and shove of criminal work. His clientele varied but typically it was Jimmy the burglar, Johnny the rapist, Jane the thief and Jack the killer. They were few but they were indeed interesting.

Skittle stuck her head in Ben's office. "Wanda Stickley is here. Should I send her in?"

Ben said, "Give me a minute. I'll come out."

Wanda Stickley sat in Ben's reception area and absentmindedly thumbed through a magazine. Although Ben knew she had been injured quite seriously about the face and neck, he was still astonished when she looked up from the magazine. She attempted a smile but it was distorted by the swelling and looked more like an effort that was having no success.

"Thanks for seeing me, Ben," she said as she laid the magazine on the table in front of her and started to stand.

Ben still a little stunned muttered, "Wan . . . , Wanda, are you all right?"

"I think so. The hospital took extensive x-rays of my head and upper body. They say I have some spider web fractures in the bones below my eyes and over my nose. Otherwise it's contusions and abrasions. I know it looks bad but it doesn't hurt nearly as badly as it looks. I go back to the doctor Monday."

Ben took her by the hand and said, "Girl, every time I see you something bad has happened to you. We've got to put a stop to this. Let's go back to the office and see what can be done."

Wanda attempted another smile and Ben noticing the effort asked, "What's so funny?"

"You. Every time I see you you are grumbling about something. I must have caught you in a good mood."

Ben barely acknowledged the compliment. "No, I'm not in a good mood. It's this assassination. It is a terrible tragedy and all I am

hearing about is how concerned everyone is about themselves. We
need to spend a little more time caring about others. Maybe it would
be a better world." Ben realized that he was giving a little lecture
and decided to stop before he got more depressed about the situation.
"Have you been able to keep up with the news about Vice President
Anderson?"

"Yeah, I watched some of it on the television this morning while I
was waiting for the doctor to read my x-rays. The local news
reported that it took place at a big pink stucco house on the south
side of Figure Eight. There is only one out there that fits that
description as far as I know. I believe I have been to the house years
ago when Ralph and I were married. It's a huge place, maybe worth
half a million dollars. Well, it was before the explosion."

Ben responded, "I believe I know which house it is now. I fish
out there in the inlet and I remember a big pink house. It's on the
side near the ocean and it's the first big house you see as you look up
along the coastline there."

"That's it," Wanda replied.

Ben caught himself staring at Wanda's face. It was swollen and
pudgy around the eyes. Her eyes were red and white dots encircled
in blue and black. She had obvious scratch marks on her cheeks that
stretched down and out of sight along her neck. It became quiet and
the stillness was a little awkward. Finally Ben spoke, "Do you have
other injuries besides those that are visible?"

"I have some bruising on my chest and upper arms where he sat
on me and I tried to push him off. And the doctor said I have some
tearing in my vaginal wall."

"Are you on medication?"

"Pain and anti-inflammatory medicine but nothing too strong."

Ben leaned forward in his seat, picked up a pen and positioned
himself to write on his note pad. "How did this happen?"

"It was last night. Well, really, it was this morning around, I
don't know, 3:30 or so. I was in bed."

"Who was in the house? Was Jeremy there?"

"It was just the two of us: Jeremy and me. Jeremy was in his
bedroom down the hall from me. I woke up and started thinking
about the things that had happened the day before and about all of
the stuff that had been happening to me when I noticed someone in
the room."

Ben scribbled on his pad. Without looking up, he asked, "Could you see who it was?"

"No, the room was dark but I could tell who it was."

Ben ignored the opportunity to ask who it was preferring instead to get some additional information concerning the physical setting. "Were there any lights in the bedroom or any street lights that shone in? Anything?"

"Not really. Just a little light from my electric clock that I keep by the bed."

"What could you actually see?"

"A large figure. A dark figure, darker than the darkness in the room."

"See the face?"

"No."

Ben leaned back in his chair and toyed with the pen. He started slowly. "When I found out that you wanted to see me, I heard at the same time that you had said that Ralph raped you. Since I knew Ralph was in prison, I went by the Sheriff's Department and talked to the detective who has the case. Frankly he's not convinced. He's . ."

Sensing that Ben was getting ready to defend the detective, she interrupted, "Look. I know it was Ralph."

"Wanda, I have represented you for years. I helped you get custody of Jeremy, helped you get child support, or at least I tried to when Ralph wouldn't pay. I helped you when he raped you. We helped the DA get the conviction that sent Ralph to prison. The detective checked. Ralph was in prison. He is confined at the Department of Correction in Brunswick and was there when the rape purportedly happened. The detective believes you were raped but he is just as convinced that you are wrong and it wasn't Ralph. Ralph has an alibi--he was serving time."

Wanda had waited patiently but when Ben stopped, she stated emphatically, "It was Ralph. It's that simple."

"And that complicated. Let me play devil's advocate for a moment. How do you know it was Ralph? It was dark. You didn't see your attacker's face; you didn't actually see his body. You didn't . . ."

"I did see his arm move as he was starting to hit me. I know how Ralph moves."

"An overreaction to the fear," Ben asserted.

"I smelled him. It was Ralph."

Ben smiled feebly. "Wanda, seriously I don't want to belabor the point but none of it will hold up in court. The identification is, well, I am going to tell you like it is: flaky. Too shaky for any DA to put up before a jury."

Wanda looked dejected. Ben sensing her frustration said, "I am willing to help but . . ."

"That's what I am here for but what can you do?"

Ben said, "Actually I can do a lot. Wanda, you have always told me the truth. The truth: good, bad or indifferent. You told me when I asked. And I believe you are telling me the truth now, that is, the truth as far as you know it. Did Jeremy see or hear anything?"

"No, he slept through it."

"How is that possible? There must have been a lot of noise."

Wanda looked directly at Ben with steely eyes. "I didn't cry out."

Realizing the agony that she must have gone through and the extraordinary courage it must have taken to withstand all of the pain and yet not cry out for fear that her attacker might harm Jeremy, Ben swallowed hard and said, "I see."

She dropped her head and tears began to fall on her hands as they twisted a tissue. Ben was angered at his own insensitivity. There is no doubt, he thought, that she had gone through a lot and here he was being the advocate when she really needed a defender. He stood up and walked around the desk. He had a seat in the chair beside her. "Wanda," he said softly, "I am here to help. Really."

As she looked up, he said, "There are several things we can do. First according to the detective, the lab has not reported back on several fibers and hairs that were found on the bed sheets. Secondly the detective believes that there was semen on the sheet. That lab result is not back. And the rape kit. The vaginal swabs will confirm the presence of semen I would bet. Your physical condition, the vaginal tear, all of it points to rape. The detective believes you were raped but he is just as convinced the case is hopeless as long as you hold to the story that Ralph was the rapist. I think though we can make some inroads on that. I suggest that you take two tests to bolster your credibility: a voice stress analyzer and a polygraph test. Both will indicate that you are being totally truthful when you implicate Ralph as the rapist. I can use both tests to convince the

Sheriff to pay for DNA tests of the semen in the rape kit. That test will reveal the probability, the high probability that Ralph was the attacker. And finally I have a friend at the DOC, the Department of Corrections. I'll have him check to see if there is any possibility that Ralph Stickley was outside of the prison fence."

As Ben had talked, Wanda began to brighten. She listened intently as Ben had gone through the process. "That's why I came to you," she said. "You always had a way, some way of making it work when no one else could."

"Well, don't get your hopes up too high. I have given you the best case scenario. And it is all designed to convince the detective to file a charge. From charge to conviction, you know how arduous that can be."

"Yeah, but at least you are doing something about it. Before I came here, I was just being victimized one more time."

Ben tried to reassure her. "The detective is exactly on point. He is right where he ought to be. He has gone as far with it as he can. It's up to us to see if we can move him a little farther."

"Oh," Ben said as he remembered what had distracted him initially before they had started talking about the details of the attack, "are you sure you are going to be safe? We can get the Sheriff more involved with security if you want it."

"I am going to buy a pistol and keep it right by the bed," Wanda retorted rather defiantly.

"I'm not so sure that is the way to go. You've got to get to it fast and you have got to be willing to use it. If not, the criminal will just take it away from you and use it on you. Are you sure you are willing to use it?"

Wanda looked at Ben as if to say, "Are you kidding after all I have been through?" When she finally spoke, it was on another subject and one more important to her at the moment. "All of these tests. How am I going to pay for them?"

"The Sheriff's office will spring for the tests. I'll see to that."

"How am I going to pay you?"

"Just like I told you before. Pay me what you can, when you can. And if you ever find any of that money that Ralph ran off with and buried before he was sent to prison, pay me with Ralph's money." Ben smiled rather mischievously. "That would be just and fair, don't you think?"

As Wanda walked to the door, she smiled again. "You are too nice, Ben."

Ben stood up and walked her down the hall. As Wanda walked out, Ben said, "Mrs. Skittleran will contact you about the dates and times for the testing."

"Thanks again," she said as she exited.

During Ben's interview with Wanda, Randy Bost had returned to her office from the courthouse. As Wanda was leaving, Randy heard the end of the conversation. After Wanda had left, Randy stepped over to Ben's office. "'You are too nice, Ben.'," she said mimicking Wanda. "Boy, I don't know what you did but that is the nicest thing I have heard said about you by anyone lately.

"Well, come on in," Ben said facetiously since Randy had already entered. "You might as well since everybody else thinks I am such a great chap. Come on in and enjoy the warmth and hospitality. As for why I am such a nice guy, I am merely helping a damsel in distress: my specialty."

Randy snickered then turned serious for a moment. "They say that she is claiming Ralph Stickley raped her. Everybody knows he's in prison. What gives?"

"I'm not sure. Wanda is certain it was Ralph. She has always told me the truth. Always. She was raped. That much I think is certain. But DOC says Ralph was in prison. So far no physical evidence supports Wanda and her opportunity for identification was almost nonexistent. So," Ben thought out loud, "so she is right and everybody else is wrong or she is so terrorized by Ralph that she believes it was Ralph. I don't know what I believe but we are going to work on it."

"What does she want you to do?"

"Nothing specific yet. She just wants help and doesn't know where to turn. The Sheriff's office isn't helping her much. The detective who has been assigned is Gerald Stanton. Have you had any dealings with him?"

"No, but I've heard he is good."

Ben continued with the thought. "Any way I remember him as a street officer but I haven't worked with him on anything since he was transferred to Violent Crimes. He is convinced she was raped but he is just as convinced it was not Ralph Stickley. I think our first efforts will be to convince him to use all of his resources to pin it down one way or the other."

"Good luck," Randy replied. "I hope you have better luck than you did with the dog. What are you going to do about that?"

"It's already in the works. We gave notice of appeal in Roy and Helen's cases for a new trial in Superior Court so that will stay the order to kill Thor. And it will give us a little time to try to come up with another plan. I can't believe Judge Wolfe ruled against us. He ruled flat out: the dog is dangerous and the dog ought to die."

Ben stood up and walked over to the small television set in the corner of the office. He turned it on and switched channels to CNN. "The President is supposed to have a press conference concerning the assassination at 4:30." He turned the volume down very low and asked, "How did your cases go in domestic court?"

After a while she said, "Want to help another damsel in distress?"

"Hey, what gives?"

"Well, I was sitting in the lobby waiting to be called in for my child support case. I was talking to my client about her income and expenses and she got off on this rambling story about her work. She was working at Big Burger on second shift. Apparently the manager suspected one of the employees of taking twenty dollars from one of the registers. The manager, a woman named Shelly, took all of them- -there were three of them-- into the storage area and, you won't believe this part, she strip searched each one of them. She didn't find the twenty dollars. She counted the money again in each register and on the recount, found that two twenties were stuck together. My client is very upset about it. She quit over it and wants to sue. In fact all three want to sue she says. Here is the problem though. And tell me if I am wrong but this is big."

Ben nodded his head affirmatively. "Oh, yes, this is big all right."

Randy continued, "The problem is I am not sure I can handle it. This has the possiblity of being one of those large punitive damages verdicts. The company will throw a dream team at us that will be unbelievable. And I'm just not sure I am ready for it. On one hand I don't want the case to walk out of the door. This is what I trained for. But on the other hand I don't want to botch the case for them. They have been woefully mistreated and they deserve, well, they deserve an attorney who won't drop the ball."

"Randy, here is my advice. Do not let them go somewhere else. You are ready for this. You are ready for prime time. If you get in trouble, and you won't, but if you do, I'll back you. Go for it."

"Well, I'll think about it," she said still harboring some serious reservations. "Thanks for the encouragement. I've still got to weigh this out. It will be tough: David taking on a corporate Goliath."

"More like Delilah taking on Sampson. You'll kill'em."

She laughed and decided to change the subject. "Oh, I heard you were assigned to the Lyerly murder case. You are going to love that. I was in District Court when they brought him in. Your client is a piece of work." Randy smiled like the Cheshire cat and shook her head indicating disbelief. "Really. He's, it's a hoot."

Ben had a quizzical look. "What do you mean?"

Before she could answer the CNN anchor said, "Ladies and gentlemen, John L Daniels, President of the United States." The screen switched to the Oval Office in the White House. President Daniels looked up from the prepared remarks that lay in front of him. Ben walked over and turned up the volume. As he sat back down, he and Randy listened as the President spoke.

"My fellow Americans, I come to you this evening in sadness charged with the awesome responsibility to inform you that Vice President William Keynard Anderson was killed earlier this morning at the hands of unknown assassins. His wife, Marilyn, was seriously injured in the bomb blast that took the Vice President's life. As we speak, she has been released from surgery and is in the intensive care unit. Her condition is serious and guarded. Though their children were present in the residence when the blast occurred, they were not injured and are presently being cared for by the family of Mrs. Anderson."

The President paused and looked out with tired eyes. He cleared his throat uncomfortably and continued. "Tonight we have lost a great American William Keynard Anderson who gave so freely and fought so courageously for this country and he now belongs to the ages. His body will lie in state at The Capitol tomorrow morning and will remain there until Sunday afternoon. After the funeral his body will be buried with the great patriots of this nation in Arlington Cemetery. Tonight we mourn the loss of our Vice President, our cherished leader and our friend."

"I encourage you to have faith and patience in our system of justice. Every law enforcement agency in this country and many in foreign countries have been asked to assist. And tonight I ask each and every one of you to do what you can for your country and provide any information that may bring this matter to a swift conclusion. So far the investigation has revealed that the killing was the work of two lone assassins who stalked the Vice President and his family to the coast of North Carolina. They planted an explosive device in the residence where the Vice President and his family were staying. The Vice President was killed by the force from the detonation of the explosive device and he was pronounced dead at 4:12 a.m. this morning."

"This evening I ask that you join me over the course of the next several days as we celebrate the life of Bill Anderson, as we say farewell and as we honor his memory. And I especially ask that you join me as we pray for the successful recovery of his wife Marilyn and for the support and care of his children."

He paused. "Tonight America goes to bed in darkness and in sadness over our heartfelt loss. Tomorrow America will arise to bury its dead and pay tribute to its fallen leader. I assure you that this country will never fall by the misguided cowardice of the assassin but it will rise by the faith, dedication and loyalty of its patriots." The President stared directly into the camera and firmed his jaw as he concluded. "And let the word go forth that when the light of day shines in the 'morrow, justice will prevail, the wrong shall be brought to the right and this land will have the truth, only the truth and all of the truth. Good night and God bless each and every one of you."

*   *   *

In Washington at the Dirksen Senate Office Building within the complex of offices of South Carolina Senator A. Fowler Worrell, Chief of Staff Wrenn Davies clicked off the TV at the end of the President's press conference. He walked down the long hall to the Senator's office. Seeing that Senator Worrell was on the phone, he mouthed the words, "Senator, I need to see you if you have a moment."

Worrell put his hand over the mouthpiece of the phone and responded, "I'm going ovah to the Capitol. Meet you down at the front desk and we'll walk ovah togethah."

In a few moments Davies was waiting impatiently at the front doorway. When the Senator approached and they had started toward the steps, Davies said, "We've got a problem."

The Senator smiled as a couple of people walked past them and entered the building. "Now Wrenn, let's wait 'til we get out. No need to get evahbody concerned." As the Senator stepped onto the sidewalk, he continued in his deep low country drawl. "Son, it's hot. You know it's hot like this in Charleston but those boys were smart enough to go inland and build summer homes." He tugged at his tie and blew out a stream of imaginary steam. "Now you'd think our forefathers who had land from heah to the mountains and beyond would've found a bettah place for the conduct of the gov'ment's business instead of heah in this swamp along the Potomac. Whew!"

They walked over to a sidewalk that was shaded. As they strolled toward the Capitol, Davies asked, "What did you make of the President's address?"

"'Two lone assassins'," the Senator said referring to the President's phrase during the press conference. "That's just for public consumption. You know those boys are diggin'. They always think the trail leads deepah in the woods. The President is just trying to calm everybody down. What'd you think?"

"Right. I didn't think he told us anything but 'two lone assassins' underscores the problem. I thought from the beginning that it was a mistake to have two involved in something this important. It's hard enough to maintain damage control with one and it multiplies exponentially with each one added. We've already got a problem."

The Senator almost stopped. "What'dya mean?"

"Well, I called our contact at the Department of Correction. He says our man is talking too much. He's been bragging that he is into something big."

Senator Worrell responded, "Good God. Loose lips sink ships, boy. What's he been sayin'?"

Davies looked around furtively and and walked a little closer to the Senator. "Nothing specific," he said softly, "but something's got to be done. What do you want me to do about it?"

The Senator felt the heat building inside of his suit. He pulled his coat open to let the slight breeze in. "Man, it's hotter than a Saturday night in a Spartanburg whorehouse."

Davies continued to wait for an answer. Finally the Senator looked over at him and whispered, "Call Chen Sheng."

CHAPTER FIVE

Deep in the tall pines of coastal South Carolina on a little knoll stood Goretown. Although it was listed in Columbia as a minimum security prison and it was lightly fortified, fenced and guarded, its outward accouterments belied the long list of felonious accomplishments of its residents. Murderers, rapists, robbers, burglars and arsonists intermingled with violent misdemeanants, drunk drivers and wife beaters. The key to access to this home away from home was twofold: be a low risk for escape and know somebody who knows somebody.

It was known as the Horry Hotel among the inmate population for several reasons. The facility itself was located in Horry County and its prisoners for the most part worked in local towns and slept at the Goretown complex at night. Having been born during the liberalism of the 'Seventies and 'Eighties which subscribed to the theory that the working prisoner is the better prisoner, Goretown was relatively new. It offered the most developed work release program of any facility in the prison system. In fact it was said that the bus drivers on the transportation staff outnumbered the guards two to one.

The rules were relatively simple. Get up and be ready to catch the bus by 6:00 a.m.; work or attend school while away from the prison; catch the bus on time and in a sober condition; and return to the prison by 7:00 p.m. When on prison property, stay out of trouble. And the most important rule, important enough to be posted in bold red letters in the prison commissary: "Stay and Play--Violate and Rotate". The regimen was straightforward and the rules were sacrosanct. If there was a violation of a rule, the inmate was returned to the rest of the prison population. To get an invitation to be "rotated" back in, the offender had to know somebody who really was somebody.

The facility was rather large and provided space for eight hundred prisoners. With prison overcrowding after the legislature's assault on drugs and drunk drivers in the late 'Eighties and 'Nineties, there were cramped quarters for the inmates. With this large bubble in the prisoner demographics, the numbers of inmates escalated by the mid-'Nineties. And given the nature of the new arrivals which by far were drug dealers and drunk drivers who had extensive networks of friends who knew friends, Goretown was packed. Even with sardine can sleeping arrangements and long lines for breakfast and dinner, it was still a desired destination for the privileged and their proteges.

In its infancy the plan that gave birth to Goretown anticipated that the inmates would provide cheap labor and an ample work force for the towns within driving distance of the facility. It was twenty miles from the Grand Strand, a tourist mecca along the coast of South Carolina, and was billed as a boon to the service industry of the coastal economy. Situated a short distance from the North Carolina line and the large urban area of Wilmington, it was also envisioned that upon the release-to-work's demonstrated success, the program would be expanded into North Carolina. Unfortunately a zeal to punish rather than rehabilitate coincided with a strong feeling that South Carolina should help South Carolinians so that the homegrown innovation turned somewhat stale and languished within the confines of the home state.

Even so, there were some prisoners from North Carolina who resided at Goretown. Most of them were criminals who had left North Carolina for what they hoped would be a greener pasture: the South Carolina coast which attracted tourists by the droves and their millions of dollars in vacation funds each summer. The pickpockets, robbers and thieves who worked the beaches were convicted and transferred upstate or served time in the capitol while the white collar criminals worked their contacts for a berth at the Horry Hotel.

One prisoner was particularly distinct. Several months previously while he was serving time in a North Carolina prison, he had been mysteriously transferred to South Carolina for trial. Upon a plea of no contest to embezzlement that had been arranged at the quiet end of a term of court, he had been carried from Florence, South Carolina, the site of the hearing on his plea, directly to Goretown to serve his South Carolina prison term. It was all arranged through proper channels upon the request of the powers that be. All in all it worked well. North Carolina had one less prisoner to clothe, feed, house and guard and South Carolina had one more worker. The powers that could open and close the prison gates were mollified and the prisoner himself was elated.   The prisoner was SC Inmate #240743078 Ralph Stickley.

Stickley had slipped into the routine with ease.   He had comfortably found work after he had arrived at the facility. In fact to more accurately state his work release status, work had been arranged for him in the nearby town of Conway before he had arrived at Goretown. Although the work was rather tedious and mundane, still it was quite an improvement over the bone numbing boredom of doing time in North Carolina he thought. He had made friends in the prison, had a knowledgeable caseworker assigned specifically to him and had relatively free rein of the grounds of the prison.

On this particular Sunday afternoon, Ralph Stickley and his fellow prisoners had access to the exercise yard and the commissary. Intramural basketball games were being held on the two basketball courts with the teams from each of the four buildings moving through semifinals then finals by late evening. The canteen had been opened and soft drinks, ice cream and pastries were available to those who cared to part with their work release earnings.

Late in the evening a large group of inmates had become somewhat disenchanted with the level of officiating at the final game. Someone had thrown a bottle into the noisy crowd and as the angry participants began to disburse and attempt to search in the direction from which the bottle had been thrown, several inmates started pushing each other. In the confusion Ralph Stickley drifted back away from the center of the confrontation. When he had extricated himself from the turmoil and had reached the yard of B Barracks, the noise had grown louder and the air was punctuated by several strident voices.   Stickley slowed to look back somewhat disinterestedly at the nucleus of the dispute when he saw his bunkmate Skids hurrying toward him.

"They're comin' after you, Stick. That's the word." Skids looked furtively around the exercise yard. He was searching for something or someone.

"What they comin' after me for, man? I ain't done nothing." Ralph looked rather alarmed and started to search the crowd as well. Not seeing anyone moving toward him from the melee, he continued, "Where'd you hear this?"

"I'm ain't talkin', Stick. They'll come after me next. But I heard it while I was in line. They said you been talkin' too much. Said you was a rat. All this fightin' is just a trick to cover up gettin' you."

Stick put his back against the brick wall and turned his head back and forth quickly as he continued to scrutinize the crowd for any untoward movement. He was beginning to sweat. "I haven't ratted on anybody."

"Don't make any difference whether . . . "

Stickley interrupted him. "Who's coming?"

"I told you I ain't talkin'. They'll come for me. May be comin' for me anyway since we been bunkin' the same cell." Skids was just as scared as Stickley and started to walk away.

Ralph slammed him against the brick wall and Skids looked even more terrified. In prison the great fear was alienating some inmate then having to deal with the wrath inside the prison walls. Your only hope was to have friends who would protect you when you could not protect yourself. Now Skids was seeing himself caught in a situation from which there was no escape and there was bound to be a lot of pain. He tried to pull away but Ralph pushed his body up against him.

"Gimme, man. Who do I need to be looking for?" Stickley demanded.

"I don't know. Really I don't. Jimmy Bob was doin' all the talkin' but a bunch of 'em was listenin'. Come on, Stick. Lemme go," Skids pleaded and tried to push away from the wall again.

Ralph slammed him again and looked around the yard at the prisoners who were moving rapidly in different directions. No one was coming toward them and he turned his attention to Skids again. "Who was there?" he asked referring to Jimmy Bob's accusations.

Seeing no way to break Ralph's hold, Skids caved in. "Dax and Shirttail. They was there. Jimmy Bob said he got it straight from the office that you were rattin' out everybody. Said you were the one who told about the sugar that was taken from the commissary and he said you ratted on C Barracks' card game. He told 'em you had been a snitch when you was in stir up in Brunswick. They put you in population here to rat. And he said the first one that stuck a shiv in ya' would live like a king."

Ralph felt a hollowness building in his stomach and released his hold on Skids. Beginnng to sweat profusely, he spoke without really talking directly to Skids. "I'm a dead man. I gotta get help."

He turned Skids loose. As Skids ran off in the direction of the door to B Barracks, Ralph fell back against the wall again. He knew he was in serious trouble and knew his options were limited. He checked the inmates who were within sight. No Jimmy Bob, no Dax, no Shirttail. Then he moved quickly toward B Barracks.

When he reached the doorway, he checked carefully. Before he entered, he listened to the noise in the prison complex. Over between B and C Barracks at the basketball court he could hear the prisoners. They were congested in a tight knot and apparently were still wrangling over the referees and the bottle. Numerous prisoners were moving back toward the four buildings that housed Barracks A through D. He started to enter and ran directly into an inmate who was running back out of B. Ralph pushed him and angrily yelled, "Get out of my way." The prisoner seemed to recognize Ralph but did not speak. He continued in his rush out of the barracks.

Ralph ran toward his bed and lifted the leg of the cot. Inside the hollow leg was a twisted piece of metal. On one end it was wrapped in black electrician's tape to fashion a handle. The other end had been abraded into a sharpened blade that came to a long point. Ralph looked over his shoulder and seeing that no one was watching him, he lifted his shirt and slid the shiv in his pants next to his body at the waistline. He walked hurriedly back toward the rear door and started out. When he reached the back of C Barracks on his way to the office, he ran into one of the guards.

"Stand, prisoner," the guard shouted. "Oh, Stick, it's you. What's going on here?"

Recognizing the guard Stick pleaded, "I need help, Dale. They are going to kill me."

"Now no need to get bent out of shape, Stick. They are just tussling over that stupid ball game. They'll calm down in a little bit. Most of the guards are over there with them and they are settling down all ready." The guard smiled in an attempt to reassure Ralph.

Ralph was covered in sweat and was obviously upset. "I'm serious. This is all about me. Somebody has put out some bad information on me. Jimmy Bob is going to put a hit on me." Dale smiled again and Ralph pressed the matter. "Really. This is no joke.

I've got to get to the office. I've got to see Gedney now. Now!" he begged.

"Aw, come on, Stick. You are all shook up for nothin'. Go on back to Barracks and all this mess will calm down. I'll walk over there with you."

"No, I'm not going back. I want to go to the office." Ralph sounded firm on his position and started to walk toward the office.

"Wait a minute. Wait a minute," Dale spoke reassuringly. "I'll walk you over." As they started in the direction of the chief steward's office, Ralph fell in beside of the guard and continued to search the prison yard for Jimmy Bob and his accomplices.

When they walked back by B Barracks, suddenly they heard a loud noise in the showers at the rear of the building. "What the . . . ," the guard mumbled as he started toward the noise. Ralph followed and felt his waistline to make sure his shiv was still in place.

Ralph was uneasy as they walked to the showers. The guard checked the showers then walked by the commodes while Ralph waited. After finding no one there, they started toward the door. As they passed the towel racks, they heard the rush of feet on the concrete. Jimmy Bob followed by Dax and Shirttail spilled into the doorway obstructing their way. Ralph stepped behind the guard and grabbed nervously at his shiv. The guard said nothing and started to walk forward toward the three who were blocking the door. Upon hearing Ralph's footsteps following behind him, he stopped and turned. He smiled again and spoke to Ralph, "Not this time, Stick."

As the guard backed toward Jimmy Bob, Ralph realized it was a set up. He threatened the guard, "You'll pay for this."

Dale stepped behind the three and smiled again at Stickley. "Not likely," he said as he disappeared through the doorway. Ralph noticed his hand trembling as he slowly removed the shiv from his pants and held it against the back of his leg.

Jimmy Bob, Dax and Shirttail spread out in front of the door. Jimmy Bob was smiling and looking extremely comfortable. Ralph knew Jimmy Bob had a tremendous cocaine addiction and was probably high from the coke as well as the excitement of the moment. Ralph had not revealed his shiv but continued to hug it against the back of his right leg. There was still a lot of noise from the disturbance at the ball courts but the moment seemed frozen in silence, an awkward silence.

Finally Ralph spoke. "Jimmy Bob, I've never done anything to you. And I don't know what they've been tellin' but it's a lie. I know I talk a lot of BS but I ain't never ratted out anybody. Not once."

Jimmy Bob tried to get his eyes to focus on Stickley but they seemed to stare out into a space. "It don't make no difference, Stick," he said as he grinned toward Ralph. "You are valuable property. You know a man's got needs in here and they ain't easy to fill. Takes money. They say you are worth a lot to somebody. Besides I hate a snitch."

"I'm telling ya' I ain't ratted on anybody."

"You told about the card game. I heard it straight from the man. You are goin' to hurt over that."

Ralph was still trying to beg his way out and thought he would try bargaining in terms that Jimmy Bob, a drug dealer who had become hooked on his own product, would understand. "Look, Jimmy Bob. I don't know what they're tellin' you but I'm no rat. And I am worth a lot more to you alive than dead. I got money. A lot of money. If you get me out of here, I can give you more money than you'll ever make in one lifetime. I'm into something really big. People want me but they won't give you a dime. Help me and you can have enough money to go to coke and smoke heaven."

Jimmy Bob laughed. "Yeah, you and Donald Trump. Gimme some money, honey. Show me the money, show me the money," he said mimicking the line from the movie and twisting a little as though he was going to dance. Then he stood still and his eyes locked onto Stickley's face. "It's time for you to die."

Ralph produced his shiv and pointed it directly toward Jimmy Bob's face. A ray of evening sunlight caught the glint from the blade and flashed it across the room. Ralph had been shaking until this point. Realizing there was no retreat, he steeled himself for the attack. He seemed somewhat relieved that it was over. He sucked in a breath of air and started twisting the knife toward Jimmy Bob. "Death. So you like death. Today you are going to meet death up close and personal. I'm going to cut your heart out and eat it while I watch you gasp for the last breath."

His show of courage caught them off guard. Jimmy Bob said nothing but grabbed for his knife from his back pocket. Dax had been holding a stick by his leg and Shirttail had a knife but was slow in bringing it out. While Jimmy Bob fumbled for his knife, Ralph charged forward and as Jimmy Bob retreated, rammed the shiv past his uplifted arm and deep into his chest. Dax hit Ralph across the side of his head with the stick and started to swing again. Jimmy Bob looked stunned and fell back.

Ralph stepped back, shaken as well from the blow, and started to turn to avoid the next swing from Dax. As he did, Dax' blow was short of the mark but Shirttail who had finally produced a knife swung toward Ralph. His blade hit Stickley in the right buttock and the area around the wound spurted blood. Jimmy Bob fell back against the wall and gasped for air. Dax and Shirttail pressed forward toward Stickley who had retreated slowly holding his hip and dragging his leg.

Reaching a corner Ralph started swinging the knife wildly. Dax lifted the stick and swung toward Ralph's arm. Dax missed and Ralph nicked him on the arm holding the stick. Shirttail tried again with his knife but the blade caught in Ralph's clothing. Ralph cut Dax again across the upper arm. Dax who had not even noticed the first cut screamed out in pain. He looked toward Jimmy Bob who was sliding down the wall. Dax ran and Shirttail who had managed to get his knife disentangled appeared to debate for a second whether he should stay and try to finish Stick or run. He fled leaving Stick in the corner bloodied and beaten but otherwise relatively intact.

Ralph ran his hand down his leg to his hip again. It had not hurt until he touched it. "Crap," he moaned. He lifted his hand back up and it was covered with blood. As he stared at the blood, he began to see movement in the blurry background behind his fingers. When he focused on the movement, he made out Jimmy Bob who was trying to stand up.

Ralph stumbled over to Jimmy Bob and stood over him with his knife still out in front of him. "You've killed me," Jimmy Bob groaned obviously in great pain.

"Not yet," Stickley said as he leaned over Jimmy Bob. Ralph turned his knife sideways and made a slicing motion along the exposed skin of Jimmy Bob's neck. He slashed deep and blood squirted from the gash. Jimmy Bob was gurgling deep in his throat and slid into a heap on the bathroom floor.

Ralph staggered as he straightened up. When he tried to stand erect, the muscles in his hip tightened and he leaned over slightly to release the pressure on his wound. He did not think he would be able to run so he decided to try to find a place to hide until he could decide what to do. He walked over to a bathroom stall and climbed up on the commode. He jiggled a large tile in the suspended ceiling as he had done many times before to hide some item of contraband. Pushing the ceiling tile to one side, he tossed the shiv into the darkness of the attic. He carefully reached for the rafter nearest the tile, braced himself against the wall and climbed into the attic. After searching for his shiv and locating it, he slid the shiv back into his waistline and moved the tile back in place.

Stickley crawled the short distance to a row of wooden planks that had served as a walkway during the construction of the rafters. He lay down gently on the planks and pulled his legs up to brace against a rafter support. His thoughts raced as he lay there trying to think of what to do next. He knew he had to get out but how, he thought. It was a stroke of good luck to have thought to hide right at the crime scene. Nobody would look for him there unless, he thought, he had left bloody prints on the ceiling tile. Maybe they would not notice even if he had since there was so much going on. As he lay there, he began to notice the sounds out in the prison yard. The commotion was still going on but as he lay there listening quietly, it seemed to get more and more distant. He focused his attention on the ray of dim sunlight that shone along the edge of the roof line. The ray seemed to shimmer and turn into a blur. Finally he closed his eyes and drifted off.

When he awoke, he was startled. How long had he been passed out he wondered. He listened but heard nothing significant. He looked at the cracks along the outside wall of the line of rafters. The cracks that had shone daylight when he had gone to sleep were now dark and indistinguishable from the rest of the trusses. He started to move and when he did, he felt a piercing surge of pain in his hip. He stopped immediately and, although unsure, thought that he had screamed out audibly. He listened again but there was no sound indicative of his being discovered.

The next time he moved slowly and deliberately. He flexed his legs very slowly several times until he thought he could move without making too much noise. Ralph crawled back to the ceiling tile and lifted it slightly. The bathroom was dark except for reflected light from the large exterior lights that were placed at intervals in the camp perimeter and as far as he could tell, was empty. He knew the routine well and except for an occasional nighttime trip to the bathroom by the older prisoners and an occasional rendezvous between lovers, the bathroom would stay vacant.

He climbed down from the attic and stepped lightly onto the commode. He listened again then stepped onto the floor. Ralph hobbled over to where Jimmy Bob had been lying earlier and studied the floor. It was almost as if it had never happened. There was no trace of him in the darkness.

As he slowly made his way out of the bathroom into the hall, he hesitated after each movement to make sure he had not been heard. Ralph was amazed that he had not been discovered after the attack. He had to remember that, the next time he was in a jam: do not run away from the crime scene but hide until all of the hoopla is over then slip away quietly. He tried with much difficulty to tiptoe to the door and went out quietly. He worked from shadow to shadow until he reached the transportation buildings. Typically they were off limits for the prisoners but tonight, Ralph thought, would be a good night to break a rule.

He pushed the door to the garage and worked his way to each bay. The only vehicle he found was a truck that the guards used for transporting small amounts of trash from the garage itself to the dump site outside of the fence. It would provide good transportation out of the prison but there was no place to hide in it and there was no certainty when the trash would be transported. After he left the garage, he went to the parking area where the buses were located. He searched the lot for the bus that he had ridden to Conway during the several weeks he had been there. Ralph knew the driver's routine and knew that after his deliveries, the driver always stopped at a little roadside cafe across from the manufacturing plant where Ralph had been assigned.

When he reached the bus, he tested the doors and found that they could not be opened. He checked and found that one of the old baggage compartments underneath the bus was unlocked. Ralph shook the door and it opened easily. He lifted it, climbed in and crawled over two old tires to the back of the compartment. The door clicked shut as he pulled on it.

He lay there in the darkness thinking about the events of the day. He knew they wanted him and wanted him badly but why. Why were they trying to have him killed he wondered. He had not done anything or said anything as far as he knew. Well, it did not make any difference he concluded. These people were powerful, extremely powerful. They were probably trying to cut any links to connect themselves to him. He knew he had just survived with luck and maybe he would not be so lucky next time. His only hope, the only way he could save himself he thought was to leave and not just leave the prison but to leave the country. To do that, he needed money, a lot of it, and he needed transportation. As he drifted off to sleep again, he thought he knew where he could get all of it.

*   *   *

Scout Troop 119 was meeting in the basement of the Ogden Baptist Church. Although the Monday night meeting was running a little late, Wanda Stickley waited patiently in the parking lot for Jeremy to emerge from the rear door. She had let him out at 7:00 p.m., completed her shopping at Food Lion and returned for the pickup at 9:00 o'clock. She checked her watch. 9:16. As she thumbed through her coupons and organized them to be used on her next shopping trip, she listened to the radio. In the background the announcer was reciting the events of the day in Washington.

"The President and the First Lady officially led the nation in what was a day of mourning and sadness. President Daniels personally visited the scene at The Capitol where the Vice President's body was lying in state. In a moment as moving as any that has been witnessed by this reporter, President Daniels and the First Lady entered the rotunda earlier this morning and walked directly to the casket. He stopped and waited for a moment, then both of them got down on their knees. As he bowed his head and prayed, others standing in the line joined him in the prayer. When he stood, it was evident that he was very moved by the experience. A tear ran down his cheek. He reached in his pocket and removed a handkerchief and wiping at his face, he turned, attempted a smile to acknowledge those who had come and then rejoined the First Lady who had stayed by the Vice President's body."

"When President Daniels returned to the White House," the announcer continued, "he attended to the difficult and lengthy process of making appropriate arrangements for the . . . "

Wanda clicked off the radio as Jeremy popped out of the door. Jeremy was directing another Scout to go out for a pass as Jeremy hoisted the football behind his head for the long pass. After the other Scout had run about fifty feet, he released the ball and it arced in a long spiraling trajectory. Surprisingly it was pulled down by the receiver. Jeremy was as amazed as the intended receiver was and Jeremy jumped up with both arms over his head yelling "Touchdown! Touchdown!"

Wanda rolled down the window and called out, "Great job. Just wait until you boys get to New Hanover High."

Jeremy trotted over to the car and the other Scout joined him. "Mom," Jeremy asked, "Mark wants to come over Friday night for pizza and a movie?"

Mark tossed the football to Jeremy and both of them waited for the response. Wanda tucked her coupons into her billfold. "We'll see. I'll talk to Nancy," she said referring to Mark's mother. "But right now. It's Monday, it's a work night. Homework."

"Homework?" Jeremy protested in disbelief. "School's out. I don't have any homework."

"Oh, yes, you do. Chores. That's home work," she responded and laughed. "Get in. Mark, tell your mother I'll call her. If she says it's okay, we'll see you Friday."

Jeremy pretended to make a lateral hand-off of the football to Mark as he circled the car. He got in and laid the football on the back seat. Mark ran back to the Scout hut and called back, "Friday. Pizza!"

As they drove home, Jeremy pulled out his Scout manual and tried to read but there was too little daylight left. He laid the book in the back seat beside the football and pretended to play drums on his knees. They rode along in silence for a little while. Finally Wanda spoke. "When does your Scoutmaster think you will be ready for your Star rank?"

"Not long," he said. "We are going to have one more camping trip this year he said. I think he said we'd go on a weekend after school starts back. Maybe September. He's arranging for us to join another Scout troop from Southport. If they decide to come, we are going to have a merit badge jamboree. I can focus on the three that I need for Star."

"Which ones are you trying to get?"

"Citizenship," he responded as he went into a drum roll. He built to a crescendo and pretended to raise the drum sticks up waiting for the announcement. "Camping and Marksmanship." Jeremy pretended to shoot a speed limit sign as they rode along then blew out the imaginary smoke.

"If I had your energy, I would have my chores done before Scouts." Wanda reminded him and did a drum roll with her fingers on the steering wheel of the car and looked over at Jeremy.

Jeremy halfheartedly smirked and reached for the ball. They turned in the driveway and pulled up to the side of the house. Jeremy started to exit. Wanda called after him. "Get your manual and come back to get these groceries. It's time to do a good turn daily," she said referring to the Scouting tradition.

"Right." He bounded into the house and then returned to the car.

Jeremy unloaded the back seat, carried the groceries in and went to get the clothes out of the dryer. He returned and started folding towels as she put away the groceries. After he had folded the towels, he went to his room and she started fixing a snack for both of them. As she reached in the cabinet for the peanut butter, a loud noise that sounded like something had fallen in the basement startled her.

"Jeremy, is that you?" she called in a loud voice.

Jeremy was in his room and called back. "No."

"Did you leave the basement door open again? I'll bet Esmeralda is down there again," she responded referring to their cat.

Wanda walked to the basement door and noticing it was closed, she opened it and called for Esmeralda. When she did not hear her or see her, she decided to go down and see what kind of mischief she was in. She cut on the basement lights and walked down the steps. When she reached the laundry room, she clicked on the light. Finding no cat she went to the furnace room. The door to the room was closed so she did not expect to find her in there but decided she would try any way. When she turned on the furnace room light, Esmeralda came walking toward her from the crawl space.

Wanda was a little surprised at seeing her, picked her up and scolded her. "What are you doing in here, you little scamp?"

When she started to go out of the room, she turned directly into Ralph Stickley. She immediately panicked and dropping Esmeralda, tried to run for the door. Ralph stepped to the side as if to let her pass but then when she ran beside him, he grabbed her by the back of her hair and jerked her down to the floor. As she fell in a thud, she screamed.

Ralph dragged her back up and tried to hold her upright by her hair. "Ralph, please," she pleaded. "Don't. Don't."

He turned her loose and pushed her into the block wall. Her body slammed the wall very hard and she slid into a clump. "Ralph, please," she begged again from the floor raising her hands in front of her. When he did not move toward her, she attempted to regain her footing. As she stood, she held her head with one hand and grabbed for the wall with the other. "What are you doing here?"

Ralph looked at her with disgust. "I'm in trouble, big trouble this time." She noticed that he moved with a limp and acted as though he were in considerable pain. "I got tied up in something . . . they want to kill me. I need money, a lotta money and I need a car. I'm taking your car."

"No, that's all the transportation that Jeremy and I have."

Her response angered him. He charged her and grabbing her by the neck with both of his hands, he lifted her up so high that her feet were barely touching the floor. She struggled and pushed away from the wall as he choked her. Her hands flapped in the air as she reached for something, anything. She knocked things off of the table next to her as she scrambled to find a weapon or anything that would make Ralph release her. She grabbed a screwdriver and plunged it directly into Ralph's side. He looked stunned and released his hold on her. She sucked air forcefully and tried to find her footing. She fell to the floor again.

Ralph regained enough to advance toward her. As he did, Jeremy yelled at him from the steps, "Stop or I'll shoot you." Jeremy was holding Wanda's pistol that she kept by her bed.

Ralph half turned and seeing the pistol, he laughed. "You think that little old pea shooter is going to hurt me. I just killed a guy, the toughest guy in prison."

Ralph turned back toward Wanda who was lying in a heap. He started to try to kick her in the head. As he braced himself on the table and lifted his leg, Jeremy yelled, "Don't"

Ralph kicked weakly but strongly enough to knock Wanda backward. As he did, Jeremy fired the gun striking Ralph in the upper left shoulder. Ralph turned toward Jeremy and walked toward him. Ralph climbed the steps slowly and Jeremy backed up the steps holding the gun between himself and Ralph. At the top of the steps Jeremy screamed, "I'll shoot again."

Ralph was not deterred but continued to advance slowly. Jeremy turned and bolted through the kitchen and out of the door to get help. When he reached the driveway, he threw the gun into the culvert that allowed drainage water to run under the driveway. Ralph staggered through the kitchen following Jeremy's route and stumbled out into the darkness. He leaned on the car and started to continue down the driveway. As he shuffled over an uneven surface in the pavement, he tripped and fell. He started to get up but was kicked from the side.

He looked up into the face of his attacker and feebly mouthed, "Chen."

As Ralph tried to scream out, the attacker held his head back and cut his throat on both sides. Ralph's arms flopped wildly in the air while blood collected in a puddle beneath his body. The blood started to roll in a small rivulet down the driveway. The attacker ripped open Ralph's shirt and carved an R in his chest. Then he undid Ralph's pants, sliced off his penis and pushed it into Ralph's mouth. The attacker hurriedly checked around him. He dropped the knife by Ralph's body as he writhed and quivered. As the attacker backed up slowly, he uttered one word, "Rat," then ran off in the darkness.

In the basement Wanda was slowly regaining consciousness. She struggled to get to her feet and remembering the confrontation, she pulled herself up by the leg of the table. She stumbled to the steps and remembered Jeremy shooting Ralph. She tried to hurry up the steps but each step seemed leaden and each movement seemed to be executed in slow motion. When she reached the top of the steps, she searched for Ralph and Jeremy. Wanda noticed that the door leading from the kitchen to the driveway was open. She reached the door way and bumped into the jam as she steadied herself. When she regained her strength enough, she looked out into the darkness and started to focus on an object in the driveway. She gasped when she realized it was a body.

Wanda descended the steps and moved as quickly as she could toward the body. When she reached it, she made out Ralph's face in the dim light from the street. She focused and saw the gashes on his neck. The reflection of light brought her attention to the blood as it drained down the driveway. Suddenly the body lurched and Wanda shrieked. When she regained her composure, she noticed an object beside the body. She picked up the knife and realizing the extent of the horror, she mumbled, "Oh, my God. Jeremy, what have you done?"

Suddenly the driveway was illuminated in a flash of headlights and blue lights from a police vehicle. The squad car screeched to a halt and an officer jumped out. With his gun trained on Wanda, he screamed at her, "Drop the knife. Now. Do it."

Wanda stood motionless like a deer caught in the headlights. "Do it. Drop it now," he demanded and braced himself in a shooter's stance.

Wanda could hear him but she could not hear him. She tried to speak. Finally words formed and she muttered, "Call . . . Call Ben Down."

CHAPTER SIX

"When it hits the fan, this is where it lands," the little gray haired woman said as she tried to make small talk. She and Ben waited in the lobby of the New Hanover Detention Center. She smiled at Ben and asked, "What are you waitin' for?"

"I am here to see a client," Ben said without lifting his eyes indicating he did not want to chat.

"So you are a lawyer," she said overemphasizing the law in lawyer and completely missing Ben's rude nonchalance. "What did your client do or is he one hundred per cent not guilty like O.J.?"

Without waiting for Ben to respond she waved some pink papers in front of her and continued talking. "They called me to come over here about these warrants to get my grandson out of jail. This is the second time. His father was hell on four wheels and looks like he's gonna be just like his daddy. I spent a boatload of money on his father. Looks like I better find another boat. But I tell ya' I'm not going to run for him like I did Herbert. Do you represent people charged with drunk drivin'?"

"Sometimes," Ben replied as he studied the door to the lawyer's interview room. While he waited impatiently to be called, he started to tell her to have her grandson come by the office when he was released from jail but she interrupted again.

"I don't know whether he needs a lawyer or not. He's guilty as sin. I hate to say it about my own but I know he is. Drinkin' and drivin'. That's what all of them Hall boys have done."

Ben was a little agitated with her assumption and her persistence. "Sometimes," he spoke up rather forcefully, "that's when you need a lawyer the most. Guilty people have rights too and often need a lawyer to make sure those rights are protected."

She seemed to stiffen a little in response to Ben's tone of voice. "Well, you don't have to get upset about it. I was just tryin' to make a little conversation. Some people . . . "

As she spoke, a jail matron stepped to the interview room door and waved Ben in. "Thank God," he muttered under his breath. He picked up his briefcase and headed toward the door as the grandmother continued to scold him for his arrogance.

"Smells like you've had a snootfull yourself." He heard her termagancy as he walked through the door into the hallway that led to the interview room. Ben was familiar with the routine and waited at the end of the hall for a pat down search and a perfunctory inspection of his briefcase. When the jailer completed the frisk and slid his briefcase back to him, Ben walked in, sat at the table and waited. Over the years he had done this hundreds of times and each time was just as unpleasant as the one before it.

In less than a minute Wanda was led down the hall from the cells. She watched her feet as she stepped over to the table and sat. Ben studied her carefully and noticed that the bruising on her face had turned dark black. Her eyes were puffy and the right side of her head seemed swollen and somewhat disproportionate. Wanda had fresh scratch marks on her neck and had patches of red on her face from her right ear to her mouth. When she changed position in her seat in order to get more comfortable, she grimaced and held her side.

"Wanda, are you all right?" Ben inquired.

In some obvious discomfort as she moved her lips, Wanda started to speak then nodded instead. Ben pressed for a clearer answer. "Where are you hurting?"

"Mostly in my face and neck but I am sore all over. They took me to the hospital. I've had x-rays and nothing is broken. The doctor said I would be swollen and sore for a couple of weeks, maybe several weeks." She looked relieved to be able to tell someone.

"You look very sleepy. Are you on any medication?"

"Tylenol and some type of anti-inflammatory medicine. I am sleepy. I was up all night with the officers. Really I'm all right now."

Ben sensed that she did not want to talk about her injuries any more and tried to focus on something else. "Jeremy is all right," he commented.

"I know," she said, "I talked to him this morning. They said as soon as we finished the interrogation that I could see him. They let him in and I got to talk to him for about fifteen minutes. He was here with some lady from the Department of Social Services. What's that all about?"

"The Department of Social Services has obtained an emergency order which grants the Department custody of Jeremy until the court conducts a hearing to determine what should be done about his care and custody while you are locked up. He will be placed in foster care and . . ."

"In foster care? What does that mean?" Wanda still had a little panic left in her even after all of the events of the night.

"It's a temporary thing," Ben assured her. "The DSS does this to protect the child. They will schedule a hearing and the court will determine what to do with Jeremy until all of this is sorted out. If you have some family member who can take him, very likely the judge would permit it if the person passes a DSS evaluation."

"I don't have anybody. Mom and dad are dead and my brother James lives in Texas. There's no one." Wanda looked even more dejected.

"What about Ralph's mother? She's still living, isn't she?"

Wanda tapped her fingers on the table indicating a little nervousness about the subject. "She never had anything to do with us. Jeremy hasn't seen her since he was a small child. She supported Ralph no matter how bad he was and never did anything for Jeremy."

"Well, Jeremy is fine for the moment. We'll work into that when the time comes. What about you? Are you sure you are all right?"

"I'm all right," she said a little more emphatically and looked off in the distance. "Will I have to stay in here?"

Ben knew this would be a difficult subject and wanted to broach it carefully. Numerous times he had had clients who thought that he could waltz them out of the jail as though there were nothing to it. "There is no easy answer to that question, Wanda. Presently you are held without bond and you will have to stay in jail until a bond is set. That is not unusual. If the State charges you with first degree murder and seeks the death penalty, then the court can keep you locked up without a bond. If the State does not seek the death penalty, then you are entitled to have a bond set. Even then though, the bond can be so high that you cannot make it. I don't want you to get your hopes up about a release. We will do what we can but it is a slow process."

Wanda seemed to be satisfied with the answer about the bond but she still looked worried. Ben's comments about the death penalty aroused a further inquiry. "Do you think they will try to get the death penalty?"

"There is no way to know at this point. We are at such an early stage of the investigation, I'm sure no one knows. Not the DA, not the investigating officers. You are charged with first degree murder but the DA will analyze all of the evidence and make several decisions: one, whether to indict you on first degree murder or some lesser charge and two, whether to seek capital punishment. We may not know the decision for several days or even months. Let's talk about what happened. Take me back to the beginning and as carefully as you can, describe what happened. Start where you first saw Ralph."

Wanda drew up a little, obviously not wanting to revisit the terror she had experienced during the last few hours. When she finally spoke, her delivery was halting and her face assumed a little more color. "I . . . we, Jeremy and I, had just returned from Scouts. I was making a sandwich for us when I heard a noise in the basement. I remember I thought that Jeremy had left the basement door open again and I thought Esmeralda--she is our cat--well, she is Jeremy's cat, anyway, I thought she was in the basement. I went down there and I saw her coming out of the crawl space. I knew something was wrong. She is so fussy she won't go in the crawl space because it is dirt, cobwebs. It's messy and she's peculiar."

"Let's get on to where you saw Ralph."

"I called her and started back out of the furnace room door. When I turned, Ralph was right there. After that it went crazy. Ralph pulled me down to the floor, jerked me around, into the wall."

"Did he say anything?"

"Big trouble. I remember him saying that. He was in big trouble and he wanted money and a car. I told him he could not take my car and he started hitting me again. I thought he was going to kill me. I grabbed a screwdriver, I think, and hit him as hard as I could."

"Where did you hit him?"

"In the side."

"How many times?"

"Once. He let go and I ran to the steps. He was still coming toward me. That's when I shot him."

"You shot him? Where did the gun come from?"

"I had carried it with me downstairs. When I heard the noise, I had gotten the gun from the bedroom and yeah, I think, that's right. I carried it with me."

Ben looked a little puzzled. "How many times did you shoot him?"

"One time. One time and he ran out of the house. The rest of it is kinda blank. The next thing I remember I was standing over him out in the driveway. The police pulled up and I asked them to call you."

"Where is the gun?"

"I don't know. I guess the police have it."

"Where was Jeremy during this?"

"He had gone over to a neighbor's house and . . . "

"I thought you said you were fixing a sandwich for both of you," Ben cross examined.

"I was but he was going to come back."

"Did Jeremy see any of this?"

"No. He didn't see anything. The police picked him up over at the neighbor's house."

"What have you told the police?" Ben had been making notes and putting question marks beside of each response that needed more inquiry. As he waited for her answer, he looked back and noticed there was a question mark beside of each response.

"The same thing I told you." Wanda spoke a little more feebly and Ben decided not to revisit the questions he had. He closed his pad and tossed it over into his briefcase.

"I'll talk to the police and see if I can find out what they have. We'll talk again later after I have talked to them. Do you know which officer or officers interrogated you?"

"No. I don't remember their names but I remember what they look like. One of them had reddish, red hair with gray on the sides. He was the same one I talked to before when I reported that Ralph raped me."

"Does Stanton ring a bell?"

"Not really."

Ben signaled the matron at the door and told Wanda, "We'll talk again. Let me talk to the officers first. Until then don't talk to anyone about any of this. Do not talk to the police, do not talk to the guards, do not talk to your cellmate. Remember: a friend today may be a witness against you tomorrow."

Wanda seemed to be paying attention but did not acknowledge the advice. Instead she wondered out loud, "You know I don't think Ralph was there to rape me. I think he was going to kill me this time. To this day I don't know why he hated me so much. I never, never did anything to cause him to feel that way."

Ben nodded in agreement. He had never seen or heard anything to provoke the anger he had seen in Ralph during the years when he and Wanda had battled each other in the courts. Wanda had always been co-operative and had almost always retreated when Ralph pushed some issue in court. She had been fiercely protective of Jeremy but even with him, she had tried to encourage Ralph to visit and do things with Jeremy. Ralph's moods had swung between icy cold and virulent heat. He was distant for long periods of time then pushy and assaultive. His reaction bore no connection to the situation and was always overkill. Ben had seen it before in domestic situations. It was a kind of insanity that had no satisfactory explanation and worse, no cure short of death.

The matron finally put out her cigarette and walked in to get Wanda. "Remember," Ben reminded her. "Talk to no one about any of this. We'll talk later and in the meantime if you need me, they will give you access to a phone. Call me. All right?"

Wanda shrugged weakly and struggled lightly to get up out of the chair. When she did, the matron took her by the arm and escorted her out of the door. Ben walked back to the front desk in booking. He noticed with some pleasure that the gray haired grandmother was not out in the lobby. When the booking officer came to the desk, Ben asked to see Noah Lyerly, the defendant he had been appointed to represent.

"Noah?" the officer said with a quizzical smile. "You mean Nora, don't you?"

Ben was not in on the joke he thought and asked, "What's that all about?"

"Counselor, your client is too pretty to be a man but a man he is. He was too disruptive with the male population in the jail so we sent him to Central Prison in Raleigh as a safekeeper. So you are the lucky one, huh? She's, he's been in before but not for anything like this. Murder. You'll have your hands full with this one." The officer noticing his pun chuckled and said, "Better keep your hands to yourself on this one or you may get a hand full if you know what I mean."

Ben did not respond to the joke and asked instead, "When will he be returned?"

"Probably next Monday. We have him down for a court appearance next week. Want to make a date with him then? Pardon me, an appointment then?" He said trying to keep a straight face.

"I'll check back."

*   *   *

Later in the week Ben filed formal notice with the office of the Clerk that he represented Wanda on the pending warrant. He also notified the District Attorney's office and served the District Attorney with a request for voluntary discovery. Since the DA's office had an "open book" policy on discovery, the request would allow Ben to have access to the investigative information as it came through the DA's office. For the time being he could talk to the investigators with the Sheriff's office while he waited for his first Prosecution Summary from the DA.

On Wednesday Ben was notified that the Department of Social Services had scheduled a hearing on Jeremy's custody for Friday morning before Judge Wolfe. Juvenile cases were distinctly different from criminal cases and civil cases. The Department would be represented by an attorney. The DSS attorney typically worked on a private contract basis and was usually very familiar with the case and its specifics. The action was begun by the filing of a petition with the District Court alleging that the child was neglected in that the child did not receive proper care or was dependent in that the child had no parent to provide for his custody and care. Jeremy was alleged to be both. The parent could be represented by an attorney who was retained or appointed if the parent were indigent. To further complicate matters an attorney was also appointed to represent the child who was presumed to be indigent. The child's attorney served as a guardian ad litem, that is, an attorney whose representation was limited to the pending litigation.

The hearing scheduled for Friday was of a preliminary nature and would deal with whether Jeremy should remain in the temporary custody of the Department or whether custody should be returned to the parent.   A final hearing would be arranged later for a determination of permanent custody.

The DSS attorney who typically appeared for these interim hearings was Mark Bryant.   The attorney who served as guardian ad litem was Caroline Markham.   Although Wanda was eligible for a court appointed attorney, Ben felt she should have the benefit of counsel who was familiar with her and with the juvenile court.   In the past Ben had volunteered for service in the juvenile court and had served in juvenile court as both appointed attorney for the parent and as guardian ad litem for the children but for the last six years, having found the work at times disturbing and frequently dissatisfying, he had removed his name from the appointive list.   Randy on the other hand had served in the juvenile court since she had come to Wilmington.   He decided to bring in Randy to represent Wanda at the Friday hearing if Randy would consent.

"Skittle, call Randy and ask her to come by my office when she gets a chance," Ben said as he came in the door to the reception area. "I want to talk to her about Wanda Stickley's juvenile case."

As she picked up the phone to ring Randy, she asked Ben, "Are you taking the juvenile case too?"

"Truthfully I haven't thought my way through it.   In fact I just assumed I was representing Wanda since she called for me.   And I just assumed I was going to take care of her in the juvenile hearing." Ben scratched his head as if he had just remembered something he should have thought about long ago.

Randy answered and Skittle gave her the information as Ben had requested.   She hung up and said, "She's coming right over.   She's just doing research she said and she was looking for a reason to get out of her office.   Ben, I never saw a Client Representation form for Wanda."

"I know.   I never had her to sign one.   Again I just assumed I was her attorney.   I haven't even talked to her about a fee yet.   I need to talk to her about both of these things."

"Ben, something is in the air.   You are representing somebody in a murder case and you haven't even discussed a fee arrangement? What's going on here?"   Skittle was a little amazed.

"Now there you go again, Skittle.   I'm not representing 'somebody'.   I am representing Wanda Stickley.   That woman has always come to me for help.   She's been so abused, she deserves all of the help she can get.   She will pay me when she can.   I can't desert her just because she is too poor to pay.   If I listened to you and Margaret, I wouldn't have a client.   I know the rule is 'payment up front' but sometimes it just doesn't work that way."

Skittle still not sure she was hearing what she was hearing remarked, "You are serious?"

Ben was a little put out that Skittle was debating the subject of fees with him and argued, "Now do I tell you how to prepare a letter?"

"Yes."

"Well, that's not what I mean.   Do I tell you how to perform your duties as a receptionist?"

"Yes."

"No, I don't.   You just want to bicker.   Even if I told you how to answer the telephone and how to deal with the public, you wouldn't do it.   You can't answer that one 'yes'.   Besides I will decide who pays and when they pay."   Ben started to walk back to his office.

Skittle called after him.   "Ben Down, you are getting softhearted. Something is in the air.   I'm proud of you."

"Now there you go again.   Don't be telling anybody that or this lobby will fill up with every bum and every sad case who wants a free ride."

Randy came down the hall and heard the tail end of the conversation.   "I'll take a free ride.   In fact I'll pay just to crawl out of those law books for a while.   I'll even sit in Ben's office and suffocate from cigar smoke rather than look at another case on punitive damages."

"Come on in, Randy.   Mrs. Skittleran has a lot of work to do." Ben enjoyed reminding Skittle who was in charge.

Skittle ignored the comment and went back to work at her word processor.   Randy and Ben wandered back to Ben's office.   As Randy took a seat and laid her legal pad on Ben's desk, Ben said, "I'm taking up Wanda Stickley's case.   It is coming rather fast and furious at the moment: criminal and juvenile.   She is in the jail charged with murdering Ralph.   She's held without bond and she has a custody hearing with the DSS on Friday.   It's just a hearing on temporary custody and she needs an attorney for that part. I was wondering," he said as he watched her eyes, "if you would like to take on the custody case for her."

"What are the financial arrangements?" Randy did not blink.

"Man, I've done too good a job with you. Get the money up front or you don't get the money."

"That's me. Legal mercenary for hire. Have money, will travel. No pay, I stay." Randy paused and grinned. "Seriously what is Wanda paying you?"

"Nothing yet. Wanda has no money. She has agreed to pay me when she can, what she can. Ralph had a ton of money. Most people think he drank it up or stuck it up his nose in cocaine but I don't think so. I've told her if she ever finds it, she can pay me with that."

"Count me out. I'd have a better chance of winning the lottery."

Ben looked disappointed and Randy said, "Seriously I'm up to my neck in research in these cases with Big Burger. I'm researching everything, everything before we file. The Big Burger Three have come to me for help. They are going to get their money's worth."

"The Big Burger Three," Ben remarked and grinned at Randy's choice of words for the three plaintiffs in the civil case. "How much do you get if you are successful?"

"Twenty-five per cent if we settle. One third if we have to try it."

"Man, I have taught you well. Too good in fact," Ben lamented referring to her refusal to help with Wanda's case. Ben had picked up a cigar from the desk and fumbled to get it out of its wrapper. They grew silent until it became a little uncomfortable.

Finally Randy spoke. "Look. Here's the deal. I'll do the custody case if you will let me second you on the murder case. I need the experience and I think it's time. I have worked in District Court for two years and I have had four felony trials in Superior Court. I know I haven't done a murder yet but a murder case would look good on my resume."

Ben lit the cigar and studied Randy as though he were sizing her up. Before he spoke, he blew out a long stream of blue smoke. When he did speak, he spoke as if he were slamming a trap door shut. "Done. You're in."

Randy shook her head and said, "I knew I should have held out for more. That was too easy."

Ben blew out a ring with the cigar smoke and assumed a certain smugness. "Well, that's what you get when you are dealing with a professional. It's the art of the deal. First things first though. We need to get Wanda to sign Client Representation forms. We need to file a Limited Representation form with the Clerk and we need to reequest voluntary discovery from the DA in the murder case and we need to file a Limited Representation form with the Juvenile Clerk in the custody case."

Randy picked up her legal pad and flipped through several pages. She pulled out a Client Representation form, two Limited Representation forms and a voluntary discovery letter to the DA. Ben leaned forward and tried to read the pages across the desk. He saw that they were filled out and signed by Randy. He leaned back and said, "I think I have been had. You were planning on entering both cases before I even asked you. You certainly assumed a lot. And doggone, you must've known I wasn't getting paid and you must have known I was going to ask you but how?"

Randy was even more smug. "Ten thousand horses could not pull it out of me."

"Give," he demanded.

"Oh, all right," Randy said pretending to cave in. She was going to tell him anyway but she enjoyed watching him suffer. "Skittle told me."

"That's impossible. Skittle didn't know I was pro bono until I told her out in the lobby just a few minutes ago. And I never told her I was going to ask you."

"Never underestimate Skittle. She knows more about you than you know about you. In fact she has more grapevines than the hills of Rome. She told me when you came back from the interview with Wanda." Randy slid the Client Representation form and the Limited Representation forms in front of him for his signature.

He signed the three forms and chewed on his cigar. "Skittle talks too much," he grumbled. "Look, here's what to do. Go . . . "

Randy took the forms back and said, "I'll go by the jail and make sure Wanda agrees to our joint representation . . . "

"Right then . . . "

"Then I'll file the two forms with the Clerks."

"Right then you . . . "

"I'll talk to Wanda and find out what options we have in the juvenile case. If she has anybody who can take custody of Jeremy, we'll start making arrangements to have them evaluated by DSS."

"Right but it's not likely she will have anyone. When I talked to her, she didn't have any family who could help." Ben laid his cigar in the ashtray and leaned forward on his desk. "Anything else?"

"Of course. What has she said about Ralph?"

He resumed his hold on his cigar and dropped back in the seat. He let the blue smoke build up and watched it meander up toward the ceiling. "Her story is pretty shaky. There are so many inconsistencies and things that do not make sense, it's hard to tell what really happened. It may be because she was beaten and was exhausted from all that had happened. I believe the police had her up all night. She says Ralph came to the house Monday night. She heard a noise in the basement, went down, was attacked by Ralph. She stabbed him with a screwdriver and then shot him. Then she blanked out. She doesn't know what happened after that. She is vague about where Jeremy was. She is shaky about how she got the gun. The detectives won't talk about it until they report to the DA. All I have heard is that it was pretty gruesome. It looks like a case of self defense but we'll see what the Prosecution Summary shows."

"After all she has been through with Ralph Stickley, there isn't a jury in the fifty states that would not find it was self defense."

"Right," Ben pretended to agree. "Since you've got it all figured out, I'll tell the DA and save him the trouble. Now if you will take the custody case, I'll try to work on a bond."

"Done." Randy chanted the word like an auctioneer reiterating Ben's earlier smug reply.

*　　　　　*　　　　　*

On Friday, District Court opened at 9:00 o'clock. Judge Wolfe concluded the criminal matters that had been set then proceeded to hear the emergency juvenile cases. "In re Jeremy Stickley, a Minor Child" was the second case scheduled.

The first case for hearing was "In re Tomeka Blackwell, a Minor Child." Judge Wolfe reviewed the file briefly then noted for the record: "This matter is before the court by way of a juvenile petition alleging that Tomeka Blackwell is an abused and neglected child. Tomeka is two years of age and is not present. Mark Bryant appears for the petitioner, the Department of Social Services; Randy Bost appears as guardian ad litem for the child and Tom Royce appears for the mother. Mr. Royce, the mother is present, isn't she?"

"Yes, sir," he replied indicating to his client to stand.

"Does she raise any issue concerning the jurisdiction of the court over the child? In fact I will ask all of you if there is any issue concerning the court's jurisdiction? I know we have discussed this before on the record but I want to be careful and make sure the record reflects proper jurisdiction."

Tom Royce spoke again. "No, sir. The child was found here in New Hanover County and by statute this court has jurisdiction over the child. Further we raise no issue concerning the content and form of the petition and the service of the petition and the juvenile summons was proper."

After both Randy and DSS attorney Mark Bryant indicated their agreement with Tom Royce, Randy said, "Your Honor, there is one matter I wanted to bring to Your Honor's attention. The maternal grandparents are here. They are Cheryl's parents." She referred to the mother of the child, Cheryl Blackwell, and then pointed to the front row of seats and indicated by pointing. "Mr. and Mrs. Horace Blackwell are here and they are sitting on the front row. Would both of you stand so that Judge Wolfe will be aware of who you are?"

As they stood up, Randy continued. "I know they are not properly parties to this action but they are vitally interested in the outcome of the case. They are here from Detroit, Michigan."

Judge Wolfe nodded in their direction to acknowledge their presence. He stated, "Even though they are not officially parties to this juvenile case, we are certainly glad to have them. Is there anything else we need to address before we proceed with final arguments?"

After each attorney reported that there were no further preliminaries, Judge Wolfe announced for the record. "We began this case about three months ago when the Department filed an emergency petition with the court alleging that Tomeka, now two years of age, was being abused and neglected by her mother, Cheryl Blackwell. Tomeka has been in the temporary custody of the

Department since the issuance of the petition and I believe by agreement, that Cheryl who is also a minor was placed in the custody of the Department."

Mark Bryant stood indicating that he would like to be heard and Judge Wolfe as was his custom hesitated and looked toward him. Picking up the cue the attorney said, "Your Honor, with regard to that, I did want to inform you that we have not been able to find a foster care placement in which Cheryl and Tomeka could be together. I know Your Honor suggested it at the first hearing and we tried, but we just could not find a foster parent who was willing to take both. Some of our foster parents will take older children and some will take younger ones. The few who will take both have been at full capacity. Sorry."

"That's all right. Thanks for trying," Judge Wolfe said. Continuing with his recitation as Mark sat down, he remarked, "We have now had three days of hearings in which the court heard from witnesses for the Department and for the mother. All evidence is now concluded, the court has adjudicated Tomeka a neglected child and has ruled the evidence is insufficient to support a finding that Tomeka is an abused child. Further all parties have been allowed to present evidence concerning the appropriate disposition of the child's custody. We are ready to proceed with final arguments. Under our rules Tom Royce, attorney for the mother, will argue first, then Mark Bryant, attorney for the Department, then we will close by hearing the attorney for the child, Randy Bost."

Mark Bryant rose again and stated, "Your Honor, I believe we can assist with speeding along the arguments. The position of the Department and the position of the guardian ad litem are the same. I will waive argument and let Ms. Bost be heard for both of us."

"Thank you, Mr. Bryant. All right then, Mr. Royce, you may proceed."

"Your Honor, if the court please," he began. "Cheryl Blackwell is fifteen years of age. She had Tomeka when she was thirteen. As the evidence demonstrates, she has made numerous errors of judgment but as the evidence also discloses, she has managed to make some important changes in her life. She has been attending parenting classes and she has been attending the adult basic education classes. Cheryl has demonstrated a remarkable maturity for a young lady of fifteen. She wants her child back and she has the ability to take care of her. We request that you return Tomeka to her and allow the Department of Social Services to monitor the placement of the child with her. Thank you."

"All right then. Ms. Bost."

"Thank you, Your Honor. As you know Caroline Markham usually serves as guardian ad litem and would have in this case except that she had a conflict of interest that prevented her from representing Tomeka. I was appointed and I have done all that I know to do to help Tomeka."

"Yes and thank you for filling in for us."

Randy acknowledged the thanks and continued, "Tom Royce is an able adversary and it is not very often that I find myself in disagreement with him. Though I admire him personally and appreciate his skill as an advocate, on this occasion though I must. Reason and sound judgment demand it. I represent Tomeka Blackwell. She is two years old and has no voice except mine before this court. I do not represent her mother Cheryl and I do not pretend to argue her case nor argue for a disposition that necessarily promotes her wishes."

She looked over at Cheryl and noticed that she was crying. "Her tears move me as I am sure they do Your Honor but reason and judgment not emotion should be the rule of this case. The guiding star for the court is to do what is in the best interest of Tomeka. Not to do what's best for the Department or do what's best for the mother. Frankly Cheryl has had a great chance and blew it. She needs to demonstrate that she can take on the awesome responsibility of raising a child. Tomeka deserves to be placed in the legal custody of the Department so that appropriate decisions will be made for Tomeka's care and supervision. As a part of that dispositional order, Tomeka should be placed by the court in the physical custody of her maternal grandparents, the Blackwells."

Cheryl screamed out, "No!"

Judge Wolfe intervened, "Stay seated and stay quiet if you want to stay in this courtroom, young lady. Continue, Ms. Bost."

"I do not come to this judgment lightly. It is based on reason. Cheryl has demonstrated such poor judgment so far. She was sexually active at twelve, she was sexually promiscuous, she became pregnant, she delivered Tomeka when she was only thirteen and she cannot state with certainty who the father is. She has been continuously rebellious. When she brought Tomeka home to her parents, the Blackwells, who are here with us in court, she continued the same lifestyle and left much of the care of Tomeka to her mother. She stayed away from her parents' home for extended periods of time without their consent and without their knowledge as to her whereabouts. During these absences Tomeka's care was left entirely to the Blackwells. Finally Cheryl ran away from Detroit taking Tomeka with her and was found here in New Hanover at Carolina Beach. When she was found, she was in possession of drugs. The baby was dirty. The mother had no food for the child and the report is that Tomeka ate ravenously when she was placed in foster care. The mother had no means of support. The officers reported that she was engaging in prostitution."

Cheryl half stood at her table and called out, "That's a lie. I never . . ."

"Sit," Judge Wolfe ordered firmly. "Sit down and be quiet or I will have the bailiff take you out." Cheryl sat down.

"Her impetuous and naive behavior continues as we have just seen her demonstrate." Randy paused, looked at Cheryl and although she continued to argue to Judge Wolfe, she directed her comments toward Cheryl. "Even with all of that, I still believe that she should have the chance to be mother to the child. She is a child herself and hopefully as she matures she will realize the great gift that God has given her and she will mature into the woman and mother that all of us hope she will be. Until then she needs help and a lot of it. Tomeka has tremendous needs, almost none of which are being met by Cheryl. Tomeka deserves someone who will make appropriate decisions for her care--not someone who will take her off and place her in an environment that is detrimental to her. The Department can fulfill this function. Tomeka needs someone who can nurture her, who love her, who can take care of her every minute of her young life. Her grandparents can do that and they are more than willing."

Randy paused then continued, "I know it does not seem so at the time to Cheryl but this course will not only promote Tomeka's best interest but will also promote Cheryl's. It has been written, 'As the twig is bent so grows the tree'. Thank you, Your Honor, not only for your patience but for the concern that you have demonstrated throughout this case."

As Randy sat, Judge Wolfe announced that he would take a brief recess to consider what had been said before he ruled on the conflicting requests for disposition. When he went out, the bailiff brought Wanda Stickley into the courtroom. As he did, Randy caught her out of the corner of her eye and walked over to where she was seated.

"Ben will be here in a . . . ." As she spoke Ben came in through the door from the judge's chambers and joined them. Randy continued, "As I had mentioned to you before, Wanda, our choices are extremely limited. I called your brother James in Texas and although he wants to help, we can't work it out. We can't arrange an out of state placement for Jeremy at this point. James will have to undergo a home study in Texas before the court will consider him as a placement possibility for Jeremy. The local DSS will not consent to a placement without it. They could take a month to two months."

Ben asked, "Were the two of you able to find anyone else that will pass muster with the court?"

Randy replied, "No. The court will not accept neighbors or friends. They will have to be approved as foster parents and that takes a long time. A family member can be considered without the formality of being approved as a foster parent but a home study has to be arranged through the Social Services or Child Welfare agency that has jurisdiction in the place where the family member lives. We couldn't find anybody."

Wanda was shaking her head in agreement and Ben inquired, "What are our choices?"

Randy said, "Trial or stipulation. The evidence is strong against us at this stage. I suggest stipulation. Stipulate custody with the DSS and placement in foster care. The advantage is we can stipulate that Jeremy is temporarily a dependent child because Wanda is incarcerated and there is no other family member available. If we proceed otherwise with the hearing, the Judge may determine that Jeremy is neglected and dependent. It may be hard to overcome that finding in later hearings. By the stipulation we can limit the amount of damage. The bottom line is Jeremy will stay in foster care no matter which way we go. We just do not have anything else to offer. I've already talked to the DSS attorney and the guardian ad litem. Both will agree to the limited stipulation and to the temporary placement. What do you think?"

Wanda looked disappointed but agreed. "If we don't have anything else, that is all we can do. Will I get to see Jeremy?"

Ben spoke up. "We can't guarantee it, Wanda, but we will try. We'll make a point of it. As for Randy's proposal, it is about all we can hope for in this difficult situation."

"All right," Randy said. "Let me talk to them again and make sure we have everyone's agreement."

Randy walked over to Mark Bryant and began discussing the case. Jeremy came in the side door of the courtroom with Caroline Markham who had been appointed to represent him in the juvenile hearing. Caroline directed Jeremy to the front row away from Ben and Wanda. When he had a seat, he looked back over the seats at Wanda and smiled. Wanda's hands were handcuffed and she made an awkward gesture trying to wave at him. Wanda looked over at Ben and said, "God, this is going to be hard."

"I know. Be strong. We've got a long way to go but there is hope." Ben patted her shoulder.

Judge Wolfe returned and announced his ruling concerning Tomeka's custody. He placed her in the custody of the local Department of Social Services and authorized the Department to place her in the physical custody of the grandparents as Randy had requested. He conditioned placement with the grandparents on two things: first, the grandparents had to pass a home study evaluation and two, the comparable DSS agency in Michigan would have to agree to supervise the placement.

After the parties in Tomeka's case went out of the courtroom, Judge Wolfe called the case of In re Jeremy Stickley, a Minor Child. After covering the preliminaries, Randy asked to be heard and when granted permission, she stated, "Your Honor, this is a case we can resolve by stipulation, that is, a consent judgment if Your Honor approves. As I am sure you know, Jeremy's mother is presently held in the custody of the New Hanover Detention Center on a criminal charge. The Department presently has custody of Jeremy by a nonsecure custody order. All of us are in agreement that we should stipulate that there is sufficient evidence for a finding that Jeremy is dependent in that no parent or guardian is available to care for him and further that he should continue in the temporary custody of the Department."

"Does everyone agree with this proposal?" Judge Wolfe asked.

Mark Bryant for the DSS and Caroline Markham for the child nodded in the affirmative.

"Mrs. Stickley, do you understand and agree to this proposed judgment?" Judge Wolfe asked being careful.

Wanda stood and answered, "Yes, sir."

Judge Wolfe entered the order and asked if there was anything else that needed to be addressed. Randy said, "Yes, Your Honor, there is one thing. Mrs. Stickley would like to have visitations with Jeremy. This is her only child and she has been his primary custodian all of his life. It would be a gross injustice to prohibit access particularly since she is only charged and not convicted of any criminal offense."

Caroline Markham objected. "Although I agree to the custody arrangement, I do not think Jeremy should visit with his mother until this matter is resolved. She is charged with killing his father. I know the attorney for Mrs. Stickley walked rather softly around this issue but it's a charge of first degree murder. She is incarcerated in the jail without bond. Jeremy is thirteen years old. He should not be required to visit her in jail. That certainly is an environment that is injurious to his welfare."

Randy started to rebut Ms. Markham's statements but Judge Wolfe intervened. "The guardian ad litem's point is well taken. The court will not order visitation at this time but will consider further requests upon a change of circumstances."

Randy looked at Wanda and noticing her disappointment, comforted her. "Sorry. We tried but I knew that was going to be a sticking point."

Ben leaned over and said, "Wanda, we have one more chance. If we can get the DA to go along with a bond, then the visitation would not have to take place at the jail. Before we go back to the office, we'll talk to the DA. He's a little late with the Prosecution Summary so we'll go by and find out what we can and we'll see if he has any mercy in his heart for a mother and her child."

As they walked out of the courtroom, Ben and Randy started down the hall toward the DA's office. Assistant District Attorney Rod Pemberton stepped out of the office door and walked up the hall toward them. Ben saw him first and mischievously remarked to Randy, "Is that Mel Gibson or . . . No, it's Rod, Rod Pemberton." Then Randy saw him.

"Oh, no. It's Rod," she whispered to Ben. "I can't be seen in these pants. These pants are screaming. I was going to lose five pounds before I saw him again. That man gives me the shivers and I don't want him to see me blown up like a hippopotamus."

Randy started to turn around and Ben caught her by the arm. "Come on, Skinny. We've got more important things to do than worry about a little bloating."

Rod continued to approach and Randy buttoned her jacket. She put her briefcase in front of her as they stopped to talk. Ben spoke first. "Hey, Rod. How is the land of felonies and fugitives?"

"As usual they're winning but we are still kickin' butt and takin' names."

"By the way," Ben said as he looked over at Randy, "Randy, that is a nice outfit you are wearing."

Rod joined in with the compliment. "Really. Looks nice, Randy."

Randy turned a little red and pulled the briefcase up a little closer. Nodding her head acknowledging the compliment, she pinched Ben on the arm hidden behind her briefcase. "Thanks, Rod. I . . . uh . . . I "

Ben overrode her comment with "Owwww. How, how's Butch? Still persecuting?" Ben rubbed his arm and said, "The Wanda Stickley case. Pretty straightforward. Self defense. End of story. Right? We need to see him about a bond in Wanda's case."

"Forget it," Rod replied. "Autopsy's in. Butch said Wanda Stickley will go to the grand jury on an indictment of first degree murder and he has specifically said, 'No bond'."

CHAPTER SEVEN

A light summer wind rose up from the Potomac through Arlington Cemetery toward the Custis-Lee House and rustled the leaves in the oak trees. A long line of mourners moved slowly along the winding road of the cemetery as the body of the Vice President was brought to join the patriots whose graves are marked with white crosses. Within sight of the final resting places of John and Robert Kennedy, the grave of William Keynard Anderson would assume a position of prominence overlooking Washington.

The late days of August in the Capitol always brought a humid heat. The moisture from the Potomac River and the radiated heat of the concrete streets and buildings conjoined to produce stifling urban heat that visibly shimmered up from the pavement. The throngs who had followed the funeral procession along its convoluted route had been slowly baked. Now they were being relieved somewhat by the shade and breeze that lifted to rise over the tall hills that were home to the Tomb of the Unknown Soldier and the former Virginia home of the Lee family.

The words of the Vice President's brother who had delivered the eulogy at the Episcopalian Church were still hovering in memory:

"We come here today not to condemn, not to accuse but to elevate the spirit as has our fallen brother for the length and breadth of his life. William Keynard Anderson, Bill, if you will permit, served his country in so many ways. All of us know of his courageous service in the military during the early years of our efforts in Vietnam and all of us know of his untiring and dedicated service on behalf of the good people of our home state, Missouri. Few people know of his devotion to our family. Over the last several years all of us saw how devoted he was to Marilyn. We have the fondest hope that she will be spared, that she will live to raise and nurture her children. Tari, Brittany and Mike are strong children as we have witnessed over the last several days. Bill was devoted to them and finally they are the witnesses to the life and spirit of their father and mother. We see in them the strength and the character that are so much a part of and the fabric of their father's legacy."

"So today we join as a nation sorrowed by our great loss but at the same time imbued with the belief that we as a people have been improved and lifted up by the short life of our Vice President Bill Anderson. He was a man of his times and he was a man who captured the spirit of an era. When he spoke, he spoke of the good and he spoke of the right. His overriding passion was his compassion, his compassion for those who were less fortunate. He worked earnestly and faithfully to make the blessings of liberty that we enjoy here in America available to those who live under the heel of the oppressor and who must seek the permission of the powerful for the enjoyment of the least privilege."

"And today we seek answers. How could this have happened again in America? Who is responsible for such a dastard act of cowardice? And more importantly what can we learn from this so that this horror will never be visited on another family, on another nation? We must know so that other generations will know. So that we in our time and they in theirs can guard against the tyranny of the assassin and the nullification of the will of the people by the violent malcontents. Today we seek answers; tomorrow we seek justice. Today we are burdened with a heavy heart; tomorrow we will wipe away our tears and . . . " He choked up and stepped back from the microphone.

After a few moments he wiped away his tears with the back of his hand and searched the crowd finally resting his eyes on the Vice President's three children who were seated with their grandparents on the front pew. "Without rancor, without enmity," he announced and continued building strength in his voice, "we commit our brother, our father, our Vice President and our friend to the world. Now he belongs to all of us."

At the cemetery the President and Mrs. Daniels placed a wreath in front of the grave site as the world watched on television. The slain Vice President was honored by a military salute and then a prayer was delivered by the chaplain who had served with him in Vietnam. After the brief graveside ceremony those in attendance began the slow walk back to their cars. Limousines lined the long drive around the entrance to the cemetery and chauffeurs waited patiently in the air conditioning for the arrival of their passengers. World leaders and other dignitaries followed each other to the shady spots as they slowly meandered back to the cars. They entered without tarrying in order to escape the heat.

Having been near the front of the long line of the motorcade when it entered the cemetery, FBI Director Fries and Assistant Director Michael Newman returned to their transportation relatively quickly. Fries had decided it would be best if they rode together in order to have a working meeting with other agents teleconferenced in as needed. As they entered, the chauffeur, who was sequestered by a sound proof lexan shield, was watching the small television screen in the limousine. Fries instructed him by the car intercom to turn the volume up so that all of them could keep up with press coverage of the event. The screen continued to show the area surrounding the grave site and the commentator was revisiting the life of the Vice President.

"You know," Fries said as he picked up on the comments, "I truly admired Bill Anderson. He was one of those leaders that this country has produced who was truly selfless. He served in the Peace Corps and then served in the Marines."

"Strange combination," Newman noted.

"True but the underlying theme was service to his country. He was poised to be our next President and I believe he would have been a good one. He certainly had the courage of his convictions. I remember when he visited El Salvador. He nearly got all of us killed. We met with the Salvadoran President and the leading members of his cabinet one morning. Anderson dispensed with much of the protocol and told them how important it was to restore basic freedoms to the people. They sat there, smiled a lot and listened politely. Who wouldn't when the Vice President of the most powerful country in the world is talking? But after he spoke to them, he took us out into the country. Now this was right after the war there and these people were still without much government then. One atrocity still led to another. It was totally insecure. We stopped at numerous places and he would send word he wanted to speak to Guillermo Ruiz who was one of the few remaining guerrilla leaders who hadn't been killed or imprisoned. By the end of the day Ruiz appeared. We sat in the courtyard of some old villa and watched his men play with their AK-47's. We kept our hands inside our coats while Anderson and Ruiz talked. Anderson gave him the same tongue lashing he had given the others, wanted a meeting between Ruiz and the Salvadoran leaders. I sweated bullets but he was as calm as though he were working out an order at McDonalds. But that's the kind of man he was. Straightforward, no nonsense, totally committed. He would have been good for this country."

"He was a great man. That same fearlessness may have been the very thing that got him killed," Newman agreed. "So far our agents have narrowed the possibles down to three. Each one has physical evidence that points in its direction and each one has been the target of the Vice President's criticism."

Fries continued to watch the television screen as he listened to Newman's speculation. He commented offhandedly after he saw the President return to his vehicle. "The President does excellent work at these official functions. He is as smooth as any chief executive we've worked with." Then he shifted the conversation to Newman's remarks. "The Iraqis. That scenario makes the most sense to me. Anderson opposed the war with the Iraqis. He supported a diplomatic solution until the last day but once we declared war, he was one hundred per cent. He felt Bush quit too soon. I still remember him telling me that it was a major mistake to leave Saddam Hussein in power. He has said privately that the war will never be over until Hussein is removed and he has supported every option to remove Hussein including military action. Saddam is no fool. He knew Anderson was going to become President and when he did, Saddam's days would be numbered. But there is one big glitch."

Newman picked up the thought. "Right. I know. The physical evidence is weak. One abandoned car out on Interstate 95 a few miles from Wilmington traced to an Iraqi operative is just too tenuous. Saddam has been quiet but several Iraqi operatives have taken credit for the kill. I agree. Except for the motive, all of it is just too disjointed to tie in the Iraqis. The Chinese connection makes more sense to me."

Fries instructed the chauffeur to turn up the volume. "I want to hear this," he said and waved Newman off.

The announcer stated, "The Vice President's brother pointed to a problem that continues to vex the investigative agencies. Although all of the nation's law enforcement resources have been brought to bear, a solution does not seem to be close at hand. FBI Director

Robert Fries spoke to Malcolm Laell on the Today show earlier this week."

The screen shifted to Laell's interview with Fries. Laell asked, "Does the FBI know who killed Vice President Anderson?"

Fries responded, "No but I do want to assure the American people that we are doing everything within our power to solve this crime."

"Are there any significant leads that point to any particular suspect or suspects?"

"There are numerous leads and we have every available agent at the FBI pursuing those leads. I do not want to set a time line for this investigation to be completed and I do not want to make any statements that will jeopardize the investigation or any of our agents in the field. The investigation will follow due course and the truth will come out. Whether it is today or tomorrow, we will solve this crime and those responsible will be brought to justice."

The screen then switched to the line of people who were continuing to make their way back to their cars from the grave site. Fries made a motion with his hand directing the chauffeur to turn the volume down. As the sound came down, Fries asked, "Where were we?"

"The Chinese," Newman reminded him. "The forensics on them are the strongest. Our lab has traced the exploded remnants of the wiring to Chinese manufacture. That by itself is not too compelling because the bomb itself is rather primitive. But when one adds C4 to the equation with Chinese components, it makes for a compelling suspicion that the Chinese are up to their necks in this."

"I agree. I saw the spec sheets on the fragments and they're of Chinese origin. Truthfully though most of them could be picked up at Walmart. Colonel Thomason's conclusion that since C4 was used so extensively in southeast Asia during the Vietnam war, the Chinese are very familiar with it and have used it frequently in their military training. So it is likely if the bomb was born in China, it would have C4 as the detonator. But I read the Rieyende report. Rieyende has the credentials. It's a think tank filled with an elite corps of analysts of Chinese policy and institutions. Rieyende concludes the Chinese would be greatly harmed by the Vice President's elevation to President since he has been so outspoken on their record of human rights violations. Further even though they would be greatly opposed to his election, they would not intervene with violence. Maybe money. Historically they have not done that and practically they would just withdraw and return to another period of isolation."

"The forensics are right but the politics just do not make sense," Newman agreed again. "One thing we do have that looks promising though is the hardened glue that was found in the hallway leading to the Vice President's bedroom on the night of the assassination and another one was found in a shoe print out in the dunes surrounding the house. The glue appears to have been used by the assassins on the bottom of their shoes to conceal the identity of their shoes. The field agents believe it just fell off of the shoe while they were walking. The glue itself is rather nondescript but the interesting thing is the sand that was found inside of the glue. It was obviously not from the North Carolina coast according to our lab. We are sending it out to geologists at the University of Nevada at Reno for a closer look. Best case scenario: we'll find out where the sand came from and that may give us another lead on our assassins."

Fries responded as he looked through his paperwork, "I didn't see the report on that. I don't have it here. When will we get the information from the University?"

"Anytime now. They've had it since Wednesday." Newman handed his copy of the FBI lab report on the glue to Fries and continued running through the developments in the case. "Well, finally our best lead is with our own homegrown anarchists," Newman reported, finding something to get excited about. "I talked to Pate Brandon in our Dallas office. He has been in close contact with the ATF and they have a line on a former Branch Davidian. The politics and the forensics match up for this one. If it is all right with you, I would like to bring Brandon and his ATF contact in by a telephone conference call. You need to evaluate their reports firsthand I think."

"That's fine," Fries responded and pointed Newman to the phone.

Newman dialed Brandon and asked him to bring the ATF officer in by telephone. When all three were connected by telephone, Newman said, "Pate, Director Fries is here with me. I am going to put us on the speaker phone." When the speaker light activated, Newman gave him the go ahead.

Brandon spoke first. "Good afternoon, sir. I have Leigh Bottoms on the line. She is presently in an adjunct office in Forth Worth and she and I have been working on a potential suspect here in the

Dallas-Fort Worth area. Leigh has been with ATF for the last fourteen years. She and I worked together on the Branch Davidians' siege and we are pretty familiar with all of the players in that."

The Director interrupted to speak to Officer Bottoms. "Leigh, nice to speak to you. I've heard a lot of good things about you from Cordell Smith, your supervisor. He says you are his best field officer out there."

She laughed and replied, "I wouldn't argue with Cordell about anything although I think he is being too kind. Sir, it's nice to speak to you and I look forward to working with you in this. You can count on me to do whatever needs to be done."

The Director responded, "Thanks," then Assistant Director Newman spoke up. "Pate, let me get you to relay what you have to the Director."

"Sure, Mike. Let's see. After Waco several of the Branch Davidians split off into smaller groups. One group in particular believed the siege was a pretext to kill Koresh and destroy their ministry. This group has been very vocal about violence being the only answer. Several of their tracts assert 'An eye for an eye' and numerous times, they have handed out literature that indicates there will be no justice until Waco is avenged. We have been calling them 'The Avengers' to distinguish them from other splinter groups who are similar but not as committed to violence. Their leader is Matthew Bryant. As you know Vice President Anderson has been very vocal in his opposition to these antigovernment groups. Although he opposes violence, he has been unwavering in his support of us as we tried to shore up these radicals. Their literature singles him out as a target for revenge. And Bryant himself has made several comments after the assassination that he personally carried out the mission."

Newman asked, "Pate, can you fax us the literature?"

"Sure," he replied and continued unprompted with the report. "We have been able to make direct contact. Leigh received information that Bryant and a couple of his followers were at the Stockyards in Forth Worth handing out leaflets. She went out there and . . . . Leigh, maybe you should pick it up from here,"

Officer Bottoms continued the report. "I found him, of all places, at Billy Bob's Texas. It is billed as the biggest saloon in the world. It was late afternoon and Bryant and two others, Shannon Best and

Roger Walton, were passing out leaflets to passersby. We had an undercover that we were using for illegal weapons purchases at the biker bars. I called him out and he was able to make contact. He has infiltrated and is attending services with them. He was the one who reported that Bryant bragged about 'carrying out the mission' and he also says they have a weapons cache and they have been training in bomb construction. Here's the kicker: they're using C4 and remote electronics for transmission of detonation signals."

Newman chimed in. "Sounds good."

Bottoms said, "We're trying to get some of the materials out for a comparison with the bomb fragments found at the VP's assassination."

"How far are we away from getting them?" Fries asked.

"I'm not certain, sir," Bottoms offered. "Our operative has a meeting with them tomorrow night."

"Any chance we can get some of the C4?" Fries was obviously interested.

"We'll try but Bryant is extremely suspicious. He has even had some of his disciples staking out our office just to see who is in the organization. We are having to be particularly careful about our contact. It's dangerous work and really our contact's a little shaky. He didn't know he would be getting into any of this."

Fries said, "We've got motive but do we have opportunity. Do we have anything on Bryant's activities during the night and morning of the assassination?"

Brandon answered. "Sir, he was in the area. We have him flying to Charlotte, North Carolina on Monday before the assassination and returning to Dallas-Fort Worth International on the Sunday following. We haven't been able to develop anything yet as to his whereabouts during the seven day period. We're still working on that."

"Anything else?" Newman asked. When both Brandon and Bottoms indicated in the negative, Fries told them that he would need daily reports. After the telephone conversation had concluded, Newman said, "I think this is the best we have so far. It's not the motherlode but it's definitely digging in the right vein." Newman handed the Director a report on the background of Matthew Bryant which included education, work, physical appearance and activities.

"Really we should have anticipated more violence from antigovernment extremists. McVeigh and Nichols in Oklahoma City were just tip of the iceberg." Fries scrambled through several other papers in a file and pulled out one titled: Assassination Analysis, Behavioral Sciences Unit, Federal Bureau of Investigation. He quickly scanned the report on Bryant and then reviewed the FBI's profile of the assassin.

"Bryant fits the profile," he said referring to his comparison of the two reports. "Caucasian, midthirties, sporadic work history, intelligent, first born son, skilled work below his ability, leader. It indicates he was a corporal in the Army. Any information on his AIT?"

"None at present. We are working on it. Bryant claims to have had ordinance and demolition training in the military. Of course he also claims he was a sergeant so he is lying about some of it."

Newman inquired while Fries continued to sift through the two sets of documents, "Should we go public with any of this? The press is getting pretty restless for an answer. It seems some answer is better than none at all. We can leak it."

Fries did not look up but continued to study the information. "No. We'll go public when we have more to offer. Too much speculation in all of this." Fries kept reading. "Let's see. It says he was a military brat and his family moved frequently. Father deceased, mother died last year. He fits as closely as anyone could." Fries laid the reports aside.

"We might've found our man," Newman said as Fries returned his attention to the television screen. "Bryant was going to go off. It's just a question of when. He could be the one."

Fries nodded while he watched the screen of the TV set. As the camera panned the area where the long line of limos waited, the screen shifted to Senator A. Fowler Worrell and his Chief of Staff Wrenn Davies who had just finished the long walk from the grave site and were entering the waiting staff car. In the background the announcer commented on Senator Worrell's role in President Daniels re-election and his work with the Vice President in South Carolina which was considered a swing state during the last election. After the Senator and his Chief of Staff entered the car and started talking, the screen shifted back to the grave site and Fries turned his attention back to Newman.

"Matthew Bryant," Fries thought out loud. "You might be right. He could be our man."

*   *   *

While they continued to wait for the traffic to start moving out of the cemetery, Senator Worrell stretched out his six feet seven inch frame in the back seat of the Lincoln and yanked at his tie. Wrenn Davies called on the car phone to the Senator's office for anything that needed to be addressed. The line of cars lurched forward then immediately stalled.

"Boy, turn that air on full blast. We're dyin' back heah," the Senator commanded. The driver turned the air conditioning unit to its maximum setting and waited in line. "Good gawd a'mighty, we're gonna be sittin' heah longer than a Strom Thurmond filibuster. What in the world is wrong with these people? We might as well just stay heah in line 'cause we'll be buryin' somebody else before we get out at this rate."

Davies, who had been half listening, hung up the phone and commented, "Senator, for somebody from the South, you hate the heat worse than anyone I know." He laughed unenthusiastically.

"They ain't nothin' funny 'bout this, Wrenn. Heat'll kill ya'. I've seen it happen. One time I was down in Orangeburg when I was a boy. We was workin' a large field of watermelons. Those things can weigh twenty to twenty-five pounds. We were tossin' up to the truck to be hauled to the State Farmah's Market in Columbia. A half cent a melon. Some of those old colored boys was gettin' on up in age. I saw one of 'em fall out. He turned cold as an icebox and turned almost white. He died right there in front of us. Don't talk to me about any heat. That stuff'll kill ya'." Senator Worrell had pulled his handkerchief from his pocket and was mopping the sweat from his forehead.

Davies wanted to speak to the Senator about some matters that had arisen at the office and told the driver to turn up the radio loudly enough so that they could hear the broadcasts concerning the funeral. When he felt the sound was sufficient to drown out their conversation, Davies spoke to the Senator in a low voice. "What do you think we ought to do about Gedney?"

"Gedney is just tryin' to take care of Gedney."

"Yes, but he is doing it at the wrong time. He is pushing us I think because he feels he has some leverage."

"Right but nothin' wrong with that. I've known the Howell brothers since I first got into politics. They can raise a small fortune off that coast. They didn't name it the Grand Strand for nuthin'. He can get a grand 'bout evahwhere he goes. Evah' time I've run he's done evahthang I've asked him. He's raised evah dollar I've asked him to. Besides we been lucky with him. He works in the Department of Corrections, cheap pay, long hours. He could've asked for a lot more and I'd have gotten him more. But he wants to be close to his mothah. She's in bad health, ain't gonna live long. So he's pretty well-satisfied. All he's askin' for is a little help with his brother, Bobby. And Bobby's all right. We gonna hep him. Just takes time. You just call'em and tell'em evahthang's gonna be all right."

"Yes, but Gedney has probably got it all figured out by now. He arranged for Stickley to be out of prison when we needed him and covered his tracks. Later when Stickley started talking too much, he got the word out that Stickley was on the government's payroll as a snitch. It wouldn't take a genius to figure it all out. Who knows? Stickley could've told him everything."

The Senator was mulling it over as Davies talked. "Naw, he's just helpin' Bobby. Those Howell boys are thicker than fleas on the back of a blue tick hound. Even if Gedney does know the whole story, he is still with us. He's smart enough to know he's in up to his neck and his butt isn't gettin' any lightah from sittin' at that desk in Goretown." The Senator laughed at his own joke. "Nah. Wrenn, you call'im and let him know personally that I said Bobby is comin' on board. Then you call the Director in Columbia and tell him that I personally said that we need Bobby Howell. What does Gedney want for Bobby again?"

"Jail inspector. He wants Bobby to inspect the jails and prison facilities."

"No problem. We always need a good jail inspectah. The people need to be safe in their homes and secure in their possessions. No bettah way to do it than have somebody makin' sure these criminals are locked up tightah than Dick's hat band. Besides Bobby would be our man and he would have his foot in evah jailhouse in the State. I can see the wisdom of that. Now surely you can, Wrenn?"

"I agree totally. It's Gedney's timing that concerns me. He is pushing this at the wrong time. He knows we owe him and he is collecting too . . . "

Senator Worrell completed the sentence for him. "He is collectin' when it's due. Plain and simple. That's all. Don't read too much into it. That's your problem, Wrenn. You're always thinkin' of the downside."

"That's my job."

"And you are doin' a fine job, a fine job. Call'im. It'll all calm down."

Davies checked the driver to make sure that he was not listening to the conversation. When he was satisfied that his attention was elsewhere, he spoke in a low voice again. "We are getting some expressions of concern from some of our associates overseas. Chen has kept them fully informed. Although they agreed with the initial plan, they are concerned that there are still some loose ends." He studied the driver again carefully then continued. "Stickley's wife. That business is a loose cannon. They feel that as long as she is around . . ."

The Senator was a little frustrated with the report and retorted, "The only loose cannon is being buried right now in the shadow of Robert E. Lee's house. Evahbody is gettin' way too nervous. That situation with Wanda Stickley is right where it ought to be. It won't evah be connected to the Vice President. In fact I see it just the opposite. As long as the attention is on her, we are Scot free. Chen did such a good job, she prob'ly thinks she killed'im. She'll prob'ly plead guilty and it will all be wiped under the carpet. Case closed and business is good. Tell them boys to put that in their pipe and smoke it."

"Still I think it is a good idea to keep an eye on the proceedings in Wilmington. She's charged with murder and since Ralph Stickley was well-known in the area, it is beginning to get a little publicity. It's being crowded out by all of the press concerning the assassination but still it is being covered."

"It can't hurt to watch it," the Senator agreed. "By the way I know the prosecutor down there. Butch Yeager and I were in school togethah at the University of South Carolina. Man, he could run fastah with a football than a mule takin' a whiz on an electric fence. I can call'im and catch up on old times if I need to."

"Senator, I don't think you ought to talk to him about it. It may arouse suspicions."

"Now Wrenn, there you go again. Quit worryin' so much."

"These ulcers have gotten me this far," Davies said as he rubbed his stomach. "No need to change now. Let's put Chen to work on it."

The line of cars began to move. This time they did not stop. As the limo pulled out onto the bridge over the Potomac, the Senator having cooled off from the Washington heat grinned and said, "Yes, by all means. By the hair of my chinny, chin, chin, call Chen."

*   *   *

Randy was down on the drops pressing her feet into the pedals of her racing bike. Although it was early evening, Oleander Avenue was relatively clear of traffic and the congestion that typically clogged each intersection along Oleander had vanished. Randy saw the light at the intersection with College Street begin to turn yellow and she kicked it. She made it with time to spare she thought but one driver blew his horn anyway. When she checked her rearview mirror to determine why he was being a jerk, she noticed she had picked up another rider who was approaching from her rear at a distance of about one hundred and fifty feet. She decided the road rage was over the approaching rider who had probably encroached upon the intersection in order to catch her.

As the rider continued to approach, he kept his body down and horizontal with the top tube of his bike to minimize drag. She watched with great interest. He was a strong cyclist and stayed down on the drops. He was probably focusing his energy on her and planning on passing her by the next intersection. She smiled and decided to give him a little competition. Reaching down to her gearshift, she indexed to the next gear and lifted off of the saddle slightly to put more weight over her pedals. As she leaned over, she felt the burn in her thighs after several hard revolutions. She checked him: he was holding tight, not gaining not losing.

She started sucking in air deeper and deeper and kept the burn going in her upper legs. The stoplight at the next intersection was coming into view and was still green. When she looked back again, the cyclist had gained a little. The light turned to yellow when she was too far out, she thought. She stood and put everything into the cranks. He was gaining and she was running out of time to enter the intersection safely. She studied the light carefully and decided she could make it but he could not. She burned everything. Thirty feet out and the light started to switch. She seized the handle bars, leaned forward over the front wheel and heaved with everything she had. Just as she made the light, the other cyclist spun past her in a blur.

That's not possible she thought: how did he do that? She kept kicking it in order to catch up to him as he slowed. When she pulled up behind him, he had slid forward on his seat, sat up slightly and maintained a comfortable pace. He looked back and grinned.

"Rod," she called out with some surprise. "Man, you blew me away. I didn't know you were a cyclist."

"Boy, you are good," he said. "A nanosecond and you would have smoked me."

"Not likely. Whew! I've never seen anyone with that strong a kick," she replied as she began to breathe harder from the effort. She pulled up beside of him. "How long have you been cycling?"

"I started in college and have kept it up pretty religiously since then." He grabbed a breath. "So about eight years. You?"

"My mom said I was born riding a bicycle. I've ridden one since I was a kid. I raced some but I was never committed enough to stay with it. College, then law school. Everything seemed to get in the way." She was still trying to slow her breathing without much success. "Wow, we burned it up."

Rod gave her a once over. "I could tell when I came up behind you that you were a veteran. Those calves. Strong. Man, you look good in lycra."

"Thanks, you look good . . . great yourself." Randy laughed. "Hey, you know what they say: cycling is sexy."

"Well," he sucked in a deep breath, "I know it makes me feel good. When things get a little tense around the office, I usually take my bike out for a quick aerobic workout when I get home. Sorts it all out for me."

Randy reached down for her water bottle with one hand. "Me too. Cycling makes the world a little more sane." She took a drink, squirted some on the back of her neck then replaced the bottle in its holder on the upright in the frame. She looked over at Rod. "You do look good. You must lift weights too."

"Yeah, I work out at the gym near the Mall. You?"

"I've been there but I've gotten lazy lately."

Rod started to pick up the pace again. "By the way where are you headed?"

"The Rice Building. Ben Down and I have a meeting this evening. We've been going over the Prosecution Summary in the Wanda Stickley case. Time to confer."

Rod said, "You'll be interested in watching the local news this evening then."

"What's it about?"

"I better not steal Butch's thunder. I'll let him tell you in person on the 7:00 o'clock report. Look, I'm going to ride along the river front. If it's all right, I'll follow you down to the office and drop off at the first street to the waterfront."

Randy dropped down over the drops on her bike. "Sure and let's do this again sometime? I'll try to keep up."

"Great. I'll call you. If you can go, we'll cycle down to Carolina Beach and back."

Randy pulled out in front and leaned forward into the wind to pick up speed. Rod tucked in behind her into her slipstream and planted his front wheel a few inches from her back wheel. They continued at speed. When they reached historic Wilmington and started toward the Rice Building, Rod pulled up beside her.

"Loved it. See ya'," he called as he turned toward the river.

Randy called back, "Carolina Beach." Rod gave it thumbs up and raced off toward the waterfront.

To cool out Randy dropped down to a crawl then stepped off of her bike when she entered the office parking lot. She walked the long way around the lot and stretched. When she pushed open the front door to the office, she could hear the television set in Ben's office indicating he was all ready at work. She brought the bike in and leaned it against the wall in the reception area and stepped back to Ben's office.

"Ben, I'm going to run over to my office and pick up my summary before we get started," Randy said. "Oh, guess who I saw coming over here?"

Ben laid down the paperwork. "It must have been a ghost. Looks like he just about caught you," he said referring to the perspiration marks on her cycling shorts and jogbra.

"Rod the Bod," she said as she started down the hall.

"Who? What?" Ben called after her. He looked exasperated and strained to hear a response.

"Rod Pemberton," she called back as she made it to her office.

Ben picked the papers up and continued to study the reports. He waited until she returned then said, "I didn't think you wanted Rod to see you unless you could hide behind a briefcase." Ben referred to their earlier meeting with Rod when they found out that the DA's office planned to proceed on the charge of first degree murder in Wanda Stickley's case.

"That was then, this is now. Thank God for spandex. Besides I've been working out. I've got it pretty good. At least that's what Rod says." She flexed her arm muscle.

Ben looked over his desk at Randy and grinned. "Rod, Rod, Rod. You've got it bad."

Randy did not respond but acknowledged the comment with a smile. She tossed her files on the desk and took a seat. She stepped over to the TV and turned it down a little. "Rod said we should watch the news at seven. Butch has apparently made some announcement in the Stickley case."

"What's it about?"

"Rod was pretty mysterious about it. He wouldn't say but when I told him we were conferring on Wanda's case this evening, he said we should watch." She checked her digital watch. After clicking off the timer that was flashing her time on the bike ride, she checked the time. "We have about fifteen minutes."

Ben noticing the perspiration on Randy's forehead said, "Do you need to cool out a little more before we start? Looks like you are all ready worn out."

Randy took a little offense at the comment and retorted, "Now to the untrained eye, I may look a little tired but that is only post

performance fatigue. It's short term and hardly a factor. I'm ready."
She leaned over to the desk and stretched the back of her legs.

Ben took a quick pull from his cigar. He was grumpy and wanted
to argue. "Now this is familiar terrain. You are reading way too
much into my statement. I only wanted to know if you were ready. I
was not commenting on your stamina or your endurance. I am an
athlete myself." When Randy smiled, Ben said, "What does that
mean?"

"You. You, an athlete? Maybe then but not now. If you would
get rid of that cigar," she said as she waved the smoke away and
pretended to have difficulty breathing, "and unload Jack Daniels
from your desk drawer, start walking and eventually get in enough
shape to run . . . ."

"Run. I could run five miles right now."

"You couldn't run fifty feet without risking a heart attack."

Ben pulled open the lower drawer on his desk and checked to see
if his "Knock'em" was still safely stored where he left it. It was.
"Look," he said, "do you want to argue or do you want to work?"

"Boy, you just hate it when I win."

Randy sat in the chair facing Ben. She waited for a retaliatory
response but he tucked his cigar to one side of his mouth and
slammed his jaw shut. He just gave her that smug look of defiance
that he used with Margaret and with the DA when he would not
budge. Margaret always said it was easier to get a turtle to turn
loose before it thunders than to get Ben to give in when his mind was
made up. Randy sensed that the skirmish was over and looked over
at the television set. "Seen any of the Vice President's funeral
proceedings?"

Ben released his grip on the cigar and rejoined the conversation.
"It's sad. It's hard to watch his children since I have two of my own.
They are pretty strong kids though. They seem to be holding up.
You know they have to be miserable: their mother is in the hospital
and their father is being buried. I never had to endure that so it's
hard to truly understand the depth of their agony. I hope they are all
right."

Randy sat somewhat mystified. Ben noticed her reaction and
asked, "What? What now?"

"Ben, you truly amaze me. One minute you are as fussy as some
of these old judges when you come into court late and another time

you are as thoughtful and sentimental as a mother with her children. Maybe that's why I like you so much: you never know what to expect."

"Nature of the beast," he said. He tossed his hands up in a gesture of agreement and acknowledged the compliment with a smile. "What do ya' say? Let's get on with this case."

"All right but first I need your advice on something. Big Burger has brought in Bayready, Fore, Paine and DeStorm in Atlanta. They've . . . "

Ben interrupted her. "They're bringing in the big boys. Who are they associating locally?"

"Diehlinger," Randy replied expressing a look of dismay.

"Ouch. Be ready for the fury. Burns Diehlinger is one of the most difficult personalities I've ever dealt with. He will dog you to death."

"That's what I want to talk to you about. I've already received a package of discovery materials from them, a catalog really, of written interrogatories, requests for production of documents, deposition notices. Since there are three plaintiffs, multiply everything by three. It's worse than fighting with the government. What can I do?"

Ben assumed a rather serious look and leaned forward on the desk. "First, do everything. Don't let anything slip. Nothing. They are waiting for a mistake. They'll pounce. Secondly, get them in front of a judge by way of a motion for a protective order. A local judge will be sympathetic. He'll stop the paper war. Try to target for Judge Perry. He was a civil attorney and will know what it's like to do battle with a giant." Ben stopped as abruptly as he had started.

Randy who had been waiting for a magic wand said, "That's it? Is there any good news?"

"That is it. You are playing hard ball now," Ben replied then hesitated. "There is some good news. They wouldn't have sent in the big boys unless you had something big." Sensing that Randy was somewhat relieved by his assessment, Ben held his hands up to outline an imaginary marquee in the sky. He said, "I can see it now. Bost Battles Big Burger. Big Burger Three Wins Big, Big, Big! Bost Gets Ben Lifetime Supply of Big Burgers."

Randy laughed. "I can see it too. Bost Bombs Bad. Bost Busted."

Ben laughed too. "All right, all right. You'll do fine. Just cover all of the bases just like you do with every other case. Enough said. Now did you get a chance to read the Prosecution Summary and attachments in the Stickley case? That's why we are meeting after all."

"Oh, yes," she said and picked up the file. She flipped through the pages to the first page of the report. "You are the pro here. What do you make of it?"

"Well, the report seems to be pretty straightforward. Butch will give us everything he's got so I wouldn't worry about the contents. We'll have what the DA has but we still need to be suspicious. Sometimes, heck, a lot of the time the investigation is not very complete. So far though the physical evidence is clear enough. No evidence of a forced entry. Inside the house everything was pretty much in order upstairs. There was evidence of a struggle in the basement. Apparently the basement is divided into different rooms. We'll have to get out there and see it. Things were in disarray in the furnace room indicating a struggle. Several items were on the floor next to a table, blood had apparently dripped in several places. A bloody screwdriver was found on the floor next to the table."

"That's consistent with what Wanda told you at the initial conference with her?"

"Yeah. He attacked her in the basement, they struggled, she stabbed him with some object she found as she tried to get away. The report indicates the evidence tech's found a blood trail up the steps down the hall to the kitchen. From there it led to the location where Ralph's body was found. Oh, yes. One of the first officers who arrived saw the blood and followed it to the basement. She smelled the odor of burned gunpowder in the basement."

"Indicating the shot was fired in the basement, right? That's still consistent with Wanda's version?" Randy asked as she followed Ben's recitation from the report.

"Yeah, we're still in the ball park," Ben replied then picked up the summary of the evidence. "Ralph's body was found in the driveway. Supine position. Extensive wounds to the neck area His throat was cut. The driveway was on a slight incline and blood was draining from the body down the driveway. Wanda was observed by an officer who was reporting to the scene. She was standing over Ralph. She had a knife in her hand."

"The blood in motion down the driveway means it had just happened?"

"Oh, yes. She was caught in the act. Eyewitness that will be reliable and credible."

"Who called it in?"

"I didn't see that in the report either. We'll have to find out. Also the knife was a little unusual according to the description given. We'll need to take a look at it. The gun is missing."

"What did Wanda say about that?"

"I thought the police would have it. I didn't ask her about it but I'll add that to the list. The list is getting longer and longer." Before Randy could respond to his comment, he said, "There are a lot of things missing but they'll come in later. Fingerprints on the knife and the screwdriver. No gun so that part is still a little shaky from the government's standpoint. There's no gunshot residue test results but I understand one was performed. We'll get the results in a few days. Should be positive showing Wanda fired a weapon on the night in question."

"What did you make of Wanda's statement to the police?"

"She told them basically the same thing she told me when I first talked to her. Ralph broke in, attacked her and she stabbed him and shot him. She doesn't know what happened after that. Given Ralph's history of abusing her--assault, threats, rape--it makes a relatively straightforward case of self defense except . . . "

"Except for that little part she says she forgot."

"Right. I couldn't believe the autopsy results. It didn't sound like we were dealing with the same case." Ben flipped to the back of the attachments to the Prosecution Summary and started reading. "1. Large wound in the lower left buttock, dried blood, some healing, estimated to be two to three days old at the time of death. 2. Wound in the upper right chest, little blood, depth 1.5 centimeters, length 1.5 centimeters. 3. Gunshot wound to back upper left shoulder, projectile retrieved in shoulder muscle. Projectile struck clavicle, embedded in shoulder muscle, retrieved projectile. 4. Large gaping wounds on both sides of the neck, both jugular veins interrupted, extensive bleeding: right--7-8 centimeters extending from beneath ear to Adam's apple; left--behind ear extending to front of neck to depth of cervical vertebra. 5. Superficial wounds on chest in area between nipples, depth 3-4 millimeters, appear to form the letter 'R'.

6. Numerous abrasions on hands, knuckles, wrists, upper arms (see diagram). 7. Penis excised approximately 2 centimeters from base. 8. Excised penis located in back of throat, compressed between rear palate and back of throat. Cause of death--severe bleeding from interruption of both jugular veins."

"So do you read it to mean that none of the other wounds were sufficient to cause death?" Randy had been reading along and thought the issue was clouded.

"Right. I think it means that but it does not say that. We'll have to find out. My guess is none of the wounds would have caused him to die except for the neck wounds. But here's the thing: the 'R' on the chest and the severed penis occurred while he was alive. Wanda did not mention any of this when I talked to her and she did not admit any of this to the police during the interrogation. She claims she does not know what happened after she shot him."

"She won't be the first murder suspect to get a little amnesia," Randy said reflecting her doubt about Wanda's statements.

"Nor the last but I can't understand why she is lying to me about it. I've represented her through the thick and the thin and it has gotten pretty thin several times. She always told me the truth but not this time. I know the woman. She's no killer."

Randy looked at Ben in disbelief. "She's not what? You think because you know her and you think because she's a woman that she would not kill and mutilate Ralph Stickley. I think it's obvious she's lying through her teeth because she did it. She probably can't believe it herself. That man kept her in terror and when she was pushed, she just overreacted. She admits she stabbed him. She admits she shot him. It follows. She carved him up. She tried to cut his head off. And she cut off the very thing he had tormented her with: his penis. I can see her standing over him ramming it down his throat hoping that the last thing he would do would be to choke to death on it."

"Stop. You're scaring me," Ben retorted as he half-laughed at her speculation.

"I'm serious. It's pretty clear she was pushed over the brink. It's the 'burning bed' syndrome all over again."

"We don't know enough about it to make any conclusion but my gut feeling is that Wanda did not kill him and she is lying about it. Why? In fact all of the information we have gotten just leads to more questions."

"Such as."

"Well, for one, why was Ralph in prison in South Carolina? The last time I knew anything about him he was serving time in North Carolina for raping Wanda. And why was he on escape? Ralph always played the inside. He wouldn't escape. He'd be a trustee if anything. Why was Ralph back at Wanda's?"

Randy replied, "That one is easy. He was going to rape her again."

"Maybe. Maybe not. Here's one that's critical. Did Ralph have a weapon? If he did, it's a perfect case of self defense. If he did not, we've got a lot more work in front of us to convince a jury Wanda was protecting herself. And oh yeah, where was Jeremy when all of this was going on? And where did Wanda get the knife?"

"And where's the gun?"

"Exactly," Ben agreed. "We've got to talk to Wanda. She can answer a lot of questions if she will. You know, I had told her I wanted her to take a voice stress analyzer test and a polygraph test when she claimed Ralph tried to rape her the last time. If she won't come across with the truth when we talk to her, I'm going to try to talk her into taking them with these questions in mind."

"I don't think she will ever admit it. I wouldn't. I couldn't. God, this is awful."

Ben laid the file on the table and stared at Randy. "Well, counselor. What do you think? Are you still in?"

"Tighter than a pair of pantyhose." Randy stared at Ben. She did not blink. "This is a tough case, maybe too tough for my first murder case but she needs us. I hope she knows that."

"Randy, that's why I like you so much. You're tough and you're ready for this case. We'll give it our best. Our first job: get Wanda to tell us what really happened. There are just too many questions."

"And here's another question for you. What do you think the DA will do with all of this?" Randy asked as she pointed to the Prosecution Summary.

"I worked for Butch for five years. I know. He . . . " Before Ben could finish, the television screen switched to a picture of Wanda Stickley. Ben stopped talking and turned toward the TV to listen. Randy stepped over to the TV set and turned up the sound.

The local news anchor said, "Today the case involving the death of former entrepreneur and tobacco warehouseman Ralph Stickley took a somewhat unexpected turn.   As was reported earlier, his former wife Wanda Stickley has been charged with his murder.   At a news conference held earlier this afternoon, the District Attorney Butch Yeager announced that he would seek the death penalty in her case."

The screen then showed a picture of the DA in his office.   He talked into the reporter's microphone.   "This is a case of first degree murder.   We plan to seek an indictment charging Wanda Stickley with the first degree murder of Ralph Stickley based on malice, premeditation and deliberation.   We will seek the death penalty because of the especially heinous, atrocious and cruel manner in which it was carried out.   No man, no matter what he has done, should have to die the way Ralph Stickley did."

CHAPTER EIGHT

"Where's the gun?" Ben pressed Wanda for a straight answer. All of a sudden the attorney interview room seemed awfully quiet. Except for some distant shouting back in the cells, it was as dead as a tomb. When she did not answer, Ben pressed further. "Well?"

"Like I told you. I don't know." Wanda was just as insistent as Ben. "I shot him and then he ran out of the basement. I followed but it's all a blur. Worse than a blur. I just don't know what happened then."

Ben slammed his pad down on the table. "Look. Randy and I are here to help you but you have got to confide in us." Wanda stared back at him and kept silent. Randy sat patiently and waited for a response as well. Ben finally broke the silence. "There are just too many questions. Where did the knife come from?"

"For the tenth time, I picked it up during the struggle in the furnace room. It must have been on the table in there. I can remember grasping for . . . for anything just to get Ralph to turn me loose. It must have been there."

"Wanda," Ben continued to argue with her, "it doesn't make sense. You told me you heard a noise in the basement. You went to the bedroom and got your gun. You went to the basement. You were attacked by Ralph. You found a screwdriver in the struggle and stabbed at him with it. Why get a screwdriver when you had the gun? Then you say after you stabbed him with the screwdriver, you shot him. He ran and you picked up a knife to go after him. Come on."

"That's the way I remember it."

Ben shook his head as he made notes. "It does not make sense. And the knife. Where did you get such a sophisticated knife? This particular type of knife is unusual, typically sold only in survival or military catalogs and is expensive. I know times were tight for you. The knife is too expensive for a Boy Scout and I know you did not need it. Where did you get the knife?"

"I don't have a clue how it got there. I just picked it up. I think I picked it up from the table. Look. If you don't believe me, maybe you shouldn't represent me."

Randy sensed Wanda's exasperation with Ben's aggressive approach and tried to change the subject to an area that was a little more supportive. "How about Ralph, Wanda? Did he have a weapon of any kind?"

Wanda turned toward Randy and smiled weakly. "No but . . . "

Ben continued the answer. "He tried to choke her. He used his hands as deadly weapons. That will be important if we proceed on a theory of self defense. She could not use deadly force unless she perceived that she was repelling deadly force herself. He was trying to kill her with his hands. Given the difference in size and strength, it should be easy to establish that his hands were deadly weapons and she was justified in using the, let's see, Wanda," Ben indicated his disbelief again, "a screwdriver, a knife and a gun, right?"

Wanda did not respond and Ben continued to flesh out the defense. "The photographs of the previous assaults and the rape for which Ralph was serving time will show what damage Ralph could do with his hands. We can use the photos of the last rape but the DA may be able to turn that against us. He would argue that we cannot show that Ralph was the rapist since Ralph was in prison so that blaming Ralph for that indicates just how bent on revenge Wanda was. The DA has photos of Wanda the morning of the alleged murder. We can use those."

Randy again tried to soften the approach during the interview and asked, "How are you holding up?"

Wanda turned again to face Randy and replied, "Pretty good. I'm having some trouble adjusting to the routine. There is noise in here all of the time. Day and night. It's hard to sleep." She stopped for a moment and looked down at the table. "If I could just see Jeremy?"

"We tried," Randy said as she tried to commiserate with her, "but it looks impossible for the time being. The DA is opposed to bond and as long as you are in here, the judge in juvenile court will not let Jeremy come for a visit. And since there is no family available to provide temporary custody, he will have to stay in foster care. I did talk to Caroline Markham, Jeremy's guardian ad litem. She said he is adjusting relatively well to foster care. He's still in school and remarkably he is doing pretty well. He wants to come to see you,

Caroline says. In fact every time they talk he has asked about it. Patience. That's all I can offer at this point."

Ben was still in an argumentative mood. He wanted the truth but was not getting it. "Let's talk about Jeremy for a moment. Wanda, when you first went through the series of events leading up to the altercation with Ralph, you said you had just picked Jeremy up from the Scout meeting and you were at home making sandwiches. You heard a noise and went downstairs. Where was Jeremy?"

"Ben, it's like I've told you a dozen times. Jeremy went over to my neighbor's, Nancy's, Nancy Wooten."

"I understand that. You say he went over to Nancy's but you never said when."

"He went almost immediately after we arrived back at the house and before I heard the noise in the basement."

"Well, explain this. Why would you be making a sandwich for him when he was gone and would not be returning for such a long time? The police found him over at Nancy's about an hour after they had arrived. It just does not make sense." Ben waited for the answer.

"Kids. Who knows about kids? Jeremy is thirteen. He's like most kids. He doesn't have any sense of time."

Ben slammed his pad down again. "Wanda, are you protecting Jeremy?"

Wanda became very visibly upset. She yelled, "You leave Jeremy out of this. He's been through too much all ready." She stood up and walked toward the door.

When the guard came to the door, Ben waved her off and asked Wanda to come back and have a seat. Ben looked somewhat apologetic and motioned toward the chair. She came reluctantly and sat in the chair again. When she finally spoke, she pleaded, "Ben, you just do not know all that that child has been through. I can't bring him into it. I can't. I can't and I won't."

Ben touched her on the hand and was a little more sympathetic. "I understand." He looked over at Randy and said, "We both understand. All we want to do is help. We can help better if we know the entire truth--the good, the bad, all of it. As your attorneys you can speak to us freely. The attorney-client privilege prevails and everything is privileged. No one can force us to tell what you have told us. The truth. We need it."

Wanda did not budge and Ben pressed on. He took Wanda's hands into his. "Wanda, I have always helped you. Always. And you have always told me the truth. All of it, all of the time. I need it. You need it. Help us help you."

She did not move but a tear trickled down her cheek. When she spoke, she said, "Ben, it's true. You've always helped me even when no one else would. I appreciate it. But I have told you all of the truth I can. Jeremy is all I've got and he has to stay out of this." She pulled her hands out of Ben's and wiped her cheek.

Ben shook his head in disappointment. "Wanda, you've cut out a hard road for yourself. We'll do what we can but I cannot, I will not stand by and watch you destroy yourself. The District Attorney has announced he will seek the death penalty. He does not come to that decision lightly and he will do what he can to see that you get it."

Wanda watched Ben's eyes as he talked. She was visibly shaken by the discussion of the death penalty. "What do you think? Can he get it?"

"I can't make any promises except to do the best we can with what we've got. The bottom line in any murder case is that the case is no better than the victim. In this case the DA has a scoundrel for a victim. Butch has even prosecuted Ralph himself. Ralph was a wife beater, a crook, an arsonist and a rapist. Butch knows all of this and he knows it will be a tough case but he also knows he has enough evidence to support each step along the way. So the answer is: no one knows whether the DA can get the death penalty, not even the DA at this point." She seemed somewhat satisfied with the answer and Ben said, " Wanda, Randy and I talked to Detective Stanton. He is the lead investigator. Well, I'm going to ask Randy to give you the report."

Randy opened her file to Stanton's report. "He won't talk very much but he did tell me that you had told him back when you charged that Ralph had raped you that you said . . . " Wanda flipped through several more pages of the attachments to the prosecution summary. "And this is a direct quote according to him, 'I'll kill him if it's the last thing I do.' Plus in your statement on the morning after Ralph was killed, you admitted stabbing and shooting an unarmed man. He believes you are lying about some of the things you said but they have enough for first degree murder. You were also found standing over Ralph's body after he had been mutilated, tortured and castrated. That's enough for an aggravating circumstance: heinous conduct. Enough to warrant the death penalty."

"So I may get the death penalty?"

Ben replied, "Yes, you may but it is unlikely. Ralph was just too evil. It isn't likely that a jury will give anyone a death sentence for killing him. Most likely we will have a chance at a negotiated plea."

Wanda looked puzzled. "What does that mean?"

"Very likely the DA will give us a chance to plead guilty to a lesser offense. In fact I would almost guarantee it. You would have to serve time in prison but you would not face the death penalty. It's a compromise."

"Prison? How long in prison? I can't do that. I wouldn't get to see Jeremy. Ralph would win then. I can't lose Jeremy." Wanda was really getting upset and started to cry again.

Ben tried to calm her down and said, "It's too early to discuss this, Wanda. It's just speculation at this point."

Randy joined in. "Let's cross that bridge when . . . if and when we get to it. We'll see what the DA has to say first."

"But no plea. I'd as soon die as to be locked up for a long prison term," Wanda insisted. "I can't lose Jeremy. He's all I've got."

Ben started packing the file in his briefcase. He did not respond to Wanda's demand but was sure that they would have this discussion again. He knew it was a case that had a lot of room for negotiation. Having served as an assistant district attorney for five years, he had seen many cases come and go that looked bad on the surface but were weak. In his assessment this one was weak for the government, really weak as a first degree murder case. Ralph was an unparalleled villain for the Wilmington area. A lot of people would have liked to have been the one to wield the knife on him. Butch would know that and would offer something. The real question was what, Ben thought.

Ben said, "Wanda, let me see what else we can find out. We'll talk again next week. We need to get ready for a bond hearing and the DA will schedule what's called a Rule 24 hearing for the court to determine several preliminary matters. Again don't get your hopes up that we will get a bond. The DA's announcement that he will seek the death penalty will control that. Ninety-nine per cent of the capital cases are 'no bond' cases. Think of anything else?" Ben stood up and walked over to the door to notify the jailer.

Wanda followed Ben over to the door and replied, "Jeremy. Keep working on my getting to see him."

Randy responded, "We'll do everything we can, Wanda. Stay strong. It'll get better."

When the jailer came to the door, Wanda stepped out into the hallway with her. The jailer checked the list on the wall beside the door to see if anyone else would need to be brought to the interview room. She asked, "Mr. Down, you are here to see a male inmate too?"

"Right. Noah Lyerly is supposed to be back from Central Prison. He was a safekeeper. He . . . "

"We have him," she said. "It will be about five minutes before we can make the transition. I'll have to take Wanda back to women's quarters. I'll alert Burt to bring him on. You're going to love this." She gave him a wink and walked Wanda up the hall.

Randy had assembled her paperwork to leave. She picked up her briefcase and walked to the interview room door. Ben went back to the table and took out a cigar. Randy turned around and came back. "You were too tough on her, Ben."

"Well, thank you for sharing."

"No, I'm serious. Wanda has been through hell. She is going through hell. You can tell that she is completely torn out of socket by losing Jeremy. She's locked up and can't see her child. She's charged with murder. She is facing the death penalty. She needs support, sympathy. She needs help and you are not giving it to her."

Ben played with the cigar wrapper and listened carefully without interrupting. When he spoke, he wanted Randy to understand what he was trying to do. "Randy, not long ago you said I was the pro. Give me the benefit of the doubt here. I am sympathetic but I can't help as long as she is lying. She is covering for somebody. I think it's Jeremy but I can't be sure. She doesn't fully realize it but she is in for the battle of her life. Missing Jeremy is a part of it, an important part but only a part. The government wants her life. I'm going to use my skills--good guy, bad guy--whatever, to get to the bottom of this and to save her life. Here it is. You work on getting Jeremy in to see her and I'll work on this case. We'll join forces later and divide the work for the trial. What do you say?"

"Okay, but be a little kinder, a little gentler," Randy replied.

"One hundred per cent," Ben said as Randy walked back toward the door.

Randy left and Ben sat at the table thinking about the interview. Wanda's insistence on 'no plea' would put this case in a much more complicated light, he thought. She will have to give in; otherwise she will very likely face a DA who has no choice but to prosecute and seek the death penalty. North Carolina case law would require it: the DA has no choice but to seek the death penalty if it is a case of first degree murder (and this one may be) and there is evidence of aggravating circumstances (and this one is particularly vicious).

He thought back to Butch's announcement at the news conference: "no man . . . should have to die the way Ralph Stickley did". He lit the cigar and inhaled deeply. If Wanda will not give in and Butch cannot give in, that would put him squarely in the middle, in the middle of a major mess. He savored the smoke and tried to release it easily but he choked as the smoke surfaced. As he regained his breath, he noticed Wanda's file and how thick it was at such an early stage in the case. He shook his head as he realized his life was going to get a lot more complicated. After a while he pulled out his file on Noah Lyerly. It was thin.

Mrs. Skittleran had obtained a copy of the warrant, the release order and bond information and had assembled them into a preliminary file: Noah Gene Lyerly. Ben wondered what he was like. He was charged with "of his malice aforethought did kill and murder Sean (NMN) Delothian". The magistrate had set a bond of $25,000 even though he was charged with murder. Since this was typically a tip off that the case would not be prosecuted as a first degree murder case, Ben liked it even better.

There are murders and there are murders, he thought. Capital murder preliminary proceedings and trials had become so detailed with motions and evidentiary hearings that he felt they were a little dull. It had gotten to the point that a researcher or librarian would make a better lawyer in a capital case. Noncapital murder cases still let an attorney shine, still had a little bit of the "gun slinger in the street" advocacy that Ben enjoyed.

He toyed with the three pieces of paper in the file as he continued to wait for the jailer to bring his client. As he reviewed each document, his mind wandered back to the words in the warrant. The warrant had language that was sufficient to charge either first degree or second degree murder. He decided he would just have to wait for the prosecution summary to know with any certainty how the DA would proceed. He checked the warrant and saw that the complaining officer was Lt. Curtis Belton, New Hanover Sheriff's Department. Ben knew Officer Belton from his days in the vice division and wondered how long he had been transferred to homicide. Ben played with the ashes on his cigar and wondered what else he had missed lately. It's tough to get old, he thought.

Ben continued to study the little information contained on the warrant and tried to imagine how his client would look. Defendant's Biographical Information: Age: 29. Race: W. Ht.: 5'7". Wt: 118. He noticed a typo in the biographical section of the warrant. Ben could not quite make it out so he took out his reading glasses. As he let his eyes adjust, he saw that the booking magistrate had typed an "F" in the box marked "Sex" then had typed an "M" over the "F".

As he continued to read the warrant, Ben was distracted by a noise up the hallway. At first he thought it was a scuffle then he decided the voices were just loud. He listened more intently. One voice sounded distinctly feminine and another was clearly a male voice. The female voice was calling back up the hallway and as the person appeared in the doorway, pointing with both hands toward someone.

"Stay cool, sugar britches. Stay cool. Love you, baby. Love-- it's you--baby!"

Ben watched as the jailer and the defendant came to the board beside the interview room door. The jailer checked off the inmate's name and the time while Ben watched. The defendant was dressed in a red jumpsuit which typically indicated that the prisoner had been disruptive in some way or had violated jail rules. Otherwise the prisoner would be dressed in an orange jumpsuit. He wore his long hair in a pony tail and had on mascara, makeup and lipstick. Ben sat up in the chair and continued to watch intently. This is going to be interesting, he thought.

The jailer ushered the defendant just inside the doorway to the interview room. The jailer was obviously reacting to the previous conversation up the hallway. He smiled and with a rather grandiose gesture announced, "Mr. Down, may I present the one, the only: Noah Gene Lyerly."

The defendant acknowledged the introduction and swung into the room with a theatrical flair. He approached the table and with long slender fingers took the barrette out of his long dark hair and let it fall down around his shoulders. It was unbelievable, Ben thought. The transformation was remarkable. Taking a seat before him was a woman, at least, he looked like a woman. Ben remembering his gentlemanly training started to stand somewhat absentmindedly then caught himself.

Slightly embarrassed at his faux pas, Ben, trying to take the lead in the interview, said, "Have a seat, Mr. Lyerly. I am Ben Down, your court-appointed attorney." Ben noticed the defendant's manicured nails as he flipped his hair back over his shoulders.

"I know who you are, sugarcakes," the defendant said in a honey dipped voice and leaned forward on the table toward Ben. "I know all about you and you can call me Nora, Nora Jean, if you like."

Ben tried to keep a straight face. He asked, "You are Noah Gene Lyerly, aren't you?"

"That cigar is going to kill you, baby. You are too pretty to go that way. I can think of a much more delicious way for you to go," Noah said as he cozied up to Ben. When Ben did not react, he said, "All right. It's no fun but yes, I can be Noah Gene Lyerly. It's just, just . . . so dull." Noah blinked his eyelashes and sighed indicating his boredom. "I prefer Nora Jean, sugarcakes."

The prisoner played with the smoke as it lifted gently from his cigar. Ben laid his cigar in the ashtray and sat back in his seat. He watched Noah, Nora Jean closely.

"I know all about you," Nora Jean said. "You are an ace criminal defense lawyer and you are mine, all mine compliments of our courts." Nora Jean leaned even further over the table and cooed, "But nobody said you were going to be this cute. I love that gray hair, makes me all gooey. I love the way it outlines that sweet little innocent face. Ooh. Ooooooh."

Ben tried to distract her. "How did you get the red jumpsuit?"

Nora Jean stuck out her arm and admired the color. She stood up and twirled around. When she had finished the fashion show, she said, "They think they are punishing me but I love it." She rubbed the sleeve and scrunched up her shoulders. "I love this color. It's so strawberry . . . so luscious. So me. Don't you think so, babycakes?"

Ben tried to get Nora Jean back on course. "What did you do so that they put you in the red jumper?"

"Nothing. Nothing. I'm as innocent as Mother Teresa. All I did was do a little dance number for the other inmates. It was kind of a celebration. I'd just returned from Central and everybody was hollerin'. I just gave them what they wanted. Helped release a little tension. I started dropping the top of the orange jump suit way down low kinda like I do in my show and I guess they got a little too excited. The guards always get shook up when they see us having a little fun." Nora Jean admired the outfit again. When she stood up and danced a little swaying number back and forth, she sang, "When I wear red, it makes it hot in bed. When I wear red, better take your med."

She added in a little bump and grind and held on to Ben's chair. She wiggled a little closer to Ben's shoulder and started singing again, "When I wear red, I'll lick . . . "

Ben was watching with some disbelief. It was interesting, funny in a way, far out, he thought. He decided this could get out of hand pretty quickly and decided he had better get everything back on track. Ben commanded, "Sit. Sit down. We've got a lot of work to do"

Nora Jean flopped in the seat. "Oh, pooh. You're no fun. Better have fun 'cause too soon you're done."

"Seriously, Noah," Ben insisted, "I need to cover a lot of ground with you and I need your undivided attention."

"Call me Nora Jean." She crinkled up her nose and begged, "Please. Please."

"Oh, all right. Nora Jean then." Ben grinned a little and said, "Tell me about show business."

Nora Jean lit up even more. She said, "Show business is my life. I started out when I was just a little girl, well, you know what I mean. Mama used to dress me up in all kinds of lingerie. I used to parade around in front of all of her boyfriends. I was good at it too. I got my first job modeling when I was thirteen."

Ben looked incredulous. "Modeling? You're kidding."

Nora Jean did not pick up on the offense and continued, "Sure. I was modeling lingerie. Mama let me do it at one of her gigs. They loved me. I thought the security guards were going to have to drag some guys out of there. They kept calling for me but mama wouldn't let me go back on. It was wild but I was hooked. Modeling lingerie. I was born for it."

"Nora Jean, you are a man, aren't you?"

"Well, yes . . . no. I mean, well, I drove mama crazy. She tried to raise me as a boy but it just wouldn't work. She'd put those jeans and cowboy shirts on me and send me off to school. As soon as I'd get home, I'd slip into a long sweatshirt. I'd wear it like a dress and dance around the house. I love to dance. Drove her crazy. She finally gave up. Huh, I knew more about wardrobe than she did. Before I moved out, she was asking me what she ought to wear. She was a red head. She just couldn't wear some things. Those big frilly green . . . "

Ben had listened as patiently as he could for as long as he could. "Do you have a penis? That's what I want to know."

"Oooooh, babycakes. You are so cute when you turn that little pink color in your face."

"Answer the question."

"Oooooh, I love it when you get angry. Ooooh, you're good. Sure I have one of those."

Ben was still a little frustrated. He asked, "Well, how do you, uh, how can you, uh, model lingerie? It's impossible."

"No, no, no, babycakes. It works fine. I learned how to conceal my peepee. That's what I prefer to call it. You can't tell anything." Nora Jean giggled. "Unless there is some stud muffin in the audience. Then I get a little excited. I can't help it. My peepee just won't stay put. Hormones, you know. Like the way I'm feeling right now when I'm around you." Nora Jean leaned forward again and looked like she wanted to snuggle.

"Down. Down. I'm not that kinda guy. I'm married, happily married."

"She's a lucky woman," Nora Jean said in her breathy voice and sighed as if she were resigned to the fact that Ben was not interested. She started to play with the smoke from Ben's cigar again. Her fingers danced playfully with the smoke so that it started hovering between the two of them. "Oooooh. Steamy, babycakes."

Ben tried to get control of the interview again but Nora Jean was difficult to reign in and would sidetrack into something sexual in an instant. He picked up the cigar to break up the little finger dance and said, "Before we get into the meat of this, let's talk about your background."

"Oh, all right," she pouted. "But I already know about you. Former mean old prosecutor. Major hitter for the DA's office several years ago. Got a reputation of being a tough fighter as a defense lawyer." Ben was sure this came straight out of the jail and enjoyed hearing the report from her fellow inmates. Nora Jean noticing the favorable reaction continued, "Hard hittin' and hard talkin'. That's what they say. Say you'll fight for the right, baby, whether you're assigned by the court or not. I knew I was lucky to get you. I'm usually lucky though. Nobody told me how pretty you were going to be."

Ben cut her off before she became too distracted again. "Got any family?"

Nora Jean turned serious for a moment and spoke more matter of factly. "Yeah," she kind of whimpered.

When she did not continue with the answer, Ben pushed the point. "Well?"

"Man, you are pushy. I was going to tell you. I was just figuring out the best way."

"Well, let's start with your parents?"

"Mama is up in Jacksonville, North Carolina as far as I know. I haven't seen her for a while. Nate says she's doing all right but she never cared that much for me so I don't keep up."

"Who's Nate? Your brother?"

"No, Nate's my sister. Her name is Natalie but we always called her Nate. Just picked it up when I was a kid." Nora Jean brightened a little and said, "She's in show business too. She's a dancer. She's been starring at The Men's Club here in Wilmington. You might've heard of her. Bree is what she goes by as a performer."

Ben smiled a little and said, "'Fraid not. Let me get this straight. Your name is Noah Gene Lyerly. Your stage name is Nora Jean. Your sister's name is Natalie. Her stage name is Bree and you call her Nate. Is that it?"

Nora Jean giggled. "Not quite. Natalie's last name is not the same as mine. She and Michael have the same daddy. She is Natalie Marie Dawtry. And oh yeah, she calls me Noodle."

"All right." Ben kept writing in his legal pad. "Who is Michael?"

"He's my brother but I haven't seen him in . . . , I don't know, years I guess." She played distractedly with the small collar on her jumpsuit then started twirling a strand of hair. " He went into military service when I was a teenager and I never saw him again. The last I heard he was in Oceanside, California."

"How about your father?"

"Don't know. I was a love child. He hit town and skipped town, mama said. Mama was a full-blooded Cherokee Indian. She grew up in the Smoky Mountains but ran away to Fayetteville when she was just a kid. She was a dancer too. I guess that's where we all got it. I mean me and Nate. Mama said she was just a girl coming into her own and a Chief wanted her real bad. And her daddy was going to do it. Just let him take her for his own. I guess he thought it would be cool to have a daughter married to a Chief. But she wouldn't do it. Ran away when she was just thirteen. She was only sixteen when she had me. She didn't tell me much about my daddy. He was in the military and when he got orders, he left town and never looked back." Nora Jean held up her arm and pulled back the sleeve. "You can tell I'm half Indian myself. Look at that dark skin. This dark hair. Do you think my eyes look smoky to you? Mama said they did."

Ben did not respond but asked, "Anybody around who can help you with bond? It's $25,000. If you have a family member who has property, they could post it for your release. Or if you can raise $3,750, a bondsman will post the bond for you."

"Nate is all I have. And I know she can't. Won't even if she could."

"Well, let's talk about the case for a moment. You are charged in a warrant with the murder of Sean Delothian. The State has not indicated whether it will proceed on first degree murder or second degree murder. The DA will give me a report called a Prosecution Summary that outlines the government's case against you. Since a bond has been set, and a relatively low bond at that for murder, I suspect that the State will not be proceeding on first degree murder. If the DA did, he could seek the death penalty. Otherwise we would be talking about a maximum of a term of imprisonment. When I find out more about the government's version of the case, I will cover the elements, the underlying basis of the crime charged, with you. Until then, we will hope for the best but expect the worst.   Got any questions so far?"

"No. Well, yes. Do you think I will get to stay here at the jail or will they send me back to Raleigh?"

Ben glanced at the red jumpsuit and said, "It's purely guesswork but I believe they will send you back to Raleigh. I don't think the local jail is like San Quentin that has entertainers in like B.B. King and Johnny Cash. They tend to frown on show business here." When Nora Jean looked a little disappointed, Ben decided to move on to something else. "Tell me about what happened. Who is Sean Delothian?"

Nora Jean started to speak then stopped. Ben watched and could tell her thoughts were racing on ahead. When she finally spoke, she sounded dejected. "I guess Nate will hate me."

Instead of trying to get her to go back to an answer for the previous question, Ben decided to keep her on the subject of Nate. "Why's that, Nora Jean?"

"She always saved me. Even from myself." Nora Jean smiled a little and said, "Always from myself. Like I said: mama didn't care too much for me. She just could not figure me out. Too strange for a mountain girl I guess. And Michael disappeared. He didn't care anyway. Nate really was the one who took care of me. I remember when I was a kid, maybe eighth grade. I got in some trouble. Well, I, uh, I just fell in love with another boy. He was a little dream. Ooooh, I still dream about him." She giggled and drifted off in thought.

"What about Nate?"

"Well, his brothers found out about it and caught us. We weren't really doing anything, just necking but his brothers beat the crap out of him. I ran before they could get me. Anyway the word went out they were going to 'beat up the little fag'. Kids can be so cruel. You know how that is. They caught me coming home from school. It started to get pretty rough but Nate showed up. They had already bloodied my mouth.   She was going to fight both of them. Scared them. Wow, scared me. She was pretty, even back then so I guess it shook them up that they were going to get beat up by a girl, a pretty girl at that. She was always tougher than she looked."

Ben checked his watch and noticed that they only had a little time left for the conference. "Better tell me about Sean Delothian."

"Sean was beautiful. He was one of the prettiest men I had ever seen. Smooth skin, white, creamy, smooth as a baby's butt."

"How did you meet him?"

"Nate met him first. She was dancing in the afternoons at The Men's Club. Sean would come by after work. He worked as a hair dresser at the Mall and had pretty flexible hours. He started staying after she finished her sets. I was working at night then dancing for the late night crowd. I like that. That way Nate and I aren't competing over the same guys. Anyway Sean and Nate became an item. He started coming out to the park, uh, the trailer park. Nate and I were living together. Things were really good then. The money wasn't tight. I didn't have anybody special I was going with then. I could have but most of the men I'd run into were gay men. I don't have anything against them but it's just not my bag. I want a man who wants a woman not another man. I'm not down on 'em. It's just, just . . . I'm a woman."

"Let's get back on track. Sean was coming out to the place where Nate and you lived."

"Right. And they were getting it on hot and heavy for a while then it seemed to cool off. Sean would come by in the afternoon when Natalie was at work and he'd want to talk. He'd say he really liked Natalie but there was something, something not quite there. I knew what he was talking about but I never told him. You see, Nate is gorgeous. She's beautiful. Her dance numbers are athletic, exciting but she just doesn't have a sense of the sensual. She just doesn't have that feminine ooooph if you know what I mean. I could see Sean was frustrated. I'd seen it before. She could start a fire but she couldn't put it out. And Sean was a man, a real man . . . " Nora Jean drifted off into her own world again with that dreamy look in her eyes.

"Nora Jean. Nora Jean. So what happened next?"

"They started fussing. It was always something. She was staying out too late. She was running around on him. You know, something all of the time. They really got into it. He hit her and she scratched him. Just a lover's spat. That's the way it started." Nora Jean put her hand over her mouth as though she had said too much. "Well, uh, that's the way it started in more ways than one. She ran out of the trailer and stayed away all night. Sean and I were there. He pulled off his shirt. God, he's got a gorgeous body. He showed me a

big scratch she'd left on his chest. I put some salve on it. The more
I rubbed, the more I couldn't help myself. I couldn't help myself.
That was the first time we were together. Oooooh, babycakes, that
man could make love. Ooooooh."

"All right. All right. Go on. What happened?"

"We'd be together in the afternoons while Nate was working.
Things went south with them. They were arguing a lot and it was
becoming more violent. He beat her up real bad one time. I told him
that was it. I couldn't let him do that to my sister. I cut him off.
He'd come around and beg but--God, it was hard; he was such a
hunk--but I wouldn't. That's when it all blew up. I loved that man
but it was all crazy somehow." Nora Jean stopped talking and just
looked off into nothing.

"What happened next?"

"He told her." Nora Jean shook her head in disbelief. "He told
her about us. At the trailer in the afternoons. They really got into it.
I got a call from her while I was at the Club. She said he was killing
her, he had a gun. I knew he could really get violent so I went
straight over there. I barged right into the trailer and he was on the
couch on top of her beating her with his fists. I saw his gun--he
always carried a gun--right beside him on the nightstand. I went
berserk. I pulled out my knife."

Ben mumbled, "Must be an epidemic. Women and knives."

"What?"

"Nothing," Ben said. "Just go on."

"I jumped on Sean and cut him with the knife. I didn't know I'd
cut him that bad. I just wanted to get him off of Nate. He jumped up
and ran toward the door. He fell right there by the telephone. I had
to step over him to call 911. They said he died right there. I held
him in my arms and told him I was sorry but he never spoke. I loved
that man. I wouldn't hurt him for the world but I couldn't let him
hurt Nate. She's all I got. All I had. I guess she hates me now. She
has every right to."

Nora Jean started crying. Ben reached in his pocket and handed
her a handkerchief. She wiped the tears as they flowed freely down
her cheeks. "You know, that's the first time I've cried since this
happened. I guess I just realized I lost Sean and Nate in one stupid
act."

"Has Nate been by to see you?"

"No, she won't. I screwed up bad. Nate always saved me. One time she saved me from a Marine that I was out with. I should've told him about peepee but I didn't. He got a little too excited and grabbed down there. Ow, he got mad and started slapping me. Nate pulled me out of that mess. Now I've messed it up so bad Nate will never speak to me again."

They sat quietly a little while. Nora Jean blotted at her eyes and Ben fumbled with the butt of his cigar. Nora Jean finally broke the silence. "How bad is it? Will they give me the death penalty?"

"I doubt it. Let me talk to the DA before I answer that question though. Sometimes their version can be a lot different than your take on it. We'll see." He checked his watch again. "We better wrap it up. Follow this advice until we can talk again. Don't talk to anybody about what happened. Not the police, the jailers, fellow inmates. Nobody. Understand?" Ben started packing up his briefcase.

"Oh, yeah. I know the drill. 'You've got a right to remain silent. Anything you say can and will be used against you.' You're the boss, babycakes." She smiled a little and folded the handkerchief up to hand it to Ben.

"Keep it. Looks like you may need it for a while."

"I need a plea, babycakes. I did it. I don't want to die. I'll do the time whatever they say but I don't want to die."

CHAPTER NINE

Reno, Nevada sits in a high valley along the Truckee River bounded on the east side by the Virginia Mountains and on the west by the higher and often snow-covered Sierra Nevadas. Settled in 1858 by pioneers as a stopover before the Donner Pass into California and connected to the rest of the world in 1868 by the Central Pacific Railroad, it is best known today interestingly enough for its casinos and night life. Certainly as important but less known is its Mackay School of Mines Museum and its attendant geological studies associated with the University of Nevada at Reno.

A short drive from Reno over the Virginia Mountains lie the remnants of Virginia City, home of the Comstock Lode, at one time one of the richest silver and gold mining regions in the United States. Its wealth and the entrepreneurs it attracted helped to create one of the most advanced centers of learning in mining and geology at the University. The campus offers quarters for some of the most elite geologists in the world, one of whom would provide the first real clue in the solution of the assassination of the Vice President.

It was late afternoon and the valley in which Reno is seated was already beginning to receive some of the shade from the high western mountains. A small jet descended from the east, dropped over the Virginia Mountains and banked to the left to turn on the down wind run for Reno International Airport. It cruised along below the peaks of the Sierra and turned again for its final approach. When it landed, a dark Crown Victoria pulled onto the tarmac and waited for the passengers to descend. Three men exited the plane and walked to the Crown Vic. After they were seated, the driver pulled onto the highway to depart the airport and then turned north toward the University.

The University lies just north of the city and occupies a collection of hills that overlooks downtown Reno. In a few minutes the Crown Vic turned into the campus and pulled to the rear of the large building that housed the geology department. They were met at the University by the geology department head and led directly to the laboratory of Dr. Abraham Werner Katzenbach. The lab was relatively dark except for an array of multicolored lights that reflected on the walls in a spectrum similar to a rainbow. After introductions were made, the three men now joined by their driver and the department head took seats and watched as Dr. Katzenbach made several adjustments to the equipment.

Suddenly the room filled with light and a piercing, almost deafening noise of scraping, screeching metal. Assistant FBI Director Newman clapped his hands over his ears and Director Fries looked toward the department head to see if there were any way to stop the penetrating sound. The department head looked apologetic and mouthed the words: "It will stop in a moment". Dr. Katzenback completely oblivious to the sound scurried about turning knobs and depressing buttons as lights flickered on the machines. The sound stopped as suddenly as it had begun and a kaleidoscope of colors splashed across two screens.

Appearing somewhat out of place among all of the sophisticated equipment, Dr. Katzenbach looked every bit the part of the old miner with his scraggly grizzled beard and his old hat. His bespectacled sunburned face gave the appearance of an old prospector who had just walked in from the mountains to have his findings assayed after days on the mountain trails returning from his claim. He spoke somewhat halting English and his voice was heavily accented with German.

"Gentlemen, if I might have your attention pleze," he inquired as he assumed a position between the two large screens. He gestured toward the screen to his right. "Dis panorama reflects der minute particle of sand contained in der rubbery substance sent to dis office from your laboratory in Vashington. Der particle was embedded in der hardened glue three to four millimeters in depth. It was excised, lasered to a sliver, cleansed, and now refracted as you see it before you by intense light. You vil notice der alignment of colors and der proportion and configuration of the spectrum of lights."

Dr. Katzenbach looked back over his shoulder at the screen and noticing a slight blurring, twisted two knobs. As the lights twinkled and the images cleared, he continued. "Dis particular particle of sand is quite unusual and bears no resemblance to any of der geologic deposits we are familiar with in der vestern hemisphere. Its angular fragments and detrital granular composition is much more coarse and augmented than ve see here in America. Or for dat matter, anywhere in dis part of der vorld."

He looked over his glasses much as a professor would to make sure his students were comprehending his remarks. Satisfied that they were following along, he gestured toward the screen to his left. "Now here, ve see an almost exact duplication of der panoramic configuration in der screen here." He gestured to the previous screen. He picked up a laser pointer and flashed the red beam on each of the most salient similarities between the two banks of refracted light on the screens. When he had finished, he continued the lecture. "You can see der verisimilitude. In fact a complete composite mirrored representation. Der particle of sand on dis second screen has been treated in der same manner as der particles received from der FBI. Dis sand particle is carbonate composed of shell, coral and minute chemical precipitates. It is found typically in deposits after gravity erosion and fluvial erosion from areas of relative frequent volcanic eruption. Der interesting ting about dese two particles is der chemical decomposition. In dis case, salt and bioclastic skeletonized accumulations extracted by chemical wash. Der conclusion reached is they both derive from der same source and are located in der same place.

He lay the laser pointer down and took off his glasses to emphasize the point. "Der place: China. And more specifically Tientsin."

Newman turned toward Director Fries with a look of "Eureka, we've found it". The professor, having concluded his presentation, looked out at his attentive audience over his glasses and asked, "Questions?"

Director Fries was first to speak. His calm exterior belied his excitement. "Dr. Katzenbach, can the methodology used to make this determination that the sand comes from China be replicated in our lab in Washington?"

"Possibly but I tink you would require some of der equipment we have here. Most particularly der laser which has been modified to accommodate sand particles down to .002 millimeters. Still it could be done."

Assistant Director Newman inquired about the time frame within which Dr. Katzenbach could reduce his method and findings into a written report. Indicating that there must have been some misunderstanding, the professor walked back to his desk and produced a stack of documents which he handed to Director Fries. Fries in turn passed a copy of the report to Newman, to Bays Covington, the field agent in charge of the assassination investigation, and to local FBI agent Bill Marston who had served as driver. After a few more questions Fries instructed Marston to serve as liaison with Dr. Katzenbach in the event further information was needed. The Director ordered the information contained in the meeting and the report to be retained as "Top Secret". Assured that Dr. Katzenbach and the department head would not reveal any of the information concerning the findings to anyone, Fries expressed his appreciation for the work of Dr. Katzenbach and the University. After a few more pleasantries were exchanged, the three FBI agents rode back to the airport with Marston and then boarded the jet bound for Washington.

Fries, Newman and Covington took the time during the ride across Reno to study the detailed lengthy report. The Katzenbach report was impressive, covering not only the geological scientific methods of identification employed but also more esoteric matters such as Chinese soil erosion charts, historical fluvial measurements, and chain of custody events. After the jet had climbed out of the valley and started ascending over Pyramid Lake, Fries called Newman and Covington together for a strategy session.

"This is it," Newman said as he laid the report on the table in front of him. "This is the magic bullet we have been needing. Our investigation finally came in out of the dark and moved ahead light years. The Chinese. Frankly I never would have guessed it."

Fries was more hesitant to make that final conclusion. "There is definitely Chinese involvement but we do not know the extent of it yet. Bays, what do you make of this?"

Bays Covington had been with the FBI since college and, after twenty years of field investigations, had moved into a position of senior agent status. He had worked on several important cases for the FBI including the investigation into the explosion and crash of TWA 800 and the bombing at the World Trade Center. He had been slow and methodical in his investigations and the success generated by his skill and dogged persistence had elevated him to senior field officer in charge of Operation Undereagle as the investigation into the Vice President's assassination had been named.

"Sir, everything is pointing toward the Chinese connection," Bays answered. He looked at Newman somewhat deferentially since he was going to indicate his divergence from Newman's implication that the assassination resulted from official Chinese involvement. "There are many unanswered questions and too many loose ends to conclude that the Chinese government, its leadership or any official agency or person is involved. Still a good argument can be made for a strong connection with the powers that be in China. If I may continue?"

"Sure, Bays, go ahead," Fries said.

"The forensics make the connection as clearly as it can be made in my view. Our lab indicates the bomb used to kill Vice President Anderson was of simple construction: C4, incendiary amplification, remote electrical activation. All of us are familiar with the conclusion that this type of bomb is consistent with Vietnam era military counter insurgency. Easy enough for us to extrapolate that into Chinese military training. And then easy enough to infer the bomb maker is at least Chinese trained. Next the components are of Chinese origin although as our tech's have advised, there is global accessibility and unrestricted acquisition."

Newman intervened to defend his position. "The thing that ties it all together is the glue, figuratively and literally. Our field agents in Wilmington inferred, and I believe rightly so, that the glue found in the hallway leading to the Vice President's bedroom on the night of the assassination and the glue found in the footprints of the assassins on the trail through the sand dunes at Figure Eight Island were used to disguise the type and manufacturer of the shoes the assassins wore. It had just the opposite effect. The glue had made a perfect cast of the tread on the shoe. We had our own scientists to analyze the glue. Here is what we know. The glue itself is nondescript. But based on measurements taken from each specimen, they were able to determine the kind of shoe worn--Fleet; the size of the shoe--6-6 1/2 American; and the manufacturer--Chiang Mai in Thailand and distributor--Macao International in Hong Kong. Unfortunately the shoes are obtainable almost anywhere including China. But and this is a big but, the whole business has China written all over it. And with Dr. Katzenbach's report, that cinches it in my opinion. Those shoes walk us right up to Beijing."

"Mike, if you are right," Fries state, "we are dealing with an act of war. This could plunge us into World War III. I'm still not so sure the syllogism follows logically. We need to be very careful here."

Fries was still not convinced and pressed Bays to continue with his assessment. Bays was more careful and would not totally disagree with Newman's conclusion although he felt the facts did not point directly toward the involvement of the Chinese government.

"Dr. Katzenbach's report," Bays said, "is the first one that actually puts the assassins on the ground in China I think. Before we had his report, we had already theorized based on one set of large shoe prints and one set of small footprints, that one assassin was a woman and one was a man. Now though our lab has determined that the small shoe print was made by a shoe designed and marketed for a man. We have no information on the larger shoe print but even so, I think our theory of male-female is weaker, much weaker. We had also theorized that the glue was put on the shoes to disguise the shoes and we had felt pretty sure that the glue was put on at the place where the sand was located. We did that based on our finding that the sand was actually found embedded several millimeters into the glue. We thought whoever the assassins were, they put the glue on then walked around while the glue was relatively warm so that the sand particles were embedded. Now we know the name of the place: Tientsin, China. There is a lot of theorization among the agents I am working with. And a lot of it is based on the same analysis Mike is making and a lot of it has been solidified by Dr. Katzenbach's analysis. I still believe we have a Chinese assassin, possibly two Chinese assassins but I do not believe we can conclude that they were sponsored by, directed by or assisted by the Chinese government."

"Yeah but China is one of the most controlled dictatorships in the world," Newman argued. "Nothing happens there without government permission or acquiescence. Besides the politics is right."

Fries put his hand up. "Wait a minute, Mike. I'm still interested in that second set of prints. What other theories are being floated on that?"

The jet shook for a moment and Bays scrambled to get control of his coffee cup. When the disturbance was over, he decided to hold on to the cup and laid his file down. Finally he replied to the

Director, "Well, we always thought the second assassin--we've been calling him Bigfoot--was there for a limited purpose. The first assassin, Littlefoot, was all over the dunes and went to and from the house. Bigfoot only went to the top of a dune, spent right much time there and then returned to a base camp where he also stayed for a long period of time. We have theorized he was a lookout and I say 'he' only because the footprint was bigger than the other. We don't know if they are male or female but presently we are inferring that both are males and the larger male, Bigfoot, was there to reconnoiter because of his knowledge of the security arrangements for the Vice President, the terrain, or the house."

"Thanks, Bays," Fries said. "All right, Mike, let's talk about the politics for a minute."

Newman said, "Of the three on our original list of suspects: Iraqis, Branch Davidians and the Chinese, the political situation was absolutely the best for Chinese involvement. The Vice President had long been a pro human rights activist particularly concerning China. He spoke out frequently and vociferously about China's record of mistreatment of dissidents. I believe we learned he had a friend from, let's see, college days that was killed over the protest at Tiananmen."

"I'll have to agree with that," Bays added. "In fact we learned when we debriefed Feinstein, his host on Figure Eight Island that Anderson had made a brief speech at the reception when he arrived at Feinstein's home about confronting the Chinese leader when he returned to Washington. And he mentioned his college friend who was killed in the massacre."

"As I recall," Newman advised, "our own people said the Chinese would have every reason to prevent Anderson from becoming President. He would have insisted that the Chinese people have greater human rights and more freedom or he would have retaliated, most likely economically. The only thing that they brought up that militated against direct Chinese intervention was the Chinese historically have not done that in the United States. Maybe this is a new era: Chinese exported terrorism.

Fries grew silent as if he were in deep thought. When he finally spoke, he said, "I agree the Katzenbach report is a magic bullet. It allows us to focus our efforts in one area. In fact the next time we talk, I want all of us to know Tientsin, China like the hometown where we grew up. But, and I want to emphasize this, there simply is not enough to conclude that there is direct Chinese involvement. It's a rush to judgment: just too much too soon. I'll need to brief the President on this."

Newman said, "Well, sir, I think we have enough for a press conference. The press is pushing us daily for a more definitive response and the public is getting restless for some results."

"No press conference. It's too soon, Mike."

"Well, at the very least, " Newman argued, "it ought to be leaked. We need to let the public know that we have at least traced the assassins to China. If we leak it and it turns out to be correct information, then we can take credit. If it turns out to be a false alarm, and I truly doubt that, we can deny it and distance ourselves."

Fries twisted the thought over in his mind and finally gave in. "All right but leak it through The Post. It's got to have some credibility."

"Yes, sir."

"Bays," Fries asked, "anything else we can do before you go back out?"

"No, everything is set. We'll redirect forces immediately."

Newman smiled slyly and said, "Well, I guess Saddam is going to get another break. And the Branch Davidians can be released from such tight scrutiny."

Bays retorted, "Maybe I ought to catch you up on Matthew Bryant. I talked to Pate Brandon in Dallas before I met you for the flight out here. Brandon said that his informer had made it into the inner circle. Bryant is a bomb maker just as we thought and he does have some pretty big plans although killing the Vice President was apparently not one of them. In fact, " Bays said as he checked his watch and calculated Central Time, "FBI and ATF are joining to bring Bryant in as we speak. Bryant and several followers are meeting this evening to work on a mail bomb to be sent to the ATF office down there. They plan to hit him with a surprise raid right about now."

*　　　　　*　　　　　*

Randy bounded up the steps to the New Hanover County Courthouse en route to the Superior Civil Courtroom. Today would be the first real test of her case representing her three clients in the Big Burger lawsuit. The law firm from Atlanta had filed an answer in each case and as a part of the answers, the firm had moved to dismiss her complaints because they failed to state a sufficient claim under existing law. Having researched the law thoroughly before she filed, Randy felt pretty confident about the outcome.

She carried a large stack of folders rather effortlessly and glided past the District Attorney's office. As she passed the door, she shot the door with her hand formed into an imaginary gun and mouthed the words: "The Man". When she reached the courtroom, she looked for Mrs. Skittleran who was bringing a large stack of law books and research documentation. Not seeing Skittle, Randy took her files to the plaintiffs' table in the courtroom and started to arrange them in proper order. She checked her watch. She still had fifteen minutes before the session would begin.

A bailiff came in the courtroom and noticing Randy's sunburn, said, "I like that tan. Where'd you get it?"

"Carolina Beach," she replied.

Before she could explain, he grinned and came back with, "Hey, counselor, your clients aren't going to be paying you to lay on the beach."

"This is a working tan. Got it while I was cycling down to Carolina Beach and back."

"That's a long way. You must be a pretty strong cyclist. You'll need it, going up against Diehlinger." The bailiff gave her a raised eyebrow and shook his head. "He can be something else sometimes."

"I know . . . ," she replied and before she could continue her response, Skittle came backing into the courtroom pulling a small wheeled carrier loaded with law books and files.

The bailiff hurried over to help Skittle with the door and sizing up Skittle's heavy load said, "Ms. Bost, it looks like you are ready for him."

"I hope so. I've worked long enough," Randy said as she went over to join them to relieve Skittle of the load. Mrs. Skittleran had developed a light perspiration on her upper lip from her efforts. Randy took the books from the cart and started arranging them on the desk. "Sorry, Skittle. I had no idea that I had such a load. It didn't look that big laid out on my desk and table."

Skittle was fanning herself and leaning on the table. "There is enough law here to win the cases straight out. Maybe they will just cave in."

The bailiff responded, "Not likely. Burns Diehlinger hasn't settled a case in this courtroom for as long as I can remember. He doesn't have anything but big cases and he won't budge until the plaintiff puts everything they got up. Then maybe, just maybe he'll offer something if he thinks the case is pretty strong. Of course by that time, he's made the plaintiff's lawyer so mad that they want to kill him. He's an A, uh, pardon my French, but he's one of the first order. The judges hate to see him coming."

Randy was busy putting everything in order and although she had been paying attention, she did not notice Burns Diehlinger enter the courtroom from a side door to her rear. She commented on the bailiff's assessment. "Mr. Diehlinger is just the local counsel. The real law firm is Bayready, Fore, Paine and DeStorm in Atlanta. We'll see who shows up for the hearing."

"If you are looking for a real lawyer, I'm it," Diehlinger spoke up in an angry tone. Randy was somewhat startled by the response and turned to see Diehlinger standing behind her. He was rather formidable in appearance, tall in stature, red hair that rose up from the sides of his head like flames and bushy red eyebrows that tended to dance as he talked. His eyes never blinked and his stare was penetrating. "In fact if you are looking for a sign from God," he said as he lay his briefcase on the defendant's table, "this is it."

Randy was taken aback by his abruptness and his intensity. "I, uh, I didn't mean anything by my comment. I'm . . . "

He stood very close to her and looked directly into her eyes. "Miss, no need to apologize. Most of us do stupid things. How long have you been out of law school anyway?"

She still had not recovered. "Uh, well, almost three years."

"These guys from Atlanta will blow you out of the water. It was ten years before I ever took on a big case and the big boys still beat me up pretty badly. Let's face it. You are not ready for this." He laughed a little. "They're going to eat you alive."

She was starting to get a little upset with his presumptuousness and his arrogance. "Not likely," she protested.

"And just between you and me. It's a mistake to show up with a sunburn. First of all, you look like you have been playing while the rest of the world has been working. Your clients won't like it. The judge won't like it. He will think you are not taking your case as seriously as you should. Really, all judges believe they work too hard already. Coming in from the beach with a suntan to play court. That will make them very happy." He rolled his eyes and gave her a look indicating she was quite stupid.

Randy felt herself getting a little redder. "Now wait just a minute. I . . . "

"And all of those law books. Who are you kidding? This is just a little 12(b)(6) motion. Nobody takes these things that seriously. You are sending a signal that you are unsure about your case. If you built your case on solid law, why do you need all of this paraphernalia? To make you look important. You're not. To make you look like a scholar? Believe me, sister, we've checked your records in law school. You're not. You're a nobody and you've taken on a giant, an international corporation that has enough money to buy you and me both over one thousand times. Get real."

Randy tightened up and found her hand forming into a fist involuntarily. Skittle took Randy by the arm and cautioned, "Easy, Randy. Easy."

"Oh, you are going to hit me. That will look good in front of the judge. I can see it in the papers now: 'Lawyer Loses Control, Hits Another Attorney'. Boy, you really are good, aren't you? You obviously can't keep your temper and you are obviously in over your head. You can't handle this case, can you? Huh, I thought we had some real competition this time."

Randy did not speak but found herself getting angrier and angrier. She turned back to her table and started counting to ten in her head. She felt her ears glow with heat. Skittle sat at the table beside her and started to arrange the books on the table as well.

Diehlinger brought his chair over from the other table and sat down beside her. "Look, if you can't take the heat, you know the old saying: get out of the kitchen. Or maybe you ought to get in the kitchen. Women lawyers are too emotional anyway."

She did not budge but kept moving the papers in front of her until they were aligned as she wanted them. When Skittle and she had the cart unloaded and the books and papers in order, Randy had overcome the surge of anger that she had felt earlier. She looked up at Diehlinger who was still too close for comfort. Randy, determined to sit on her feelings, attempted a smile and said, "When will Bayready be here?"

"He's not coming. This isn't that big a deal. Who do you have helping you? Somebody obviously has to be."

Randy started to feel that upsurge of heat again. She drew Ben's name out like she was drawing a pistol in a gunfight. "Ben Down," she said between gritted teeth.

"That drunk. And he's out of his element. This is a civil case. He works with the criminals. That's where he ought to be. Ben Down. Boy, you have gone out on the high wire without a safety net. It will hurt badly when you fall. And believe me, you are going to hit the ground hard, sister. Ben Down." He laughed out loud.

Randy's face turned scarlet red as she felt the anger rising within her. She pushed her chair back and stood. She started to speak but nothing came out. Diehlinger watched her begin to lose her temper as he had done with countless others. The chair fell over and startled everyone.

"Look, honey, no need to overreact." Diehlinger spoke so everyone could hear and backed up as though he were about to be attacked.

"I'm not your honey and . . . and furthermore Ben Down is no drunk," Randy stuttered as she glowered at Diehlinger.

The bailiff rushed over and positioned himself between the two of them. "Easy now," he said. "Mr. Diehlinger, maybe you ought to return to your table."

Skittle who had been folding up the book cart was stunned. Everyone waited to see what was going to happen next. Finally Diehlinger smiled and threw his hands up. He dragged his chair back to his table and the bailiff picked up Randy's chair. Skittle sat down then Randy sat. Skittle reached over and patted Randy on the arm.

Randy said, "It doesn't mean anything."

It was quiet for a few awkward moments then Randy went back to reviewing her documentation for the motion. Skittle and the bailiff started talking about the latest news in the clerk's office while other people started filtering into the courtroom for the session of court. Diehlinger opened his briefcase and started fumbling through some papers. A few more moments passed and Diehlinger cleared his throat.

"Look," he said in a low voice to Randy, "I've got an offer for you."

Randy did not look up but stayed busy with the paperwork on her desk. Diehlinger waited a moment then said, "Look, you do know you are required by the rules of ethics to inform your client of any offers. Here it is: the Bayready firm has asked me to inform you that in exchange for a voluntary dismissal with prejudice of each claim, we will pay the costs and the attorney's fees you have involved so far."

Without looking up, Randy said, "I'll tell my clients."

Diehlinger laughed again. "You won't find one of them," he said.

"What do you mean?"

"Our investigator can't find Louise Shelton. The last report we had was from her family. She's left the country and left no forwarding address." When Randy did not appear to be interested in the report, Diehlinger continued. "As for your client, Stella Barton, she is a former stripper. And to further complicate matters, she has a kid. I doubt you can show she was harmed and furthermore, I doubt she will want her sordid past to come out. She might lose her kid. She's in a custody fight right now, you know." Randy still did not respond although all of this was news to her. Diehlinger could tell he was sharing some information she had not heard before. "And your other plaintiff, Phoebe, what's her name, is a flake. She won't even come out of her house. Besides all of them just got a little out of hand down at the Big Burger. That's all it was just a little misunderstanding."

Randy finally spoke. "No, it's not. Your manager humiliated and embarrassed them. She assaulted them, she stripsearched them over a measly twenty dollars that was actually there. She had just miscounted the money. The corporation condoned it and covered it up. It's outrageous. You know it is and I know it is. And a New Hanover jury will know it is."

"Well," Diehlinger replied, "you better settle while you've still got a law license. You have just felt the tip of the wrath that we are capable of." With that said, he stood up, picked up his briefcase and started toward the door. "You have until Monday."

Randy was nonplused that he was walking out. "Aren't you going to stay for the hearing?"

"Nope. We just filed it to provide you a little education in legal hard ball. I believe you've got the message. Tell the judge we don't desire to be heard on the motion if you like." The last thing Randy saw was his flaming red hair as it disappeared out of the courtroom door.

Randy looked over at Skittle and said, "I can't believe it. My first real test on this case and I blow it. I got mad and I got stupid."

"No, you didn't," Skittle disagreed. "You got lucky. You are going to win this motion without a fight."

Thinking back over Diehlinger's repeated attacks, Randy said, "Well, I know one thing. I just got stripsearched."

*   *   *

"Margaret, I'm home," Ben said as he walked in and laid his keys on the bar in the kitchen. He went over to his chair and deposited the magazine he had purchased. He listened for Margaret in the house but heard nothing.

"Margaret," he called out again. Hearing no reply he went back to the kitchen and retrieved his bottle of Jack Daniels from the cabinet. He poured a couple of fingers into a glass, dropped in a couple of ice cubes and finished it off with a splash of Coke. He walked down the hall jiggling his drink as he checked the rooms. Nothing. He turned to go back up the hall and caught a glimpse of Margaret though a bedroom window as she came in from the backyard.

"Where were you? I called for you and you weren't here," he groused.

"Boy, you're in a fine mood. What are you doing home so early?" Margaret replied as she checked the clock in the kitchen. She put her tomatoes on the bar and took off her large hat revealing long tresses of black hair highlighted with gray and smooth lightly tanned skin. She loved to garden and even more she loved to collect her harvest from their large plot and distribute it to friends and neighbors.

As she started washing the tomatoes in the sink, Ben replied, "Worn out. Thought I'd come home and take it easy for a while. Get an early start on tomorrow."

Margaret stopped washing tomatoes. She came over and gave Ben a hug. "Now, now. I knew you were working too hard. Come over here to your chair and let's get you relaxed. Dr. Mom suggests plenty of rest and no work for you for a while." She led Ben over to his chair and picked up his magazine to make room for him to take a seat. "Fitness Today," she noted as she read the front cover. "Thinking about starting an exercise program?"

"Well, I don't know. Maybe. What do you think?"

"It would be good for you. You are down in the dumps too much lately. You need something to occupy your mind besides murder and rape and all of those things that make up your law practice." As he sat down, she pulled off his shoes and handed him the magazine. "You know I saw a man on TV the other day who started lifting weights in his sixties. In about four months the results were amazing: he looked ten years younger in the face and had the body of a young man. Diet and exercise make all the difference."

Ben skimmed the first couple of pages of muscular men and women in the magazine. "Yeah, maybe I could do that."

Margaret walked over and turned on the TV. "He was on one of the exercise channels." She flipped through several channels then laid the remote on the end table beside of Ben. "Guess who I saw out for an afternoon of exercise the other day?" Ben raised his eyebrows somewhat disinterestedly indicating he did not want to guess. "Randy. Randy Bost in your building. I was driving down to the garden club outing at Fort Fisher, you know, when we check on the sea oats and she was at a convenience store down at Carolina Beach. I think she was riding bicycles with some man I have seen at the courthouse."

"Probably Rod Pemberton. He's one of the DA's in Butch's office. Both Randy and Rod are exercise nuts."

"Rod. That's it. I've got something even juicier. They are nuts about each other. Randy was smiling from head to foot and she was giggling like a school girl when she introduced me to him. She has definitely got a thing for him." Margaret went back to the kitchen and retrieved the errant tomatoes that had rolled off of the cabinet top into the sink. "She looked like a woman in love."

"We'll see how 'in love' they are. She and I are going head to head with Butch and Rod in the Wanda Stickley case."

"Yeah, I saw that on TV the other night. The DA wants the death penalty for her. That's ridiculous. Everybody knows that that Stickley man was the devil. Nobody will give her the death penalty for killing him. I mean it's bad she killed him but come on, that man took everybody around here and everybody knows how badly he treated his family."

Ben soaked in the comments with great interest. He knew that Margaret always had a good sense of what people on the street would be thinking. And they would be the ones who would fill the jury box. Ben had always sought out her opinion about cases when she had worked for him as his secretary and now he wanted to talk about Wanda's case a little more. He said, "I think you're right but there is some pretty bad evidence. The DA gave us a prosecution summary that Wanda may have stabbed him, shot him, and possibly tortured him by carving something into his chest, cutting off his penis (while he was still alive) and ramming it down his throat."

Ben watched Margaret. She stopped washing tomatoes, a bad sign he thought, and she offered, "Oh, that's what they were referring to. The newsman never did make it very clear. That's bad. That's really bad. Could make a lot of difference."

Ben was a little discouraged with the comment and went back to his magazine. He continued to give it a little attention and at the same time give a little attention to the TV. He was still not very committed to the magazine and the news was a rather dull rendition of events of the latest rift in Mexican-American relations over the border. As he tried halfheartedly to keep up with the story, he mentioned in passing, "By the way I met an interesting person the other day. Strange really. The court appointed me to represent a man who looks like, acts like and talks like a woman. It's the most bizarre tale of twisted love between a man and my client and my client's sister. Any way my client wound up getting charged with murdering the man."

"What? What did you say?" Margaret said having been absorbed in bathing the tomatoes.

Ben kept thinking about Nora Jean and asked Margaret, "Do you think I'm cute?"

Margaret heard that. She stopped washing tomatoes and came into the living room. She wiped her hands on her apron. She gave Ben a big grin. "Why, Ben Down. You must be going through a middle age crisis. I thought you men had those long ago, you know, in your forties. What is going on with you? The next thing I know you will be wanting to buy a little red convertible and moving in with some little beach blonde."

Ben grumbled, "Not likely."

Margaret came over to him and sat in his lap. She cupped his head in her hands and said in a rising voice, "Not likely. Not likely. You're going to have to do better than that." Ben smirked at all of the attention he was getting from her little jealous streak. "Besides you're cute, really cute. You are the cutest thing in the world to me. Cuter than a room full of teddy bears."

"All right. All right," Ben protested softly.

Margaret grew quiet for a moment and snuggled in his arms. "I don't know what I'd do without you," she whispered.

"I don't know what I'd do without you either, Margaret," Ben said in a serious tone and gave her a hug. "You and Sandy and Mary Lee have been my life. Guess I am just dragging for some reason. Sorry I've been so negative but these cases, something is getting to me. Same old, same old, I guess."

Margaret commiserated. "I know what you mean. I've been feeling like I don't have much energy lately either." She hesitated for a moment as if unsure of whether to tell him something. "I have . . . had some sharp pains in my chest too. It probably doesn't mean anything but I have felt a little tired too."

"You never know about something like that. You had better let the doctor take a look. Chest pains. That's not good at all. You'd better . . . "

"I wish I had never told you. It's nothing. You are worse than an old mother hen. I'm going for a check up with my gynecologist in about a month. I'll get him to check. Right now we need to get dinner up and running," Margaret said as she got up out of his lap. "Oh, by the way, Sandy called. She says she might have some very interesting news for us in a couple of weeks. She was pretty mysterious about it."

"What's that all about?"

"For a lawyer you can be a little thick sometimes, Grandpa."

"Huh? Do you think?"

"I don't know. We'll see." She walked back into the kitchen and picked up the washed tomatoes. She put some in a plastic bag to give to the neighbors and packed the others in the lower part of the refrigerator. She leaned back and looked at Ben until he finally looked up from his magazine. She raised her eyebrows a couple of times as though she were flirting with him. "Oh, you're cute. Really cute all right," she said.

Ben smiled and laid the magazine down. He started to get out of his chair to go to the kitchen when he was distracted by the news report on the TV.

The television screen shifted to a scene of chaos and smoke as FBI agents and ATF agents stormed a house in a residential neighborhood. The newsman announced, "Today in Irving, Texas, a small town between Dallas and Fort Worth, a small army of FBI and ATF agents raided the residence of a person identified as a former Branch Davidian. As the accompanying footage from local affiliate WDFW in Dallas indicates, there was a violent confrontation. At least one ATF agent was wounded and two persons were killed. Those who died were apparently killed not by gunfire but by a large explosion which occurred shortly after the siege by the federal authorities. Only one of those killed has been identified. He is believed to be (by the unofficial report) Matthew Bryant who has headed a splinter group from the Branch Davidians. This group known as The Avengers by reason of their advocacy of a violent reprisal against the ATF for its role in the siege at Waco, Texas several years ago has been investigated (according to sources close to the investigation) for possible explosives and illegal weapons violations. They were believed to have been getting ready to blow up the ATF office in nearby Fort Worth when this purported arrest attempt was made by federal authorities. No identification has been made of the wounded ATF agent nor has the name of the other person killed in the confrontation been made public. We will keep you updated as the story progresses."

The TV screen then turned to recent television footage of the funeral procession of the Vice President as his body was transported through the streets of Washington en route to Arlington Cemetery.

The announcer reported, "In other news a high ranking source close to the investigation of the assassination of Vice President Anderson has revealed that a major breakthough has occurred. For the details of this report at this time, we are going to take you to Sanders Norris, our correspondent in Washington."

The screen shifted to the journalist standing in front of the FBI building in Washington.   He said, "In a rather surprising development in the case involving the assassination of the Vice President, the assassins have been linked to China. Apparently the assassins had used a type of adhesive glue on their shoes on the night of the assassination to help conceal their identities. Sand found embedded inside the glue has been traced to Tientsin, China, a major manufacturing and port area in China."

Margaret having noticed that Ben was paying very close attention to the TV walked into the living room and joined him in listening to the report. The screen then switched to aerial footage of the mangled second floor of the Feinstein house on Figure Eight Island.

The reporter continued with the report. "According to our source, in a rather unusual twist in the investigation, FBI agents at the scene on the night of the assassination found at least two large specimens of glue that had apparently worked themselves free from the shoes of the assassins. Initial analysis of the glue revealed very little but a collection of geologists, anthropologists and forensic scientists working at a feverish pace have finally concluded that the sand could have only come from one location in the world: Tientsin, China."

The TV screen then shifted from the reporter to a wide angle view of the port city in China. He closed the report with the following: "So far there has been no official comment from Chinese authorities nor has our source been willing to speculate on the extent of the involvement, if any, of the Chinese."

Margaret was the first to speak. She said, "That's amazing. They may solve this case from one little grain of sand."

"Science and technology," Ben agreed, "may be able to tell us the truth about everything one of these days."

"Not everything."

"What do you mean?"

"I know you are cute and I don't need a scientist to tell me that." Ben smiled and took Margaret in his arms. "And you know what else?" she asked.

"No."

"I don't need a scientist to tell me how much I love you."

CHAPTER TEN

"Mr. Yeager," the DA's secretary said as she entered his office, "Rod just called from the courtroom. He said they are about to complete sentencing in the Foster case. He has arranged for Wanda Stickley to be brought to the courtroom and Ben Down and Randy Bost are there. So he said to give him about five minutes and he will be ready to proceed on her Rule 24 hearing."

He nodded without looking up from the files on his desk and she continued, "Oh, you may want to look at this." The secretary handed him a letter with an attached envelope. "I just clocked it in."

He took the letter, assembled the documents into a stack and closed the file. As he scooped up the file, he told the secretary that he would be back in about twenty to thirty minutes and to delay his calls for about fifteen minutes after he returned to give him sufficient time to make journal entries on the Stickley case.

"The Honorable Allen D. "Butch" Yeager, District Attorney," he read in the letter as he walked down the hall. He checked the letterhead and noticed that it was from the WOA, Women of America, an organization that devoted its efforts to securing equality and fairness for women in "the work place, the home place and every place" as its motto indicated. He read:

"Dear Mr. Yeager:

I write to encourage you to reconsider your stance in the case of State of North Carolina versus Wanda Stickley. Recently you have announced that you will seek an indictment charging her with the crime of first degree murder and you will seek the death penalty. Your decision in this matter is not merited by the evidence or the law. Wanda Stickley was victimized by Ralph Stickley for the last thirteen years. She and her son were abandoned by him; she was left without his support to care for herself and her son Jeremy. Your court records reveal that at the time of Ralph Stickley's death, he was $48,386.23 in arrears in child support.

His abuse of Wanda is legend in our area. He assaulted her repeatedly, he beat her unmercifully in the presence of their child, he raped her and he tried to kill her. There is not a woman, and for that matter, not anyone who could endure what she has had to go through at the hands of Ralph Stickley. Although the evidence in this case would tend to show that she killed him and that she committed harsh acts of violence against him, the evidence is equally clear that what she did was done in defense of herself, her home and her child.

Finally I write to plead that you release her and that you not prosecute her. She has suffered enough. I also write to inform you that our organization will resist any effort to prosecute, convict and imprison her one moment further. Sincerely yours, Carrie Pestoff WOA President"

He opened the file and slid the letter inside. When he entered the courtroom, he walked down the center aisle toward the DA's desk while Rod Pemberton was making the State's final argument to the judge in a case before the court for sentencing. He walked through the small gate quietly and laid his file on the DA's table. As he turned to look back over the courtroom, he caught the eye of Ben Down, gave him a brief look of acknowledgment, and took a seat at the DA's table. He turned his attention then to the jury box where the prisoners were usually held temporarily until their cases were called. It was a busy day and the jury box was filled with orange uniforms. Finally his eyes settled on Wanda Stickley.

Wanda sat leaned over somewhat and watched the proceedings as each prisoner had been called before the court. Her face was still swollen and streaked in black and blue from the beating. Remembering Ben's advice she tried to sit up and to look interested in the proceedings. She also hoped desperately that Jeremy would be present so she scanned the audience for him. As she did, she made eye contact with the DA. He did not blink and gave her no indication of what was going on in his mind.

Allen Dayton Yeager, nicknamed Butch in elementary school because of his similarity to one of the Little Rascals a la Spanky, Alfalfa and Buckwheat, had served as District Attorney for twenty-six years in New Hanover County. He had served beyond the age when he would have received full retirement benefits. In point of fact it actually cost him money to continue to serve. He served for two reasons: one, he really enjoyed the duties of the office and two, he had nothing else he wanted to do.

Those who were familiar with his tenure said he had served longer than the office had existed which was in one respect true. The position had been called Solicitor in North Carolina until about twenty years ago when it was modernized to the more common term District Attorney. He was first elected as Solicitor in the old days and then was continually re-elected District Attorney after the name of the official position had changed. Even so he still kept the title "Solicitor" on the door to his office.

At seventy-two years of age, he looked and acted much younger. Butch had been a football player at the University of South Carolina and he had been an amateur boxer in the Army. He wore his hair military short and he kept his five feet nine inch frame rifle erect as he stood. His chest was barrel shaped and his shoulders were wide. His voice was clear and projected as he addressed the court. Indeed when he called the docket of scheduled cases at the courthouse in Wilmington, it was said that there was no need for the bailiff to call anyone out when they failed to appear because they could hear Butch all of the way to South Carolina.

In a way Butch admired Ben Down. After all Butch had hired him years ago. Both of them shared many of the same qualities including a love of the law and an addiction to the courtroom. They had worked well together when Ben had worked for him. Butch often called Ben his "push button DA" meaning that Ben would do his job without a great deal of instruction or oversight. But since Ben had left the DA's office, the relationship had soured somewhat. Ben said it was Butch's gung-ho, got to be right attitude; Butch said it was Ben's constant grumbling. The courthouse regulars said it was simply a case of alcohol intolerance: Ben loved to drink and Butch was a teetotaler.

Strong drink and strong personalities made for some pretty interesting confrontations in the courtroom. Several years ago the schism erupted into a shouting match in a simple assault case. It was a simple case really with the wife claiming that she was the victim of an assault by her husband. Ben claimed that she had nagged his client until he could not take it any more. When the husband started to leave, the wife had stood between him and the door. Ben claimed that she invaded his constitutional right to come and go as he chose and further that she had used fighting words when she invoked the name of his mother in rather unceremonious terms.

Butch countered with an accusation that the husband was drunk and on a rampage and that is what you should expect from someone who partakes of strong drink. Ben objected claiming that was a rather conservative, narrow view. Butch and Ben moved toward each other during the heated exchange and balled up their fists. Bailiffs rushed to intervene and separated them. When the dust settled, the judge directed them to report to chambers. Although it only merited a judicial lecture, it added an edge to their court appearances after that with the courthouse regulars taking odds on who would have won. Ben was the odds on favorite because of his youth; Butch on the other hand had his adherents because of his previous training as a fighter. Egged on by their various supporters, the tear in the relationship never healed.

Rod had just about concluded his remarks in the sentencing case when Assistant District Attorney Jack Krait came in the courtroom and spotting Ben, took a seat beside him. Krait stared at Ben obviously wanting his attention. Ben never looked over to acknowledge him but stayed busy reviewing some papers from his file. Finally Krait whispered to Ben, "Got some good news."

Ben still did not look up and Krait whispered again, "Butch is transferring me to Superior Court."

Ben looked a little stunned. Krait had stayed in the lower court much longer than any other Assistant District Attorney because of his rudeness and ineptness. It was generally assumed by the practicing bar that Krait would remain at the District Court level because of these traits. Krait and Ben had had several unpleasant rounds, not that that was unusual since almost everyone had been a victim of Jack Krait, but the prospect that Ben would have to deal with Krait in another court was rather unsettling. Ben whispered back, "You've got to be kidding."

Krait rather than being offended by Ben's disapproval missed the point completely and whispered back, "No, seriously. Butch and Rod are going to be really busy on this Stickley case and they wanted to bring me up so that when the trial starts, I can take over the other sessions of Superior Court."

"Butch has lost his mind." Ben shook his head in disbelief.

"No, he hasn't. It's time. I've worked those crummy little old cases down there long enough. I'm ready to handle the big court. Speaking of which, we need to deal with the Kitners and their dog.

Butch said I need to start out with some of the cases I handled in District Court that were appealed to Superior Court. What do you say? Let's get that case over with."

"Jack," Ben whispered, "has it ever occurred to you that if Butch and Rod are going to be busy in Wanda Stickley's case, that I might be just as busy myself?"

"Well, you appealed the case. I'm going to call it when I'm good and ready."

"Jack, you are the quintessential jerk."

Krait reacted to the comment by raising his voice at the same time Rod had finished his remarks and was sitting down. "I'm the DA up here and you'll have to be ready when I say so."

Everybody turned to look at Krait and the judge looked up from the probation report in the sentencing case, took off his glasses and stared at Krait. Krait shrugged his shoulders indicating he was not aware he was creating a disturbance. The judge let the interruption pass without comment and went back to reading the report. Ben went back to his paperwork.

Krait stood up to leave and whispered to Ben, "Be ready."

Randy came in as Krait was leaving and took the seat beside of Ben. Ben closed his file and whispered to Randy, "Where have you been? We're up next."

"I've been working on something juicy, wonderful really. Girl stuff. I'll tell you about it later."

As the judge pronounced the judgment in the sentencing case, Rod looked behind him to see which attorneys were present for the call of the next cases. He saw Randy and gave her a warm smile. Randy smiled back and leaned forward in her seat.

"You look radiant today. Ready to do battle in the Stickley case?" she asked.

As Rod looked back and grinned at her, Ben whispered, "I'm going to have to get somebody to throw a bucket of cold water on you two so we can get on with the business."

Randy cooed, "Ooh. Cold water. Sounds steamy. Ooh. Quit talking dirty, Ben."

Ben smiled and shook his head. "Worse than a couple of teenagers."

Before Rod or Randy could respond, Butch was announcing that the State was calling the case of Wanda Stickley. The bailiff walked over to the jury box and started escorting Wanda to the defense table. Ben and Randy moved up to the table and left a chair between the two of them for Wanda. When Wanda joined them, Butch said, "Your Honor, at this time we are calling the case of Wanda Stickley for a limited purpose. The grand jury has returned a bill of indictment charging her with first degree murder and under Rule 24 of the General Rules of Practice, she is entitled to have a hearing on several preliminary matters."

The judge looked over at Ben and asked, "Defendant ready?"

Ben stood and said, "We are, Your Honor. If the court please, I would like to announce for the record that the defendant is present and I make a general appearance on her behalf and Randy Bost makes a general appearance as second counsel."

"Thank you, Mr. Down and Ms. Bost. At this time then, I will recognize the District Attorney to be heard on whether this matter will qualify for treatment as a capital case."

Butch spoke up. "Yes, sir, Your Honor. If I might offer a brief synopsis of the case?" Receiving the judge's nod, he continued. "The State's evidence indicates that the victim in this matter is Ralph Stickey. Mr. Stickley and the defendant were formerly husband and wife at the time of his death. Our investigation reveals that Mr. Stickley went to the home of his former wife and entered without permission. An altercation ensued between the two of them. Mr. Stickley was not armed with any weapon. The altercation which had turned violent began inside the house and continued out into the driveway of the residence. Mr. Stickley, although completely unarmed, was stabbed, was shot and mutilated by Wanda Stickley. She was found by an officer to be standing over the body of Mr. Stickley as the blood drained from his body. She was holding a knife, the same knife that killed him. She had cut his throat, she had cut off his penis and rammed it down what was left of his throat. She had claimed and we say falsely on at least one occasion that she had been previously raped by Mr. Stickley. Further when Mr. Stickley was found, he had an 'R' carved into his chest. We believe, given the hatred and anger she held for Ralph Stickley, that she carved that 'R' into his body while he was alive. Somewhat like a scarlet letter, she marked him 'R' for rapist. The evidence will show he was alive when he was castrated and when he was carved up like a Christmas turkey."

Ben stood. "Objection, Your Honor. The District Attorney's remarks are a statement of his opinion and should not be permitted. And certainly they are outside the purpose and purview of this simple Rule 24 hearing."

Before Butch could argue with Ben's objection, the judge ruled. "Objection overruled. The court will observe this is just a hearing for announcement by the District Attorney of the charge and the underlying basis for the charge. No need to go into the evidence here, gentlemen."

"Yes, sir, Your Honor," Butch replied. "We do say this is a case of first degree murder based on the theory of malice, premeditation and deliberation and on the separate theory of torture. And we do intend to proceed with this case as a capital case in that the defendant's conduct was heinous, atrocious and cruel, which, as Your Honor knows, is a basis for imposition of the death penalty in this State."

"Thank you, Mr. Yeager. That will suffice for purposes of this hearing. What says the defendant?" the judge inquired.

Ben stood again and said, "We take issue with almost everything the DA has said about his case. Although this case is not before this court for arraignment at this point, I can tell you that Wanda Stickley pleads not guilty. We contend that she was the victim not Ralph Stickley. If he hadn't been drunk and on a rampage, after all, what do you expect from someone addicted to strong drink and . . . "

"Objection. Objection, Your Honor," Butch challenged as he stood. He stared at Ben knowing that Ben was referring to the allegations Butch had made in a previous case that had resulted in a confrontation between the two of them.

Before the judge spoke, Ben defended his statement. "Your Honor, I was just quoting our DA from another case. This is a central part of our case."

Butch started to speak again and the judge cut him off. "All right. All right, gentlemen. No need to tread over old ground. Let's just stick to the preliminaries in this case."

"Yes, sir, Your Honor," Ben agreed and Butch sat down. Ben watched Butch out of the corner of his eye and when he was completely seated, Ben continued. "We do say that Wanda Stickley is not guilty. We also ask that Your Honor consider granting her a bond. She is presently held in jail without bond. That improperly impinges on her right to defend herself. She is presumed innocent and she needs the opportunity to prove it. She can't do it sitting in jail."

"What says the State, Mr. Yeager?"

"This is a capital case. She should not be allowed bond. We oppose her release."

"Given the State's announcement that this is a capital case, Mr. Down," the judge said, "and the fact that the defendant now faces the possibility of the imposition of the death penalty and concomitantly the likelihood of flight increases dramatically, the court could not in good conscience grant a release on bail. Motion for bond is denied. Any other matters that you gentlemen need to address?"

"Yes, sir," Ben said. "We will be filing motions in this case and we suggest a schedule for hearing the motions."

"How many motions will be filed?" the judge asked.

"At least thirty, possibly more," Ben replied.

"You're serious?" Butch stared at Ben.

"As serious as one hundred proof white Wilkes County whiskey," Ben replied as he handed copies of the motions that were being filed to Butch.

Butch handed the copies over to Rod and told the judge. "We'll be ready whenever Your Honor says. We do not want anything to delay the trial of this case."

"Your Honor," Ben said, "Miss Bost will be handling the bulk of these motions and she has indicated she will be ready to proceed whenever Mr. Yeager and Mr. Pemberton are."

Randy leaned forward and looked over at Rod who was thumbing through the motions. Rod stood and looked back at Randy with a smile. "We'll be ready," he told the judge, "whenever Your Honor states."

"All right. The court will set arraignment in thirty days and will grant these additional thirty days for the filing of any further motions and then the hearing on all motions to be scheduled within sixty days from today. Anything else, counsel?"

Butch and Ben indicated that there were no additional matters to be taken up. As Wanda was led back to the jury box and the attorneys moved away from the tables, Ben told Butch he wanted to talk to him about the case. Butch told Ben to give him about thirty minutes then to come by his office. When they made it out into the hallway, Randy asked Ben, "How do you think it went?"

"Fine. Butch was just puffing his wares. We are going to meet in a few minutes to find out if there is any soft underbelly in the DA's hard line. Want to join us?"

"No," Randy responded. "I have arranged a surprise for Wanda, in fact, a couple of surprises. I have been talking to Caroline Markham who is serving as the guardian ad litem for Jeremy in the juvenile case. Caroline loves kids and although she has officially been opposed to visitation between Jeremy and his mother, she is pretty softhearted underneath. She has had Jeremy brought to the courthouse ostensibly to work on the juvenile case but more importantly so that Wanda and Jeremy can visit for a few minutes while I'm in conference with Wanda."

"Wow," Ben said. "You are better than I thought. There is more than one way to skin a cat and more than one way to get a kid in to see his mother. Good job." Ben hesitated for a moment as though he was unsure of how to approach the next subject. "I want to talk to you about another matter. It could be a potential problem. You and Rod. Looks like the two of you are heating up. I just wonder . . . "

Randy cut him off. "No need to worry about that. We are professionals. We know we are advocates. Our personal lives will not interfere with the case."

"No, I don't think it will but the case could interfere with your personal lives. Look, Randy, I like you and I don't want you to get hurt."

Randy brushed it off. "No one is going to get hurt. We are like most couples: we can make love all night and make war all day. It's no problem."

"Well, I hope so. With that said, tell me about the other surprise."

"No, I'm going to wait and let you see it for yourself. It will be out on the sidewalk when you exit the courthouse. You'll know what it is. Well, I'm off to make a mother happy. I'll talk to you back at the office about the conference between Butch and you."

Ben checked his watch. Seeing that he had another twenty minutes before he would meet with Butch, he decided to go to the law library, one of the few places in the smokefree courthouse where he could sneak a smoke on a cigar. As he walked down to the end of the hall to go in, he noticed a rather attractive lady waiting by the steps. She appeared to be rather nervous and acted as if she were waiting for someone. As Ben walked by, she spoke.

"Mr. Down, sir, are you Ben Down?"

"Yes, what may I do for you?"

"I am Natalie Dawtry, Nora Jean's sister, well, uh, Noah Gene Lyerly's sister. I understand that you have been appointed by the court to represent her and I wanted to talk to you about Noodle, I mean, Nora Jean."

"Certainly," Ben said. "Come into the library and we'll talk."

They entered the library and found that it was not occupied. Ben pulled out a chair for her and after she was seated, took a seat himself. There were several law books on the table so Ben moved those to one end of the table. After he had cleared out a space for them to sit more comfortably at the table, Ben asked, "I believe Nora Jean calls you Nate, isn't that correct?"

Natalie was very nervous and Ben's inquiry made her smile a little. "Yes, she's Noodle and I'm Nate. Goes back a long way to when we were kids."

"Nora Jean said you and she were very close when you were growing up." Ben laughed. "Nora Jean also said you were very pretty and you are. Prettier than I imagined."

"Well, thank you." She appeared somewhat distracted from her purpose and reached in her purse for a tissue. "How is Nora Jean?" she finally asked.

"She is doing very well for someone incarcerated. From the reports I get, she is very popular with the inmates." Ben checked his watch and seeing he had enough time, he reached in for a cigar and began working it out of the cellophane wrapper.

"Noodle always did have the personality. She always had a way with men."

"Oh, yes. She still does." Ben smiled. He continued fumbling with the cigar and was somewhat anxious to move on to the subject of the meeting. He asked, "What can I do for you?"

"Well," Natalie said then hesitated as if unsure of what to say next. "I guess the question is what can I do for Noodle? I want to help if I can."

"That's good to hear," Ben replied. "What happened out there when Sean was killed?"

Natalie changed position in her seat indicating her discomfort at revisiting the events that led to Sean's death. She choked up a little and her face filled with a slight pink tint. "Sean," she started. "Sean went a little crazy. He and I had been dating for a while. He was a little too far out for me. I think he was a little sex crazy or something. Anyway we were breaking up and he . . . " She hesitated again. "He started hitting on Nora Jean. Well, she has always been oversexed. I mean that's all she thinks about. You know, life is strange. I mean, well, you know. She hasn't got all of the equipment but she's got a lot of interest. Too much I think. Anyway I could see how she and Sean got into it. He was about as crazy about it as she is."

"What happened when Sean was killed?"

"She was just defending me. Sean had a mean streak. If things didn't go his way, he would get angry and start throwing things or make a scene. Really he was selfish, childish even. He could be really mean too. He beat me a couple of times and he would try to hurt me too. That's what was happening when I called Noodle. I believe he told me that he and Noodle were lovers just to hurt me. Anyway she came straight away. He would have killed me if she hadn't come in and got him off of me. I really don't think she meant to kill him but she knew how he was. That's why she had her knife out. He was bad when he wanted to be."

"Nora Jean mentioned a gun. Where was it?"

"It was lying on the coffee table."

"That's too bad. That's where Nora Jean said it was."

"What do you mean 'too bad'?"

"Well, her defense of self defense would be a lot stronger if he were using the gun. I'm not sure that a jury would believe she needed to use deadly force, lethal force to protect you from a beating by Sean with his fists."

"Well, I'm going to testify that Sean was holding the gun in his hand and was going to shoot me."

"No, you are not," Ben stated emphatically. "You are going to tell the truth, plain and simple. All of the truth, no more and no less."

"But I've got to save Noodle. She's all I've got."

"I am sympathetic," Ben said. "I know you want to help her but perjuring yourself to save her will not help you or her. Look, Nora

Jean knows she did wrong. She is strong and she is able to handle whatever the court deals out. You will tell the truth and the truth will help her enough."

Natalie looked down at her hands and said softly, "Really. I already told them Sean was holding the gun."

"What?" Ben expressed his surprise.

Natalie did not look up. "At first I told them the way it really happened. I was really mad at Noodle right after it happened. Then when they locked her up, I couldn't take it. I changed my story and said Sean was beating me with the gun and told me he was going to kill me with it. I wasn't going to let Noodle go to prison because of what I said. Then the detective came back out there and said that Noodle confessed and didn't mention anything about him holding a gun. Anyway the long and short of it is, I went back to my original statement. But for Noodle I'd go back to him holding the gun. I can't lose Noodle."

"No, you tell the truth and Noodle will be all right. There's no way out of it. She knows that. She will have to do some time but given the way this thing has come down, she should not have to do too much."

Ben picked up his briefcase, checked his watch again and said, "It will turn out all right. I will get the prosecution summary pretty soon. We'll see how it looks after I go over that. In the meantime I've got to get to a meeting with the DA about another case and I'm going to suggest that you make arrangements to go by and see Nora Jean in the jail. I believe from what she has told me, your telling her that you are not mad at her will do more to uplift her spirits than anything else that we can do. What do you say?"

"No. I can't do that. I can't let anything happen to her. She's my sister. But I can't forgive her."

Ben stood and walked her out into the hall. "I hope that you will think about that, Natalie. She feels terrible for what she's done to you and for that matter, to Sean. She needs you. In fact you are all she's got."

Natalie did not respond and walked up the hall toward the stairs. Ben walked toward the DA's office. When Ben went in, he asked Mrs. Carlton, Butch's secretary with whom Ben had worked when he was with the DA's office, "Is the Grinch in?"

She smiled mischievously at Ben. "Still stirring up trouble I see. Mr. Yeager said for me to bring you on back when you came in." They walked down the hall toward Butch's office and Mrs. Carlton noticing that Ben was carrying an unlit cigar, remarked, "I see you are celebrating our smokefree courthouse."

Ben, who had been carrying the cigar somewhat absentmindedly, was still thinking about Natalie's continued anger at Nora Jean. He lifted the cigar up and said, "You know this world could use a little more forgiveness. Maybe we smokers wouldn't have to sneak around to find a place to smoke if these 'do gooders' were a little more forgiving."

Mrs. Carlton, a smoker herself, replied, "I know what you mean."

She showed Ben to the large office at the end of the hall and when they entered, Butch said, "Take a seat, Ben." Butch also noticed the unlit cigar and said, "Don't light that thing up in here. It's against the law, you know."

"It's a fascist law. Today they are coming for the smokers. Tomorrow," Ben said as he pointed to Butch's coffee cup, "they are coming for the coffee drinkers. Caffeine, you know. Next," Ben continued as he breathed in deeply, "Mrs. Carlton, the nose police will be coming for the perfume. That intoxicating, alluring smell will be classified as a nasal irritant."

Mrs. Carlton smiled at Ben and shook her head. Butch finally looked up from the paperwork on his desk and said, "Ben, you always did know how to make friends and influence people."

"Butch, you always were defender of the faith."

"As long as they come for your so-called 'Knock'em', I think this will be a better world."

"Butch, you know what, you need a stiff drink. Sure would . . . "

"Well, if I recall correctly, you went to Wake Forest. Now that's a good old Baptist school. I don't think you learned to drink there. They were milk drinkers if I recall all right."

Ben winced a little. "No, the last time I looked they were drinking some beer up there and it seems like they had even started dancing on campus."

Mrs. Carlton interrupted, "All right, boys. I refereed you two for five years. Do I need to stay and do it again?"

Ben replied first, "No, but thanks just the same. You were always such a darling. You might see if Butch has any of the strong drink hidden anywhere as evidence, or God forbid, for drinking purposes. It would make this meeting go a little smoother."

Butch smiled at Mrs. Carlton and said, "We're all right. I'll call you if I need you. Remember 911 if he goes into DT's."

Mrs. Carlton smiled at both of them again and walked up the hall toward her desk. Butch went back to reviewing the paperwork on his desk and it became quiet in the office. Ben was familiar with the routine: Butch always gave him the "I'm important; you're not" routine when Ben came in for conferences on pending cases. Ben listened to the pleasant hum of Mrs. Carlton's word processor and wondered if Skittle were busy making any money for him or was on the phone idly chatting with one of her friends at the clerk's office. Ben looked around the office and his attention finally fell on a sign that Butch always kept posted behind him and just over his head. It was the quotation from Shakespeare: "The first thing we do, let's kill all of the lawyers".

Finally after Butch had made him wait for what he thought was an inordinate length of time, Butch looked up from the mound of paperwork and asked, "So Wanda Stickley. Want to plead guilty and go right into the sentencing phase?"

"Want to do the right thing and take a voluntary dismissal? This is self defense and you know it."

"It may have started as self defense but it got way out of hand. You've seen the pictures. My God, the woman went crazy, overreacted, tortured him and killed him. Can you imagine the agony that he must have gone through?"

"I don't have to imagine the agony my client has gone through over the years at his hands and the misery she is still going through right now because you have her locked up in that nightmare of a jail."

The preliminary skirmishing was over and it grew quiet for a moment. Ben knew the drill all too well. Butch would always focus on the victim next. Butch led off with: "Ralph Stickley. He was no angel but he did not deserve to die like that. No one does."

"Butch, save the propaganda for the TV. Ralph was a monster. You know it and I know it. More importantly everyone out there knows it. You can't pick a jury without most of them knowing how bad he was. And besides that, you taught me well. One of the things you always said is, and let me quote you here: 'Your case is never

any better than your victim.'   Applying that principle, Ralph
deserved what he got and your case stinks."

Butch smiled as if he had caught something in his trap. "So you
are saying she did it and your defense is she did it in self defense."

"I'm not saying that at all. I am saying she is not guilty. It's all
up to the State to show she did it and if you are successful in that, to
show she did not do it in self defense. There is no burden of proof on
Wanda to do anything except to look like a poor abused wife. And
believe me, she will."

"Where's the gun?" Butch asked.

"That's my question. Where *is* the gun?" he asked emphasizing
the "is". "And for that matter why was Ralph in prison in South
Carolina? You convicted him and sent him to prison in North
Carolina. And why was he on escape? Ralph wouldn't escape from
anywhere. He'd try to buy his way out or bargain his way out. And
why was he at Wanda's? This case is full of questions that you can't
answer."

It grew quiet except for the hum of the word processor up the
hall. Finally Ben broke the silence. "Enough sparring. What's the
bottom line here, Butch?"

Butch opened the file and glanced at the letter from the Women of
America. He looked back at Ben. "Here it is. We've got enough to
go forward with first degree murder and we've got enough to seek the
death penalty. But. You talk to her about a second degree murder
plea, open end on sentence, and we will consider it."

"I'll tell her but I don't think she will do it. She has already given
me marching orders for 'no plea'."

"Well, tell her how it works. She can plead in and take the time
or my hands are tied. Second degree is as good as it will get. She
can't plead on first degree because I will have to seek the death
penalty if she does. If she won't plead guilty to second degree
murder, the evidence is straightforward on first degree murder and
the Supreme Court says I have to seek the death penalty if there is
enough evidence to support it. This case has plenary evidence for the
death penalty. And Ben, they are finally starting to execute some of
the scum so it's real. She better get on board or . . . . Well, you
better have a prayer meeting with her."

"I'll talk to her but I don't believe second degree murder will
budge her one inch. She won't take a long prison term. She loves

that boy, Jeremy, and she's told me she'd rather die than lose him." Ben searched Butch's face for any emotion. Nothing. "I might get some movement with a voluntary manslaughter plea with sentencing in the mitigated range. I'm not promising but maybe . . . "

Butch threw up his hands. "Get back in the real world. This is a case of torture. We might have a little problem with Ralph's background but no jury will cut her any slack when she carves her signature on him and castrates him. Ralph was bad but he wasn't that bad. Second degree. Take it to her; otherwise get ready for battle."

Ben stood up and put his cigar in his mouth and rolled it to one side. "You are a hard man, Butch."

"A hard man is hard to find in this lily-livered world. Take it or leave it."

Ben walked up the hall and as he passed Mrs. Carlton's desk, she remarked, "Glad to see you are still alive. How did you leave the boss?"

"Just like I found him: hard-headed and hard-hearted."

Mrs. Carlton grinned and said, "Oh, by the way, Rod has been assigned the Noah Gene Lyerly case and asked me to give you this copy of the prosecution summary."

"Thanks," he said and took the manila envelope from her. He walked out of the door and made his way outside to the walk leading back to the parking lot. He noticed two women walking back and forth. They were carrying placards. Protesters, Ben thought, we have not had those since the 'Sixties. When he was close enough to one of the signs, he read: "WANDA STICKLEY--VICTIM NOT MURDERER". The other sign read: MOTHER NOT MURDERER--NO WAY--WOA. Ben smiled and looked up at the window at Butch's office. The old boy is getting some pressure, Ben thought, it is about time.

He looked back at the protesters and watched them march back and forth. Several drivers slowed their cars to allow them to read the signs and pedestrians moved over to the side to give them enough room to walk. One car pulled up and a news reporter exited. He took a picture and began interviewing one of the protesters. As several people gathered and Ben slipped through the crowd, he thought: Randy Bost, you are full of surprises.

CHAPTER ELEVEN

The bailiff carried the judge's two catalog briefcases up the steps toward the judge's chambers on the second floor of the courthouse. The judge, His Honor Meykus Allgood, carrying his robe followed along in tow. When they reached the chambers, the bailiff sat a briefcase to the side of the door and started to open the door with his free hand. Ben,who had seen the difficulty he was having negotiating the door and the briefcases, approached and picked up the judge's briefcase and followed them into chambers.

"Ben Down, Your Honor," Ben said introducing himself. "I'll be one of the attorneys who will be adding to your workload while you are with us for the next six months."

The judge put out his hand and shook Ben's hand saying, "Thank you, Ben. Judge Meykus Allgood at your service. Have a seat and let's visit for a while."

He hung his robe in the closet and Ben took a seat. The bailiff waited for further instructions from the judge before he left. Ben who had known the bailiff since he had come to Wilmington commented, "Your Honor is in good hands. Kyle Cook is one of the best officers to serve the courts. He has worked at this court longer than anyone else I know of including our DA Butch Yeager."

"Thanks, Ben," the bailiff responded. He continued to wait by the door until the judge was situated in his chambers. "Your Honor," he said returning the compliment, "Ben Down is one of our best lawyers. He won't give you a hard time. He's just kidding about adding to your workload. But he will chew on Butch Yeager until he wins or Butch says uncle. Ben is like an old beagle. He keeps chewing on 'em until they see it his way."

The judge laughed and Ben said, "Guilty. You've got me Kyle but in my defense I will say that I learned a lot of that from Kyle. He was a former alcohol law enforcement officer in this area and in the old days he'd lay out in the woods for days and nights until the moonshiners came back to their still for a visit. Then he'd spring the trap. He'd look so ragged by the time he brought them into the justice of the peace's office that he would have to have someone to identify him before the justice would take his warrant."

They laughed again and Ben perceiving the judge had a good sense of humor continued with the report about the judge's bailiff. "Kyle was good too. Probably the best. He had one shortcoming though."

"I knew it. Here it comes, Your Honor," the bailiff interrupted.

Ben winked at Kyle while he continued to talk to the judge who had now assumed a chair behind the desk and listened with interest. "They said Kyle was thorough. Too thorough sometimes. Now Kyle can tell you whether this is true or not but it is told that one time back in the old days when one of the dispatchers had to step out of the Sheriff's office, he asked Kyle to sit by the phone and take emergency calls. When a call came in, Kyle scrambled to the telephone and said, 'New Hanover Sheriff's Department. What can I do for you?' The caller was somewhat breathless and said, 'It's a UFO. That's what I want to report. A UFO has been sighted out by the Cape Fear River.' Kyle reached for a pen and pad and asked, 'Uh, did you happen to get the tag number?'"

The judge burst out laughing and said, "No, that didn't happen, did it, Mr. Cook?"

"Well, I thought everyone had forgotten about that," Kyle said and scratched his head. "Ben, you can tell 'em. I just wasn't thinking I guess. I thought the guy that called it in was a nut and I would bet he thought I was about as crazy as he was. Anyway, Your Honor. Anything else I can do for you? If not, I am going down to help move the prisoners over from the jail to the lockup for this session of court."

"Thanks, Kyle. You've done enough already. I can tell I am going to enjoy working with you fellows over the next several months. I've got everything I need and I'll let Ben entertain me for a while," Judge Allgood replied.

The bailiff balled up his fist and playfully made a gesture toward Ben. "One of these days," he said as he walked out of the judge's chambers.

Ben grinned at him and then watched as the judge started removing things from his briefcases. He removed several law books, pads, pens and pencils and laid them on the desk. Then he removed three small pictures that were framed and positioned those on the desk. When he had arranged things as he thought they ought to be, he said, "Very well. Open for business." He looked over at Ben and said, "Let's trade information. I know you fellows call my home district to find out what kind of judge I am. What are they saying about me back home?"

"Personable. That's the first thing we heard about. The lawyers up in Manteo said you were pleasant. None of this: 'I'm somebody, you're not.' Also they said you are hardworking, no nonsense, good temperament, treat people with respect. Also you have a reputation of being quite the scholar. That's quite an improvement over some of the judges we have been getting. We've had a few who were a little difficult in court too."

"Come on. There is not a negative in there. Let's here the rest of it."

"Well, Your Honor, they call you 'The Velvet Hammer'. You kill them with kindness then send them away for as long as the law allows. Tough in sentencing. I heard that from several people. That's about it. Oh, yes, I did see that you received the Bar Association's award for outstanding service in the law by an African American. Looks like we are in for a good six months."

"Fair enough," he said. "Could be a lot worse." He laughed a little and commented, "Looks like I'm going to have to be a lot tougher on those fellows back home. They are saying too many nice things about me."

"Well, fair is fair, Your Honor," Ben said. "What are the judges saying about the lawyers down here?"

"You fellows are getting a good report. Good bar. Straightforward lawsuits, no nonsense. No snakes in the grass although there are one or two difficult personalities. Somebody mentioned some ADA named Krait, a couple of civil lawyers but nothing major. As for you, I've been reading about you in the papers. What about this Stickley case? Are we going to have to try it or are you and Butch going to plead it out?"

"We're talking. There are plea discussions on the table but there are strong feelings both ways in this case. My best guess is we will be going to trial, probably during your six months assignment to Wilmington. As usual Butch and I do not see things quite eye to eye. I think she is as innocent as the Mother Mary and Butch thinks she is the Devil incarnate."

The judge laughed again. "You two are still at it. Actually I was supposed to be assigned here about six, maybe seven years ago now, but at the last minute I was assigned back to my home district and did not get to come. Even back then the judges said that Butch and you were keeping them entertained."

Ben smiled at the thought of being endorsed by the judges and remarked, "I don't think we will disappoint Your Honor during this term. We still have an item or two on the agenda to scuffle over."

The judge reached into his coat pocket and pulled out a pack of cigars. He flipped open the top and offered one to Ben. "Panatella?"

"No, thank you, Your Honor, but you are a man after my own heart." Ben reached in, produced a stubby cigar and took off the cellophane wrapper. He lit the judge's cigar then his. After the stogies were fired, the judge leaned back in his chair, took a long draw and exhaled slowly.

Judge Allgood asked, "Are ya'll still swarming with FBI agents? We heard that this place looked like an armed camp after the Vice President was assassinated."

"No, actually it has been two or three weeks since I have seen any agents here. And out at Figure Eight Island the owner of the house where the Vice President was assassinated has been given permission to rebuild that section of the house. Most of one side of the house was blown away by the blast. I was out there about a week ago in the evening fishing for flounder in the Inlet and I noticed that a work crew had reassembled most of the framing. It's probably under roof by now. There are still a lot of gawkers though. It's almost impossible to get to the upper end of Wrightsville Beach because of them especially on weekends."

"While I'm down here, I'd like to ride out there and see it during lunch someday. Maybe we'll get the chance later in the session."

"Sure. I'll be glad to be the tour guide. I know the area pretty well. In fact I can probably find someone who can get us onto Figure Eight and we can see the damaged house and go out to the trail the assassins took. I've heard the FBI markings are still in place."

"Oh," the judge said, "I just heard on the radio on my drive down here that the Vice President's wife, Marilyn, has been released from the hospital."

"That's wonderful news. That has to be joyous news for their children. They have been through such a horror. I'm glad they are getting some good news. The last I had heard the hospital had reported that there was the possibility that she might lose a leg from the injuries she received from the bombing."

"No, according to the report this morning she will likely recover almost fully."

The bailiff came back by the door and poked his head in. "Anything I can do for Your Honor before we get started?"

"No. Thanks, Kyle. Come and get me as soon as everything is ready in the courtroom."

Ben took that as a cue to leave and stood. When he did, he happened to notice the pictures that Judge Allgood had placed on his desk. Of the three pictures, one was of a woman and two were of a dog. Ben touched the picture of the woman and said, "She is a nice looking lady."

"That's my wife Helen. She'll come down and stay with me in a few weeks. Please come by and let me introduce her to you."

"I will," Ben said. "I'll bring my wife Margaret. Maybe Margaret and Helen can take on the town when she comes to stay with you."

"Great," Judge Allgood replied. He picked up one of the other pictures and said, "This is Chase. He's our pug. We never had any children and Chase has become one of the family."

Ben took the picture and looked at the little black bulldog type dog. The judge grinned and said, "He's so ugly, he's cute. I know he's almost human. You know, some dogs are almost human. That dog is smart, too smart sometimes. He knows what I'm going to do before I do. You know, if Helen had to choose between us, she would have a hard time. I guess he's the child we never had."

Handing the picture back to him, Ben said, "You know what they say: a dog is man's best friend."

He set the picture down beside of the picture of Helen and said, "It's true. They are remarkable animals." The judge checked his watch and said, "Well, I guess they are about ready to start court. I enjoyed meeting you, Ben, and I look forward to working with you while I am here. Come by when you can."

"Yes, sir, Your Honor. It was my pleasure entirely. You are just as they said you are: quite pleasant. We will enjoy the collegiality. Thanks."

Ben stepped out of the door and started down the hall. As he walked among the people who were assembled there for the opening of the session of Superior Court, he saw Jack Krait coming toward the courtroom. He walked directly toward Krait and said, "Top of the morning to you, Jack."

"What's up with you, Down?"

Ben smiled and said, "Oh, I don't know. Something's in the air I guess." He started to walk past Krait but Krait stepped over and blocked his path. Ben laughed out loud.

"You are sick," Krait said. "Something's up all right. I don't know what it is but I do know it's time to do something about the Kitners. They aren't on this docket but we can add them on if you are ready to quit pussyfooting around with it. How about it? The animal control officer is driving me crazy. He says that dog Thor is eating enough food for a pack of wolves. We need to do something about it. What d'ya say? Let's do it."

"Krait, you are always pushing somebody. If it's not me, it's somebody else. Why don't you do the decent thing: dismiss the Kitners' cases and let their dog go? They are good people and the dog has been locked up a long time. You know what that dog means to them. You've scared them enough. They will keep that dog up and that's punishment enough."

"That dog needs a deep breath of cyanide. I'm going to see that he gets it."

"You are heartless, Jack." Ben thought for a moment then said, "All right. Here it is. Add the cases to this docket. We'll do it this afternoon."

Krait was a little surprised. "You're kidding?"

"No. Two o'clock. Take it or leave it."

"Guilty or not guilty?"

"They won't let me plead them any way but guilty. They are willing to sacrifice themselves for that dog. Look, you don't even need your witnesses. I'll stipulate there is a factual basis for the plea of guilty to allowing their dog to be at large. I just want a chance to plead it out in front of the judge. Maybe he will have a heart."

Krait grimaced. "Not likely when he hears the evidence. Get everybody in here at two o'clock. What do you say?"

"Done. Two o'clock." Ben slid the cigar over to the side of his mouth and slammed his jaw shut.

*   *   *

The sandy road was crooked and puddled in places from a recent rain. Randy checked the address again from the legal pad lying on the seat beside her. Long leaf pines and thick bushes hid most of the swamp that lay on both sides of the road. Randy read the mailbox that was barely connected to the stump that served as its pedestal and seeing the numbers matched those on her pad, she turned into the driveway. She was immediately met by a large dog that was growling and biting at her tires as she dodged large mud holes and stunted cypress tree stumps.

Randy pulled up to an old trailer and waited. The dog retreated to the wooden porch that had been added to the front of the trailer and continued to growl. No one came out immediately and she blew the horn. Still no one came. She blew again and this time the door of the trailer opened slightly and someone peeped out. Finally an old woman stepped out onto the porch and stared at Randy.

Randy began to roll the window down and as she did, the dog became more aggressive approaching and barking loudly. Randy called out. "Hello, I am here to see Phoebe. I am her lawyer, Randy Bost."

The old woman did not speak but walked out to the dog and took him by the collar. She led him with some difficulty to a tree and clipped a rusty old chain to his collar. When the dog appeared to be secured, Randy began to exit the vehicle. When she did so, the dog ran out to the length of the chain with such force that it jerked it up in the air and flipped him onto his back. The dog immediately jumped up and leaned into the chain continuing to emit an angry growl.

"Sorry about the dog," the old woman spoke up, "but we live so far out here in the country, you never know who is going to come up." She looked back at the dog and continued, "He's all right now. Shut up, Rex. He won't bother you. Come on up."

While watching the dog out of the corner of her eye, Randy stepped up to the porch and spoke to the old woman. "Thank you. That dog can be a little unnerving." As the lady nodded in agreement, Randy said, "I want to talk to Phoebe about her case. As I said, I am Randy Bost, her lawyer. Am I at the right place?"

"Yeah, Phoebe lives here. She's my daughter," the old woman said as she studied Randy carefully. The old woman went over to a chair on the porch and indicated for Randy to be seated. Both of them sat down and the old woman remained quiet for a while.

Randy broke the silence. "I need to see Phoebe. I am beginning to get a lot of discovery requests from the other side in her case and I need to get her assistance in answering a lot of the questions they are asking. I've tried to call without any luck and I have tried to find out where she lives without any luck until today. She is very hard to find."

"She won't come to the phone and lately," the old woman said as she looked off in the distance, "she won't do much of anything."

"Is there anything wrong with Phoebe?"

"Yeah, since all of this happened down at Big Burger, she's a different person."

Randy said, "She seemed fine when she was in my office as we went over the complaint that we were going to file. What's happened?"

"I don't know. Phoebe has always been quiet. She was always kind of backward and shy even when she was in school. She has always had a hard time getting to know people. She's just quiet and has her own ways. That's just her way." The dog began growling again and the woman yelled at him. "Shut up, Rex. One time when she was in school, I remember that she had to make up some kind of a speech or something and she was going to have to stand up in front of the class and make it. She couldn't do it. She had it prepared, all written out and everything, but when the teacher called on her, she just wouldn't get up there. Her teacher, Mrs. McGee, rode all of the way out here to try to get her to go into some special program that would help her, I don't know, she said, 'socialize'. I took it to mean she was going to help her meet other people without being so upset. It didn't work too good. As soon as Phoebe turned sixteen, she dropped out of school and got a job in the mill. She was working with some kind of packaging machine and she was doing pretty good with that. But the work got short and they laid her off. That's when she got a job down there at Big Burger. I don't know, but she was meeting people every day. Seems like she was doin' all right. Then

that thing happened with the manager. They made her pull her
clothes off right there in front of several of those women. She won't
even let me see her without clothes. She's pretty backward. Anyway
she's been pretty upset about it."

Randy was surprised to hear that Phoebe had had so much
trouble. "How is she doing now?"

"Not too good. She won't come out of the house. There was a
man here the other day who said he was with an investigation service
or something like that. He just wanted to talk to her and she
wouldn't come out for him. You know, I don't think she would have
ever even thought about lawing those people if those other two girls
hadn't pushed her into it. She's just not that way."

"Would you mind if I went in to see her? Maybe I can help."

"I don't mind. You seem nice enough to me and somebody needs
to help her. Somebody needs to do something."

"Thank you. Oh, I'm sorry. I didn't get your name."

"I'm Lila Barefoot, Phoebe's mother."

"I'll go in then if it's all right." Mrs. Barefoot nodded and Randy
stood. She walked toward the front door and said, "I won't be very
long but I would like to talk to her about her case. I need to see what
she wants to do about it."

Randy opened the front door and walked into the living room.
The trailer was dimly lit and she made her way slowly down the hall
looking for Phoebe. A flickering light reflected off of the door at the
end of the hall. Randy checked each room as she went down the hall
toward the light. Finally she found Phoebe sitting in a chair by a
curtained window. Phoebe's attention was drawn to the television set
that was providing the light for the dark room.

As Randy's eyes adjusted to the stark contrast between the
changing light patterns from the television set and the darkness of the
room, Phoebe spoke first reflecting her surprise at seeing Randy.
"Miss Bost, what are you doing here?"

"I came to see you, Phoebe. I came to talk to you about the case
you have with Big Burger. The lawyers from Big Burger are sending
me a lot of discovery materials. They are asking a lot of questions
and I need you to help me answer them." Randy stared at Phoebe
and noticed that she seemed rather pale in the light. "Are you all
right, Phoebe?"

"I'm fine." She pulled a blanket up over her lap. "I just haven't felt like doing too much lately. Been kinda blue, I guess."

"Maybe that is the reason that you haven't been returning my phone calls."

"I meant too but I just kept putting it off. It's a hard subject to talk about."

"I know it is Phoebe but unless we talk about it, they are going to win the lawsuit. They will get away with treating you like they did." Randy located a chair next to the wall and pulled it beside of Phoebe. She sat down and said, "Mind if we cut the TV down a little?"

"Oh, no. That's fine." Phoebe reached up and cut the television off. She asked referring to the other two plaintiffs in the lawsuit, "How are Louise and Stella doing? They lost their jobs too when we complained about the search."

"They aren't doing too well, Phoebe. Louise cannot be found. I finally located her mother who lives down in Yaupon Beach. She said that Louise was gone and she didn't know where she was. She said that was not unusual for Louise though. Apparently she travels with a pretty rough crowd. Her mother thinks she may be in Florida with a motorcycle gang. I will probably have to take a dismissal in her case or let the lawyers from Big Burger force the judge to enter an involuntary dismissal for her failure to appear and proceed with her action. As for Stella, I also had a lot of trouble finding her. She has been dancing at an all night club down toward Carolina Beach since she left Big Burger. She wants me to dismiss the case. She says she's in a custody dispute over her daughter and doesn't want the people in this lawsuit to stir up a lot of trouble for her. Big Burger's investigators have already talked to the child's father. She is pretty scared. The bottom line is that she insists that her case be dismissed. We would have to dismiss it anyway I think. I don't know how we could claim she was damaged by a strip search if she strips voluntarily in a room full of men every night. So that leaves you, Phoebe. In the beginning all three of you were intent on making Big Burger pay for the humiliating way you were treated. Do you still feel that way?"

Phoebe wouldn't look Randy in the eyes but continued to stare at the blank screen on the TV set. She wadded the blanket in her hands as she started to talk. "That hasn't changed. I'm still, well, I still can't talk about it without crying. They ought to pay for it but I don't know if I'm strong enough. I can't seem to get the courage to go back out into the world. Every time I see somebody I think that they know about it and it makes me fell like . . . well, like I'm nothin'. Like I'm dirty or somethin'."

"They will get away with it unless you are strong enough to go through with it. Really I think they put pressure on Louise. That's why she skipped town. I believe that's her way to deal with any serious problem. And Stella. I can see how she would cave in. She doesn't want to lose her kid. But you, Phoebe. They have hurt you the most. They've virtually made you a prisoner. You shouldn't let them get away with that."

Phoebe was silent.

"If not you, who?" Randy continued. "If you don't stop them, then they will get away with it again. They will mistreat somebody else unless they are stopped. Did you know the night manager who strip searched you is still on the payroll and is still working right now at Big Burger? Who else will she mistreat?"

Phoebe spoke at a whisper. "I'll do it. I've, I've got to do it."

"Good. That is the right decision." Randy reached over and put her hand on Phoebe's. "I won't try to convince you it will be easy. It won't be. It will be hard. But we can do it together. All right?"

"What do I have to do?"

"Well, for starters, you have got to let your mother bring you into my office so that we can start to unravel this mountain of discovery requests that I have received from Big Burger. And I want you to speak to a psychiatrist I know."

"I'm not crazy."

"No, I know that but she can help you deal with the stress and with the pain that you are going through. What do you think?"

"I'll do what I have to do. I have to. I can't stand it like this any longer."

"Good." Randy stood and walked to the door. "I'm going to leave the time for the appointment at my office with your mother. And I am going to call back with a time to go to see the doctor. Phoebe, you must be there or else we will lose this case. Understand?"

Phoebe nodded indicating she understood and Randy went back to the porch. She gave the information to Phoebe's mother and encouraged her to make Phoebe attend the appointments. Satisfied that she had done all she could do, Randy drove back down the sandy road through the swamp. As she drove, she thought about Phoebe: just as there is one way out of this swamp along this road, there is only one way out of the nightmare and that is through the case.

*   *   *

Two p.m., Superior Courtroom, New Hanover County Judicial Building.

Ben Down walked into the back of the courtroom followed by Roy and Helen Kitner. Ben directed them to a seat on the bench in the back of the courtroom. After they were seated, Ben reached in his pocket and pulled out the typed note from Skittle.

He smiled when he saw the phrasing: pure Skittle he thought, no wasted energy.

Randy called--BB3 hanging by a thread, possibly down to BB1.
          Randy needs to talk to you.

James Wilkes came by--he has the info, Ralph Stickley in SC
          prison after extradition, pled to embezzlement in
          Florence, sentenced to prison, Goretown, he says
          he can pull it all up by e-mail and fax if you
          want it?

Margaret said Sandy called, false alarm, maybe next time
          Grandpa.

Animal Shelter called back--Thor bathed, will do. Save Thor,
          Knock'em out.

Ben flipped the note over. There was nothing on the back side. He turned back to the front. Did Skittle mean his Jack Daniels Knock'em was out, he wondered, or did she mean to knock'em out in the dog's case? He decided it was the latter since Skittle was almost a dry herself.

Ben stuffed the note in his pocket and wished he had a little Knock'em. To fill the wait until court started, he watched Jack Krait arrange the files on the DA's desk in the front of the courtroom. He tossed the files around with the same disinterest and flippancy that marked his treatment of the people they were about. Several people continued to mill about in the hall and occasionally one or two would filter in and take seats for the court session which was scheduled to begin any minute. Mrs. Morrison, the Kitners' neighbor and Ben's witness in Thor's case in District Court, pushed open the door and stepped in. After she searched the courtroom for a moment, Ben finally got her attention. She came over and joined them. Ben assured them it would not take very long and then he started walking up front to have a seat in front of the bar.

Krait finished sorting the files and turned around toward the audience. He put his hands on his hips as he surveyed the people who were moving about the courtroom. When he made eye contact with Ben, he pretended to pull an imaginary gun and shoot Ben. Ben ignored the bravado and opened the gate to enter the area at the front of the courtroom. When he started to sit, Krait said, "No need to sit there. Get everybody up to the table, Down. You are my first victim."

Ben moved over to the defendant's table and motioned for the Kitners and Mrs. Morrison to come to the front. As they approached, the bailiff entered the courtroom followed by the judge. The bailiff called for all to rise and opened court. "Oyez, oyez, oyez, the honorable court for the County of New Hanover is now open and sitting for the dispatch of its business. The Honorable Meykus Allgood presiding. God save the State and this honorable court."

As soon as everyone was seated and Krait was recognized by the judge, Krait called the cases of Roy and Helen Kitner. Ben entered pleas of guilty and after the formalities of accepting the pleas, Krait chose to render a summary of the events that led to the charges against the Kitners for allowing their dog Thor to run at large. Krait told the judge how the dog had been off his own premises, how he had chased a jogger and how he had grappled with the animal control officer when he came to apprehend him. Krait wrapped up his presentation with his "the dog is dangerous and must be destroyed for the safety of the community" argument.

When Krait concluded, Ben acknowledged that Thor had broken free of his chain and even though his clients were unaware of it, they insisted that he plead them guilty. Ben told Judge Allgood that the Kitners were extremely concerned about their dog Thor and could not bear the thought of Thor being destroyed. After those few opening remarks, Ben offered to call witnesses who could attest to the dog's good and peaceful character.

When Judge Allgood indicated his willingness to entertain the testimony, Krait leaned over to Ben and whispered, "God, let's not make another circus out of this."

Judge Allgood listened intently as Mrs. Morrison testified that as a neighbor of the Kitners, she had known Thor since he was a puppy and he was not vicious, aggressive or dangerous. On cross examination by Krait, she did admit she did not know anything about Thor's actions on the day the Kitners were charged: she had not seen him chase the jogger or growl at the animal control officer. Helen Kitner cried on the stand when she told how she had received Thor from her father who was now deceased. Judge Allgood appeared to nod his head up and down in agreement with her statement that Thor was "just a big ol' fluffy dog". Repeating his performance in District Court, Krait had her to admit that a dog that would growl and attack someone was dangerous.

Krait finished his cross-examination by saying, "Your Honor, I rest my case. The evidence shows this dog chased the jogger and shows he growled at and tried to bite the animal control officer. It follows that this dog is dangerous. We say we are entitled to an order of destruction."

"Objection," Ben said. "This case is not over. I have over twenty letters from neighbors of the Kitners who assert that Thor is a neighborhood pet and there is no danger in him." Ben handed the letters to the bailiff so that he could pass them to the judge. "And I have one more request, Your Honor. I would like to offer Thor himself as an exhibit in this case."

"Objection, objection." Krait jumped to his feet. "That dog is too dangerous to bring into this courtroom. Someone could be injured."

Judge Allgood said, "What do you have to say about that, Mr. Down?"

"Your Honor, I have made arrangements with the animal control officers at the animal shelter to bring Thor here. They are trained and they can manage him. And really as an officer of the court, I assert that there is no danger. He is being held just outside of the courtroom in the basement of the courthouse. I can have him here in two to three minutes."

The judge scratched his head and grinned. "Now we don't want people to think the courthouse has gone to the dogs but in all fairness, I'll permit it."

Krait moved from his seat and started toward the far side of the table. "Your Honor, with the court's permission, I am going to get over here and keep this table between that dog and me."

"Granted."

Ben had the clerk to call downstairs to the animal control officer and in a couple of minutes, the back doors of the courtroom swung open and Thor appeared. Thor strained at the end of his chain as he drug the dog warden through the doors. When he entered the courtroom, he looked like a big floppy fur ball bouncing in ten directions at once. When he saw Helen Kitner, he pulled at the officer even harder until he was bucking at the end of the chain. The officer gave in and Thor pulled him along in quick fashion. When he reached the gate at the bar, he burst through it. Krait recoiled and moved even further away.

Thor went directly to Helen Kitner and laid his head in her lap. She put her arms around his big head and murmured, "There, there. He's a good boy. Good boy." As she stroked his head, he calmed down immediately.

Ben said, "Now. Your Honor can see. He is big all right but he's no monster. He is just as Mrs. Morrison and Mrs. Kitner testified: he's a gentle giant."

Thor slobbered as his head lay there seemingly tranquilized by Helen's long gentle strokes on his back. She took her handkerchief and blotted his mouth to keep from getting her dress mussed.

"Your Honor," Krait argued as he stood at the other side of his desk appearing ready to leap to the safety of the table top if there were to be an attack, "there is nothing to be learned from this show. That dog is going to be gentle around the Kitners. It's just when a stranger comes around that he becomes a teeth-bared, growling, attacking monster."

Ben remonstrated, "I see it just to the contrary, Your Honor. This big ol' mutt is a pushover. You can see it." Thor moved over to Ben and put his head under Ben's hand as Ben spoke. Ben patted his head and Thor stared up at him with big eyes. "He is loved and he loves back. Besides, there is nothing quite like a dog. There is no animal more devoted to mankind than the dog. He is a friend when you are down. He is a supporter when you are low. He is the same to you whether the world loves you or hates you." Ben reached down and held Thor's head from underneath his jowls. "He is . . . " Ben choked up a little. "He is probably the best client I've ever had."

Krait could not stand the melodrama and blurted out, "Oh, come on."

"Really. Although he has been held on death row these many weeks, he's never complained. Instead each time I have gone to see him, he has greeted me with excitement. And he is that way with everybody who has shown him any attention."

Thor seemed to realize that everyone was focusing on him and as Ben talked, he walked around to the side of Ben, cocked his head to one side like the dog listening to the old phonograph in the RCA advertisement. Ben removed his white handkerchief and wiped his forehead. Krait groaned audibly. Thor stepped over and laid his head on Krait's chair while he listened to Ben's final argument.

Ben's voice lifted. "Your Honor, the love of a dog is straightforward, simple and true." As he talked, Ben noticed that Thor had drooled all over the seat of Krait's chair. It was so profuse that it had started to collect in puddles and drip down the legs of the chair. Ben continued. "Quoting Senator Vest in State of North Carolina versus Wallace, Your Honor: *'And when the last scene comes and death takes the master in its embrace and his body is laid in the ground, no matter if all other friends pursue their way, there by the graveside will be found . . . "*

Judge Allgood picked up the line and continued it. " '. . . *the noble dog, his head between his paws, his eyes sad, but open in alert watchfulness, faithful and true in death.'* Well said, Mr. Down."

Judge Allgood looked down at Thor and said, "Here it is then, gentlemen. Let the word go forth that every dog shall have his day and this day is the dog Thor's day. Stand up, Mr. and Mrs. Kitner."

They stood and the Judge pronounced the judgment of the court. "I order that prayer for judgment be continued in the cases of Roy Kitner and Helen Kitner. The court orders that Thor be released to the care, custody and supervision of the Kitners." He looked over at the Kitners and admonished, "Now you are going to have to keep this dog up or next time there may be no way to save him. Understand?"

Both of them responded that they understood. Krait grew a little red in the face and threw the files on the table. Ben replied as he looked over at Krait, "Thank you, Your Honor. Certainly this is justice tempered with mercy. They will repay your kindness with obedience. Thank you, sir."

"All right then, gentlemen. Let's get on with the next case," the judge said.

Ben nodded for the animal control officer to lead Thor out of the courtroom. Ben, the Kitners and Mrs. Morrison followed. When they reached the back doors of the courtroom, Ben whispered for them to go out to the lobby and he would join them as soon as he completed one item of unfinished business.

Ben stood at the back of the courtroom and watched as Krait came back around the table to his seat. After moving a couple of files in front of him to prepare to call the next cases, Krait pulled his chair out without giving it much attention and sat. A couple of seconds passed and his facial expression revealed his pained discomfort. He shoved his hand between his bottom and the seat. As he pulled it out dripping with dog drool, he cried out, "What tha'?"

Ben smiled to himself and quietly slipped out the back door.

CHAPTER TWELVE

"Second degree murder."

Wanda shifted in her seat and grew silent. The prisoner interview room in the jail was relatively quiet although there was a great deal of distant noise. Ben studied Wanda as she thought about the plea. Her appearance had improved dramatically he noticed. The red marks were healed and were reduced to a few pink lines. The blue and black bruising on her face had faded to a slight shade of yellow, only a suggestion of the violence they evidenced. When she spoke again, she had a question. "How long would I actually have to serve in prison?"

Ben replied, "Sentencing is in the judge's discretion within certain limits. The very least that you would have to serve would be one hundred and forty-four months and the maximum would be three hundred sixty-nine months. Realistically speaking, given your clean record, sentencing at the least level within the presumptive range: two hundred forty months."

Randy who had been silent to this point in the interview added, "That's real time, day for day, Wanda. No early release and no parole."

Wanda hurriedly made the calculation. "That's twenty years. Twenty years. Jeremy would be thirty-three years old when I would be released from prison. I can't do it. I can't."

"That's all the District Attorney is offering: plead to second degree murder and no agreement on sentencing. In other words sentencing is up to the judge." Ben showed Wanda the punishment chart. "Here, this shows the three ranges from which the judge can enter sentence: aggravated, presumptive or mitigated range. There is plenty of evidence to allow the judge to sentence from either the aggravated or the mitigated range. My guess is the judge would come down in the middle: the presumptive range. And that's twenty years."

Wanda studied the chart and looked at the numbers in each category. She slid the paper back to Ben and said, "What happens if I don't accept it?"

Randy said, "We go to trial almost immediately on the charge of first degree murder with the State seeking the death penalty. My guess is the DA will calendar it within a month unless we object."

Wanda looked dejected and stared at the sheet of paper as it lay between them. Ben picked it up and put it back in his briefcase. He had been through these discussions hundreds of times and he knew the realities of sentencing possibilities were harsh. Sometimes the client would get angry, sometimes the client would be so stunned she could not speak and occasionally the client would try to reason her way through the process.

Finally Wanda swallowed hard and spoke. "What are my chances?"

Randy looked at Ben. Ben answered. "Frankly they are not good with regard to conviction on first degree murder. They have your statement during the rape accusation that you were going to kill Ralph. They have your admission that you stabbed him and shot him. They have a credible eyewitness who observed you standing over his mutilated body with a knife in hand."

"Yeah, but I had to defend myself," Wanda argued.

"I agree but will the jury see it that way? Your defense is self defense. The jurors could easily find that Ralph was not armed and your use of a weapon in defending yourself constituted excessive force. The law says you can only use reasonable force. The use of a knife and a gun to fend off a physical attack that consists of blows struck by fists could easily be determined to be excessive. And that's true even given the difference in your size, weight, strength and gender."

Randy added, "And to assert self defense, you are almost always required to testify. You will have to go on the stand and tell your version of what happened. And seriously Wanda, there is no doubt that Butch Yeager could make you appear to be an untruthful witness. If there was ever a professional at cross examination, it is our DA."

Ben ruffled through his briefcase and began pulling out several documents as he rejoined the conversation. "Even if you are successful at holding off Butch, part of your story will not be believed. No one will believe that you do not know what happened or that you do not remember what happened after you went outside of the house and were found standing over the body with a knife in your hand."

"Well, that 's my story and I'm sticking to it."

"Wanda," Ben remonstrated, "help me help you. The polygraph test indicated that you were being untruthful about that part of it. The psychological evaluation concluded that you are competent, were sane at the time the killing occurred and you are malingering, that is, not telling the truth about parts of the events of that early morning. You know what happened and you just will not tell it. And I'll tell you something else that flies in the face of your version of the facts. We have just received the results of the gunshot residue test. You tested negative for gunpowder and exploded debris on the night of Ralph's killing. It is possible that the test is inaccurate but it is very unlikely. Do you know what this means?"

Wanda shook her head. Ben pulled out his copy of the gunshot residue report and placed it in front of her. "It means that you did not fire a gun that night as you admitted to the detectives. It means that you did not shoot Ralph. It means that someone else did. Who?"

Wanda gave Ben a hard look. "I told you how it happened," she insisted.

"I know you did but the facts do not support what you said. Wanda, I've always been straight with you and up to this point, you have been straight with me. What could possibly cause you to tell me something other than the truth?" Wanda did not budge. "Well, all right then, I'll tell you what. You are protecting someone. Someone who was there and someone you care about deeply. Someone who . . . "

"You leave Jeremy out of this. He had nothing to do with it. Nothing."

Randy interjected. "He had everything to do with it, Wanda. We know that and you know that. Tell the truth and I believe the truth will set you free."

"The truth. The truth." Wanda lifted up in her chair and raised her voice vehemently. "The truth is Jeremy is a good child who had a scoundrel for a father. The truth is he was abandoned by his father. Ralph did not love Jeremy. He never did. It was hard for me to accept it but it's true. The truth is Jeremy has never had a fair chance. He is a great son, greater than I have a right to expect in view of all that has happened. The truth is I am not going to let Ralph Stickley pull him down. He is going to have a life. The truth is . . . " Wanda broke down crying.

Ben reached into his pocket and removed his large white handkerchief. He handed it to Wanda and she wiped her eyes. Ben pressed on hoping to break down the barrier between them. "We can protect Jeremy. He is a child. As I have told you, they will not do that much to him."

Wanda talked back through the handkerchief without looking up. Although her voice was strained with emotion and was breaking up as she talked, she remonstrated, "Jeremy had nothing to do with it."

"Well," Ben spoke hesitatingly, "the DA says he did. Jeremy told the detectives that night that he heard voices in the basement. He went down there and Ralph was attacking you. He says he ran for help. Then later after he talked to you at the police station, he told the police that he was not there, that he had gone over to a neighbor's house and did not know anything about what had happened. Although he has equivocated about it, if it comes to a trial, I believe the District Attorney will put him on the stand."

"No," Wanda protested as she continued to wipe the tears from her eyes. "Can't you stop it?"

"No, the DA can call Jeremy and anyone else he would like."

"The nightmare is never over," Wanda cried. She shook her head in disbelief.

"Tell us the truth, Wanda," Randy insisted. "That's all we want. And that can be the beginning of the end of the whole thing."

Wanda firmed her jaw and laid Ben's handkerchief on the table. She looked directly at Ben. "You've got the truth as I know it. This is the truth. I killed Ralph Stickley in self defense. If they don't believe me and they convict me of first degree murder, I would rather die than lose Jeremy. I can't rot in prison for twenty years. That would be like a death sentence to me. In fact I would rather be sentenced to death than lose my child."

Ben said, "It's possible. Really, Wanda. If you are convicted of first degree murder and the jury believes that you tortured Ralph while he was alive, carving an initial into his chest, castrating him, shoving his penis down his throat. It's gruesome enough that they might not forgive you even though Ralph repeatedly abused you. Frankly I believe it is unlikely that they would give you the death penalty but it is entirely a possibility. It's real and it can happen."

Silence filled the room. Wanda stared at the table and said nothing. Ben waited hoping that she would finally confide in them with the truth. Time seemed to stand still while neither side budged.

Distant cell doors slammed shut. The clank of heavy metal broke the momentary truce. Ben spoke. "It's not guilty then?"

Wanda replied emphatically, "Yes."

"It's all or nothing. I'll tell the DA."

"What happens next?" Wanda asked.

"The DA will set a trial date. We'll get our motions heard in a few days. We have filed, uh, how many, Randy?"

"Thirty-seven. Most of them are pro forma but some will take a while to hear. We have one important motion: the motion to suppress your confession. We have asserted that you were questioned in violation of your constitutional right to counsel and your Miranda right to remain silent. We think we have a pretty good chance on that."

Ben said, "As soon as we get a firm trial date, we will start a series of interviews with you to develop information for the trial. We'll break the trial down into specific events and determine as best as we can what the DA will do and what we will do. Anything we can help you with now?"

"I want to see Jeremy again."

Ben looked at Randy as he began to pack things back into his briefcase. Randy said, "I believe it can be arranged. So far Caroline Markham has been supportive. We'll see. If she agrees, we'll set up an interview at the courthouse and have the Sheriff to bring you over. We'll try to get Jeremy in then."

Ben closed his briefcase and spoke up. "Wanda, don't get the wrong impression. We are on your side. I am disagreeing hopefully without being disagreeable. We will defend you to the best of our ability. I think we can do that better with the truth, that's all."

Wanda got up and walked to the door. "Thanks," she said. "I've never doubted you, either of you. I know you are trying to do what's right but so am I. I'm sorry it had to work out this way but I have to do what I have to do."

"Sorry, Wanda," Randy offered, "so do we."

Ben nodded without speaking. The jail matron opened the door and escorted Wanda up the hall. After she had gone, Randy spoke first. "Looks like we are stuck."

"I had a law professor once who had a name for it. He called it a 'psychic vortex'. Basically you get caught between strong ideas and cannot escape. They lead uncontrollably and undeniably to one conclusion. On the one hand our client gives us marching orders: plead not guilty, go to trial. The DA tells us: plead guilty or go to trial. We tell ourselves: it is our duty, go to trial. No one wants a trial, not Wanda, not Butch, not us, but we are going to get one anyway."

"I thought she would cave in," Randy offered. "Really I thought she would tell us last week when you explained to her that if Jeremy did it, he could not be held beyond his eighteenth birthday since he is a juvenile. And today when we told her we knew she was lying because of the lie detector and the gunshot residue report, I felt sure she would finally tell us what really happened." Randy grew quiet as though she were in deep thought. Finally she asked, "What do you think really happened the night Ralph was killed, Ben?"

"There is nothing really solid to go on. I think Ralph was on the run. He had escaped from prison. I do believe Ralph broke in and Wanda found him there. A confrontation developed between the two of them. The altercation took place in the basement and spilled out into the driveway. Her fingerprints were on the screwdriver. Ralph's blood was on the screwdriver. I believe one can infer she stabbed him with the screwdriver. I do believe Ralph was shot but Wanda did not shoot him. Truly I believe Jeremy could have shot him. Neither the stab wound from the screwdriver nor the gunshot were fatal though. The fatal wounds were the cuts on Ralph's neck. Randy, frankly, I cannot get consent of mind to believe that Wanda or Jeremy cut his throat, castrated him and carved him up. I've known Wanda too long. There just is not the level of evil in her heart that this kind of vicious assault requires. And you've seen Jeremy."

"Right. There is no way anyone could convince me that kid could do this. For one thing I don't think he would be powerful enough physically. Ralph was a big man. But most importantly I don't think Jeremy could do it mentally. I've been with him numerous times and I just don't see it. He could be the poster boy for the Boy

Scouts. I don't think that ripping out Ralph's throat is in the Boy Scout Manual."

"You see where this takes us though: a mystery killer," Ben said. "Who? Why? The theory makes sense until you actually state the conclusion. There are just too many unanswered questions too. What was Ralph doing serving time in South Carolina? Why did he escape? Why did he come to Wanda's? Why was he tortured when he was killed?"

Randy joined in. "Why was an R carved in his chest? Why was his penis cut off and rammed down his mouth?"

"The questions are endless and I believe the answers lie with Ralph. I've asked James Wilkes to help. He's already gotten a lot of information from South Carolina through the internet. Apparently while Ralph was serving the sentence for raping Wanda in North Carolina at the Brunswick prison unit, he was extradited to Florence on an embezzlement charge. According to the paper work as soon as he was sent to Florence, he was tried. He was allowed to enter a no contest plea, sentenced and transferred the next day to the South Carolina prison unit at Goretown. He was immediately eligible for work release. Now to get all of that done, Ralph had to have a lot of help from people in high places. In the space of a couple of days he went from a highly guarded medium security gun camp in North Carolina to a minimum security prison in South Carolina that allowed him day passes and night bed checks. Really. I've had clients who served in Goretown. It's a soft berth, top of the line for prisoners."

"I see what you mean," Randy said as though a light were turned on. "Why would he want to escape from there? And why would he return to North Carolina where he might be put back in a North Carolina prison? It doesn't make sense, does it?"

"Not for a second."

"And Wanda told us that Ralph told her on the night he was killed that he was into something big," Randy thought out loud.

"I've had Skittle to try to arrange a meeting for me with the superintendent of the Goretown prison unit. He is being awfully coy for some reason. He has come up with some reason to avoid seeing me every time she has called. I think I am going to drive down and surprise him. It's only about an hour and half from here."

"In the meantime what do you think we should do about Butch? Want me to tell him about Wanda's decision?"

"No, let me talk to him one more time. There might be a chance, however slight, that he might give a little more. After all the Women of America are keeping protesters down at the courthouse and the letters to the editor section of the newspaper are keeping the pressure on Butch." Ben smiled a little at the thought of Butch squirming under the pressure that was being brought to bear by those who felt Wanda was being made the victim again. "Maybe he'll want to offer a little more. We'll see."

          *   *   *

Later that afternoon Ben watched the television as he stood in line to purchase four fifths of Jack Daniels. With the weekend coming, the line at the liquor store was a little longer than usual. Somewhat bored he shifted from one leg to the other then rearranged the bottles in the basket. When he moved a little closer to the TV, he became more attentive as the screen displayed a ship moving into a bay filled with other ships, junks, fishing boats and sailboats. The reporter's name and location appeared on the bottom of the screen: Charles Banks, Tientsin, China. The reporter in an English accent confirmed what other newsmen had been reporting for the last several weeks on CNN.

"The main thrust of the investigation," he reported, "into the assassination of Vice President Anderson has shifted to mainland China and most particularly to the busy port of Tientsin. Forensic evidence has made a direct link to this industrial and port city. Officially the Chinese government has offered to provide plenary assistance to U.S. investigators who have been focusing on the Chinese connection. Privately though our sources close to the investigation here are complaining that the Chinese have offered little in the way of assistance and indeed have at times been dilatory and obtrusive. FBI agents who have worked this case from the beginning believe that the key to breaking this case is right here in Tientsin. They have repeatedly found their efforts to penetrate the bureaucratic maze that is so much a part of life in China obstructed by lower level government officials."

As the camera panned across the waterfront, the reporter said, "As you can tell from this view, Tientsin is a very active port city. It serves as a conduit for a great deal of the import and export trade that is so vital to the Chinese economy. In the background you will notice the official prison for this part of China. Several years ago this prison received attention around the world from Amnesty International because of the numbers of prisoners that were executed here. Representatives of Amnesty International charged that prisoners were being executed for their vital organs which were sold abroad for transplants. Also great numbers of dissidents were being held here on political as opposed to criminal charges. Their only crime: opposition to official policy of the Chinese government."

The screen shifted to the busy urban area and the reporter continued with the description of Tientsin: "This is a rather large city in China and has been a center of trade with the rest of the world. Prior to the Chinese assuming control of Hong Kong, Tientsin had served as a major eye on the rest of the world with foreign investment being attracted to the technological, medical and computer industries that have proliferated here. As China has slowly evolved out of its almost total isolation from the rest of the world, Tientsin has been a window of opportunity for foreign investors. After President Nixon's easing of tensions with China, trade was reestablished and Tientsin found itself in the middle of not only the economic but the cultural exchange. It remains an active port although speculation persists as to its future in view of the Chinese access to Hong Kong. It is still the base for a large presence of the Chinese army. So far investigators have been unable or at the very least unwilling to speculate what part China, and for that matter, this city may have had on the assassination of Vice President Anderson. This is Charles Banks reporting, Tientsin, China."

As the screen shifted back to America, the news anchor reported, "In other news here at home Marilyn Anderson, the Vice President's wife, is shown in this footage as she is moved by wheelchair to an appointment with her physical therapist. She . . . "

Ben had moved to the front of the line and was unloading his basket as the clerk said, "Ben, I thought you did all of your business up on the north end."

"Well, I have been but I'm out on a little road trip this afternoon. Going down to see some of our South Carolina neighbors."

The clerk laughed and said, "If that's the case, you might want to take a little Rebel Yell with ya'. My experience has been that that crowd still loves a great hurrah in a whiskey."

Ben smiled and paid the bill. He scooped up the bag and carried his purchase to the car. After he had packed everything away in the trunk, he got in and called Skittle on his cell phone. He backed out of the space and turned onto the road south out of Wilmington. Skittle came on the line. "Ben Down, Attorney at Law," she answered.

"Skittle, have you had any luck making an appointment with the warden at Goretown?"

"No, Ben. His secretary says he has a heavy schedule this afternoon and will not be able to see you. She said he would be happy to speak with you but she was pretty vague about when. I set an appointment for you on a Friday afternoon at 2:30 in two weeks. I'll bet they will call and cancel though as they have done with the two previous appointments."

"You know, I think they are trying to avoid me for some reason. I don't know why but I do know that the superintendent does not want to talk about Ralph Stickley. I am on my way down there now. I have a little time so I'm going to show up unannounced. We'll see what happens. Anything else going on I need to know about?"

"No. Everything is quiet here. I like it. Friday afternoons when you have cleared your schedule is awfully nice. Oh, it looks like it's not going to last though. Randy says Wanda's case looks more and more like a trial. We'll be busy if it is."

"Yeah, I think so, Skittle. We are going to get really busy I think."

"Oh, one more thing, Helen Kitner brought you some canned green beans and said to tell you one more time: thank you. I know she has told me thanks ten times since you saved Thor. She really appreciates it. On the other hand Jack Krait called. He sounded pretty upset, said he has a bone to pick with you."

Ben smiled again remembering the look on Krait's face as he realized he had sat in a pool of dog drool. Ben remarked, "Now if Krait could be as nice as Helen Kitner, this would be a better world.

Thanks, Skittle. I'll come by the office on my way back so leave me a note if there is anything I need to address before the weekend."

Ben clicked the phone once and then punched in the DA's number. When he finally was put through to the DA, he said, "Butch, what are you doing working so hard on Friday afternoon? Trying to figure out a way to make the lawyers' lives even more miserable?"

"Not likely," Butch said. "I'm just trying to make sure you fellows don't snatch anymore from the jaws of justice. I heard about the deal with Krait. I believe you have moved to the top of his enemies list."

"He had it coming. He's a jerk."

"Now come on, Ben. He's just a little rough around the edges. He'll come around. How about you? Wanna make a deal on Wanda?"

"That's basically the reason I called. We cannot accept a second degree murder plea." Ben wanted to remind Butch of the continuing protest and said, "Besides, those protesters would probably start harassing me if I pled her guilty. She won't do it. She can't stand twenty to thirty years in prison."

Butch's voice turned serious and he assumed that ominous tone. "This is a serious mistake, Ben. You know what that means. I've got to prosecute her for first degree murder and I've got to seek the death penalty. And nobody wants that. No choice about it."

"Well, actually there is," Ben replied.

"What do you mean?"

"Voluntary manslaughter. She might take a voluntary manslaughter plea. I mean I can't guarantee it but she might."

"Are you out of your mind? Manslaughter. She wouldn't serve two, maybe three years in prison at most. Can't do it. Don't be ridiculous."

"You've got some real problems with this case. No gun, negative gunshot residue test, courthouse lawn covered with protesters. It's got to affect the jurors."

"I'll set a trial date." The phone line went dead.

Ben smiled at Butch's rudeness. He knew that Butch was not mad about the discussion concerning voluntary manslaughter. Butch was in a tight spot. He had a case, a strong case of domestic violence and he did not want it. Butch was getting forced into a trial that he did not want. Sometimes, Ben thought, that is just the way things worked out. Sometimes you just get pushed down into the psychic vortex toward the inescapable conclusion, like it or not. The smile waned when Ben remembered that so was he.

He flipped the top back on his cell phone and dialed Randy's number. When she picked up, he said, "Randy, I talked to Butch. Boy, is he in a bad mood. We had better get ready for trial."

"I'm already getting ready. I've been researching the North Carolina law on self defense. Self defense, that is it, isn't it? I don't see anything else."

"Right," Ben replied. "We only have two weapons for the trial: reasonable doubt and self defense. We'll attack the State's case. It's a circumstantial case. We'll cast as much doubt as we can. Our defense will be self defense. Maybe between a little doubt and a little mercy, we can hold off the executioner. How about Rod and you? Are the two of you going to be able to take the strain of squaring off in court in a big case?"

"I think so," Randy said somewhat haltingly.

"You sounded a lot more certain when I asked you this earlier."

"Things have changed a little bit since then. He and I had better talk."

"Right. Well, I . . . "

"Ben, before you get off, I did want to tell you I appreciate your help with the Big Burger case. I took Phoebe to the female psychologist that you suggested. That is working wonderfully. She seems to be coming out of her shell. As you said, she won't take Diehlinger's offer, if you can call it that. We are dismissing the other claims of the other two plaintiffs and I am pressing Big Burger to make us a legitimate offer on Phoebe's case."

"Down to BB1, huh?"

"Yes, but it's a righteous case, thanks to you."

"I just passed over the South Carolina line. I'm going to Goretown. It's time to start unraveling some of these questions. Guess I better get off. See you Monday."

After several miles Ben turned off of the main highway and worked his way across country on several back roads. He turned on one long straight road that cut through a large stand of pines. As he reached the top of a knoll, the Goretown complex loomed as a rather stark break in the tree line. Ben turned into the parking lot, located the visitors spaces and parked. He walked the short distance to the administrative building. When he went in, he identified himself to the secretary and asked to see the superintendent of the facility. She directed him to take a seat while she checked. Ben noticed the lobby was empty except for a prisoner trustee who was mopping one of the hallways that led back to the offices.

In a few moments the secretary motioned for him to come back to her desk. She related how busy the superintendent was and asked Ben to make the appointment that had been scheduled in a couple of weeks. Ben refused. He told her that his office had been trying for several days to firm up an appointment with the superintendent, his business was important, a matter "of life or death" he said, and he would wait until the superintendent could find time in his busy schedule for a brief conference with him. Ben took a seat and waited. Ben checked his watch. He knew that since it was late Friday, the superintendent would very likely be leaving work. With the additional pressure of someone staking him out, maybe the superintendent would give in and meet with him Ben hoped.

Ben waited. A few minutes before five o'clock the secretary called him to the desk again and said the superintendent would see him now. She led him down the hall past the prisoner who continued to mop the long hall. When they went into an office, Ben noticed the sign on the desk: Superintendent. The graying bespectacled man rose and walked around the desk. He said rather coldly, "Gedney Howell, Mr. Down. I'm very busy this afternoon. What can I do for you, sir?"

As the secretary closed the door behind her, Ben said, "Thank you for taking the time to speak with me." Howell nodded. He did not acknowledge the thanks but waited impatiently for Ben to state his business. "I'm here to check on one of your former prisoners, Mr. Howell. I need to know more about Ralph Stickley. I am the attorney for Wanda Stickley who is charged with killing Mr. Stickley just across the border in Wilmington, North Carolina."

Ben watched Howell for any indication that he was interested. Howell said, "I believe that central records in Columbia forwarded everything to your man, a Mr. Wilkes, upon request. I can't think of anything else that we can add here."

"Well, I would like to know a little more about Ralph if you don't mind."

"For example?"

"Well, how did he get to Goretown? I understand that only a very few prisoners in the system get to take advantage of the work release program here. My understanding is that it usually takes a sponsor, someone willing to vouch for the prisoner so to speak. Given Ralph Stickley's prior history of violence, rape, arson, assault, I didn't think he would be a good candidate to be released back into the population."

Howell had listened carefully but gave no indication that he was familiar with Goretown's reputation. When he spoke, he remained rather cool toward Ben. "Your information is incorrect. Prisoners are assigned here by the central office based on their potential to work productively under a supervised program."

"I understand that each prisoner has to be individually approved by you."

"No, again your information is incorrect. I have nothing to do with approving a prisoner for assignment to this unit."

"Well, in looking at the documents furnished about Ralph Stickley, I saw that you had signed his transfer to Goretown. It looks as . . . "

"That's just a formality. I am required to sign each prisoner's transfer. Anything else?"

Ben and Howell were still standing and Howell walked toward the door signaling to Ben that the conference was about over. Ben said, "What information do you have about Ralph's escape?"

"He left here during the night. He did not appear for the count the next morning. There was nothing unusual about it."

"Well, it's unusual for anyone to escape from Goretown, isn't it?"

"Yes, we have a minimal escape problem here."

"What did the investigation reveal about why Ralph escaped?"

"Nothing unusual. He was involved in an infraction or two but nothing serious. My guess is he just did not fit into the atmosphere here. After all it is for people who are willing to work. Maybe he just did not fit that category. Really, Mr. Down, it's end of the week and I have several things to do. So if you don't mind." Howell opened the door and gestured toward the hall.

As Ben walked out, Howell closed the door behind him. Ben walked up the hall toward the lobby. As he walked by, the prisoner who had kept his head down and stayed busy mopping when Ben had been escorted to the warden's office earlier looked up at Ben and stared at him as Ben passed. The prisoner looked as though he wanted to say something but immediately dropped his head again when Ben came beside him. Ben walked out into the parking lot and entered his car.

He turned onto the road and headed north toward Wilmington. The long pines began to swish by as Ben became lost in thought. Ben who had been totally absorbed in trying to understand the strained and strange conference he had just had with Howell thought out loud, "Something stinks to high heaven."

Back in the superintendent's office, Gedney Howell peeped out of his window and watched as Ben's vehicle sped up out of sight on the long road. He called his secretary. "Get me Wrenn Davies. Right now."

*   *   *

The bicycles rode easily over the packed sand as they made their way along a meandering old road bed. The trees were tall and added a welcome shade holding the heat from the late Saturday afternoon at bay. Dodging mud puddles and the limbs from the underbrush that protruded into the old road, Rod Pemberton agilely held a line that kept them out of the marsh that lay on either side of the road. After a sharp turn the old road widened into an opening. Rod stepped off his bike and started pushing it along a narrow path that trailed off of the back of the opening. Randy followed.

The path twisted and descended through thick foliage. It cut zigzag fashion through the marsh until it started getting less wet and more sandy. Finally it went up slightly and then opened onto the bank of the Cape Fear River. The bank gave way to a small sandy beach that extended for several yards along the River. In the distance a ship appeared like a small dot making its way up the deep water channel.

Randy who had dropped back slightly as she maneuvered through the brush was startled when she stepped out into the sunlight on the bank beside of Rod. "It's gorgeous. How did you find this place?" she exclaimed.

"I found it last summer when I was out exploring on my mountain bike. It's beautiful, isn't it? It's a little cove that's hidden along the Cape. I don't believe anyone has used it in years. The road that we took to get out here was probably an old logging path and after the trees were cut years ago, it was abandoned. Perfect place for a picnic," Rod said as he released the bungee cords that held a large blanket on the back of his bike.

"Lovely," Randy replied as she looked out over the River.

He placed the blanket on the bank in a lightly shaded spot. Both Randy and he started unloading their panniers. After they had spread everything onto the blanket, Randy picked up a bottle of red wine and noticing that it was chilled, remarked, "How did you do it? I mean there is enough food here to last several days. And how did you keep this wine cool?"

"When it comes to a beautiful girl, there is no limit to my imagination."

Randy smiled at him and started preparing lunch. Rod served the wine in glasses and Randy produced huge cheese and ham sandwiches. They sat comfortably as they ate and watched the merchant traffic as it maneuvered through the channel. After they had eaten, they lay lazily on the blanket and sipped the last of the wine. The breeze carried the sound of some distant ship as its engines strained against the current. The sun leaned into late afternoon and cast long shadows out into the water.

Randy watched two leaves floating easily on the current near the bank. Randy sat her glass down and said as she continued to watch the leaves, "This is a beautiful place. It's almost dreamlike. It looks like you could just reach out and touch the ships although they must be a long way off."

"Everything is miles away," Rod whispered as he rolled over to his side and stretched his body out beside of Randy. He put his arm around her and pulled her gently to him. She put her hand on his arm and lightly rubbed her hand against the hair on his forearm. She toyed playfully with his fingers then slid her hand slowly up to his upper arm and onto his chest. She watched her hands as her palms glided gently over the hair on his chest. Rod's back arched and his chest moved closer under her hand. She began to feel the muscles of his upper chest and let her hand kneed into his strength.

Rod put both of his arms around her and pressed his fingertips into the small of her back. He leaned his head foreword slightly and kissed her on the forehead, the eyes, the nose, the cheeks and then her lips. As their lips brushed lightly, Randy whimpered slightly. Rod smiled and cupped her face in his hands.

"You are beautiful, Randy. I have dreamed about this and I have dreamed about you."

Randy was breathing hard. She slipped her hands up to his hands and brought them down to her breasts. He lightly touched the outside of her jogbra arousing the skin just above her nipples. As he did, Randy trembled and pulled him close to her. His hands rubbed the sides of her breasts and then underneath them. He gently lifted her bra and slipped his hands underneath the elastic band until his hands were directly on her breasts. He could feel the perspiration begin to build between their bodies.

As he slid down slightly to kiss her neck, he felt her nipples harden as they pressed into his chest. His tongue slid along the side of her neck and he tasted the sweet sweat. At the base of her neck he sucked lightly making a little noise.

She reached down to her jogbra and started lifting it up to remove it. She lifted partially up and Rod helped remove it the rest of the way. When she lay back, she felt the hair on Rod's chest rubbing against her bare breasts. She pulled him to her and tried to pull him over on top but he resisted. Instead he moved down and kissed her between her breasts. He moved his hands along the hot smooth skin of her upper chest. He let his hands slide down and began to massage lightly with his hands cupped around her breasts.

Randy began to breathe even harder and Rod kissed the sides of her breasts as he held them in his hands. Then his lips pursed on each nipple and Randy whimpered again. He felt her fingernails tighten into points that pressed into his back. Their bodies began to move slightly, rhythmically and Randy reached down to Rod's cycling shorts. She started pushing down at the top of the band that held them up. Rod lifted up and slid them down his legs until they were off and lying at the edge of the blanket. Then he helped Randy remove her shorts.

Randy pulled Rod to her again and started to slide under him as she pulled him to move over her. Rod continued to resist and let his hands glide all over her body arousing her skin to a tingle. Their lips

met and he kissed her. She kissed him hard. Her mouth opened
slightly and Rod's tongue slid inside her lips and skirmished playfully
with her tongue. She pulled at his body again.

He slid his hands down to her navel and began sliding his hands
slowly up and down Then he let his hands glide from her navel
down. Again she pulled at him and he did not resist. He lifted his
weight over her bracing himself on his arms and his legs. Randy let
her hands explore the hardened muscles in his arms and in his thighs.
She pulled him down to her but he held back. He kissed her on the
neck and shoulders. She squirmed under him and pulled again. His
body felt rigid as he suspended himself just above her. She held onto
his upper back and lifted herself up to him. "Now, please," she
whispered.

He moved his legs inside of her legs and slowly lowered his body
until he could feel the heat and dampness of her body as it glided
along his.

Rod extended his body and let the front of his body slide over
Randy. He did this until she could take it no more. She pulled
forcefully down and lurched her body up until they were just barely
coupled, joined in a flash of heat. Randy cried out and their bodies
unified as though they were one. She buried her face into the hair on
his chest and bit into his chest. They moved rhythmically, slowly at
first then building into a crescendo of exploding heat and wet. It
seemed to last forever then imperceptibly it subsided. They clung to
each other and finally slumped.

Randy slid her hands over his body for several minutes as they
regained their breath. At first Rod was inanimate but as she touched
him, she awakened an arousal that was more physical, more sensuous
than the first. Soon they were rejoined into a frenzy of thrashing
bodies. Both of them exploded again. After a few moments they slid
down breathless into an afterglow. Rod moved easily to the side and
Randy curled up with her back into his chest. Rod wrapped his arms
around her and held her tight as he pulled her into a ball. They slept
for a short time then Randy stretched slightly. When they awoke,
Randy looked out over the River. Everything was hazy and beautiful
as the early evening light brought a golden glow.

"This could be our place," Rod said as he squeezed her in his
arms.

"What do you mean?"

"It's for sale. We could own it." Rod started lightly rubbing the lower part of her tummy with his fingertips.

Randy felt the tingle in her stomach and felt it run down to her toes. She crunched her toes and pushed into the blanket with her feet. "What do you really mean?" she asked.

"Well, I'm crazy about you. I believe you are crazy about me. Maybe we ought to think about taking our relationship to another level. Maybe we . . . "

Randy rolled over and gently gave him a kiss. He put his arms around her again and started to continue talking. She put her fingertips over his lips. She put her other hand on his chest and lightly pressed into the muscles, "Let's talk about something else. Something that worries me: Wanda Stickley."

CHAPTER THIRTEEN

The battery at Charleston was filled with tourists. Many were enjoying the scenery: the beautiful bay at the confluence of the Cooper and Ashley Rivers surrounding Fort Sumter and providing the peninsula for the pastel ante-bellum homes that lined the old cobblestone streets. The sun filled the park which consisted of a city square anchored by a large cupolaed gazebo and landscaped with ancient trees and cannons. Sunshine glistened off of the water and through the Spanish moss in the trees to create a relaxing, even surreal atmosphere. Several people were throwing Frisbees and others were walking their dogs while a couple of inline skaters circled the park. Most though were enjoying the sun in supine fashion.

A large limousine circled the park until a parking place was located near the promenade. While the driver waited, two men stepped out and strolled onto the large elevated walk which had served as the heavily artilleried fortification for Charleston during the Civil War and now served as a bulwark against the occasional storm's tide. They walked quietly for a few moments then after they had strolled past the crowd, they began a conversation in whispered tones.

"I told you Gedney was out of control," Wrenn Davies whispered rather vehemently as the Senator studied the broken pavement before him. "I believe he totally blew it when that Stickley woman's lawyer came to see him."

"I agree," the Senator responded as he continued to weave his way along the uneven pavement, "but at least the boy had enough good sense to call us and let us know what's goin' on."

"He should have given that lawyer every thing he wanted. The paper work was meticulously documented. I saw to it myself. Our connection to Ralph Stickley is so deep, no one could pull it out with a submarine. Our connection at best is by word of mouth. Unfortunately we've got some big mouths."

"You know, Wrenn, you'd think ol' Gedney would be more appreciative. After all we got Bobby on the payroll. What was it?

Jail inspectah? That boy is gettin' a little unnerved. Gonna have to watch him, Wrenn."

"Yes, sir. He's becoming a loose cannon."

"What'd he do about that inmate Ralph killed before he escaped?"

"Gedney put it down as an accident. No one has questioned it; after all the victim was a scumbag. No one cared about him one way or the other. And the officials at the prison know how it works. If it had gone down as a murder, there would be an investigation and heads would roll. I think everyone was content to let it be swept under the carpet."

The Senator stopped and leaned on the railing as he watched a sailboat making its way down the Ashley River toward Fort Sumter. A slight breeze kept its sails filled and it moved swiftly down river. The sun was bright and the Senator searched his pockets for his sunglasses. When he found them, he slipped them on and stared down directly at the water as it reflected bright rays back toward him. "This is the time to be in Charleston, Wrenn. Even with this big ol' sun boilin' like a peanut, the early autumn breeze keeps ya' cool. Charleston, little bit a heaven on earth."

The waves from a distant ship finally reached the shoreline and began lapping onto the rocks at the base of the sea wall. The noise was just enough to break the spell. The Senator cleared his throat and asked, "What do ya' heah about the investigation in China?"

Davies looked around to make sure no one was listening. Satisfied that they had enough privacy, he still spoke in a whisper, "Chen says not to worry. He says it's like the Keystone Cops over there. They can dig all they want but it's not like it is here. When the FBI goes behind the bamboo curtain, it has to get permission from the Chinese authorities before it can get an agent into a bathroom to take a pee. Even if they accidentally stumbled across anything, and that's what it would take, our involvement is so remote that we'd never be identified."

The Senator seemed satisfied with the answer and changed the subject. "What did you find out about the case up theah in Wilmington?"

"They are going to trial I believe. The DA has offered second degree murder but she has refused to plead although there has been some discussion that she might plead guilty to voluntary manslaughter. The DA is getting a lot of pressure from women's groups. It's quite a domestic violence issue there locally. They say he's got a strong case on the evidence but you know Ralph, he had a mean streak in him. The DA is afraid that will jade the case so he is offering the second degree plea."

"Well, I know ol' Butch. He'll do what he's gotta do and he hasn't been around all these years for nothin'. He knows how it works. Maybe he needs a little more pressure to plead that case out. What did you say? Voluntary manslaughter? What da'ya know about Wanda Stickley's lawyer?"

"Mixed bag of information. His name is Ben Down. Wake Forest Law School graduate. Former prosecutor in Wilmington, even worked for Butch. Has a good reputation as a trial lawyer. Knows what he's doing but he's got a major flaw, they say. Likes to drink. Makes him irascible and cranky. His practice is a one man firm although he shares offices with two other attorneys who are helping him with the case. One of them is a woman. Bost, I believe, is her name. The other is a black lawyer. Name's Wilkes. He's the one that's been contacting the Department of Correction in Columbia about Ralph. Down is up to the job if it comes to a trial but I hear he'd like to plead."

"Well, it sounds like those two ol' boys just need a little push and they'd get in bed with each other on a voluntary manslaughter plea."

Davies raised his voice. "I know what you are thinking, Senator, but I don't think we ought to get involved. Really it could jeopardize things. After all, what interest do we have? It would just be too suspicious."

"Not necessarily, Wrenn," the Senator said and smiled a little mischievously. "We've got constituents who want this woman helped. Women's groups are callin' our office to see what we can do. There is still a lot of residual feelin' up theah in Florence ovah that warehouse deal. They knew ol' Ralph up theah and they remember he was meaner than a striped snake. And that's what we do is help people. I think we can help heah."

"It's too risky."

"Life's a risk. Take a look out there at Fort Sumter." The Senator gestured across the bay to the Fort that stood guard over Charleston where the Cooper River and Ashley River spilled into the Atlantic. "Those good ol' boys who had all they could stomach of Yankee domination took a chance and went out theah and took that

Fort away from the Federals. They risked it all for what they thought was right."

"But they lost."

"But they was right," the Senator argued back and looked sharply at Davies. "They was right. And we are right heah. This case has got to go away. Theah is way too much snoopin' goin' on because of it. It's got to be knocked in the head like an ol' cottonmouth or it's gonna bite us, boy."

"But . . . "

"No buts, Wrenn, heah it is. We are gonna help 'em put this case to rest. And we are gonna keep our eye on that Wilmington lawyer. Down, did you say his name was? You get Chen and tell him what we need. I want that lawyer covered up like the dew covahs Dixie, heah?"

*   *   *

Ben and Randy walked through the protesters and noticed that their numbers had grown somewhat. Four carried placards and walked the sidewalk at the front of the Judicial Building. Their messages were more strident than they had been. "Free Wanda Now" and "Wanda Stickley--Victim Not Murderer" were hand written in large block letters on two of the signs.

James Wilkes who had been brought into the case to help with research and investigation negotiated the sidewalk and caught up with Ben and Randy as they entered the door to the courthouse. Ben held the door for James who was attempting to juggle a briefcase, a stack of files and his laptop case. When they reached the lawyers lounge, Randy went on to the courtroom and Ben asked James to come in so they could discuss the case.

As they stacked everything on the large table among the coffee cups and old law books that had not been returned to the law library, James commented, "Randy told me about your experience with the prison warden at Goretown. It sounds like he is trying to cover up something but what?"

"Exactly, James. That is the question. He couldn't get rid of me fast enough and he wouldn't talk about Ralph Stickley. Something is definitely wrong there."

"What do you think he is covering up?" James asked.

"It's hard to say. It may be a red herring. It may be as innocuous as a bureaucrat who is just trying to cover his butt because of Ralph's escape. Stonewalling may be the only way he knows how to do that. On the other hand, if I were a betting man and I am, I would wager that Ralph was up to his neck in some serious criminal activity at the prison and Gedney Howell was treading water right beside of him."

"What do you want me to do?"

"I've got a 'to do list' for you a mile long." Ben looked somewhat mischievously at James and reached into his case and searched for the list. "Get everything you can on Gedney Howell: political connections, family, friends, associates . . . "

James began making notes as Ben talked. He asked, "Financial information?"

"Sure. Everything. And see what you can find out about Ralph. There must be a way to find out how the transfer was arranged from the prison in North Carolina to the prison in South Carolina. Oh, check the DA's office in Florence if you can without stirring the waters too much. Who put the pressure on the DA to bring Ralph to South Carolina for trial? And see what you find out about Ralph: family, friends. Who did he associate with at Goretown and for that matter, who did he bunk with when he served time here in Brunswick? Maybe they heard something and are willing to tell it?"

James grinned and said, "You know, this stuff is not on the internet. I thought I was being brought in for my knowledge of the great wide web. A lot of this is shoe leather work to be done by a private dick."

"James, James," Ben chided gingerly as he finally located the list and handed it over to James, "when you volunteer for duty, you have to do what's assigned."

"Uh, let's go back to 'volunteer'. I believe you asked me to find out via internet what I could about Ralph Stickley's transfer to South Carolina. I did that. Then you asked me to find out what I could about the South Carolina Department of Correction and especially Goretown. I believe the word you are looking for is 'drafted'."

"Come on now. You know you love this stuff. Skulduggery, clandestine operations. You know it beats a title search through the records at the Register of Deeds."

James still did not look convinced and Ben said, "And besides a woman's life hangs in the balance here."

"All right. All right." James caved in rather quickly as Ben knew he would. "What's next?"

Ben patted him on the shoulder. "You are a hundred per cent, James. Now back to Ralph, I really need to know who he associated with at the prison. They will know a lot, if they will just tell it."

"I can check with some of the brothers on this. You get my drift, man?"

Ben grinned and started to load the papers back into his grip. "That's what it will take. Somebody who was in prison when Ralph was there will know. Oh, we are gearing up for trial. I need a background check on the list of jurors for the session."

James opened his briefcase and pulled out a computer printout. "I thought that is what I would be doing in the beginning. I've already obtained the list and I've started a workup on the ones who have been called to appear on the first day of the session. By the time you get into jury selection I should have the information you want."

"You are sharp, James. You are the man for this job."

"All right. No need to butter me up. I'm doing it already."

"One more thing. Butch is pretty good about getting us the State's list of witnesses. As soon as I get it, I will get it to you for a background check of each of the witnesses. It's usually pretty long. Butch puts down everybody and then some."

"Will be done. Anything else?"

"Only the most important thing of all." Ben picked up his briefcase and started toward the door.

"What's that?"

"Thanks."

As Ben started out of the lounge en route to the courtroom, Jack Krait started in the doorway. Krait blocked Ben and glared at him. "Down, you think you've got something over on me but it hasn't happened. You will rue the day you ever messed with Jack Krait."

Ben replied, "Come on, Jack. You had it coming. You are impossible to deal with sometimes and you were completely unreasonable in Thor's case. That dog was not vicious and you knew it but you had to push the issue. Look, a little compassion goes a long way. Besides I didn't make you sit in that chair of dog drool. You did that."

"It was more than that, Down. You knew that Judge Allgood is a dog lover. The bailiff told me about the pictures of his dog on his desk. You knew he was going to let that dog go and you knew that dog had messed all over my seat. You, you set me up," he fumed.

"Come on, Jack. You can dish it out but you can't take it."

Ben started to walk on by him and Krait pushed Ben back. Krait drew back his arm as though he were going to take a swing at Ben. Ben stepped back and prepared to counter punch. James Wilkes who had been watching the confrontation jumped between them.

"Cool off. No need to get into anything here," James spoke sternly and put his hand on both of them.

Ben and Krait continued to stare at each other. Finally Krait relaxed his arm and stood up straighter releasing the tension in his body. As he continued to lean into James' hand, he was still very angry and spoke to Ben in a growl. "I'm going to get you if it's the last thing I do."

Krait stalked off and James turned toward Ben. "I think you've got an enemy, Ben."

Ben grinned and replied, "No, I think I've got him right where I want him."

As soon as Ben reached the courtroom, Rod called Wanda's case for the hearing that had been scheduled to determine whether Wanda's statements could be used in the trial. The defense had raised an objection by way of a motion to suppress her statements as being violative of her right to counsel and her right not to incriminate herself. Since this was the last motion that needed to be addressed in the case, the DA's staff had pushed for a hearing during this last week before the trial was to be held.

Ben and Randy waited with Wanda at the defense table while Judge Allgood reviewed the contents of the motion. After his cursory review the Judge inquired if all parties were ready to proceed. Each side responded affirmatively and he directed Rod to call his first witness.

At Rod's direction officer Morgan Creed approached the witness stand for the administration of the oath. As he walked, he was a combination of noises: creaking leather, scraping starched uniform and jingling keys. He assumed the witness stand with a flair indicative of an officer who was proud of his work and eager for attention. Ben thought it was a good sign and expected a straightforward rendition of the events of the morning when Wanda was taken into custody.

Rod picked up the examination as soon as the witness was sworn and seated. "Sir, state your name and where you are employed."

"Officer Morgan Creed. Deputy Sheriff with the New Hanover County Sheriff's Department."

"On or about the alleged date of this offense, did you have occasion to see the defendant Wanda Stickley?"

"I did, sir."

"How did you become involved in this matter?"

"On the night in question, a call came into the dispatcher's office at the Sheriff's Department concerning a shot fired at a residence off Highway 17 in Ogden. I was closest to the area and was dispatched."

"What did you do in response to the dispatch?" Rod asked.

"I went straight to the area. Only a couple minutes away. When I arrived in the neighborhood, I had a little difficulty locating the house. The street name was well-marked but the house numbers were not visible."

"What did you do after you arrived in the neighborhood where the residence is located?"

"I drove until I found it."

"How long did it take from the time you were dispatched until you arrived at the residence in question?"

"About five minutes."

"What did you observe when you located the residence?"

"Well, I turned into the driveway and immediately observed something shiny in the driveway. The driveway kinda went up from the road and my headlights were reflecting off of this shiny substance, a liquid, as it ran down the driveway in a little strip."

"What were you seeing at that time?"

"At the time I didn't know what it was but it was long and shiny. Maybe twenty, twenty-five feet long. Like a little stream. Later I learned that it was a small stream of blood."

The courtroom until that point had a little noise from people going in and coming out of the courtroom and from people who were whispering relatively quietly to each other. The courtroom grew very silent. The only sound that emanated for a couple of seconds was Officer Creed's leather belt as it creaked when he moved in the chair.

"What did you see next?"

"My eyes followed the stream of blood and as the beams of my patrol vehicle began to point in a more upward direction as I started the drive up the driveway, I saw a white female."

"And what was she doing, if anything?"

"She was standing. She stared directly into the lights of the car. Then I noticed that at her feet was an object. As my eyes focused on the object, I saw that it was the body of a man. The body was lying on its back and it was not moving. Then I noticed that the woman was holding an object in her hand. As my headlights pointed more directly toward it, she moved it slightly and I could see it was a knife."

"What did you do then?"

"I called for backup. I stopped my patrol car, drew my side arm and exited the vehicle, all in one motion. I stood behind my driver's side door and pointed my gun at her and told her 'Don't move' or 'Freeze'. I can't remember which."

"What did the woman do?"

"Nothing at first. I then told her to drop the weapon. She hesitated for a few seconds like she did not understand what I was saying. I said it again and she snapped out of it. She dropped the knife and I went to her. I cuffed her and walked her back to my patrol car. I radioed the information of what I had found."

"What happened next?"

"We waited. I checked the man on the driveway."

"What did you observe about him? Was he alive or dead?"

The officer swallowed hard and hesitated. "He was dead, sir."

"How were you able to determine that?"

"No one could be alive with those kinds of wounds." Officer Creed screwed his face up tightly as he remembered the disfigured body. "He wasn't breathing and I didn't feel a pulse."

"What wounds did you observe about the man?"

"Objection," Ben responded. He knew the press would cover the details, particularly the most gruesome parts and their reports would be printed the week before jury selection was to begin. "That's irrelevant. Your Honor, that's for another day and time during the trial. To go into it now would just risk contaminating the jury pool who will be reporting Monday I believe."

"Sustained." Judge Allgood looked at Rod but talked to both of them. "I agree. Let's just stay on the issue of whether the defendant's confession is admissible."

Rod did not argue the point and moved onto another area of the examination. "Officer Creed, were you able to identify the man on the ground?"

"Yes, sir. Later I learned that he was Ralph Stickley."

"What happened next, that is, after you had taken the woman into custody?"

"We waited. In a couple of minutes another road deputy arrived. Then my supervisor arrived. In about fifteen minutes a detective arrived. I turned the defendant over to him."

"Which detective arrived?"

"Perry Foster."

"Was the woman in your custody the entire time?"

"Yes, sir."

"Did you interrogate her or ask her any questions?"

"No, sir. I figured the detective would take care of that. I just secured the scene."

"All right, sir. Do you see the woman that you took into custody there that morning? And if you do, point her out."

"Yes, sir." He pointed to Wanda.

"Your Honor," Rod asked, "I would like for the record to reflect that Officer Creed pointed out the defendant in this matter, Wanda Stickley?"

The Judge looked at Ben and Ben nodded in agreement with Rod's request. Judge Allgood noted, "Without objection, so ordered."

"That's all I have, Your Honor."

Judge Allgood turned his attention to Ben and asked, "Questions on cross?"

"Yes, sir. Thank you, Your Honor. Officer Creed," Ben began, "I do not want to ask you about the events of that evening except to determine what statements my client, Mrs. Stickley, may have made.

So I'll ask you to think back to the evening hours of the night in question. Did my client make any statements in your presence?"

The officer wrinkled his brow as if he were having difficulty recalling. Ben said, "To help refresh your recollection, I am looking at your report of that evening and you mentioned that she said something about calling someone."

"Oh, yes," he blurted out remembering the entry in his report. "The defendant said 'Call Ben Down'."

"Was that the first thing she said in your presence?"

"Yes, sir. As she stood over the body with the knife in her hand, she looked somewhat dazed when my headlights flashed on her. I got out, pulled my revolver and when she looked at me, she said, 'Call Ben Down'."

"And that was the first thing she said?"

"Yes, sir."

"Do you know who Ben Down is?"

The officer began to look puzzled again. Thinking it must be a trick question, he stammered a little as he spoke. "Uh, uh, that's you."

There was a little laughter in the audience at Officer's Creed's strained response to the simple question and Ben continued with the examination. "And who am I?"

"You are you," Creed responded without cracking a smile.

Several in the audience broke out in laughter. Judge Allgood tapped his gavel lightly and spoke to the officer who had completely missed the point of Ben's questions. "I think he wants you to say he is a lawyer."

"Oh, I see. Yes, you are the lawyer."

Ben grinned at Judge Allgood and asked Officer Creed, "So you knew she wanted to talk to her lawyer, correct?"

"Yes."

"And you knew that from the very first thing she said, correct?"

"Yes, sir."

"So did you ask her any questions?"

"No, sir. I secured the area and held her in custody while I waited for my supervisor and then the detectives to arrive."

"Did she make any other statements in your presence?"

"While we waited, she wanted to know if we knew where her son was."

"And did you?"

"No, sir. Not at first but later we learned that he was at a neighbor's house."

"Did she get to see her son Jeremy while she was in your custody?"

"No."

"Did she say anything else to you or to anyone else while she was in your presence?"

"No, sir."

"Well, did you tell any of the detectives what she had said about wanting to talk to her lawyer?"

"No, sir, but I did put it in my report and they would have had access to that."

"When did you complete and file your report?"

"The next day," he said as he checked the date on his copy of the report.

"Finally let me ask," Ben said as he concluded the examination, "did you specifically tell Perry Foster, who I believe is the lead investigator in this case, what Mrs. Stickley said about wanting to talk to her lawyer?"

"No. Well, only in my report ."

After Ben indicated that he had no additional questions and Officer Creed was released from the stand, Rod called Perry Foster, the New Hanover County Deputy Sheriff who had served as the primary detective in the investigation of the death of Ralph Stickley. After he had identified himself for the record, he indicated that he had taken custody of Wanda Stickley from Officer Creed at the residence of Mrs. Stickley in Ogden on the morning of the incident.

"To clear up a point raised by Mr. Down's questions," Rod said, "tell the court whether Officer Creed made any statement to you concerning what Wanda Stickley had said on the scene."

"No," Foster replied. "In fact I did not talk to Officer Creed but talked to the supervising officer on the scene concerning the events of that morning. No mention was made of that statement, that is, that she wanted to talk to a lawyer."

"And when did you see Officer Creed's report?"

"Probably a couple of days after the arrest of Mrs. Stickley."

"Well, what happened after you arrived at the scene of the killing?"

"As I mentioned I obtained the underlying information from the supervising officer on the scene. Detective Jimmy Watson arrived shortly after I did. I observed the body of Ralph Stickley. He appeared to be dead at the time I saw him. I noticed that Wanda Stickley was being held in the custody of Deputy Morgan Creed. After Detective Watson and I did a walk though of the crime scene, I asked him to direct the evidence technicians in preserving the crime scene and obtaining physical evidence."

"What did you do next?"

"I took custody of Wanda Stickley and transported her to the New Hanover Detention Facility. I told her I would like to interview her about what happened."

"Where were you at that time?"

"In an interview room at the Detention Center. Only the two of us were present."

"Had she made any statements of any kind to you before that?"

"No. Basically I had just introduced myself as a New Hanover Deputy Sheriff and a Detective in the Department. I told her that I would be investigating this matter and I would want to talk to her about it. She had said nothing and at that point I had not asked her anything."

"What did she say in response to your statement to her at the Detention Center that you wanted to interview her about what had happened?"

"She did not respond directly but said that she wanted to see her son Jeremy. She said she wouldn't say anything until she could see her son."

"Did she ask for a lawyer then?"

"No, only her son."

"What did you do?"

"I contacted the officers at the crime scene and learned that her son had been located. I asked them to bring him to the police department and they did. Mrs. Stickley talked to her son for a few minutes then I told her I wanted to speak to her."

"Did you advise her of her Miranda rights before you asked her any questions?"

"Yes, sir."

"Did she appear to have complete control of her mental and physical faculties at that time, that is, did she appear to understand the rights as you gave them to her?"

"Yes, sir. I gave her the rights orally and in writing. She signed a waiver of rights form indicating she understood them."

At that point Rod stood and had Detective Foster to identify the written rights form and Wanda's signature on the form. After he introduced the written form into evidence, he asked, "After the rights were administered and she had signed the written form waiving her rights, did she agree to answer your questions?"

"Yes, sir."

"All right, Detective Foster, what happened then?"

"I asked her to tell me as clearly as she could what had happened. I asked her to begin at the beginning and slowly tell me each thing that had happened leading up to her being taken into custody. I informed her that her statement was being recorded. She gave me a brief sketch of what had happened. I made notes as she went along then I asked her questions about what she had told me. After we had gone through that, I asked her to reduce her statement to writing and had her to sign it."

"Briefly," Rod stated as he reached for his copy of her written statement from his table, "tell us what she told you."

"Mrs. Stickley said she had picked her son up at a Scout meeting and returned home shortly after 9:00 p.m. on Monday night. She said she was fixing sandwiches in the kitchen while her son went across the street to a neighbor's house. She heard a noise in the basement that she thought was the cat. She went to investigate and was attacked by Ralph Stickley. She fought him off she said. In the process she stabbed him with a screwdriver and she shot him with a handgun. She stated that Ralph Stickley went upstairs and after being dazed from the attack, she followed him. When she got upstairs, Ralph Stickley was in the driveway. He was lying there. His throat was cut and he was dying. She saw a knife beside him, picked it up and then the police car pulled up."

Rod introduced Wanda's written statement into evidence and after having Detective Foster to identify the tape recording of her statement, introduced it into evidence and played it for Judge Allgood.

Ben cross-examined seeking to show that Wanda was in no
physical or mental condition to make a statement at the time.
Detective Foster described each of the visible injuries and testified
that even though she was dazed, she understood the questions and
gave cogent, responsive answers.

Ben honed into his real point of contention. "Detective Foster,
you do not deny, do you, that the first thing she said when she was
taken into custody by a law enforcement officer was that she wanted
a lawyer?"

"No, sir, but I didn't know anything about it at the time I
interviewed her. In fact she . . . "

"In fact," Ben butted in, "in fact she was in no condition to
answer any question when you interviewed her?"

"No, her statement was 'knowing and intelligent'," he said
referring to the language of the case holdings that required a judge to
find an accused's statements were made after a knowing and
intelligent waiver of her constitutional rights.

"Sir, she never initiated the conversation or interview with you,
did she?"

"No, but she co-operated fully and raised no objection to
answering any question."

"And you would not have asked her any questions if she had said
she wanted a lawyer present or wanted to consult with a lawyer
before answering any questions?"

"I would not have asked her any questions."

"And the fact is this: she asked for a lawyer the very first thing,
didn't she?"

Upon Rod's objection, "Argumentative and repetitive," Judge
Allgood sustained.

Ben stated that the point was made and indicated he had no
further questions. Rod next called Deputy Sheriff Gerald Stanley.
Deputy Stanley identified himself and testified that he had been the
Detective who had investigated Wanda's complaint several days
prior to the present charge that Ralph Stickley had raped her.

"Detective Stanley, as I understand it, Wanda Stickley had
complained to you that Ralph Stickley had raped her?"

"Yes, sir."

"Were you able to confirm her charge?"

"No, in fact Ralph Stickley was actually in prison at the time serving a sentence for previously having raped her and he was also serving a sentence in South Carolina for embezzlement. He had an alibi."

"So basically you did not believe her story, did you?"

"Well, I couldn't prove it. I mean, she appeared to have been attacked. She was scratched and bruised and really, she looked like somebody who had been raped."

"Did you talk to her again after you learned that Ralph Stickley was in prison at the time of the alleged rape?"

"Yes, sir. I spoke to her attorney Ben Down and then later I spoke to her."

"What did you tell her?"

"I told her that the evidence did not support her claim and that I would not be able to file a charge against Ralph Stickley."

"What was her reaction?"

"She was very frustrated and she was angry."

"What did she say?"

"She said she would kill him if it was the last thing she ever did."

Rod looked over at Ben and said, "Your witness."

"Detective Stanley," Ben asked, "you've known Wanda Stickley for a long time. You investigated the first rape in which Ralph Stickley was convicted and you made an exhaustive inquiry into the background of Ralph and Wanda Stickley in preparation for the trial of that case, isn't that correct?"

"Yes, sir."

"And you have never known of Wanda Stickley to be a violent person, have you?"

"No, sir."

"In fact she has been just the opposite. She has been the victim time and again of Ralph Stickley's abuse, assaults and rape, correct?"

"Yes, sir. She went through a lot."

"You do not know whether her statement that she would kill him was just her way of venting her feelings over the abuse, do you?"

"No."

"And you never knew of her to take any action toward carrying out such a statement?"

"No."

"With regard to her statement that Ralph Stickley raped her on this second occasion, you are not saying that he did not do it, are you? You are saying at the most that you just could not prove it?"

"Yes, sir. I could not prove it."

Ben looked at Detective Stanley carefully and decided to take a chance with the next line of questions. "How long have you been a law enforcement officer?"

Stanley smiled obviously proud of his record as a law enforcement officer and said, "Twenty-six years, next month."

"How many cases of domestic violence have you investigated?"

"I don't know, sir. Probably thousands."

"In all of those cases, and take as long as you would like to think about your answer, you cannot name one woman, or for that matter, one person, who has been more abused than Wanda Stickley was by Ralph Stickley, can you?"

He did not hesitate. He looked directly at Wanda and as he spoke, all eyes focused on Wanda. "Not one."

"Thank you, sir. You may step down."

Ben and Randy offered no evidence on the motion and with the evidence completed, Judge Allgood announced that he would hear final arguments after recess. During the break Ben received a telephone page from Skittle. He stepped out to the hallway to obtain better reception as he called her on his cell phone.

"Skittle, what's up?"

"Margaret called and said her doctor was sending her to the hospital. Now don't get excited. It's not an emergency but she wanted you to know. Apparently they are going to run some tests. She said she will see you at home."

"Is she all right? I'll come right now if I need to," Ben inquired.

"No, she specifically said not to let you overreact. She said to take care of business and she will see you this evening."

"All right, if she says so but keep me informed if there is any change."

Skittle said, "I've got some more juicy news for you. Guess who wants to speak to you as soon as you get back from court?"

"All right, Skittle. Don't start these guessing games again. Who?"

"Guess."

"Give."

"Oh, all right, but you won't believe it." She hesitated for a moment to give it the solemnity she thought the news required. "Senator Fowler Worrell."

"Who?"

"Senator Fowler Worrell. From South Carolina. He wants to talk to you. I told him you had an important hearing this morning but would be back in the office in a couple of hours. He is going to call back in about an hour."

"I'll be there," Ben said as he wondered what it could be about. "And call me if anything comes up concerning Margaret. ASAP."

Ben went back to the courtroom and continued to puzzle over why the senior Senator from South Carolina would want to speak to him. He had never met him and frankly knew very little about him. What little he did know about him did not offer any possible reason for wanting to speak to him. As Ben continued to try to determine why the Senator wanted to speak to him, Judge Allgood returned to the courtroom and announced that he was ready to hear final arguments on the motion.

"Mr. Down," he announced, "since the District Attorney has the burden of proving that the statements are admissible in evidence, I will hear from you first then let the State close the arguments."

"Thank you, sir," Ben said as he stood. "Your Honor, first I would like to comment on behalf of my client Mrs. Stickley and my colleague Ms. Bost. All of us thank you for the serious attention you have given this matter. As to the merits of the motion, I would like to present Your Honor with a brief that deals with the issue of admissibility of the defendant's statements."

Randy pulled the brief and several copies from her briefcase and handed a copy of the brief to Rod and two copies of the brief to Ben. Ben motioned for the bailiff and gave him a copy which was then delivered to the Judge. The Judge momentarily thumbed through the brief then laid it to the side. When he looked up, Ben continued with his argument.

"I know Your Honor will want to review the brief and take this matter under advisement. I would also like to cover the salient points briefly with you. First the statement that Mrs. Stickley made to Officer Creed is inadmissible. She said 'Call Ben Down' and . . . ," Ben smiled at the Judge, "as admirable as that is, it is not admissible because she was asserting her right to an attorney. Our courts have held such a statement cannot be used to incriminate her. The brief is replete with cases holding to such an effect. Secondly, her statement to Officer Foster, the primary detective in the case, is inadmissible because it violates her Fifth Amendment right to counsel and not to incriminate herself and her Sixth Amendment right to counsel. She clearly asked for an attorney and our cases hold that the officer cannot question, interview or interrogate her further after she exercises her right to counsel. It makes no difference that she made the request to one officer and another officer then questioned her. Finally her statement to Detective Stanley after the second rape is not admissible evidence because it was not a voluntary statement--she was a victim required to tell the officer the details of the crime. It is not relevant under Rule 401 and is not admissible under Rule 403 because its probative value is outweighed by the danger of unfair prejudice to the defendant. And with that, we rest. Thank you, sir."

Ben sat down and Rod stood. "As persuasive as Mr. Down is, Your Honor," he began, "the law and the facts are against him in this motion. The first statement, 'Call Ben Down', was a spontaneous, voluntary statement by the defendant. The statement to Detective Foster at the Detention Center was made after a knowing, intelligent and voluntary waiver of her Miranda rights including her right to have counsel present. The officer told her specifically she did not have to make a statement and told her she could have a lawyer and even one appointed for her if she could not afford one. She still made the statement. Although we contend much of her statement was self serving and untruthful in parts, she admits stabbing and shooting Ralph Stickley. It is critical to the State's case. Finally her statement to Officer Stanley that she would kill him if it was the last thing she ever did is a clear, unequivocal statement of her premeditated and deliberated specific intent to kill. All of it is admissible and it's probative value outweighs the danger of unfair prejudice. In fact it is a confession to first degree murder."

Rod sat down. Judge Allgood was silent for a few moments then spoke in an even voice as was his temperament. "This is an important ruling. It is a complicated area of the criminal and constitutional law of our nation and State. Frankly I am leaning toward ruling in favor of admissibility but I should review the evidence, the arguments and the brief presented. I will rule later, certainly by the time trial is to start on Monday morning. Are all parties ready to proceed?"

Rod stood and announced, "We are, Your Honor."

Ben was a little slower to stand. "As usual, Your Honor, we are ready when called upon. We are ready to defend against the allegation and to fight the allegator."

The Judge and Rod laughed at the pun and Judge Allgood closed the proceeding: "So be it."

              *   *   *

"What is all of this mess?" Ben asked as he walked in the office. The lobby was full of boxes and large envelopes.

"I believe all of it is from the attorneys for Big Burger." Skittle gestured at all of the boxes across the room. "Randy said after she had refused to settle the case, the defendant's attorney said to expect 'The Wrath', whatever that means. I believe all of these boxes contain requests for information."

As Ben listened to Skittle's report, he leaned one of the boxes over looking for an address. "My God," he mumbled, "it looks like we are the repository for UPS shipping.

"If all of this is discovery requests, we are in trouble," Skittle said. "The two of you are going to start Wanda Stickley's case Monday and Randy will never have time to answer all of these questions and get all of the information requested. They don't know what they are doing."

Ben smirked. "They know exactly what they are doing." He leaned the box back and sat it down. "Has Randy seen this?"

"Not yet. She won't be in until this afternoon."

The telephone rang and Skittle answered, "Ben Down, Attorney at law." As she listened, she put her hand over the mouthpiece and whispered to Ben, "Right on schedule. It's Senator Worrell's office." Then she took her hand off and said, "Yes, ma'am. Mr. Down is here. I will transfer your call immediately. Thank you."

Ben walked back to his office and when Skittle buzzed him, he picked up line one and said, "Hello, this is Ben Down speaking."

"Yes, sah. Mr. Down, Ben, this is Senator A. Fowler Worrell in Washington. How are you doin' this aftahnoon?"

"Fine, Senator. Thank you for calling. What may I help you with?"

"Yes, well, I wanted to talk to ya' about that case, you know, involving Ralph Stickley. You represent his wife who is charged with killin' him, isn't that right?"

"Yes, sir."

"Well, ya' see, for a while Ralph Stickley was a business man down in Florence, South Carolina and several of my constituents have expressed an interest in that case. I knew him when he worked down theah in South Carolina. I don't like to speak ill of the dead but it was pretty much common knowledge that he was pretty hard on his wife, uh, what is her name?"

"Wanda, Wanda Stickley."

"Yes. Wanda. It seems of late that my office has been bombarded with several complaints from women's groups who believe that Wanda is bein' treated unfairly. They think that the gov'nment has gone overboard trying to get the death penalty for her when she was really the victim heah. Now I don't usually try to interfere with the courts. It's none of my business but this time feelings are pretty strong down heah. I have been asked repeatedly to do something. Frankly I'm at a loss but I want to try to hep my constituents if I can and when I can."

"Yes, sir," Ben said as he continued to try to sort out what the Senator was after. "How does that affect Mrs. Stickley, sir?"

"Well, aftah gettin' all this pressure, I had to do somethin' so I had my staff to make a few discreet inquiries, so to speak. I learned that the DA theah, Butch Yeager, really didn't want to try this case. He wanted to offer a plea to second degree murder. Is that correct?"

"Yes, sir. We have discussed a plea agreement including second degree murder but so far we are unable to agree."

"Well, now, you tell me if I'm right or wrong heah, but I heard that Mrs. Stickley might accept a plea of voluntary manslaughter with a couple of years of prison time if it were offered."

"I can't say that she will but certainly she would consider it."

"Now look, Ben. You are not in this thing alone. I know Butch. He and I were buddies down at the University a long time ago. I can talk to 'im. I believe I can explain to 'im how messy this thing is and how important it is to settle this case on somethin' reasonable. And voluntary manslaughter is reasonable. We got a woman's life at stake heah and that's not right. Meet that thing in the middle and do what's right. That's what I'll tell'im. Now Wanda'll go along with that, won't she?"

"I can't promise anything. I'll have to speak to her."

"Well, if voluntary manslaughter's offered, and it will be Monday morning. You mark my words: ol' Butch will see the light. You'll recommend she take it, won't ya'?"

"Senator, if it's offered, I'll take it to her. As to a recommendation from me, I'll have to see how it is finally packaged."

The Senator laughed and said, "Now don't you two go gettin' hardheaded on this thang 'cause we want justice and we won't be satisfied with anything less." He hung up the phone.

CHAPTER FOURTEEN

It was a cold, harsh wind that blew across the coast of North Carolina. Waves buffeted the shore and the wind blasted and blew away anything that was not firmly attached. At this time of year it was called a nor'easter and at times it blew as hard as the fall hurricanes that appeared to threaten various parts of the coastline. By Monday morning the surf that had been a boiling angry cauldron over the weekend had diminished to a choppy soup and the wind had released its fury. Even though the flagpoles could stand erect again, the surviving tattered flags whipped and popped in the unsettled air.

The people of Wilmington were familiar with the phenomenon. Though things slowed over the weekend, by Monday business continued as usual. Even the ice cream vendor on the waterfront along the Cape Fear River in downtown Wilmington was open though there were few takers. Traffic snarled and slowed during the early morning commute then finally released as the gawkers looked for damage. The destruction was minimal with a few trees down and a few shingles ripped out of place. Considering the degree of intensity of the storm, Wilmington was lucky. They were ready to get back to work and ready to try the case of Wanda Stickley.

Confused jurors who had been able to follow the directions to courthouse parking pulled their coats and hats tightly as they negotiated the windy gauntlet from the parking area to the Judicial Center. Once inside they were directed to the jury assembly room for orientation and instruction concerning what was expected of them.

One bus unloaded a group of protesters catching the attention of the film crew from the local television station. Although reporters and cameramen were aware that they could not film jurors at any time, they knew that protesters were not only fair game for television coverage but made excellent background visuals for on-site news reports. The cameraman followed by the reporter moved into position and filmed several protesters as they exited the bus.

At the door of the bus Carrie Pestoff, State President of Women of America, gave marching orders to each person. As they assembled outside, she called a list of assignments including the group to which each person was assigned and the area around the courthouse where each group would be located.

"Now does everyone know where you are supposed to be?" she asked.

There was no response except for a few heads nodding affirmatively as they huddled together and tried to master their placards in the whipping wind. Of the twenty or so who had appeared for the bus ride from the organization's office in Jacksonville and the fifteen from the local WOA chapter who had joined them, most of them held signs protesting the treatment of Wanda Stickley. Some of the signs were tearing loose from the wooden stakes.

"Listen a minute. The wind is going to be horrific out here this morning so you may not be able to use the posts. The wind is probably going to rip your placard loose. Use the post as long as you can. It makes for a lot more visibility. If your sign is ripped loose, you'll have to hold it out in front of you and as long as you can, over your head. And turn them toward the cameramen who will be here." She noticed the camera from the local television station at some distance behind her. " . . . who are here," she interjected.

When everyone started turning their signs toward the camera, Pestoff noted, "Great. That's what I mean. We are here to be seen and we are here to be heard. When we were in Charlotte last year for the trial of Gina Davis, we had twice as many people to show up for the first day as we have today but they wouldn't speak out, wouldn't hold up their signs. We barely got coverage on the nightly news. Listen, you know the old saying: the squeaky wheel gets the grease. Be visible out there and make sure you cover your area."

"Will we be out here all day?" one protester asked. The wind flipped her sign as she reached to grab her hat.

"Probably not. The press is pretty good about showing up the first day to get some video of the courthouse and the activity associated with the case they are interested in. After that, it gets very slow especially during jury selection. Once the trial itself starts, well, once the evidence starts, they will be back to get video of the people who will be testifying. Usually they will be at the entrances to the Judicial Center. Since we do not know which entrance will be used, we need to be represented at each entrance."

"Will somebody be bringing sandwiches and drinks?" another one called out.

"Right. We'll come by your position and tell you when the food is here. You'll be relieved and you should come to the bus. The bus is headquarters. Eat here, drink here, report all news here. Understand?"

Again several of them nodded and a few mouthed the word "Yeah".

"Oh, when you need to use the restroom, go into the facilities in the Judicial Center. But be careful. Leave your placard with someone else. Do not go into the courthouse with any sign or anything indicating your political stance on the case. It could bring the judge down on us. The sidewalks are ours but the courthouse is his. So be careful."

All of them seemed to have congregated into their assigned groups and she tried to yell above the wind. "Any more questions?"

When there were none, she said, "All right now. We know why we are here. We are here for Wanda Stickley and we are here for women everywhere who have been the victims of oppression. We march today for those who cannot. Even though it may seem hard and thankless work, remember: Wanda Stickley is in this every day. She is fighting for her life in there and the least we can do is give her the support she needs. All right let's . . . . "

"Oh, I had a question," one protester spoke out. "How long will we be here? I mean how long will the case last?"

Pestoff replied, "There is no way to tell. Usually these cases last about three or four weeks. We need to make a strong showing on opening day. Then we'll get a break for about a week. We just need a skeleton crew for that. That's when jury selection is going on. Then we need another big showing on the day opening arguments are to begin. Then we need to stay at full force for the remainder of the trial."

Noticing that some of the protesters were looking at each other with a little disappointment at the length of their possible involvement. "Remember this," Pestoff pointed out. "We are not in this alone. We will have people coming from all over to help with this. I know all of you have obligations at home and at work but today we need your best effort. Tomorrow we'll do what we can with what we've got. Anything else?" Checking her watch and sensing no additional questions, she said, "You know where your assignments are. Let's get there and let our message go forth."

Pestoff picked up a placard and checked over her shoulder to make sure the camera was still rolling. She yelled, "What are we here for?"

On cue several of the protesters held their signs over their head and yelled, "Free Wanda Stickley."

"I can't hear you," she called back. "What are we here for?"

All of the protesters called back even louder this time, "Free Wanda Stickley!"

On the second floor overlooking the meeting of protesters was the DA Butch Yeager. As he stood at the window in his office, he made a mental note of the number of protesters. It was a lot he thought for a case that had received only a modest amount of attention from the press. He had seen more, many more protesters when some of the civil rights cases had been tried in Wilmington. Still it was one more headache that he did not need and one that he did not deserve he thought.

Rod Pemberton came in and asked, "Did you get any damage from the storm?"

Butch did not answer and Rod, noticing that Butch was absorbed in something out the window, walked over and stared down at the people on the street below. "It looks like the Stickley case is finally getting a little publicity. I saw three different news organizations set up in the parking spaces as I came in this morning."

"Did you see the protesters?" Butch asked as he pointed to the group that was splitting up and making their way to the entrances of the courthouse.

Rod leaned forward and tried to read the placards. "Free Wanda Stickley," he read out loud. "Looks like we are into the siege."

"Oh, this is just the beginning," Butch said with a great deal of chagrin in his voice. "I got a call over the weekend that there would be busloads of protesters coming from South Carolina. It seems that Ralph Stickley has aroused the ire of some of our neighbors to the south. I got a call from Senator Fowler Worrell. He and I used to be fellow students together at the University of South Carolina."

"I didn't know that. He looks a lot older than you."

"He is older. He had gone into military service as I did but he stayed in a lot longer than I did before he entered the University. We were classmates even though there were several years' age difference. Anyway he said that the people around Florence were hopping mad about Ralph. They have been ringing his phone off the hook saying that we were being too hard on Wanda Stickley. Apparently some of them think Ralph got off way too light for raping Wanda and for sticking several of them with big debts as he cleaned out that warehouse business down there. Fowler says his phone lines are hot from women's groups around the State and mostly from people in the Florence area."

"What is he wanting done?" Rod asked.

"He says we are taking too hard a line on the case. He said he had heard that Wanda Stickley would plead to voluntary manslaughter and he thought we ought to offer the plea."

"What did you say?"

"I told him we had offered second degree murder and she wouldn't take it. We've got a strong case on the evidence of first degree murder. He wouldn't hear of it. He said it didn't make any difference about the evidence. He said the public wouldn't stand for it either. Ralph was a two-bit hoodlum and he deserved what he got. That's the way his people are seeing it. He said he'll back us up, even on the floor of Congress, if we will just let it go at voluntary manslaughter."

"What are you going to do?"

"I've thought about it all weekend. This case is a loser. We've known that from the beginning. Even if we try it to a jury, and even if they convict her of first degree murder, which I doubt, they will not give her the death penalty. Really the more I hear about Ralph, the more I think they ought to pin a medal on her. Voluntary manslaughter is too light but there are several important things about it. She admits that she is guilty. She is sentenced to imprisonment. We save several weeks of trial. God knows we can spend the time more valuably on other cases. Politically, as Fowler says, the manslaughter plea is a winner. Nobody is going to fuss with us for being too light on her and most people will probably believe it's fair and just. Who is going to complain anyway? Ralph Stickley fans? I can't think of one. After listening to Fowler, who is a political expert in my opinion, I think it's the way we ought to go with this case."

Rod had spent a lot of time getting ready for trial and was a little surprised at the turn of events. He understood the reasoning for the proffer of the lesser plea but still he decided to suggest the down side. "And if she doesn't accept it?"

"I've thought about that too and my response is that we've done all we can do. And we'll let everybody know that. We offered but she refused. The anger should focus on Ben Down for not making her take the plea." Butch smiled lightly. "Let Ben take some of the heat for a while."

"Did you get a copy of the fax this morning from Judge Allgood?"

Butch stepped away from the window and went back to his desk. As he picked up the fax, he answered, "It looks like he is denying her motion to suppress her statements as evidence. No surprise in that. I thought we would get to use her confession. It does concern me though that he said he was sick this past Friday when he sent the fax and he wasn't sure he was going to be able to be in court this Monday."

"I thought when I saw it that it was a little unusual to fax us the order. I'll bet he was getting really sick. Do you think we'll have to delay starting the case if he doesn't make it?"

"No, the Administrative Office of the Courts will probably assign another judge."

"I didn't see Judge Allgood's car in the parking lot this morning and he's usually here by this time. I'll bet he is sick."

Butch was still thinking about the plea and did not respond to the speculation that another judge would be assigned to try the case. "You know," he said, "if he had allowed the motion and we couldn't have used her statements against her in the trial, that would've been a good thing to hang our hats on for the plea bargain. We could have said that the case was weakened substantially by our inability to use her confession in evidence and as a result we felt we needed to offer the reduction in charge on the plea. But with his ruling in favor of the State, I think I won't even mention the ruling in any statements to the press. If Ben takes the plea, we'll say we did it because of the serious problems we had with the victim and his reputation in this area. After all Ralph had escaped from prison, had broken into his wife's house and had attacked her. So we'll say the State's case is weakened by evidence of the victim's reputation and weakened by the strong case of self defense. What do you think?"

"I don't have a problem with the plea," Rod responded matter-of-factly. "Voluntary manslaughter based on excessive force used to defend against an attack by a larger, stronger person. That's a legitimate plea but do you think Ben will take it?"

"Oh, yeah. I know Ben. He is a realist. He'll take it and run with it if he can. The real question is whether Wanda Stickley will take it. I've heard from the jailers that she is saying she didn't do it. Heck of a time to get self-righteous about it."

The intercom buzzed and the secretary said, "Mr. Yeager, Judge Godboldt asked to see you in her office immediately, sir."

Butch looked crestfallen and shook his head. "I guess the speculation is over. God has cursed us. Judge Millicent Godboldt has been assigned to try the Stickley case."

"I've heard stories about her but I've never met her. She is an emergency judge, isn't she?"

"Millie Godboldt," Butch said somewhat dazed by the turn of events. "She is a Marine in a dress."

Rod smiled at Butch's description and Butch responded, "You might see some humor in it now but I assure you it will not last long. She used to be the District Attorney up in Elizabeth City many years ago then she was elevated to Superior Court Judge. You are right: she is a retired judge who is called back to serve in an emergency. She is a pistol in court." Butch swallowed hard and continued. "You see, she and I have a little history too."

Rod was very interested and asked, "What's that all about?"

"When we were DA's together back in those days, we would attend the biannual training conferences. Like most conferences the real training went on in the hallways and the hospitality rooms at night. Anyway, and you probably ought to hear this from me first, she and I got into a fight."

Rod tried to imagine the straight as an arrow Butch and a woman in a fight. He stammered, "What? Are you talking about a fist fight?"

"Exactly," Butch said and continued to shake his head. "One night after the conference, we had a pretty good poker game going. Just a friendly game. I mean the stakes weren't that high but . . . " Butch drifted off into deep thought.

"Butch, come on. What happened?" Rod prodded.

"All right, now this is between you and me. It doesn't go any further than right here, agreed?"

"Agreed."

"I can still remember the hand. Five card, draw two poker and I had two jacks and two sevens. I was drawing for a full house. It was an unbelievable hand. I had been watching the cards pretty closely and I had been having some great hands all evening. I drew and pulled the card. It was a seven and completed the full house. I raised. It went around the table. When we laid cards, nobody had anything. At least no one had me beat. I raked the winnings over and all of a sudden Millie threw her cards at me. She shoved the table and spilled everybody's liquor. It took everybody by surprise. I can still remember Brooks, the DA up in Greensboro. He must have been pretty high. He started trying to scrape his drink off the table back into his glass. Now Millie could drink you under the table. I knew she had had a few like the rest of us but I didn't realize how screwy she was. She didn't come straight out and say I was cheating but she implied it. We were in each other's face and out of nowhere, she hit me on the side of the face with her fist. I should've backed up and let it go but instinctively I popped her right on the chin. She didn't go down to my surprise. I had seen guys just as big as she is go down with a punch lighter than that. She's six feet two inches to my five feet ten. They jumped between us before it got any worse. It's a good thing. Truthfully she might have killed me."

"How did it go after that?" Rod asked still trying to imagine his boss trying to deck a woman and not just any woman, but the woman who would be the judge trying the capital case scheduled to start in less than an hour.

"Well, as you can imagine, it has always been strained. After she was appointed Superior Court Judge, she would occasionally rotate into our district. I always avoided her. In fact when Down was my assistant. I would send him in to prosecute in front of her." Butch smiled for the first time since he started remembering Godboldt. "You know, Ben and she have a little history too. I'd love to see his face when he finds out Millie the Mauler will be presiding."

Rod asked, "Do you want me to go with you when you meet her in her office?"

"Oh, yeah. She always likes to talk to the DA's who will be prosecuting in front of her. She likes to take them through the drill.

Come to think of it, let's call Down and get him over there for a visit too. We'll offer him the voluntary manslaughter plea during our meeting with her. Then if he doesn't take it, maybe she will turn her anger toward him instead of dredging up old memories."

*   *   *

Ben opened the door for Randy as they stepped into the judge's chambers on the second floor of the Judicial Center. As they walked in, Ben told the secretary that he and Ms. Bost were present whenever the Judge was ready to see them. Learning that the judge wanted to wait until the DA arrived before starting the conference, Ben laid his briefcase on the coffee table in the office and took a seat. He opened his briefcase and started a review of the witness list for the trial.

Randy took a seat beside Ben and asked, "What did the doctor say about Margaret?"

"She had gone in for a mammogram and when the results came back, he noticed something. I'm not sure what it is but it is a small place, maybe a centimeter in size. The doctor told her that given her history, you know, her mother had breast cancer, and given the size and location of the growth, she needed to see a surgeon for a needle biopsy to be performed. So last week he sent her to the hospital for several tests to make sure she could handle the procedure. When she gets the results of these tests back, the doctor will arrange the procedure for the biopsy."

"How is Margaret handling all of this?"

"Like a trooper. She went through this with her mother so she knows what to expect. Margaret always seems to be pretty strong but I don't know how she will take it if it turns out to be cancer." Ben had a worried look and laid the list down.

"Well, how are you taking it?"

"Not as well. Margaret is my life. If anything happened to her, . . . " he said without finishing the thought. "She's the anchor on this ship."

"Margaret is special," Randy observed. "In fact both of you are special to me. When I came to Wilmington, I didn't know anybody and now I feel like both of you are my second parents." She hesitated and laid her hand on his. "Hope you get good news, Ben."

Ben agreed and then remained silent. When he spoke, he asked, "How are you coming with the Big Burger discovery requests?"

Randy turned a little red in the face as she thought about the UPS shipment of discovery interrogatories and deposition requests from Big Burger's attorneys in Atlanta. "I am swamped. I worked as much as I could over the weekend but I didn't even make a dent in it. They knew that I was involved in this murder trial and timed it so that I would get the material just before the trial began. I wonder what else they have in store for me."

"Can James help?"

"He's offered but frankly between his practice and the work we've asked him to do on the Wanda Stickley case, I don't think he can do very much."

"I'll be glad to help if I can."

"No, you've got the first chair in Wanda's case. You need to stay focused on her defense."

Butch and Rod came into the judge's office. Rod smiled at Randy and went over to where they were seated while Butch asked the secretary to let the judge know that all of the attorneys were present for the conference.

Butch joined them and said, "Glad you were able to come on over. The judge wants to meet with us before court starts."

"Always glad to accommodate, Butch," Ben commented dryly.

"Did you get a copy of Judge Allgood's fax denying your motion to suppress the defendant's statements?" Butch asked.

Randy answered, "We have it but why didn't he just announce his ruling in court? Why did we get faxed?"

Butch grinned a little sheepishly and said, "Oh, yes. I forgot to mention but there has been a change in plans concerning the trial. Judge Allgood is sick and will not be available for the trial. He wanted to get his ruling to us as quickly as he could so the case would not be delayed because of his illness. Another judge has been assigned."

"Who?" Ben asked.

Butch smiled ear to ear as though he were about to explode with the news. He announced with a flair, "The Honorable Millicent Godboldt."

Ben started to respond with "Oh, my . . ." when a tall woman walked out of judge's chambers into the hallway and started toward the lobby. She had red hair that was flecked with gray and rolled into a large bun. Though she was in her late sixties, she stood upright and towered over all of the attorneys. Her face wore a grim expression as though she had just heard the worst news. She carried her hands behind her and walked stiffly as she approached them.

When she was close enough, she stared directly at Butch and in a stern voice stated, "You people are slipping down here, Butch. I didn't see a bailiff in sight when I drove into the parking lot this morning. I had to come in and call the Sheriff to have a bailiff meet me in the parking lot to bring my books and things in. Wouldn't've happened in my era, not for a minute."

"Yes, ma'am," Butch responded. "I'll talk to the Sheriff about it myself. We'll see that that doesn't happen . . . ."

She ignored Butch's promise and talked over Butch. She looked at all four attorneys and said, "Come on into chambers and let's get started."

As they all filed in, they stood and waited to be seated. Judge Godboldt assumed the chair behind the desk and motioned for everyone to sit down. When everyone had located a seat, she spoke again.

"Mr. Down, long time, no see. I hear you are no longer with the DA's office here and they say you've made a pretty good lawyer. Any truth to it?"

Ben smiled at the compliment especially since it came from someone who did not usually share a pleasant conversation. "Let me say with all modesty that Your Honor is correct on both counts. I've done my duty with the right honorable DA and I've taken to defending the poor, the pitiful and the innocent."

Judge Godboldt did not let a smile disassemble her firm visage; nevertheless, Ben continued, "Judge, I would like for you to meet Randy Bost. She is an attorney here in Wilmington. We share offices together over at the old Rice Building. She is joining me in this fight for the right."

Judge Godboldt nodded at Randy and tapped her finger lightly on the table in annoyance at Ben's second attempt at humor. She still did not smile but asked referring to Rod, "Butch, I see you've got a new face in your office. Who is this gentleman?"

Rod nodded and smiled pleasantly at Judge Godboldt. Butch made the introduction. "Rod Pemberton, Your Honor. He has been an assistant with me for about four years. He's one of the most able young men I've had working in this office. He will be assisting me in prosecuting this case on Wanda Stickley."

"Carrying you, more than likely," she responded again without smiling.

Butch attempted a feeble smile and looked over at Ben. Ben pretended not to notice Butch's awkwardness and continued to watch the judge. Judge Godboldt took command immediately and said, "Now you need to know this is not a conference about the Wanda Stickley case. I know I have been assigned down here to try this one case but as you also know, our case law does not permit the judge and the attorneys to meet in a capital case without the defendant being present. This is a meeting about right and wrong."

She looked harshly at the four attorneys as if waiting for someone to challenge her assessment of the meeting. She continued her pronouncement in the same high pitched tone as though she were giving marching orders to her troops.

"Now is that Miss or Mrs. Bost?"

"Miss, Your Honor," Randy replied.

"Now Miss Bost and Mr. Pemberton, all of this will be new to you but it will be old hat to Mr. Yeager and Mr. Down. They have heard all of this before but they could use a refresher." She stared directly at Butch and said, "There is a right way and a wrong way to do things. We will do them the right way, right?"

Butch nodded dutifully and she turned her attention to the other attorneys. "This is a meeting about court in general and how it ought to be conducted. You need to hear this directly from me and you need to hear this up front," she said as she reached back and punched the bun of hair at the back of her head to make sure that it was in place. "It's important and I will cover this one time."

Ben smiled and she asked, "Did you have a point to make, Mr. Down?"

"No, Your Honor. but I did want to say it is nice to see that you haven't lost your charm."

"I've been flattered by the best. Stow it, Mr. Down." She leaned slightly forward in the chair and talked directly to Ben as she continued with the instruction. "Now, first, call me Your Honor. Do not call me Judge. Judge is a title not a form of professional address. Call each other Mr. or Miss or Mrs. And specifically not Ms. Do not get personal or informal by using first names. Neglect your duty and you will spend the night in the jail."

She hesitated for a moment and made eye contact with each attorney in the room. "All right then. Next stand when you are speaking to me; sit when you are questioning a witness. Never speak directly to your opponent. And never, never argue with each other. Neglect your duty and you will spend the night in the jail. Never ask to approach the bench. There is no worse sight in the courtroom than a bunch of lawyers draped over the judge's bench like a bunch of monkeys."

The judge looked around the room at each lawyer again and announced. "Dress like a lawyer: black, gray, blue, maybe brown. Accouterments are to be businesslike. No Mickey Mouse ties like you are wearing Butch."

Butch looked down at his tie and Ben smiled again. The judge noticed. "Mr. Down, wear socks."

"Your Honor, this is a beach community and at times it is the custom to be bare ankle. Even businessmen . . . "

"Socks, Mr. Down. Neglect of duty is a night in jail."

Before Ben had occasion to argue the point further, the judge turned her attention to Randy. "Miss Bost, nothing tight fitting in the courtroom. You want the jurors thinking about your case and your client. We don't want them distracted and thinking about a roll in the hay with the attorney."

"Yes, ma'am."

"No chewing gum, no candy, cigarettes, cigars, chewing tobacco, or snuff. And stand up on your hind legs when you are addressing the court like God meant for you to. And when you come into court, stay in court. Go out at the recess."

As she said the words, "Neglect of duty", Ben mouthed the words with her, "and you spend the night in jail."

"Now Mr. Down, except for an episode or two, you were a pleasure to work with when I served here many years ago. That hasn't changed, has it?"

"No, Your Honor."

"Good," she snapped and stood up. "Now let's get out there and pick a jury."

As everyone started to stand, Butch said, "Oh, there is one more thing, Your Honor. We have been talking settlement and so far we have not been able to reach an agreement concerning a plea. I did want to say that just so that everyone understands, we are offering a plea of voluntary manslaughter to the defendant with sentencing entirely in Your Honor's discretion."

Ben cut his eyes at Butch and started to speak directly to him. Remembering the rule he spoke instead to the judge. "Your Honor, this is hardly the place or time to be discussing a plea since it puts us on such a spot with Your Honor. I will carry the plea offer to my client and we will attempt to resolve it as soon as we can."

Judge Godboldt responded, "Plea bargain all you want but it will not slow down the trial. We are going out there and we are going to select a jury. If you reach an agreement about the plea, put it in writing and we'll take it up. Until then let's go to trial."

*   *   *

Jury selection began promptly at 10:00 a.m. with Judge Godboldt's order to the bailiff: "Lock all the doors". Of the six hundred and fifty jurors who had been summoned to appear over the next three days in groups of two hundred per day, due to excuses and attrition from nonservice of summons approximately eighty jurors waited patiently on this first day of court for instructions from the judge. Judge Godboldt turned her attention immediately to the jurors.

"Welcome, ladies and gentlemen. I am Millicent Godboldt. I am a Resident Superior Court Judge from Elizabeth City and I've been assigned by the Chief Justice of North Carolina to preside over this session of Superior Court in New Hanover County. For those of you who are appearing for jury service, I will have detailed instructions for you later but first let me speak to all of you here in the courtroom. These are the rules. The doors are locked for a reason. No one enters and no one exits until recess. So be here on time and plan to stay until we recess. Our schedule is posted on the courtroom door. Suffice it to say that we will adhere to the schedule."

She stopped abruptly and swept the courtroom with a steely glare giving each person the impression that she was looking directly at them. After a few moments of silence she continued. "Now about hats in the courtroom," she boomed.

A couple of jurors who had neglected to remove his hat immediately removed it. One juror was so self-conscious about it that he slipped his hat off of his head and slid it down the side of his face so as to be less conspicuous.

The judge continued with numerous orders of decorum in the courtroom giving everyone "due notice" as she put it that the court would be conducted with respect and dignity. When she was satisfied that sufficient instructions had been given about what was expected of the spectators, she turned her attention to the jurors. After hearing several requests for excuse from jury service and then having the panel of jurors sworn to serve for the duration of the case, she introduced the attorneys, related the basic information concerning the case and informed the jurors of the possible penalties: death or life imprisonment without parole, if the defendant was convicted of first degree murder. When she concluded her general orientation she directed the clerk to "call twelve into the box".

"To the twelve of you as you presently constitute the jury in this matter, I will tell you before we start the voir dire or questioning of the jurors that there are no cameras in this courtroom. I won't permit it. Too much television in court already. Even if there were cameras in here, the reporters could not cover jury selection. I tell you that so that you understand that we need frank, complete responses from you in regard to questions from the lawyers and from the court."

The twelve jurors listened attentively as they tried to adjust to their new role of being seated up front and faced with the prospect of having to answer questions by the judge and the lawyers.

Judge Godboldt said, "Well, let's get right to it. How many of you have heard, read or seen something about this matter in the press, that is, newspaper, radio or television, or for that matter from any source, for example, a neighbor, a friend or family member? Indicate by raising your hand."

Eleven hands went up. Judge Godboldt tapped her finger on the table and directed her next question to the lone juror who had not heard anything about the case.

"Sir, you haven't heard anything about this case from any source?"

"No, Your Honor."

"And how is that, sir?"

"I just returned from South America. I work for American Tobacco and I was there for the last six months on business."

Several people in the audience laughed and Judge Godboldt turned her grim visage toward the audience. She did not speak for several moments. "There is nothing humorous here," she scolded. "This is serious business and if you want to stay among the free, treat it that way."

When she returned to the jurors, she explained that hearing something about the case would not necessarily be a ground for excuse and in order to be removed from the jury, the juror must have formed some opinion about the guilt or innocence of the defendant or must be so influenced by what he had heard or read that the juror could not set that aside and enter the trial with an open mind. After the instruction she inquired of each juror and was assured that each had formed no opinions about the case and could be fair and impartial. Next she turned to the subject of the death penalty.

"Well," she said, "here it is then. As you know the possible penalties in this case are death or life imprisonment without parole if Mrs. Stickley is convicted of first degree murder. I want each one of you to take a look across this courtroom at the defendant seated at the table across from you." Each juror looked at Wanda who was seated between Ben and Randy. "Now. If you are chosen as a juror in this case and if you are convinced beyond a reasonable doubt that she is guilty of first degree murder, could you and would you be able to consider and impose on her, if it's called for by the evidence and the law as you find it, death?"

The courtroom grew quiet. Each juror studied Wanda, some carefully and some very quickly then turned their attention back to the judge. Judge Godboldt stared directly at Wanda and then at her watch. "Time for a recess," she noted. "I want each of you to consider what I have just asked you and when we return from recess I will ask for your answer."

After the jurors were taken out and the bailiff announced the recess, Ben leaned over to Wanda and whispered, "We've got some important business to discuss during recess. I'll come back to lockup in a few minutes."

The courtroom officers led Wanda back to the holding cell while Ben and Randy had a whispered conference in the hallway behind the courtroom.

Ben asked, "What do you think about 'The General'?"

"Judge Godboldt?" she asked.

"Yes, that's what we used to call her in the old days. She hasn't lost much of her punch."

"She's pretty tough but at least she is telling us up front what the rules are. I can live with that. What do you think about Butch's offer?"

Ben did not respond directly. He looked around to see if anyone was listening. Except for a couple of probation officers at the far end of the hall, they had the area to themselves. "I got a call last week from Senator A. Fowler Worrell from South Carolina. He was interested in Wanda's case, said he was getting pressure from women's groups to do something to help Wanda. He wanted to know if we would plead guilty to voluntary manslaughter. He also said he knew Butch because they were students together many years ago. He said he would call Butch and get him to offer us the voluntary manslaughter plea."

"That's pretty strange. What's it all about?"

"You are exactly right. Something strange is going on behind the scenes. I don't know what it's about and I'm not sure we will ever know but at least it's working in our favor."

"Do you think the Senator called?"

"I don't know but Butch is offering us voluntary manslaughter," Ben remarked with a look of pleasant surprise on his face.

"I can't believe it either. I thought my heart was going to jump out of my chest when he said that. I never thought we would get that from the DA."

"I know it," Ben said. "It's a slap on the wrist. But, you know, Butch is setting us up. He announced the plea in front of Judge Godboldt. If we don't take it, the judge will think we are fools, and we will be, and worse she will know we are the reason she is sitting there for several weeks to try this case. It could generate a little heat in the courtroom and guess whose butts will be on the skillet."

Randy smiled and replied, "Not necessarily. Maybe The General will have you doing push ups. After all," she said as she punched her index finger into his stomach, "you could use a little work."

Ben smirked and retorted, "All right, all right. Let's get on with it. Let's go sell this plea to Wanda."

"Do you think she will take it?"

"She'd better. This is a great deal. She could get out in two years, four years tops. Now is the best time to discuss it. The State's case is strong, our case is weak and the judge has the jurors trying to decide over recess whether they could put her to death. Let's give it our best shot."

Ben and Randy were let into the holding cell where Wanda was being held during the trial. Wanda was standing at the window staring out at the Wilmington skyline. Although the injuries on her face were gone except for a few light lines on her neck, she looked gaunt. Although most prisoners adjust to imprisonment after the first thirty days and typically gain weight, Wanda had done just the opposite. She looked very thin and tired as she leaned against the window frame. When they came in, Wanda joined them at the table.

Ben led off. "Wanda, it's been a long time but we are finally up to bat."

"Five months," she remarked.

Randy spoke next. "At least the waiting is over. We will find out what is going to happen."

Wanda smiled and nodded in agreement. Ben asked, "Do you know Senator Fowler Worrell from South Carolina?"

Wanda asked, "Why do you want to know?"

"I believe we have some powerful people helping us in this case and I am trying to figure out why."

"I don't really know him," Wanda said, "but I met him years ago. He and Ralph were in politics together and they were going to invest in some land deal. I met him at Figure Eight Island at a reception. It was supposed to be about buying some land out on Figure Eight. Ralph grew up hunting and fishing off the Island and he knew a lot of the people out there. He had found a pretty large tract of land that had some drainage problems. He and Senator Worrell were going to buy the land and develop it but the EPA got involved and it pretty much fell apart. Then Ralph got into some trouble and I never heard any more about the Senator. Is he the one trying to help?"

"I'm not sure," Ben responded, "but we've got a plea offer. This morning when we met with Judge Godboldt, the District Attorney offered voluntary manslaughter." Ben searched her eyes for any sign of acceptance or relief. "Sentencing is in the discretion of the judge."

"What sentence can be imposed?" she asked. "I know you told me earlier when we were going over the charge and the elements but what can happen?"

"The judge can sentence you to prison for up to forty-seven months. In order to do that, she would have to find aggravating factors. As we have discussed before, there are aggravating factors. Since you have no prior criminal record, I believe that she would not find any aggravators and sentence in the presumptive range which would be twenty-five months."

Randy added, "You have credit for five months awaiting trial so you would be eligible for release in less than two years."

"Do I have to plead guilty?"

Ben responded, "Yes, but only to voluntary manslaughter not murder. I know the DA and he will not allow a no contest plea or an Alford plea in which you plead guilty but deny in fact you are guilty."

Wanda was silent. She got up from the table and walked back over to the window. In the distance she could see the location of the USS North Carolina, a ship from World War II that had been docked in Wilmington for tourists to visit. She remembered visiting there a couple of years before with Jeremy and his Scout troop. As she watched, she could make out a distant figure climbing the steps to the fore deck. "You know," she spoke quietly and unemotionally, "I may never get out of here."

Ben looked at Randy and shook his head. He could feel a tightness in his chest as he thought back to his law professor's description of the psychic vortex. He was slowly being squeezed into the focus of the vortex, the trial that no one wanted.

"Wanda," he said as he joined her at the window, "what's wrong with this plea?"

"It's not the truth. I didn't kill Ralph."

"Well, who did?"

"I don't know."

"Jeremy?"

"No," she snapped back emphatically.

"Wanda," Ben pleaded, "think about Jeremy. You have been away from him for five months. If you plead not guilty, the State of

North Carolina wants to put you to death. You could die. Even if you are not sentenced to die, you could spend the rest of your life in prison. With this plea you will see Jeremy. You will be out of prison while he is still a young man."

"The plea is a lie. It's not the truth."

"But.´ But it may not be the truth but it's a lie you can live with. Literally."

She continued to stare out of the window. "Ralph would love this. He is still torturing me even in death." She turned toward Ben and stared directly into his eyes. "Ben, I have thought about this a long time. I have lost Jeremy. There is no way I can get Jeremy back. Even with a voluntary manslaughter plea. The State will never give him back to me. And by the time I get out, he will be a man not the little boy I cooked for, drove for, sewed for. It's a harsh reality but Ralph has won. I lost. Jeremy is gone."

"That's not . . . ," Ben argued.

Wanda raised her hand. "It is true." She turned to stare out of the window again. Ben noticed that all of the marks and bruises had healed on the outside but the pain inside had hardened. He saw the resolution on her face and heard the strength in her voice.

She spoke calmly. "Jeremy turned fourteen the other day. I wasn't there. I won't ever be there. My only hope is to stand by the truth. I did not kill Ralph Stickley. What I did I did to defend myself. If I am found not guilty, I will walk out of this courthouse in a few weeks and I can get my son back. That is my only hope and that is the only way I can win. If I am found guilty, I know that I may be sentenced to die or spend the rest of my life in prison. It's the only choice I am willing to make and it's the chance I have to take. God help me."

CHAPTER FIFTEEN

"Fowler, this is Butch. How are you doing this morning?"

"Fine, Butch." The Senator cut off the speaker, picked up the phone and pressed it close to his ear. "It was nice to talk to ya' the other day. You know we oughta stay in closer touch but life gets real busy. Y'know how it is."

"Oh, yes, sir," Butch replied. "How long has it been?"

"Too long, buddy," the Senator responded half-heartedly as though he were still working on some project at his desk.

"I saw you on C-SPAN the other day at the memorial service for Vice President Anderson," Butch said as he slowly worked up to the main reason for the telephone call.

"The Senate finally paid tribute to 'im. I don't know what took so long but you know how Congress is. I tell you, people are funny, Butch. They love politicians a lot more when they're dead. I wished they loved us half as much while we're alive."

Butch laughed at the Senator's joke and then turned serious. "I saw his widow and their children. She looked like she had recovered pretty well from her injuries."

"Yeah, Butch. I think she is gonna be all right. She's still in that wheelchair. I talked to her for a moment and she said she was hopin' to be walkin' by next spring. She's a strong woman. Southern by birth. She can take it, boy. By the way how is that case goin'? Ya'll able to put that little matter to bed?"

"That's what I'm calling about, Fowler." Butch hesitated then blurted out the bad news. "They wouldn't take the voluntary manslaughter plea."

"They what?" The Senator was immediately irate and Butch could hear his hand slamming the table. "My Gawd, are they a bunch a fools up theah? You offered 'em the courthouse. I mean it's a fair deal and all but they musta lost their mind."

"I'm as disappointed as you are. We are going to be trying a case that doesn't need to be tried and we have been as fair and reasonable as we know how."

"What's that lawyer's name again?" he asked in disgust.

"Down, sir. It's Ben Down."

"He's a fool. You are tryin' somebody for murder and tryin' to get 'em executed and he won't take a little ol' plea, a manslaughter plea, that's going to save her life. He ain't got no business bein' a lawyer if he can't do any bettah than that. Does he know how much trouble he can be in? I mean, my Gawd, man, he will have a rain of hell and fury down on 'im for being so stupid. Worse than Sherman burnin' Georgia."

Butch found himself in the uncomfortable position of having to defend Ben and feebly offered, "It's his client, Fowler. She just will not take the plea."

"That's crap, Butch, and you know it. What lawyer, what good lawyer can't even persuade his own client to step out of the shadow of the gas chamber? I mean, ya'll still gas 'em up theah, don't ya, Butch? Christ, that boy will pay the piper ovah this." The Senator grew quiet for a moment after he realized that he had become way too angry over the subject. After he calmed down for a moment, he asked, "How far are ya'll along in this case anyway?"

Butch was a little relieved. He hated to disappoint his old friend and especially someone as powerful as the Senator. It was nice to be able to report on something that was a lot more favorable. "We have finished jury selection and Judge Godboldt has us scheduled to start opening statements later this morning. Our case is quite strong: a confession, murder weapon with defendant's prints all over it, lot of circumstantial evidence, maybe a surprise or two along the way. We've got an excellent case."

The Senator took a deep breath and sounded a lot more relaxed. "Right. How long will the trial take?"

"We'll take a couple of weeks to put our witnesses up. Down will very likely offer evidence. I guess two or three days for defense evidence, maybe a week. All of it shouldn't last more than four more weeks."

"Well, heah it is, Butch. Our people ain't gonna like this. We're still holding back the floodgates. Telephone calls worse than when Strom Thurmond was filibusterin' the Senate over segregation. You keep workin' on ol' Down. Make him take that plea, heah?"

"I'll do what I can, Fowler, but he's tough-minded. Once he makes up his mind he won't budge."

"We'll see about that."

*   *   *

Judge Godboldt punched the bun in her hair and turned toward the jurors. "Ladies and gentlemen," she announced, "you have now been selected and impaneled to serve as the jurors in the case of the State of North Carolina versus Wanda Stickley. There are fourteen of you, twelve regular jurors and two alternate jurors. We need your undivided attention over the next several days. We expect it and justice requires it."

She stopped and punctuated the silence with a stare into the eyes of each juror. When she was satisfied she had them sufficiently indoctrinated, she continued. "Your duty is simple. Hear the evidence, find the facts from the evidence, apply the law to the facts that you find and finally let your verdict speak the everlasting truth. Now we are ready to begin this case with the opening statements of the attorneys. Bear in mind these statements are not evidence. They are given as a forecast of what the attorneys believe the competent, admissible evidence will be. Under our rules the State goes first, then the defendant. I will now ask you to give your attention to Mr. Yeager."

The District Attorney stood and approached the jury box. When he assumed a position squarely in front of the jury box, he looked at his watch then stared for several moments at the clock in the courtroom. When the second hand reached the twelve on the clock face showing ten o'clock, Butch spoke.

"Life is precious. In fact every minute of life is precious." He checked the courtroom clock again. "Ralph Stickley has been dead for 215,976 minutes. Yes, it's a long time." Butch paused again and let several seconds tick off. When he had all of the jurors watching the clock, he continued watching the clock himself and began speaking again. "He will be dead forever. For as long as the hands on that courthouse clock tick off the minutes. He will be dead when those hands have turned to rust and finally to dust. When he lost his precious life, the world was changed forever. Time stopped for him. But it continued for us. We have been given an important duty. We must use our time on this earth, our precious time to pursue justice for Ralph Stickley, a man whose time was cut short."

Butch walked over to the defense table and stared directly at Wanda. He lifted his hand slowly like the hand on the clock and pointed at her. "Cut short by this woman. Wanda Stickley."

Butch walked back to the jury box and looked at his watch again. "Time. Precious time. I would like to speak to you about your time over the next several days. I would like to give you a forecast of what is to come. You will hear Ralph Stickley and Wanda Stickley were formerly married and at the time of his death, they were divorced. You will hear their relationship was stormy. You will hear that Ralph was at times violent. You will hear that that was only one side of Ralph Stickley. The side that Wanda Stickley brought out in him. You will hear from Ralph's mother. She will tell you that Ralph did a lot of good for a lot of people and it was only when Wanda Stickley was involved, that Ralph was, well, less than he should have been."

Butch began pacing back and forth in front of the jury box as he talked. "And you will hear evidence that will make your skin crawl. Officers will tell you how they found Ralph, you will hear from a small army of evidence technicians, and you will hear directly from the detectives who investigated this crime. And when it is all said and done, you will hear how Wanda Stickley overreacted to Ralph's return to her property, how she stabbed him with a screwdriver, how she shot him, how she cut him with a knife. You will hear how he was unarmed. You will hear, and I can barely say this without a shiver running up my back--and I have tried more gruesome murder cases than I care to remember--you will hear how Wanda Stickley used a knife to kill Ralph Stickley, an unarmed man. Sure you will hear he should not have been on her property, but you will also know that no one, not Wanda Stickley, not anyone has the right to do what she did to him."

Butch leaned over and whispered to the jurors. "In the dead of the night. After she had stabbed him and after she had shot him and after he retreated trying to get away from her, she stalked him, stalked him right out into the night. Can you see her as Ralph labored with his injured body trying to escape the wrath of Wanda Stickley? She is carrying a knife. She trails him out into the driveway. He falls, never to rise more, and she stands over him."

The courtroom was silent as Butch spun his web of violence and evil. His voice began to ascend as he related the events leading up to Ralph's death. "He's down, he's unarmed, he's injured. He's defenseless. She leans over him and cuts his throat in long, slow slashing cuts on both sides of his throat. While he is still alive and drowning in his own blood, she opens his pants and cuts off his penis. Ralph is helpless, powerless at this point. She drives his penis into his throat and finishes the job by ripping open his shirt. While the blood drains from the gaping wounds to his throat and flows down the driveway, and while he chokes on his own penis, she who has done the unspeakable now does the unthinkable. She slowly carves an R into his chest."

Butch stopped and let the horror of it all sink in. He noticed that a lady on the back row began to shake her head. He looked directly at her and said, "That's right. That's right. And it happened right here in our little ol' neck of the river, not in New York, not in L.A. but right here. I know it's hard to believe and at first you don't want to believe it but you will believe it."

He stepped back and spoke to all of the jurors. "You will believe it in time." Butch looked up at the clock and watched the second hand move. He looked back at the jurors who were watching the clock as well. "You will believe it in Ralph Stickley's time. He's got all the time in the world to be dead forever, dead by her bloody hands." He sat down.

Judge Godboldt recognized Ben who stood, removed his watch and laid it on the defense table. Ben walked to the jury box and said, "This case is not about time. We'll take the time necessary here to see that everyone is treated fairly and to see that justice is done. This case is about the truth. The truth, plain and simple."

Ben walked over to the judge's bench and pointed at the Great Seal of the State of North Carolina which was posted on the front of the bench. He pointed at the Latin phrase across the bottom of the seal. "Esse Quam Videri," he read. "Does anyone know what that means? Sure we do. We learned in school that it means 'to be rather than to seem'. It's our motto here in North Carolina and it's a standard that we believe in. The truth rather than what appears to be the truth."

Ben scanned the jurors and walked back to the jury box. He said, "A trial is the search for the truth. The judge just told you that your duty is to find the facts, the truth, and not just what seems to be the truth. The truth. Well, let's talk about the truth that you will hear in this case. You will hear about Ralph Stickley. And the truth about Ralph Stickley is that he was at one time a good man, a respected man, a man with whom Wanda Stickley fell in love. Out of that love was born a child Jeremy. But things changed, Ralph Stickley changed. His business went bad and he went with it. He became violent, unbelievably brutal in fact. He separated himself from Wanda, he assaulted her, he attacked her, he served time for assaulting her, he was so angered at serving time for assaulting her that he came back and raped her. He was sentenced in this very courtroom for raping Wanda to a term of imprisonment. It seemed he was serving a sentence but the truth is he had escaped from prison when he returned to Wanda Stickley's house. He returned to finish the job he had started long ago. He had returned to kill her. And the truth is she was terrified of him. And she had reason to be. And the truth is he came back, broke into her home under the cover of darkness, hid in the basement and attacked her. And the truth is it was a brutal, vicious attack. She defended herself as well as she could. She does admit she hit him with a screwdriver, she did shoot him to repel his attack. She had to. It was live or die. As you will learn though, he did not die from being hit with the screwdriver or from being shot. He died from the wounds to his neck that were so graphically described for you by the DA."

Ben walked back to the defense table and stood behind Wanda. "And the truth. The truth is she did not kill him. She did not inflict the wounds that caused his death. The DA's evidence will make it seem that she did kill him. But the truth is she did not. She did admit what she did and she has denied cutting his neck, cutting off his penis, and cutting an R into his chest. Remember this: there is no direct evidence that she produced any of these wounds. The DA's evidence will only make it seem that she did. She has admitted what she did. She has explained what she did not do. And there is no eyewitness, there is no one, absolutely no one who will tell you she caused his death. The evidence will show she was terrorized by Ralph Stickley, that what she did was in self defense, and that the evidence is not convincing beyond a reasonable doubt that she committed the acts that caused his death."

Ben assumed a position in front of the jury box again and pointed back at the Seal of the State of North Carolina. "To be rather than to seem. The truth rather than what seems like the truth. And the truth is when you have used your precious time, as the DA referred to it, you will very likely not know who killed Ralph Stickley. And the truth will be that you very likely will suspect who killed him and it will not be Wanda Stickley. And the truth will be that Wanda Stickley did not kill him and the truth will be that Wanda Stickley is not guilty."

Ben turned and walked by Butch's desk. He turned back to the jurors and stated, "I thank you for your time and I'll thank you for the truth."

As Ben sat, Judge Godboldt startled everyone when she spoke loudly interrupting the silence as everyone contemplated what had been said by the attorneys. "Mr. Yeager, time is awasting. We await your first witness."

Butch stood, picked up The Bible from his desk and quickly responded, "The State calls as our first witness Mrs. Ruth Leslie Stickley."

A woman stood up at the front bench and walked toward the District Attorney who held out The Bible for her to be sworn. As she received the oath, she stood firmly then walked to the witness stand without looking at Wanda. Although she was in her early seventies, she was alert and maintained a stern visage. She arranged her dress and adjusted one of the several rings on her fingers.

"Ma'am, state your name for us and where you live," Butch directed in a loud, firm voice.

"I am Ruth Leslie Stickley. I live in Wilmington."

"Tell the men and women of the jury how you are related to Ralph Stickley."

She looked a little surprised at the question but answered without hesitation. "I am Ralph Stickley's mother."

Butch showed her a picture of Ralph. She identified it as a picture of Ralph which was taken at a wedding of his cousin about five years earlier. He wore a suit and tie and had a charming smile. She did not remark except to note it was the last picture that she had of him. Butch introduced the photograph into evidence, placed it on an evidence table near the witness stand and turned it to face the jurors during the trial.

Butch quickly took her through Ralph's personal history: an only child, a star athlete in high school, college student, excellent business man, budding politician. Her report was devoid of much feeling as she remembered the events of his life but she did get a little animated when she mentioned the marriage to Wanda.

"After he married Wanda, Ralph changed." She said without acknowledging Wanda's presence. "His interest in his business properties declined. In fact he started a long slow decline. She kept him in court over every little thing. He resorted to alcohol and wound up losing almost everything. If it weren't for his friends helping him with his finances, he would have, well, ..."

Butch gave her a moment or two to see if she would finish her thought. When she did not, he asked, "When was the last time you saw Ralph?"

"Here in this courtroom. He was being sentenced over something with Wanda. The so-called rape I think it was."

Butch asked for permission to approach the witness. When the judge granted the request, Butch picked up a photo from a stack of photos of the autopsy of Ralph Stickley, marked it State's exhibit two, and walked to the witness. He handed her the photo and waited for her reaction to the gruesome picture. She briefly viewed the photo, laid it on the bar at the witness stand, and without conveying much of what she was thinking or feeling, turned toward Butch.

"I know this is difficult for you, Mrs. Stickley, but I must ask, can you identify the person in this picture which I have marked State's exhibit two?"

"Yes, that is my son Ralph. Obviously taken after he was deceased." She did not look back at the picture.

Butch retrieved the exhibit quickly, asked that the picture be received in evidence and laid it by the other picture of Ralph. When Butch returned to his seat, he said, "Your witness, counsel."

Ben looked at Mrs. Stickley and said, "Ma'am, we are sorry for your loss and sorry that you had to go through this. We have no questions."

As she stepped down and returned to her seat, Judge Godboldt declared a fifteen minute recess. After the courtroom cleared somewhat, Ben, Randy and Jim Wilkes huddled in conference.

Randy spoke first. "I don't know, Ben. I know we agreed that we would not ask her any questions from a tactical standpoint but she said several things that need to be refuted."

"I agree but she is not the witness to do it with. That jury will be sympathetic to a mother who has lost a son even if she was somewhat emotionless. No need to get the jurors angry with us right at the start. Jim, what did you think about her testimony?"

Jim leaned in. "I know one thing. She lied."

"Yeah, I noticed that," Ben retorted. "Your records showed she visited Ralph in Brunswick Correctional Center several times after he was sentenced. Strange. I don't know why she would say that the last time she saw him was here for the sentencing in the rape case. And another thing she said troubled me. When did Ralph Stickley ever have any friends that helped him with his finances? She hesitated after she said that too. I believe she didn't mean to say it. Something is not right."

Jim pointed to his briefcase where he kept a dossier on Ralph's business dealings. "He didn't have any friends, just complainants and creditors."

"And another thing bothers me," Ben continued. "What mother can look at an autopsy photo of her only son showing him butchered and mutilated without showing some emotion? She's a hard-hearted woman. Hard. I believe we had better take another look at Mrs. Ruth Leslie Stickley. Something is not right. I can't put my finger on it but something."

Jim made a note and stated, "I'll dig a little deeper."

After the recess Rod led off with Officer Creed who had been the first officer on the scene. Officer Creed described the wounds in some detail then by the end of direct examination, he placed Wanda, in his words, "like a deer caught in the headlights" standing directly over Ralph's body with the knife in hand. He admitted on cross-examination by Ben that he did not see Wanda pick up the knife, did not see Wanda do anything toward Ralph, and did not see Wanda make any of the wounds he had graphically depicted. Officer Creed was confused on whether she had the knife in her left hand or her right hand and waffled on his opinion of whether she had sufficient strength to produce the wounds he had seen.

Ben tried to exploit the weakness in his testimony by arguing with him. "Well, she is five feet four inches to his six feet two inches, isn't she, Officer?"

Creed stumbled over his words. "Uh, well, she'd shot him."

"And the truth is you don't know that, do you? You say she said that. But you didn't see it, now did you?"

When he did not respond for a moment, Ben half raised up from his seat implying the hesitation was important and raised his voice trying to make a big point for effect out of something that was of little consequence. "Did you? Did you?" he demanded.

Judge Godboldt thumped the bench with her fingernails. She was very familiar with the ploy, did not like it and intervened. She growled, "Give him time to answer, counsel."

"No, but I just meant that I thought she was strong enough to do that." He pointed to the photograph of Ralph's body.

Next Rod called Detective Foster as the lead investigator for the purpose of putting the case on the ground as the phrase is used. Foster testified to the chronological order of his investigation beginning with the call to go to the residence of Wanda Stickley. When he arrived, he said, Wanda was in the custody of Officer Morgan Creed and Ralph Stickley was dead. His body was in the driveway and in Foster's opinion, due to the fresh stream of blood that flowed from the body down the driveway, Ralph had just been killed. His description of the grotesque wounds on the body was emotionless and his detailed analysis of the scene was disjointed and lackluster. Even so, he basically diagrammed the murder.

The battery of forensic scientists who followed were even more boring but they astutely fleshed out the schematic with conclusions and opinions that explained the significance of the evidence and connected the events to Wanda.

Randy held the technicians and scientific experts to the limited area of their expertise but even with that, the noose tightened dramatically around Wanda.

As they moved into the second week, a paint by numbers picture was beginning to emerge from the testimony. The physical evidence in the basement included drag marks beginning at the basement door and lots of hair on the basement floor. The hair was of the same color and type as Wanda's. Scuff marks on the back wall of the basement were photographed, marked and introduced into evidence.

The things on the table beside the place where the attack took place were in disarray as though "they had been knocked off in a scuffle".

A bloody screwdriver was found on the basement floor. The fingerprints belonged to Wanda; the blood belonged to Ralph. The small jagged hole in Ralph's side was consistent with a wound caused by the blunt end of the screwdriver.

The air in the basement was damp and had a distinct odor of gunpowder. "Consistent with the air where a gun had just been fired," an officer offered. No gun was ever found. There was blood on the floor and blood drops that trailed from the basement to the body in the driveway. The blood was Ralph's.

Wanda had scratch marks on her face, bruises on her neck and hair had been forcefully removed in several places from her head. The side of her face was swollen. She "gave the appearance of having been involved in a scuffle," another officer testified.

A bloody knife was identified as having been retrieved from beside of Ralph's body. The fingerprints were Wanda's; the blood was Ralph's. Officer Creed had identified the knife as being the one he observed Wanda holding as she stood over Ralph in the driveway.

The autopsy was lengthy due to the number of wounds. When Rod asked the medical examiner to sum up in layman's terms, he said, "Okay, but it's not easy. He had an older wound in the hip. He had a gunshot wound to the upper left shoulder. An entry wound in his side. His throat was cut on both sides, almost ear to ear. An R was carved into his chest. His penis was excised, that is, removed, and located in the back of his throat."

"Anything else, Doctor?" Rod inquired.

"Well, that's all I can think of. That's about enough, isn't it?"

Rod nodded in agreement and asked, "And in your opinion and to a reasonable medical certainty, can you tell us what caused the death of Ralph Stickley?"

"Oh, yes, sir. None of the wounds as bad as they were would have caused death except for the wounds to each side of the neck. The victim died as a result of exsanguination."

"And what is that, sir?"

"He bled to death."

Rod walked to the evidence table. He picked up the knife and approached the witness. "Doctor, let me show you what has been marked as State's Exhibit Thirty-eight, a knife bearing the fingerprints of the right index finger and ring finger of Wanda Stickley and still showing the blood of Ralph Stickley. Can you tell us if the wounds, except for the gunshot wound you described, could have been caused by this weapon?"

"Yes, sir. This knife could have produced these wounds."

"And finally, sir. Can you tell us whether he was alive or dead when these wounds, all of these wounds, were made?"

"He was alive."

"So he was alive when his throat was cut on both sides. He was alive when his member was cut off, that is, his penis was cut off. He was alive when it was rammed down his throat. And he was alive when the R was carved into him."

"Alive."

"Your witness, Ms. Bost."

As Randy made it clear on cross-examination that the witness's opinions only dealt with the cause of death and not with who caused the death, Rod leaned over to the defense table toward Ben.

"Butch assigned me the Noah Lyerly case," he whispered and checked to see if Judge Godboldt was noticing. "We're going to finish up our part of the case a little earlier than we thought this week and Judge Godboldt will probably not hold the jury over on Friday. What do you think about a little entertainment? Let's bring up Noah or Nora for a plea on Friday morning?"

"Voluntary manslaughter?" Ben inquired.

"I think so but let me run it by Butch to be sure."

"Sounds good to me but let me talk to my client first. I think she'll take the plea. It's fair enough but it's still up to her, him. I'll let you know tomorrow morning."

Randy concluded the examination and the judge announced recess for the evening. After everyone filed out, Ben and Randy moved to the lawyers' lounge and reviewed the case for purposes of an assessment.

Ben fumbled with his cigar while Randy started sipping on a soft drink. Ben reached for his briefcase to locate his file on Noah Lyerly. As he did, he mentioned that Rod wanted to call the Noah Lyerly case on Friday for a plea bargain. "They are getting pretty cocky when they want to do another murder case while this case is going on. Must think they have it sewed up."

"I think the wagons are circled. The Indians are closing in. And we are about to run out of bullets." Randy yawned and stretched reflecting the fatigue that was beginning to build from the case.

"Too pessimistic for me. We're doing all right. Everything they do to build a case of first degree murder adds fuel to the defense. It was self defense and the evidence is showing that too." Ben lit his cigar and shook the match slowly. "Besides nobody saw her do it. Residual doubt. If the jurors can't see her do it through the eyes of an eyewitness, they will still have that nagging doubt that our version is right. Somebody else did it."

"Rod will call Foster again for Wanda's confession. That will cinch it, I think," Randy tendered.

"Not necessarily. Wanda's version introduces the phantom. The one item the State cannot explain. I mean: she said she stabbed him, she shot him. Why lie about cutting his throat? She wouldn't know at the time she gave the statement that the wounds she said she inflicted would not cause his death." The match was still burning and Ben shook the match again to put out the flame.

Randy tried with some difficulty to follow the logic but it was late and she was tired. She watched the match through bleary eyes. When she finally commented, she said, "You know, one thing bothers me. Why is Butch letting Rod do just about all of the case? That's not like our illustrious DA."

"Yeah. Yeah." Ben pulled on the cigar as he pondered what it meant too. "Well, Butch is always in for the kill. Maybe there is something or someone we don't know about. Some . . . ." Before he could finish the thought, the match had burned down to his fingers. "Yeooow," he called out and shook his hand. He looked over at Randy and noticing how tired she was, he said, "We've got to get some rest. Go home. We'll talk about it tomorrow."

The next morning Rod led off with Detective Foster and went through the details of Wanda's statement about what had taken place during the attack in the basement. Ben crossed and emphasized that Wanda had not provoked the attack and was defending herself according to her version. Foster admitted that no weapon had ever been found and acknowledged that the gunshot residue test indicated that Wanda had not fired a gun on the night of the confrontation with Ralph.

Butch who had been out of the courtroom during the beginning of Foster's testimony entered quietly and sat beside of Rod. After the examination of the detective was concluded, Butch whispered to Rod then stood. As he spoke, he looked over at Ben and smiled slightly and slyly.

"Your Honor, if the court please. We would like to call our last witness Itzak Dundail."

A middle age gentleman arose and walked to the witness stand. As he was sworn and took a seat at the witness stand, Ben whispered to Randy. "He's on the witness list but he shouldn't have been last. He's going to tell us more than we knew about. Brace yourself. This is it. The smoking gun."

"Give us your name, sir." Butch stated confidently.

"Dundail. Itzak Vari Dundail."

"And where did you live in relation to Wanda Stickley on the night Ralph Stickley was killed, Mr. Dundail?"

"On the same street. About three houses down from Mrs. Stickley."

"Were you at home on the night in question?"

"Yes, sir."

"All right, sir. Tell us what you saw that evening."

"Well, I was in the living room reading the paper when I heard a noise. It sounded like a car had backfired or maybe gunfire. I walked outside to see what was going on. The sound came from the area where the Stickley house is located."

"What did you see when you went outside?"

"I didn't see anything at first. I was looking up toward the Stickley house. It was dark but I could see pretty good because of the streetlights in our area. Anyway. I saw one person come out of the house and fall. Another person came from the house and stood over him."

"What did you see the person who was standing over the other person do?"

"The one standing up bent down and made several motions toward him with their arm."

"What kind of motions?"

"Like they were slashing or striking at the other person."

"What was the person on the ground doing?"

"Holding up their arms like they were defending themselves."

"Go on."

"Well, I went inside and called 911. Just took a few seconds. I came back out. The two people were still there."

"What were they doing?"

"Same thing. One was standing up and one was layin' on the ground."

"What happened next?"

"I saw the lights of a car coming up the driveway. The lights of the car were on the two people."

"Were you able to see well enough to identify the person standing up?"

"Yes, sir."

"And was it a man or a woman?"

"A woman."

"And were you able to identify the person who was lying on the ground?"

"No, sir, but I could see it was a man and his arms were still flailing about."

"And is the woman you saw in this courtroom?"

Butch leaned forward in his seat and paused for effect. He looked over at the jurors then at Ben. His mouth turned up at the corner and he restrained the effort to let his face break into a full blown smile.

"Point her out."

He pointed directly at Wanda.

CHAPTER SIXTEEN

"We're in trouble," Ben said as he laid his briefcase on the table in the jail interview room. "I didn't think they had it but somehow they found an eyewitness."

Randy looked at Jim but spoke to Ben. "I'd say we are in trouble. I heard that you were at Childrey's Grill and Bar last night." She had a hardly concealed angry tone in her voice.

"Had to go for a consultation. It's no problem," Ben defended himself. "I always go there when it gets tough. The owner is a friend of mine. Jack's a former detective. Retired now but still pretty sharp especially in sizing up a case. I like to get his insight."

"Oh, yeah," Randy complained. "A consult with your friend Jack? Jack Daniels, I'd say. Come on, Ben. Let that stuff go while we work on this. There is too much at stake."

The detention center was busy for a Friday morning but even with the commotion of people moving about the facility, it grew uncomfortably quiet. Jim watched Ben and Randy to see what was going to happen next. Knowing the two personalities, he expected fireworks but Ben did not ignite over the criticism. He continued to look through his briefcase. Finally after he had rummaged through the stack of files and had laid out the case files for Wanda and Noah Lyerly, he looked up at Randy and did not seem to be very perturbed with her suspicion.

"Randy, keep your eye on the prize. You worry too much. Especially about the wrong things. I did have a couple of Jack Daniels on the rocks last night but my mind is as clear as the view over the ocean after a storm. Seriously here it is." He sat down and pointed toward the chairs for Randy and Jim. "When the State rested yesterday and Her Honor sent the jurors home until Monday, the government's case was strong. Too strong. Butch and Rod had laid out a pretty good case of first degree murder. Better than any of us thought it would be. The last witness, Dundail, nailed us to the wall on first degree and even worse, he laid out a death by torture which gets them into the penalty phase."

Randy, who had taken a seat across from Ben, seemed to let the Jack Daniels' comments slide for a moment as well. She offered some conciliation. "I thought you did a great job with him when you got him to agree with you that he must have been at the telephone more than a few seconds for the 911 call. That segway left plenty of time for 'the phantom'."

"I agree, Randy," Jim chimed in. "And he admitted to you that he could not say that the person he saw, who came out and slashed at Ralph Stickley, was Wanda Stickley. He could only identify her after the lights from the police vehicle shone on her."

Ben checked his watch to see if it was time for the turnkey to bring Wanda to the interview room. He still had a few minutes. He blew off the peace offering. "Save it. I didn't make enough head way with him. That jury didn't see a phantom when Dundail testified. The jurors saw Wanda cutting Ralph's throat while he was down. That's all they needed: a picture worth a thousand words of testimony. And I can hear Butch now. 'Ladies and gentlemen, there might have been self defense when she resisted Ralph in the basement but the case took a sharp turn when Wanda Stickley stabbed him, shot him, beat him off. She went too far. It became cold-blooded murder when she pursued him, tortured him while he was down and helpless, and killed him. I could see her do it just as Mr. Dundail did. First degree murder, plain and simple.' And if they get first degree murder, they get a shot at the death penalty. Who knows what a runaway jury will do?"

"Well, let's give them another picture," Jim argued. "Let Wanda testify."

Ben responded first. "Can't do it. Butch will eat her alive."

Randy agreed. "She has told too many lies about it. The DA will be able to show she lied about too many things. Her statements do not match the physical evidence. Butch will blow it up. He'll tell the jury: 'she's a liar, she's trying to protect herself and the reason: she's a killer.'"

"But," Jim tried to support his position, "she can tell the history and that may be enough to save her. The violence from Ralph, the assaults, the rape, the . . ."

"We can do that with Detective Ray Stanton. He investigated the first rape and the second rape. He will know the family background and the trail of violence. We can do that without submitting Wanda to an impeaching and potentially devastating cross by Butch. Besides a lot of it is already before the jury in my cross of the lead investigator, Foster. I'll have to hand it to Judge Godboldt. She might be a pain but she's really been straight up on evidentiary rulings. We've had a good shot at it."

"She's been all right," Randy partially agreed, "but you can sense something about her. Like she's looking for something."

Ben remembered the story he had told them about the fist fight that Butch and she had had years ago. "Probably wants to give ol' Butch the one-two. You know, take up where they left off at the card game when she accused him of cheating." Ben demonstrated with a jab and an upper cut.

Randy smiled for the first time that morning. Ben went back to Wanda's testimony. "You know, one thing we are not in control of is Wanda. She'll do what she wants to. I believe we can convince her not to testify but if she wants to, that is her right. In fact as careful as Godboldt is, if she does not testify, she will make inquiry of Wanda on the record to make sure that the decision not to testify is entirely hers and is voluntary. Probably doesn't make any difference though. I think we are sunk unless. . . ." Ben drifted off into thought.

"Unless what?" Randy demanded.

"Unless we have a surprise witness of our own."

"Who?" Jim asked somewhat puzzled.

"I know what you are thinking, Ben," Randy added, "but I doubt it will work. We'll never get that."

Ben had that quizzical look on his face like he knew something that they did not.

"Who? For God's sake, who?" Jim was exasperated.

Randy looked at Jim. "Jeremy. He can undo the State's case."

"Exactly," Ben offered. "My retired detective thinks he will make or break the case. Without him, we've got a solid first degree murder case against us. With him, we can shake ol' Butch to the foundation. I believe Jeremy knows what happened. He saw the fight. He can make it a life or death struggle instead of a little ol' scuffle as Butch has been saying. He can tell us it was so bad that he felt he had to shoot his own father to save his mother. He can tell us whether Wanda's version is true. Who knows? Maybe he can tell us who actually killed Ralph."

"Yeah, but how do we get to him? He's got a wall of protection around him." Jim stated.

"That's right, Ben," Randy agreed. "I've tried numerous times to convince his guardian ad litem, Caroline Markham, to let me talk to him. She won't do it. She is willing to let him see his mother but that's as far as it goes. When I mention how much we need to know what he knows about the case, she won't budge. No dice."

Randy noticed the grin on Ben's face again and interrupted her report. "What? What? Come on. Out with it. You know something."

Ben relented. "Well, let's just say that problem is solved."

"How so?"

"Last night let's say somewhere between the first and second Jack Daniels, I was mentioning to my friend Jack Childrey the details of the case. I happened to mention how much we needed to talk to the child involved. And out of the blue he said he knew Jeremy. You see he is a member of the Fraternal Order of Police. This Saturday the organization is giving a hot dog cookout for the area Scout troops. One of the Scout leaders in Jeremy's troop is also a member of the FOP. Jack met Jeremy several months ago when Jack spoke to the troop about law enforcement for the FOP. Anyway, to make the long, short, Jack is inviting me to the cookout and is going to help arrange a meeting with Jeremy tomorrow."

"You can't, Ben. It's against the rules," Randy chided.

"Oh, yes, I can and I must. Unless you have been watching a different trial, you gotta know we are down for the count. Wanda's very life may very well be hanging in the balance this weekend. I've got to find out what Jeremy knows. Besides it's a public place and it's a free country. I can talk to anybody I want to."

Jim agreed. "There is no rule against it I'm aware of. You don't need the DA's permission to talk to the witness. Look, why don't you just subpoena him as a witness and put him on the stand?"

"No way. I'm not putting him up there without knowing what he has to say. Too risky."

Jim said, "Well, since he is a child, you may need the guardian's permission to talk to him. But if you don't have it, what's the penalty?"

"I can answer that," Randy replied vehemently. "The wrath of Judge Godboldt and the censure or suspension of the State Bar for an ethics violation. Need I go on?"

"Well, it's got to be done. We've got to do everything we can . . .
"

"Ethically can," Randy interrupted.

"to vigorously defend our client." Ben looked askance at Randy and continued without stopping to debate. "These words will never be chiseled on my gravestone: Here lies Ben Down, Ineffective Assistance of Counsel."

Jim mused out loud. "It's the proverbial horns of a dilemma: unethical or ineffective. Wish there were another way."

Randy was still unsatisfied. "What will Wanda say?"

"She won't like it but this is bigger than Wanda," Ben said. "This is bigger than any of us. The truth. We've got to know it. I'm not losing a case and Wanda is not going to lose her life over a lie. The truth. And I believe we will know it when we meet again on Sunday afternoon."

Randy would not budge and announced it. "Well, I don't like it and I do not approve, join or condone the tactic."

"Jim, what do you say?" Ben asked.

"Count me in. I think it has to be done."

"Good. Great. Glad to see we are all of one mind," Ben said rather smugly and stared at Randy.

She relented but reluctantly. "Oh, all right then. 'It's all for one and one for all.' Just be careful, Ben."

Jim checked his watch and reported that he had to go to a real estate closing at his office. "So. Anything else we need to go over before they bring Wanda in?"

"How about Ralph's mother? Any luck yet?" Ben asked.

Jim responded, "Working on it as we speak. Nothing of any consequence yet but a check at the Register of Deeds revealed that she purchased a new house for $327,000 this past fall. Must've paid cash, no deed of trust. She moved from a neighborhood off Oleander where the houses are $85,000 to $125,000. I'm checking her bank records through a friend, backdooring it through the Net, but I haven't heard anything back yet. I'll let you know as soon as I get anything."

"I want to know more about her. She just doesn't fit the mold of the grieving mother," Ben added.

Checking his watch again, Jim asked, "Anything else?"

Ben replied, "Yes, there is one more thing. Apparently I am being watched."

Randy looked a little alarmed. "Now what's that all about?"

"Jack told me that someone came into Childrey's asking questions about me. He didn't know who the person was. He said he was a male, late twenties, muscular, well-dressed, Asian. No real cause for alarm as far as I can tell but still I would suggest that all of us be careful. There are some strange things in this case, things that just do not add up. This is one of them. Butch wouldn't send out a PI to investigate us. The law enforcement agencies involved in this are straight up on this case as far as I can tell. So be careful and report anything suspicious. Anything."

"Wow, what else is going to happen? Surprise witness, mysterious spy asking too many questions. What else?" Randy commented.

"How about the phantom killer revealed?" Ben replied.

"Yeah, you wish," Randy said.

"All right," Jim said. "Will do. I'm out of here. If you need me, call me. If I don't hear from you, I'll see you at the office on Sunday afternoon for our last conference before the trial resumes Monday."

"Sounds good, Jim," Ben remarked. "See you Sunday."

Jim left and Ben noticed that Randy was busy writing notes on a set of written interrogatories. He inquired, "BB3 or 2 or 1 or whatever it is now?"

"Yes, I'm snatching every moment I can to make sure I have responded to every deposition request, interrogatory, motion and letter. And by the way it's BB1."

"How's it going? Everything on track?"

"I hope so. We're chugging right along. I'm sure they thought that I would drop the ball while we were trying Wanda's case but every I is dotted and every T is crossed so far. It has taken working day and night around Wanda's case. We're up to speed I think but I can sense it's a losing battle. As soon as I miss a deadline, they'll be in court seeking a dismissal. It is boring with a capital B but I said I'd do it and I am."

"Can I help? You know I'm willing. I can . . ."

"No, stay focused on Wanda's defense."

"All right but I'm willing to help when you need me." Ben remembered how strongly Randy felt about Rod Pemberton. "Well, how about Rod? How are the two of you holding up under the pressure of being major competitors in this trial?"

"We're staying apart during the trial," she commented and looked a little disappointed. "You know, Ben, he is just as good as I thought he would be. He's beating our pants off and doing it like a gentleman. I hate to lose but if I had to, I'd choose him. I'm crazy about him, really, and even more, I admire him."

"You are sounding more and more like a woman in love." Ben grinned and pretended to look a little nauseated.

Randy picked up on the innuendo and said, "Don't kid yourself. You know your whole world revolves around Margaret."

"Well, back to my original point. Remember: all work and no play will make Randy a dull girl."

Randy shrugged and started to scribble on the interrogatories again. Ben said, "Listen. If you would like a little fun, come to the courtroom this morning. Rod is calling the case of Noah Lyerly for a plea."

"What did you get out of the DA? Second degree?"

"Oh, no. We quibbled about it for some time but they gave in. They were stuck on second degree murder, sentencing in the mitigated range but we finally settled on voluntary manslaughter, sentencing in the judge's discretion. We have a strong issue of defense of a third person. The victim was on top of Nora's sister beating her badly. He had a gun right by his hand. Nora Jean came in, saw what was going on and just overreacted. She killed him with a knife. Immediately called for help for him. Even held him in her arms while she waited for the ambulance. It was clearly a killing in the heat of passion."

"What does Noah say about the plea?"

"He loves it. He knew he was in serious trouble and really thought the State would stick him with murder. So when I brought the manslaughter plea in and explained how it worked, he, she jumped up and down like a kid at Christmas. Tried to give me a hug but, hey. But back to the fun for a moment. She told me some things that will make for an interesting sentencing hearing. You will want to be there. Seriously. This will be the best show in town." Ben rubbed his hands together as he thought about it.

Suddenly a noise diverted their attention toward the hall. There were several cat calls then Nora Jean appeared in the door of the interview room with the jailer in tow. She was pointing back up the hall and wiggling in a little dance.

Randy looked at Ben and shook her head in disbelief. Ben hailed the jailer. "I thought you were going to bring Wanda Stickley first."

"No," he argued checking the interview list posted by the door. "The sheet plainly says Noah Gene Lyerly for Ben Down at 8:30."

Nora Jean continued to dance to some music in her head and stared at Randy. Ben talked to the jailer again. "Well, sorry about the mix up but we've got to have Wanda first while Ms. Bost is here. I'll talk to Noah later."

"So this is Miss Randy Bost, sugarcakes. Sharp."

Ben grinned and said, "Why, yes. Nora Jean, may I present Randy Bost, attorney at law?"

"Yes, you may. Yes, you may, baby," Nora said as she continued to stare at Randy.

"Nice to meet you, Mr. Lyerly," Randy said rather coolly.

"No need to get icy, baby. I'm not going to take your man," Nora said in her honey voice. She looked over at Ben, "but he is so sweet. Oooooooo."

Randy shook her head and looked at Ben as if to say, "Do something."

"Okay, Nora Jean. I'll talk to you in a little while. Ms. Bost and I have to talk to Wanda Stickley first."

"Oh, I know about her, sugarpie. They trying to give her the gas for killing one mean ol' rotten man. Ain't right. I tell'ya it ain't right." She wagged her finger back and forth to emphasize the point.

"Exactly," Ben said as the jailer pulled Nora Jean toward the door.

She sashayed back up the hall accompanied by hoots and whistles. Ben looked over at Randy who was still shaking her head in disbelief.

Ben said, "I told you. You won't want to miss this. Better come to court this morning."

*   *   *

It was the same courthouse: same tables, same bench, same bailiff, same clerks, even the same lawyers but somehow it seemed different. Ben waited in the courtroom at the defense table for the Sheriff's deputy to bring Nora Jean from the jail. He watched the morning light streak in a ray from the window across to an empty chair. Except for the particles of dust in the light, nothing was moving. Ben's eyes began to blur and he started to drift into the sleep he had been missing.

The squeak in the side door to the courtroom broke the silence and Ben jerked. Rod followed by Jack Krait entered carrying a metal bucket full of criminal files for the Friday morning session.

Rod gave Ben a smile and said, "Wake up sleeping beauty."

Ben groaned in acknowledgment of the comment. Krait smirked and sat with his back to Ben. Ben checked the clock and noticed it was 9:28, two minutes before the always prompt Judge Godboldt would walk through the door from her chambers. He leaned forward slightly in the chair, put his elbows on the table, rubbed his eyes and yawned. When the door from the lockup popped open, Ben watched the bailiff point Nora Jean toward Ben's table. They walked over and Nora Jean who was familiar with the drill lifted her arms for the bailiff to remove the handcuffs.

As she sat, Ben cleared his throat and spoke first. "Morning. Everything okay?"

"Yes."

"Ready for this?"

"Yes."

Ben yawned again. "Why so subdued?"

She looked at her prison attire: red jumper, orange sandals over gray socks, plastic identification bracelet on her right wrist. "I don't know. I just imagined it differently, sweetie. Somehow I thought that on this day I would be dressed in scarlet, you know, some fetching thing that would add to the drama of it all." She looked at Ben with adoring eyes. "But you," she continued as her eyes took a stroll over Ben, "you are everything I thought that you would be. Gray, distinguished eyebrows, neatly trimmed hair, blue suit, conservative tie. My knight in shining armor. Makes me juicy just thinking about it."

Ben was awake now. "All right, Nora Jean. Remember what I told you. This is important. Everything you . . ."

Nora Jean spoke over Ben, "Everything I do and say can make a difference. I know, I know."

"Right. No sugarcakes, no sweet britches, no honey. Just straightforward: yes, sir; no, sir; yes, ma'am; no, ma'am. Got it?"

"Yes, sir," Nora Jean sat up and saluted gingerly.

Ben winced slightly. "Nora Jean, seriously, do everything I tell you to do. Sentencing is entirely in the judge's discretion so don't do anything or say anything to arouse the ire of this judge. She won't put up with it."

Nora Jean seemed to drift off during the lecture. "Where's Nate? I thought she was going to be here."

"She'll be here. The DA will have her here."

She pulled at a strand of her hair. When it tangled in the band holding her ponytail in place, she pulled at the band and shook her long hair over her shoulders. Krait who had been watching Nora Jean looked a little uneasy and started to get up out of his chair. Rod tapped him on the arm and pointed toward the clock. As Ben prepared to admonish her to put her hair up, the bailiff opened the judge's door and called everyone to attention.

Everyone stood while the bailiff gave the customary opening for court. When he concluded, Judge Godboldt obviously in a rush told Rod to call his first case as soon as everyone was seated.

Without hesitation Rod announced, "Your Honor, at number 69 on Your Honor's docket, the State calls the case of State of North Carolina versus Noah Gene Lyerly. This is a matter that is before Your Honor upon a plea of guilty to voluntary manslaughter."

Ben stood and said, "Your Honor, Ben Down for the defense in this case. Noah Gene Lyerly is present. On his behalf I enter a plea of guilty to voluntary manslaughter and I have prepared a transcript of the plea. If I might approach with the transcript?"

The judge nodded. She studied Nora Jean as Ben approached with the plea form. After questioning Nora Jean about the voluntariness of the negotiated plea, she instructed Nora Jean to be seated and looked at Rod for a presentation of the State's case.

"Your Honor," Rod said as he picked up on the judge's cue, "we have two witnesses: an eyewitness and the detective who investigated the case. The State calls Natalie Dawtry."

He walked over to the door and motioned for the witness to come into the courtroom. A stunning woman entered and walked to the witness stand. Nora Jean, who had been watching her intently along with everyone else in the courtroom, pulled on Ben's sleeve and whispered, "I told you Nate was beautiful."

Natalie was sworn, seated and asked to identify herself. After the introduction, Rod asked, "What is your relationship with Noah Gene Lyerly?"

"I am his sister. We've been close all of our lives."

Ben smiled to himself and spoke softly to Nora Jean, "She's going to help. Great. I thought she would."

She recited at Rod's direction the events leading up to the killing of Sean Delothian. Her report was very favorable. She spent a great deal more time on Sean's anger and violence rather than the personality that had won over both Nora Jean and her.

On cross-examination, Ben exploited the opportunity and built a strong defense for Nora Jean. Natalie testified that she and Nora Jean had had to fend for themselves a lot during their lives and both were very protective of each other. "There is no doubt," she testified as she cried from remembering the events of the night Sean was killed, "I would have died that night if Nora Jean had not come to my rescue. You may find this hard to believe but I loved Sean and in my heart I believe Nora Jean, uh, my brother Noah loved Sean. But Sean was a violent man. He had a terrible temper. He just couldn't control it."

"Did he have a gun?" Ben queried.

"He always had a gun. He used to sell drugs and he said he got in the habit of it then. That night he had pulled the gun out and put it on the table beside the couch. He . . . "

"Did he do anything with the gun toward you?"

"Yes, he pointed the gun at me several times." She started trembling and her voice broke off. "Uh, in between, between the times he'd point it at me, he'd lay it on the coffee table and slap me or hit me with his fists. The last time he pointed it at me he said he was going to kill me with it at midnight."

Natalie's vivid description of her fear and Nora Jean's speed in responding to her distress call convinced Ben he had accomplished enough with her testimony. He asked, "Anything else you need to say?" Ben concluded.

"Yes," she said and looked directly at Nora Jean. "Sean is not completely dead."

"What?" Ben asked matter of factly. He knew what she meant since they had talked on several occasions over the last several months but he was the only one. Everyone else including Nora Jean looked puzzled.

"What did you say?" Ben asked again.

"Sean's not completely dead. At least in a sense he's not." Tears began to form in her eyes and one slipped easily down her cheek.

After a long silence Judge Godboldt intervened. "What's this about? Speak up now. What are you talking about?" She punched the bun in the back of her hair and turned directly toward Natalie. Natalie kept crying and did not speak.

Ben said, "Your Honor, I believe I can help." When the judge relented with a nod, Ben continued the cross-examination with a warm approach. "Natalie. Natalie. You need to tell us what you mean."

Finally she spoke. "I'm, I'm pregnant."

"It's Sean's child, isn't it?"

"Yes," she said lightly as she stared at Nora Jean. "Sean still lives inside of me."

Nora Jean whispered to Ben. "I knew there was some reason she had gained some weight. A baby. Our baby. Well, I'll be."

Judge Godboldt turned around in her seat and cleared her throat. She did not betray her thoughts with any gesture or statement. Ben watched her carefully for any indication of what she thought about the testimony.

Ben asked Natalie, "Why are you crying? Are you upset about it?"

"Oh, no," Natalie protested, "God has blessed me with this child. It's wonderful. It's just, just . . . I don't know. I don't know if I can do it by myself. I don't know what I'll do without Noodle." She looked at Judge Godboldt apologetically. "Sorry, Your Honor, I mean Mr. Lyerly, uh, Noah. He knows more about babies than I'll ever know. Ever since we were children, Noo, uh, Noah was always crazy about babies. I don't know if I can go through this alone."

Ben sensing he had accomplished as much as he could indicated "No further questions" and tendered her to the judge and to Rod. When she was released from the witness stand, she walked by Nora Jean and patted her gently on the arm before she took a seat behind her.

Rod called the detective in order to lay out a factual background for the plea. After the investigator's rather antiseptic report, Rod informed the judge that the DA's office had notified the victim's next of kin concerning the hearing but the office had received no response. Next the District Attorney notified the other known family members but again received no response. Rod turned toward the benches and called for anyone representing the Delothian family to come to the front. No one spoke or came forward.

"With that said, Your Honor, the State rests," Rod announced.

Ben stood then bent over and whispered to Nora Jean, "Remember. This is it. Mind your manners." Then as he stood again, he stated, "Your Honor, we'll have one witness. I call Noah Gene Lyerly to the stand."

Ben felt a little tension begin to build in his chest as Nora Jean bounced a little as she approached the witness stand. He gave her a hard look as she was being sworn in. She winked at him and took a seat.

Ben took no chances and introduced her rather than allowing her to introduce herself. "You are Noah Gene Lyerly, is that correct?"

"Yes. I mean yes, sir," Nora Jean said in her honey-dipped voice. Great, Ben thought, she remembered the instructions. Suddenly she turned toward the judge and spoke directly to Judge Godboldt. "Judge, I mean, Your Honor, I just want you to know that I am trying to be on my best behavior. My lawyer," she looked at Ben who wanted to curl up and crawl under the table, "Ben Down, instructed me plain and simple to be on my best behavior and I'm trying. If I do anything or say anything that I shouldn't, Your Honor, I want you to let me know and I will stop and I mean stop immediately."

Judge Godboldt looked at Nora Jean sternly and said, "Rest assured, Mr. Lyerly. Now listen to your attorney. Mr. Down."

Judge Godboldt was so pleased with the instruction that Ben had given Nora Jean about how to be courteous during her testimony, she almost smiled at Ben. Before Ben had a chance to speak, Nora Jean still speaking directly to the judge, offered, "Yes, ma'am, Your Honor, and I want to thank you for letting me say my peace today. Thank you."

"Mr. Down," Judge Godboldt insisted.

"Yes, Your Honor," Ben said. "Now listen Nora Jean, let's clear up something that needs to be clear from the beginning. You are a man, are you not?"

"Oh, yes, sir, physically I am a man. Yes. But and this is a big but, I am a woman in my mind, my heart and my soul." She held out her arms and spread them wide. "I can't help it. God made me this way and I believe this. I really do. I believe it can't be wrong. Now I know a lot of people think . . . "

Ben knew he was going to have to rein her in and broke into her explanation. "All right, I believe we understand you. Now, your given name is Noah Gene Lyerly, is that correct?"

Nora Jean nodded.

"But you go by the name of Nora Jean and sometimes your sister, Miss Dawtry, calls you Noodle, is that correct?"

"Yes, sir."

"And which do you prefer that I call you?"

"Why, Nora Jean, of course, Ben. I mean Mr. Down." She looked at Judge Godboldt to see if she was in trouble.

"Now, let's go over the events that led up to the death of Sean Delothian, all right?"

"Yes, sir."

For the next few minutes Ben directed her through the chronology of events that began with her life with her mother, the closeness between Natalie and her, and the stormy relationship with Sean. For the first time since Ben had been representing her, she stayed focused on the question asked and did not slip away into some distant space that made her seem disconnected and vacuous. She was careful to respond with "Yes, sir" and "No, sir" and she only became emotional when she mentioned her betrayal of Natalie with Sean.

"After Natalie had called you for help, what did you see when you walked in the trailer that evening?" Ben inquired.

"Sean. He was furious. He was on top of her. Beating, beating with his fist. I knew his temper. Lord, he was glorious when he was sweet but when his mood changed, he was like a pit bull. He would rage out of control. The gun was right by his hand. I couldn't let him hurt Natalie. She's all I've got." Nora Jean started crying. She turned toward Natalie and blurted out, "It was all my fault, Nate. I'm sorry. I'm so sorry. I love you, Nate. I'm sorry."

Ben looked behind him at Natalie to see how she was reacting. Natalie was reaching for a hankie as she mouthed the words, "I love you, too, Noodle." Except for the obviously bored Jack Krait, who laid his head in his hands and emitted a slight groan, everyone in the courtroom seemed genuinely moved by the show of emotion. Even Judge Godboldt, a veteran of the courtroom pugilism, had a little softer look.

"How do you feel about Sean, Nora Jean?"

"I am truly sorry for what I did. People who don't know me will not understand but I loved that man. I wouldn't harm a hair on his head or on anybody else's for that matter. He was as close to heaven as I will ever get when he was a little sugarcake. I had an awful choice that night as I saw it: Sean or Natalie. I made the choice and now I have to live with it. It's all my fault." She whimpered slightly.

When she settled down again, Ben asked, "What would you have the judge know about you before you are sentenced, Nora Jean?"

"I'm not a bad person. Really I'm not. I know I've done a bad thing and I have to be punished for it but there is good in me too." She turned toward Judge Godboldt and begged, "Judge, if you give me a chance, I will use it. I will love that baby just like I love Natalie. I ask you to please give me a chance to help Natalie with the baby. She needs me and I need them."

Ben tendered Nora Jean to Rod for cross-examination. As he did, he noticed that Randy who had been watching the proceedings from the rear of the courtroom had moved up to a chair behind him. Ben leaned back and asked, "Well, what do you think?"

"I don't see how it could have gone any better," she whispered, "but I thought you said it was going to be exciting, 'the best show in town' to quote you. This has been sad, too sad for me."

Ben smiled and motioned for Randy to move a little closer. He whispered, "Show's not over yet. You know how many times Krait has taken great pleasure in making life miserable for us. Well, what goes around, comes around. That man has tormented us for the last time. Keep your seat. A bomb is getting ready to explode."

Rod's examination was brief and dealt mostly with the details of the killing itself. Again Nora Jean was courteous and careful to answer the questions asked without digressing. When Rod finished, Ben told the judge he had one or two more questions on redirect examination and his evidence would be completed.

"Nora Jean, I forgot to ask you this earlier but have you been in any trouble with the law before?"

"Well, nothing really. Just small stuff. Nothing like this."

"Well," Ben said and looked over at Jack Krait who continued to conceal his face in his hands, "do you even know any of the law enforcement officers or any of the officials here at court?"

"No." Nora Jean thought for a moment. "Uh, yes, I do. I know one person."

"And who is that?"

"That man," she indicated and pointed.

Ben stood up and walked behind Krait's chair. Ben pointed toward Krait and asked, "Is this the man, Assistant District Attorney Jack Krait?"

"Yes, but I only knew him as Jack."

Krait's face turned red and he sat as though his face were frozen onto his hands.

"And how do you know him?"

"He was a regular out at The Men's Club where I worked. He hit on me a couple of times but I wouldn't go out with him. He was too, uh, icky, creepy, I thought."

"No more questions," Ben announced nonchalantly as though he had just concluded a perfunctory task.

Rod refused to look at Krait whose ears were turning a shade of purple. Rod indicated, "Nothing further, Your Honor."

When Nora Jean stepped down and returned to her seat at the defense table, she quietly asked Ben, "How'd I do?"

Ben chuckled under his breath and whispered, "Perfect. You were a perfect lady.

                    *   *   *

"Ben, that's what you need," Jack Childrey said as he pointed to several Boy Scouts who were scuffling playfully with each other.

Ben waved the smoke from the grill away from him as Jack flipped the wieners. He watched the boys bump into two other Scouts who joined the fray. They were obviously having a good time and grew louder.

"What? I didn't hear you," Ben raised his voice above the din.

"Kids. You need some kids. Keep you young."

Ben laughed and shook his head in disagreement. He rattled the ice in his empty cup. "This Coke needs something."

Jack raised one eyebrow and laid the tongs beside the grill. "Thought you might think so. Follow me," he said motioning toward the office area of the Fraternal Order of Police hut.

When they walked into the room, Jack reached underneath a table and pulled out a bag containing a bottle of whiskey. "It's not your favorite, Ben. It's not Jack but it's pretty smooth I think."

Jack poured some into Ben's cup and then poured himself a small amount in his own cup. Ben took a drink and smiled. "Yassir. It's rough but it's right."

Jack grinned and they walked back to the grill and all of the commotion. The weather had co-operated with warm sun and light wind so that the event could be held outside. Approximately seventy-five Scouts from eight area troops had shown up for the annual appreciation day and including parents, Scout leaders and FOP members, the yard at the hut was filled with people.

Ben nursed his drink and listened to the radio in the background while Jack cooked. As the Scouts began to line up for hot dogs and drinks, Ben surveyed the crowd for Jeremy. When he heard the words "Vice President", he leaned back toward the speakers to hear the news.

The reporter said, "For the last several weeks the focus of the investigation into the assassination of Vice President Anderson has been in Tientsin, China. Investigative efforts have been repeatedly stymied and slowed by a resistant Chinese government. Today Secretary of State Madeline Baker has filed a formal protest with the Chinese concerning the lack of co-operation by Chinese authorities. Earlier this year Chiang Ching-kuo, minister of security, pledged the full support and co-operation of the Chinese in pursuing the inquiry.

The official policy of the Chinese has been complete co-operation; however, American investigators have repeatedly complained of stalling by government officials, bureaucratic red tape and interference by local Chinese leaders in Tientsin. Perhaps the strongest statement to date has come from FBI Director Fries who indicated on Wednesday of this week that, to use his words, "the investigation leads directly to China and we are extremely frustrated by the lack of support by the Chinese". The latest imbroglio has centered around the FBI's request to search a certain business identified as Shang Chou International by American agents. The Chinese have steadfastly refused indicating that granting such a request would compromise national security. At any rate Secretary of State Baker has made the denial of the request to inspect the facilities at Shang Chou a central part of the official protest. On a brighter note, Marilyn Anderson, wife of the Vice President, has . . . "

Ben was interrupted by Jack who handed him a plate with a couple of hot dogs on it. "Want anything else?" Jack asked. When Ben replied in the negative, Jack spoke in a hushed tone, "Go back to the office and wait. I'm going to bring the Stickley boy back there for you to talk to him. But look, we have to be careful. Jeremy is here with his guardian Caroline Markham and she won't know I'm bringing him to you."

Ben nodded, walked to the office and waited. In a few minutes Jack appeared with Jeremy. Jeremy was holding a drink and a plate full of hot dogs and chips. Ben indicated for Jeremy to take a seat and Jack stepped out to go back to the grill.

As Jeremy sat his plate and drink on the table and took a seat, Ben spoke first. "Jeremy, do you know who I am?"

"Yes, sir. You are mom's lawyer."

"That's right." Ben smiled and said, "I'm Ben Down. I am representing your mother in the trial."

"How's mama doing?" Jeremy played with his chips and nervously took a drink from his cup.

"As well as can be expected. She's a strong woman. How are you holding up?"

"I miss mama. I mean they are treating me all right but I miss mama." He furtively stole a glance at Ben and started to tear up.

Ben did not want to upset him and tried to divert his attention. "I know you do but . . ."

"When can she come home?"

"I can't answer that with certainty. She is in the trial and no one knows how it will turn out. We're doing the best we can but . . ." Ben noticed that Jeremy was getting a little pink in the cheeks and Ben stopped talking.

It grew silent. A tear streamed down Jeremy's face as he stared at a chip he was turning over and over between his fingers. Ben watched and when Jeremy seemed to have settled a little, Ben continued. "Jeremy, your mother is in serious trouble. If we stopped now, we would lose this case. They have enough to convict her of first degree murder. But I know and you know that she is not guilty. I think I know what happened out there that night. Your mother was defending herself and you were defending your mother. I know that you shot the gun that night. And I know that you did it to protect your mother. And I know that you did not kill your father. You only wounded him. He died from the slash wounds to his neck."

Ben watched Jeremy carefully for any reaction. Jeremy was taking everything in without getting overly emotional. Ben continued, "I know that but the jurors do not."

"What can I do?"

"You can tell the truth if I call you as a witness."

"Mama don't want me involved. She told me to stay away and not say anything."

"And ordinarily I would tell you to obey your mother but I can't this time. It's literally a matter of life or death. Your mother needs your help. She needs the truth. The truth that only you know. The truth that you shot your father."

"What do you want me to say?"

"I want you to tell them you did it," Ben said.

Caroline Markham, who had just walked up to the office, partially stepped in and glared at Ben.

"Jeremy, it's time to go. Now."

CHAPTER SEVENTEEN

"I call Jeremy Stickley to the stand," Ben announced when Judge Godboldt recognized him for a presentation of the defendant's evidence.

The courtroom seemed to explode. Wanda jumped to her feet and screamed out, "No!" At the same time Butch stood and emphatically stated, "Objection."

Judge Godboldt rocked forward in her chair and rapped the bench with the gavel. "Here, here. We'll have no such outbursts in this courtroom. Be seated and be quiet." She stared directly at Wanda as the bailiff moved to a position behind Wanda's chair. Randy put her hand on Wanda's arm and tried to get her to sit down. Judge Godboldt instructed the other bailiff to take the jurors out of the courtroom. After they were led out, she turned her attention to Ben. "What's, what's the meaning of this? Mr. Down?"

"Your Honor, my client and I have reached a disagreement about what should be done in the case. The witness I have called is her son, Jeremy Stickley. She does not think that he should testify. I think it is not only important but imperative, crucial that he tell what he knows about this matter."

"Mrs. Stickley," the Judge inquired, "is that correct?"

"Yes, Your Honor." Wanda was shaking, she was so upset. "Jeremy is my child and this is my case. I flatly do not want him to testify."

"Is there anything else you want to tell the court about this, Mrs. Stickley?" the judge asked further trying to give her the opportunity to explain herself.

Ben leaned over and whispered to Wanda. "Wanda, it's time for the truth."

Wanda hesitated and started visibly shaking then as tears streamed down her face, she responded to Judge Godboldt's question. "No. Apparently I can't stop it."

The judge did not rule immediately but turned her attention to Butch who was still standing. "What's the basis for the objection, Mr. Yeager?"

"This, Your Honor," Butch argued. "This is a child and he should not be allowed to testify unless he is shown to be qualified by reason of understanding and ability to communicate the truth."

Ben did not wait for the direction from the judge to respond. He said, "Your Honor, that's ludicrous. The young man is thirteen, almost fourteen years of age. He's an A student and a gifted, talented athlete. The DA knows that. I can qualify him if I have to but I think it will be just as expedient to hear his testimony and determine from that if he is competent to testify."

Butch was just using the delaying tactic to get a chance to examine Jeremy before the jury was brought in. Butch badly wanted to know what Jeremy was going to say so that he would be better prepared to react to it in front of the jury. "But," Butch began to argue.

"All right, enough," the judge said. "As for Mrs. Stickley's objection, I rule that this is a matter of tactics and the attorney can determine which witnesses to call. As for the State's objection concerning competency, we can hear the testimony and if at any time, Mrs. Stickley's son appears incapable of being a competent witness, I will stop the proceedings and we will make further inquiry outside of the jury's presence."

Clearly perturbed, Butch sat down. Ben nodded at Randy who walked to the hallway and escorted Jeremy and Caroline Markham into the courtroom. While the jury was being brought in, Wanda stared at Jeremy and shook her head in disagreement. Jeremy kept his eyes on the floor. When Jeremy was sworn and it was quiet in the courtroom again, Ben began the examination with the usual introduction and led Jeremy through his background including his relationship to Wanda and Ralph, his education, and the events leading up to the night of the killing. Through it all Jeremy did not look at his mother and stayed riveted on Ben and although obviously nervous, did relatively well.

"All right now, Jeremy, you had just returned from your Scout meeting and your mother was fixing sandwiches, what happened next?"

"I, I was in my room. I had the radio on and the next thing I knew, Esmeralda came into my room. She had spider webs all over her head."

"Esmeralda is your cat?"

"Yes, sir."

"Continue."

"I walked out to see what was going on and I heard mom in the basement. I started down there and I heard her scream." Jeremy started turning a little pale as he revisited the terror of that night. "I, I ran back to her bedroom and got her gun."

"Why did you do that?" Ben asked to try to slow Jeremy down.

"I knew mama was in trouble. I thought somebody had broke in the basement." Ben nodded at him to continue. "I, uh, went down the steps. It was my father. I told him to turn her loose. He, he wouldn't. He just kept beating her."

Ben again tried to calm Jeremy. "Let's stop right there. Now how did your mother look?"

Jeremy quickly glanced over at Wanda who was looking down at the table. His face turned very red. "She, uh, . . . she was bloody."

"Did she say anything to you?"

"No, she just had a look like . . . like, uh, she was going to die. He kept hitting her and hitting her. I fired the gun. I didn't mean to hurt him. I just wanted him to stop. He turned mama loose and came after me and I ran."

"Where did you go, Jeremy?"

"I ran up the steps and out of the kitchen. Down the, uh, driveway." He started hyperventilating.

"All right, Jeremy. Take just a moment." Ben waited. Jeremy seemed to calm down a little. Finally Ben asked, "What happened next?"

"I ran by the shrubs at the end of the driveway and stopped. When I looked back, my father was coming out of the house after me. So I ran."

"What happened to the gun?"

"I threw it in a storm drain."

Jeremy struggled with his pants pocket and suddenly pulled out a rusty handgun. He held the gun up. A woman in the rear of the courtroom shrieked.

"What the . . . ," the bailiff called out as everyone ducked.

Ben pointed at Jeremy and instructed him, "Put the gun down on the table. Now, Jeremy. You are scaring everyone."

Jeremy looked around at everyone with a bewildered expression on his face. As he obeyed the instruction and lay the gun on the bar in front of him, the bailiff approached the witness stand with his hand on his revolver. The bailiff picked up the gun by the trigger guard between two fingers and started carrying it to the evidence table. Judge Godboldt called the attorneys and the bailiff to the bench for a conference on courtroom security which ended with a very red-faced Butch. The gun was bagged in plastic and marked as a defendant's exhibit.

When the trial resumed, Ben tried to assure everyone. "Okay, Jeremy, no more surprises, okay?"

Jeremy nodded sheepishly. Ben was relieved that the incident had not provoked more of a reaction from Judge Godboldt. "I take it that you went back and retrieved the gun from the storm drain and this gun is the one you used to protect your mother?"

"Yes, sir."

Ben led Jeremy through other details of the night hoping to get more information to the jury concerning the possibility of a third person being the killer. Jeremy knew nothing about anyone else being present at the scene the night of the killing but the sequence of events still allowed the possibility that someone else had killed Ralph.

Ben closed with this question. "Jeremy, why did you tell everyone that you did not know what happened the night your father was killed?"

Jeremy grew very uneasy again and blurted out, "I had to."

"Why did you have to?"

"Mama said it would be best. She did not want me in any trouble. She said she wanted me to stay out of it."

"And why are you telling this now?"

"I have to." He looked at his mother apologetically. "I have to, mama." He looked back at Ben and explained, "I can't let anything happen to mama. She's all I've got."

On cross-examination Butch made a lot of headway with Jeremy's falsehoods but the truth, at least part of it, was out, Ben thought. Jeremy was a credible witness and his version fit the physical evidence. The picture was much more complete: it was a life and death struggle between Wanda and Ralph and finally Ralph appeared to be what Ben had known all along, the epitome of evil.

At the recess Ben assembled everyone in the conference room just off the lockup. James had a raft of paperwork concerning the second rape: DNA showed the semen on the sheets was Ralph's and DNA of the rape kit proved the semen in Wanda's vagina was Ralph's.

"We can get this in through Detective Stanton," Ben lectured. "Butch won't give us any trouble about it especially since we didn't get this in discovery as we were supposed to. This further corroborates Wanda. I say let's wrap it up with Stanton's testimony. He'll take us back through the history of violence and he'll tell us that Wanda was being truthful: Ralph really was out of prison and Ralph committed the second rape. It's as good as we can get it. Good chance at a 'not guilty' verdict and certainly no worse than a second degree verdict. . Randy, what do you think?"

"I'm in."

"James?" Ben asked.

"You're the pro, Ben. If you think so, let's do it."

"Wanda?"

She did not speak but continued to look down at the table. She started haltingly at first. "Where does that leave Jeremy? If they find me guilty, can't they say Jeremy was part of it?"

Ben responded, "They wouldn't do that."

"I don't care. Could they?"

"Well, yes, but it would never happen."

"They could. I can't let that happen. I've got to go on the stand."

"Absolutely not," Ben remonstrated. "I know what you're thinking. You will take all of the blame and try to exonerate Jeremy. It will backfire." Wanda looked unconvinced and Ben pressed the point. "I'm telling you, Wanda, Butch will eat you alive. Friday we were sunk. A guilty verdict of first degree murder seemed almost certain. Now we've got a chance. And I mean a real chance, a chance at not guilty. Not guilty. Think about it."

"No." She was adamant. "I have to save Jeremy. First and foremost, Jeremy. He's all I've got left in this world."

"But," Ben continued to argue.

"No buts. I'm testifying."

Ben who had half risen out of his seat slowly sat and appeared as though the steam was slowly being released from him. He was convinced that her testimony would be nothing short of a bloodletting. "Look," he said, "let's put Detective Stanton up and see what we can do with him. Maybe he can put things in a different light." Ben was trying to buy some time with the hope that he could come up with something to convince Wanda to stay off of the stand.

He started to speak again when the bailiff stepped to the door and called for Wanda. She got up, walked to the door and as she started to step out, she turned and repeated her resolution, "I'm testifying."

After she went out, Ben looked nonplused at Randy. "We've got to do something. Randy, talk to Rod and see if the voluntary manslaughter plea is still on the table."

Randy said, "Don't you think you ought to talk to Butch about it?"

"Butch is mad. Been mad since this morning about something. He won't talk to me. But look, we've got to have a backup. If Wanda testifies, we're sunk. She'll take all of the blame again to save Jeremy from some perceived danger. If we can get the manslaughter plea, maybe she'd rather go that route. I know I'd rather for her to plead than testify."

They filed out of the conference room and returned to the courtroom. After the jurors were returned to the courtroom, Ben called Detective Stanton who turned out to be very skillful in providing the picture of the tortured relationship between Wanda and Ralph. He had actually known Ralph and was familiar with his drug use, his descent into drugs and violence and painfully, Ralph's unmitigated hatred of Wanda. He like everyone else could not understand it but knew that it was one of the horrors that he had contended with in the assault and the rapes. Just as Ben had thought, Butch did not object when Ben introduced the DNA evidence through Stanton that corroborated Wanda's report of the second rape. Ben, still thinking about trying to convince Wanda not to testify, was able to get the detective's opinion into evidence that Jeremy was a good young man and, in the officer's opinion, "would not be untruthful".

At the next recess Wanda was still adamant about taking the stand. "It's all about Jeremy. I'm nothing in the scheme of things. Ralph is not getting another victim. I'm saving my child."

Ben asked, "Randy, what does Rod say about a plea?"

"Nothing doing, Ben. Butch won't permit it. He says we've gone too far, whatever that means."

"All right, Wanda," Ben acquiesced. "Here it is. You have a right to testify. I can't stop you. If I could, I would. I am advising you as your attorney not to do it. It will be devastating to your case. However, if you choose to testify, I want to put it on the record that I am opposed to this and if you choose to testify, I will still try my best to save you. But bottom line: don't do it."

"Ben, I've always trusted you but this is different. I must. Really I must," she said pleadingly.

When they returned to the courtroom, Ben addressed the issue of her testimony on the record and indicated his disagreement with her decision to testify. After Judge Godboldt queried Wanda about whether her decision to testify was her own and whether she had had sufficient time to discuss the issue with her attorney, the judge ruled that she could testify even over her counsel's opposition.

Wanda admitted everything: the battle in the basement, the stabbing with a screwdriver, the shooting by Jeremy that was "absolutely necessary to save her" as she testified, and the pursuit into the driveway. She admitted telling Jeremy not to tell what had happened in the basement. She made it clear that none of it was Jeremy's fault and that Jeremy's shot was to protect her and "did not kill him anyway". She denied cutting Ralph's throat, his penis and his chest. When she concluded, Butch was so excited he was salivating.

Butch slipped to the front part of his chair as if he were a race horse getting ready to charge out of the gate. His voice filled the courtroom. "You lied," he bellowed. "You lied from the beginning of this case, did you not, Mrs. Stickley?"

Before Wanda could answer, Butch asked a second question, "In fact you could say the lies you've told about this are enough to fill one of those law books on the shelf there behind you?"

Again before Wanda could answer, Ben jumped up. "Your Honor. He is badgering this witness."

"No, I'm not," Butch argued back. "I'm . . . "

Ben continued to address the judge. "Well, he is calling for a conclusion, is argumentative and he won't give her time to answer."

The belligerence caught Judge Godboldt by surprise. It had not been there before and had just exploded without any notice. She banged the gavel several times as the argument blew up. "Stop. Stop this instance." Before they could continue the oral pugilism,

she ruled, "Objection sustained. Mr. Yeager, one question at a time
and I direct that you allow the witness to respond."

Butch, who had yielded gracefully to the rulings she had made
earlier in the trial, would not budge. He kept up the same forceful,
argumentative style. He wanted the jurors to clearly understand that
he did not believe a word Wanda was saying and he wanted the
jurors to see it the same way. Ben followed each question with an
objection with relatively good results from the judge. He too wanted
to emphasize to the jurors that Butch was being an unreasonable
bully. Hopefully, he thought, Butch's plan would backfire so that the
jurors might be somewhat sympathetic with Wanda.

"Now let's see," Butch growled, "not only did you lie about your
involvement with the killing of Ralph Stickley but you put your own
son, your own son, Jeremy up to lying about this as well?"

Wanda admitted that and everything else Butch asked except for
the final coup de grace. Ben studied the jurors as Butch took her
through each detail of the scuffle, as he continued to call it, and each
physical assault. Ben was unsure how the jurors were reacting to
Wanda. She was hazy about where she got the screwdriver. She
admitted she kept a weapon for the very purpose of using it "on
Ralph if she had to". And she frequently repeated her reason for
going on the stand: "Jeremy had nothing to do with it."

Butch went through each agonizing step of the case. He literally
stopped on each step of the stairs leading from the basement for a
description of what Ralph was doing and what she was doing.
Wanda steadfastly denied any involvement with the stabbing and
slashing that resulted in Ralph's torture and death.

"I didn't do it," she pleaded, "and I wouldn't do it. As much as
Ralph had done to me, I still did not have the desire to kill him. I just
wouldn't do it."

Butch looked at her with his head tilted back and with his chin
tucked in to give the appearance of disbelief when she answered.
When she finished her answer, he spoke somewhat quietly and said,
"Well, Mrs. Stickley, if you didn't kill him and if Jeremy didn't kill
him, who did?" Butch looked at the jurors with a look of great
doubt.

"I don't know."

"You mean, to use your words, you fought with him, you stabbed
him, you followed him out of the house to the driveway where he was

killed, and, again to use your words, it all took a matter of seconds, and you are telling us, you don't know who killed him?"

Butch turned toward the jury and shook his head in disbelief. He was smiling an incredulous smile. As Wanda responded, "Yes," he put both of his arms out in front of him and pointed toward Wanda as if to tell the jurors: I can't believe she is saying that.

"Do you expect us to believe that some other person besides you and Jeremy, some interloper, got in there 'in a matter of seconds' and killed him before you could do anything about it?"

"Objection," Ben asserted.

"Overruled."

"Well," Butch demanded as he stared at Wanda, "what do you say?"

"I, uh, . . . I," Wanda stammered.

"Well, I'll answer for you. Right or wrong, Mrs. Stickley? You lied before to protect Jeremy and you are lying this time to protect . . "

"Objection, objection, Your Honor," Ben interrupted.

"Lying to protect yourself because you are guilty as sin?" Butch pushed on through like a bull in heat.

"Objection!"

"I have no further questions, Your Honor." Butch responded and looked at Wanda with disdain.

Judge Godboldt sustained the objections but it was too late. The damage had been done. Ben tried to rehabilitate Wanda on redirect examination but he could feel the cool indifference of the jury. Butch had operated with a hatchet during the cross-examination but he had done it with the skill of a professional surgeon with a razor sharp scalpel. To the jurors Wanda was a liar and they would discount her testimony, Ben believed. The real questions he felt were whether the jurors would punish her for her perfidy and whether they would give more credence to the evidence against her because of their negative feelings for her. Ben rose to rest the defendant's case feeling that it could not get much worse.

Butch announced he had one witness on rebuttal. He called Caroline Markham. As she approached the witness stand, Ben began to get a sinking feeling it was about to get a lot worse indeed.

"State your name, please," Butch directed.

"Caroline Markham."

"And what do you do for a living if I might ask?"

"I am an attorney practicing here in New Hanover County."

"And are you familiar with the young man, Jeremy Stickley?"

"Yes, sir. I have been appointed by the court to be his guardian ad litem. I am his representative before the court."

"Did you happen to be at a cookout or a picnic this past Saturday at which the Boy Scouts were being given a day of appreciation by the local Fraternal Order of Police?"

"Yes, sir. Jeremy is a Boy Scout and I had taken him to the appreciation day cookout."

"What happened when you got there?"

"Jeremy got in line to get hot dogs and I walked over to see some people that I knew. When I checked on Jeremy, I saw that one of the men who was cooking was walking Jeremy into the building there. I was curious so I followed them. After the man came back out, I walked in and I saw Jeremy sitting in a room. I started to go in and get him when I heard someone talking to him. I don't think they knew I was outside of the door and I moved a little closer."

"Did you see who was talking to Jeremy?"

"Yes, sir."

"Is that person in this courtroom?"

"Yes, sir."

"Well, point him out," Butch demanded.

She pointed to Ben and said, "It was Ben Down."

"And what did he say to Jeremy?" Butch looked at Ben with disgust.

"He said and I quote, 'Tell them you did it.'"

Ben turned red at the suggestion that he was trying to obtain perjured testimony but he did not want to react immediately since it would give it more importance than it was due. He chose instead to deal with it on cross-examination. He cross-examined and tried to make it clear that she had not heard all of the conversation. He got away with asking her what she had not heard so that he could reconstruct the conversation that Jeremy and he had had. When the jury was sent out, he moved to strike the evidence from the record and for an instruction from the judge to the jurors to disregard the testimony. The requests were denied. Ben countered with a motion for a mistrial which was likewise denied. The rulings were wrong, Ben thought, and grounds for an appeal but the damage was done.

After two weeks and two days of trial, Ben was tired and disappointed. He was convinced that the cause was lost. He still felt there was a good chance Wanda would not get a first degree murder conviction but she would not get a 'not guilty' verdict. As the judge prepared the jurors for final arguments, Ben assumed the worst and studied the sentencing manual to see what mitigating evidence was needed to reduce the sentence to its lowest level.

By law Randy and Ben would argue first and Rod and Butch would get to close the arguments. Randy led off the arguments with a careful comparison of the evidence with the requirements to convict on each offense. She reasoned her way through the evidence and concluded that it led to one result: not guilty. Ben was more emotional contending that Wanda had "absolutely no history of violence and there is absolutely no explanation for her actions except self defense."

"Wanda Stickley has admitted to you everything she has done," Ben argued. "She would not, she could not do the things the State says she did. You've seen her, you've heard her. You be the judge. And Jeremy could not and would not do the horrible things the State has put forth in this case. So who killed Ralph Stickley? I argue and contend to you that you do not know. The State has not proven it and Wanda Stickley does not know. Do you know?" Ben slowly canvassed each juror and received one slight nod. There's hope, Ben thought, but not very much.

"There is no doubt there was a killer," Ben continued, "but who? It has to be a third person. There is somebody else and something else going on in this case. Nobody has been able to tell who or what but mark my words, the truth will come out. If you share the same doubts, then I say to you, you have a reasonable doubt and a reasonable doubt means not guilty."

The jurors sat expressionless. Ben decided to focus on the down side and offer the jurors a possible lesser verdict if they were not going to accept the defendant's version of the events that night. "Even if you believe it happened just as the State has contended, and we say there is no way that you can, but if you do, I say to you there is no way the State has proved premeditation and deliberation and there is no way the State has proved a specific intent to kill. These are required for first degree murder. And even if you believe there was malice which is required for you to convict of second degree murder, you must also believe that Wanda acted in the heat of passion. And if you believe she acted in the heat of passion as the judge will explain to you in her charge, then the most, the very most you have, is voluntary manslaughter."

"So, in closing I ask you one thing: give Wanda the justice our court system could never give her, give her justice and give her peace. There is but one way to do that." Ben surveyed the jurors again for any indication of support. He found grim faces and steely eyed stares. He braced for the worst but asked for the best: "Return a verdict of not guilty."

Under the court's rules, the State has the right to close the arguments when the defendant has offered evidence. Rod took the same approach as Randy and covered the "nuts and bolts" of the case: the elements of each offense and the facts that supported each element.

"There is one verdict and one verdict only by that approach," Rod analyzed. "If you find these to be the true facts of the case and if you follow the law as you told us you would during jury selection, there is only one verdict that reflects the truth. That verdict is guilty of first degree murder and the State of North Carolina asks you to return that verdict."

Butch charged out like an old time preacher. He started arguing before he stood up then walked straight to the jury box. "We can talk about the law and we can talk about the facts all day but I tell you this: my mama taught me some law. I remember it to this day and I'll bet you do too. Yes, sir, my mama taught me the law." He turned and pointed his finger directly at Wanda. "Mama taught me this law: caught red-handed."

A couple of jurors smiled at his homespun down to earth approach. It was refreshing and entertaining after all of the slow days of testimony and the repetitive nature of direct and cross-examination. He talked about the law that they understood: the law that you learned as a child, what you can do and what you cannot do. The law of the case required that they analyze the case much more carefully and exactly than Butch's approach would permit so not too many lawyers used the tactic any more. Still it was having an impact so Butch kept it up.

"And even though my mama tried to teach me everything I needed in this world, I still learned a thing or two when I came to this courthouse. I learned you can't leave your common sense at the door. Lawyers are great at cookin' somethin' up and making it appear more than it is. And that's what the defendant's attorneys are doing here. They are conjurin' up some mystery person, some spook out in the woods who just comes up and kills people. No reason. They've told you no reason. He, she, it, or whatever it is, just killed Ralph Stickley. Well, we have a phrase for that here at the courthouse: 'smoke and mirrors'." He stopped and laughed. "Don't leave your common sense at the door."

Butch continued with the show for over an hour. When Judge Godboldt's patience gave out, she rapped her fingernails on the bench a couple of times. Butch took it as a cue to close the performance. "Now I've talked long enough," he said. "Let me say one more thing and I'll quit. Let's go back to the beginning: mama's law. Remember: caught red-handed. Well, mama had another law and I'm sure your mother did too. I call it, 'tell the truth and the truth will set you free'. Don't let Wanda Stickley lie her way out of this. She's lied from the beginning and I contend to you she lied right there from that witness stand. And I can understand it." He picked up one of the more gruesome pictures of Ralph with his throat cut away. "If you did this, would you want to admit it. Well, mama wouldn't let her get away with it and don't you."

With Butch's argument concluded, Judge Godboldt instructed the jurors on the applicable law and sent them to the jury room to deliberate. She informed the attorneys to stay at the courthouse during the recess and be prepared to proceed as soon as the jury had reached a verdict and was ready to pronounce it. Then she directed the bailiff to recess court. Wanda was returned to the detention center and placed on twenty-four hour watch. Butch and Rod returned to the DA's office and Ben, Randy and Jim camped out in the lawyer's lounge.

"What do we do now?" Jim asked as Randy paced back and forth and Ben fumbled with a cigar wrapper.

"We wait," Ben explained. "We just wait."

"How long will it take?" Jim asked.

"A long time I believe," Ben said. "You can never predict what a jury will do or how long it will take them to do it. This jury has a lot of evidence and a lot of conflicting issues. I guess they will take a long time and sort it out." Ben watched Randy as she continued to walk a line on the floor. "Better take it easy, Randy. This could take awhile."

"Just burning out some nervous energy. I can do anything except wait. Drives me absolutely bananas."

"Well, that's the nature of this business: hurry and wait," Ben offered.

Randy continued to pace for a few more minutes and Jim worked at his laptop. Finally when the boredom was too much for Randy, she said, "What do you think? It's been thirty minutes."

"We've just started. Take awhile." Ben remarked disinterestedly as he thumbed through a magazine. He pulled on his cigar and let the smoke escape from both nostrils.

Randy waved the smoke. "I hope something happens soon or we may have another casualty." She pretended to cough. "Whew, second hand smoke. It's a killer."

Ben who was a veteran at the wait, the interminable wait, lifted his eyebrows barely acknowledging the complaint. He kept his head buried in the magazine as though he were involved in something important and Randy went back to walking. After another long period of silence, Randy sat down at the table across from Ben. Ben still did not look up. She cleared her throat. No response.

"What about Nora Jean?" Randy asked.

Ben finally decided he was going to have to entertain Randy whether he wanted to or not. "Well, what about what about Nora Jean?"

Randy smiled mischievously. "You caved in a lot sooner than you usually do."

Ben puffed the smoke directly toward Randy and argued, "Now I didn't cave in. I merely chose to help a neurotic, frenetic friend who is slowly driving herself crazy and will soon be sending us all into the loony bin if she doesn't find something constructive to do."

"I'm not."

"Not what?"

"Neither. I'm not frenetic and I'm definitely not neurotic."

"You are neurotic if you are a nail biter."

"I am not, repeat not, a nail biter," Randy protested.

"Let me see your little finger on your left hand."

Randy hid her hand. "I will not."

"All right. I rest my case." Ben picked up the magazine and started to turn the pages. It grew silent again except for Jim's keyboarding his computer. Finally Randy broke the impasse.

"You never did answer the question."

"What? Nora Jean?" Ben laughed. "Randy, you've been hanging around me too much. I believe you like to argue just for argument's sake."

"Do not."

"Do."

"Do not."

Ben started to speak then opted for a pull on his cigar. He savored the smoke and let it expire in a slow steady stream from his lips. "By the way," Ben remarked, "you did an excellent job on final argument. Very analytical, thought-provoking. Great summation."

"Thanks. I learned from the master: the great Ben Down."

Ben acknowledged the compliment with a nod. They had reached a truce for the moment and Ben went back to the magazine article he had been trying to read. It was a pithy, very biased statement, he concluded, on male egos. He gave up and started to flip the pages again.

"Nora Jean? Let's hear it." Randy insisted.

"What about it?"

"What did the she male, the shim, think of the sentence?"

"Twenty-nine to forty-four months. With the credit for the time she has already served, she'll be out in about two years. Now that's the way a case ought to go."

"What do you mean?"

"Nora Jean listened to everything I had to say and did it. I wonder where we would be in this case if Wanda had listened to us."

"Yeah," Randy agreed, "A lot better off for sure."

"Every now and again, you get a client that follows your advice," he mused. "Nora Jean adores me. She cried when I left her at the jail."

Ben grew silent for a moment as he thought about their last meeting then chuckled. "I told her to take care of herself while she was in prison. Well, actually I said, 'Watch your back side'. She just laughed and said, 'Are you kidding? They've put the fox in the hen house.'"

Ben laughed again. "She is different." Randy nodded in agreement and Ben said, ""You know she said she was going to figure out some way to help me out while she was in prison. I don't know what she meant but it'll definitely be interesting."

"She's already helped with Krait. I don't think I've ever seen anyone get that red before. Rod said Krait was thinking about leaving the DA's office."

Ben looked concerned. "Maybe I went too far. I just wanted him to know if you treat people badly, the people are going to treat you badly. I didn't want him to resign."

"Don't worry about it. He brought it on himself."

Randy stood and started pacing again. Ben went back to his magazine and Jim who seemed unperturbed by the tension continued to bang away at the computer in his own little world. After a while Randy pulled out her cell phone and called Skittle. When she hung up, she looked upset. She tossed the phone into her hand bag.

"Christ. I can't believe it. Those bastards," she complained out loud. "Skittle said I was just served with a motion for sanctions in the Big Burger case. They want a dismissal and they want me to pay their attorney fees."

Noticing Randy's angry tone, Jim stopped working. He said, "I thought we had answered everything."

"We did but . . . "

Before Randy could finish the report, the bailiff stuck his head in the door of the lawyer's lounge and announced, "We've got a verdict."

CHAPTER EIGHTEEN

Ben watched each juror's face carefully as they filed into the courtroom. After they had assumed their seats in the jury box, Ben leaned over and took Wanda's hand. "Remember what I told you," he whispered. "No matter what happens, do not react. We will still have to deal with this judge." He squeezed her hand lightly and said, "Good luck."

Randy reached over and took Wanda's other hand. Wanda glanced at her quickly and tried to smile but her attention was riveted on the jurors. They sat with blank stares and did not look at anyone.

"Let me have your attention please, ladies and gentlemen of the jury," Judge Godboldt announced and sat up stiffly in her chair. "Mr. Foreman, if you will stand please." As the foreman of the jury stood, she asked, "Has this jury reached a verdict?"

"We have, Your Honor," the foreman announced.

"Please hand the verdict form to the Sheriff and I will direct that the bailiff hand it to me."

The foreman and the bailiff did as directed and Judge Godboldt briefly scanned the verdict form. "All right, ladies and gentlemen, in the case of State of North Carolina versus Wanda Stickley, your foreman has returned as the unanimous verdict of the jury that the defendant is . . . ," Judge Godboldt raised her voice and gingerly adjusted the bun at the back of her head. "Guilty of second degree murder. Is that your verdict so say you all?"

Some jurors nodded and some answered out loud in agreement with the announced verdict. As the Judge polled each juror concerning whether the verdict was the juror's verdict and was still the juror's verdict, Ben felt Wanda pull her hand away. He had felt no perceptible movement when the verdict was announced but when he glanced at her, a tear slid down her cheek and she was reaching to her face to wipe it with the back of her hand. Ben felt in his coat pocket and retrieved a handkerchief. As he handed it to her, he whispered, "Stay strong. We still have a battle in front of us. Sentencing."

At the conclusion of the judge's poll, the verdict was accepted and recorded. Ben made several routine motions to set aside the verdict which were just as routinely denied. Judge Godboldt moved directly into sentencing and recognized the State for a presentation of the evidence on sentencing.

"Your Honor," Rod offered, "we will rest on the evidence presented during the trial and after the defendant has concluded her evidence, we would like to be heard."

Ben presented several mitigating factors for the judge's consideration, the most salient of which was Wanda had no criminal record. He argued for leniency based on her lack of criminal record, the great provocation by Ralph, the fact that she had been the sole support and a good mother for Jeremy, and the continuing residual doubts about what actually happened the night Ralph was killed. Ben argued for a sentence in the mitigated range based on these factors.

"Your Honor," he concluded, "this case cries out for justice, justice tempered with mercy. The lady you sentence today is a victim. A victim of Ralph Stickley. I ask that you not make her a victim again, a victim of our system of justice."

Judge Godboldt listened patiently without revealing how she was reacting to the request. When she recognized the State, Butch stood and appeared as agitated as he had been during his cross-examination of Wanda.

"Thank you, Your Honor," he began. "I have served the State of North Carolina for thirty years and I have served in these courts for longer than that. I have never seen anything like this. She murdered, she maimed, she tortured. You know everyone has speculated about that R that was carved in Mr. Stickley's chest. I say she carved the R to stand for rapist. She made a tombstone out of his own body."

Butch's voice began to quiver. "She is evil, she is dangerous, and she is a perjurer. She tried to lie her way out of it and those representing her tried to use her own son's perjured testimony."

"Objection," Ben called out and jumped to his feet. "He goes too far, Your Honor. He's . . . "

"We'll see," Butch challenged.

"All right, all right, counsel. Approach the bench," Judge Godboldt demanded.

When the four attorneys assembled for a side bar, Judge Godboldt led off. "Enough. I think the jury is still out on whether the defense sought perjured testimony."

Ben winced and started to argue the point. "But . . ."

She put her hand up and stopped Ben. "I think there is still a strong question of whether it was all a set up. Who knows? Maybe the DA sent Ms. Markham out there to the cookout to entrap defense counsel. It's all too pat." She looked at Butch with a steely glare. "It's like cheatin' at cards, Butch. Sometimes it's hard to break old habits."

Butch was outraged and turned a dark color. He tried to speak but nothing came out. Finally Rod tried to break the tension. "Your Honor, we want to make the point that this is an aggravated situation and . . . "

Judge Godboldt did not give an inch and continued to glare at Butch while she spoke to Rod. "I see the point, Mr. Pemberton. Now go back and make it some other way." She announced to the record, "Objection sustained."

When they returned to their tables, Butch continued the argument but without the force and fury he had brought to the beginning of the argument. He closed by focusing on Ralph's wounds. "She tried to decapitate him. She did cut off his penis. She stuffed it down his throat. She carved an R for rapist into his chest. She had plenty of time to stop but she slashed, carved and tortured over a long period of time. She premeditated and deliberated this killing and that's the factor in aggravation that makes this call for the maximum sentence in the aggravated ranger."

"Stand up, Mrs. Stickley," Judge Godboldt instructed. "Anything you want to say before sentence is pronounced?"

Wanda stood and trembled as she tried to speak. "Your . . . Your Honor, I'm, uh, I am innocent. I . . . love my son. I . . . " Tears streamed down her face and she stopped talking.

Judge Godboldt was unmoved by the tears and pronounced sentence as Wanda cried. "Clerk, make this entry. This is aggravated by premeditation and deliberation. There is a mitigating factor present: no record. Aggravation outweighs mitigation. I sentence you to the maximum for second degree murder: a minimum of sixteen years and a maximum of twenty years in the North

Carolina Department of Correction, no parole, no early release. Mr. Sheriff, she's in your custody."

Wanda started shaking uncontrollably and sunk into her chair. Randy put her arm around her and tried to console her without much success. Ben stood and announced that the defendant appealed to the North Carolina Court of Appeals. As soon as the appeal was entered in the record, Judge Godboldt instructed, "Take her out, Mr. Sheriff."

Wanda was led back to the holding cell and Ben and Randy followed. After the bailiff left, Wanda was standing and looking out of the window. She was still crying but seemed to have calmed considerably. Ben took a seat at the table and Randy, too tense to sit, stood by the door. They waited until Wanda stopped crying. She still had Ben's handkerchief and turned to hand it to him.

"That's all right," Ben said declining to take the handkerchief. He motioned toward a seat at the table and said, "Come and have a seat. Let's talk for a moment about the appeal."

Wanda lay the handkerchief on the table and continued to stand. The tears had slowed to a trickle and she started to speak.

Ben could see that she was still upset and said, "It's not over, Wanda. It's never over until the appellate courts uphold this trial. There are things that could overturn this . . . "

"I don't care. It's over for me."

"It's not," Ben argued quietly.

"You might as well have killed me yourself. Without Jeremy, I'm dead."

"I just saved your life. They had us on murder one and they had a good shot at the death penalty. You are still alive, Wanda. Still alive."

"Yeah, and ruined Jeremy's in the process. You had to bring him into it." She walked toward the door of the interview room and called the bailiff to take her to her cell in the lockup. The bailiff opened the door and positioned herself to take Wanda.

"I'm sorry you see it this way, Wanda, but we did all we could do," Ben pleaded.

As she walked out past Randy, she looked back at Ben. "I'll never forgive you for this."

After Wanda was led back to her cell, Randy and Ben collected their briefcases in silence. After a few moments Randy spoke. "God, this is awful."

Ben replied, "This is just a part of it. She is devastated. She'll come back around. I hope."

They walked down the hallway toward the lawyer's lounge to pick up Jim who was waiting for them. When they arrived, he asked, "How'd it go?"

Randy replied first, "Not good."

"I've got some more bad news for you," Jim added. "This morning when I came in I noticed that my computer had been moved. Just slightly but I'm so peculiar about it. I thought that the cleaning people might have come but I checked and they hadn't been there. I went through my computer files and I've been violated. Nothing missing but somebody took a tour of my software. So. I told Skittle and she checked your office," he said indicating Ben, "and she says someone has been through your desk and the file cabinet that you keep in your office behind the door."

Randy looked concerned and Jim said, "I don't know about your office. I asked Skittle to check but she says she can't tell."

"What's going on here?" Ben interjected. "This is screwy. Something is really rotten in Denmark. I'm telling you, there is something sinister going on in this case and we are just on the tip of the iceberg. Has anyone reported it to the police?"

"Yeah," Jim said, "Wilmington P.D. is on the scene now."

"Well, let's get over there," Ben said and picked up his briefcase.

They started out of the door and down the hall when Butch and Rod were coming up the hall carrying a stack of criminal files. Butch stopped in front of Ben and laid the files on a bench.

"Down, you oughta know," Butch stated. "That was some piece of work in there. I never knew you to be so shady but that was about as stinking a mess as anything I've ever witnessed."

"What are you talking about, Butch?" Ben demanded.

"You know very well what I mean. Trying to get that kid to lie for you. It's outrageous."

"What? You know that's not true."

"I know full well what Caroline Markham told me, told everybody in that courtroom."

"I could not and I would not do that. I can't believe that you would believe it for a moment."

"Oh, I believe it, all right," Butch charged. His face reddened and he grew louder. "Caroline Markham would not lie about it. And I can tell you one more thing. We're not going to stand for it."

"What do you mean?" Ben was visibly angry and stepped closer to Butch.

Rod took hold of Butch's arm and started to pull him back. He yielded and took a step toward Rod.

"You've lost your mind, Butch?" Ben charged and got into Butch's face.

They were almost chest to chest. Randy and Jim grabbed Ben and pulled him back and Rod did the same with Butch. They were ready to blow up and glared at each other. Again Rod tried to keep the peace. He shook his head at Randy and said, "I'm sorry about all of this, Randy. Really. Come on, Butch. Let it go."

Before Randy could speak, Ben said, "Me too but your boss is a fool."

Rod pulled Butch back to the bench and finally Ben released and started to walk on with Randy and Jim. As Ben walked past Butch, Butch turned toward Ben and stated emphatically, "I can tell you this, Down. I am going to see that you are indicted for what you did. Subornation of perjury and for tampering with and intimidating a State's witness. And I will personally make the complaint to the State bar. I will have your law license over this."

*   *   *

The weight room at the health club had the familiar smell of perspiration and muscle balm. Several bulky weight lifters helped each other as they worked through their sets. The Rolling Stones were blasting on the sound system with "Satisfaction" which intertwined with the beat music from the aerobics room to create a jumble all of its own. The bright lights, loud music and cheerleading staff put everyone in the mood to, as the sign over the door read, "Be strong or be wrong".

People moved in and out of the exercise area until late evening when the tide of sweat bathed, parttime athletes began to ebb. At the stationary bikes men and women in multicolored lycra rode several miles without ever leaving the room.   Rod, sweat drenched and muscle-bound, wore a large towel around his shoulders as he left the weight room. As he walked past the stationary bikes, he put his hand on Randy's shoulder as she spun the pedals at high revolutions. She lifted the earphones and let them slide to her neck.

"About to finish?" Rod asked.

"Just about. I've got about ten more minutes. What'ya got in mind?" Randy asked.

Rod lifted the towel to his forehead and wiped the perspiration. "Thought I would like to run about three. Wanta go?"

"Sure. Give me a few minutes to wind down and I'll join you."

"Great. I'm too hot to go out in this cold. I need a few minutes for a cool down. I'll wait for you up front."

Randy slid her earphones back on and watched as Rod walked to the locker room. She felt a surge of energy and put the bike on a hundred plus rpm's.   When she concluded the cycling circuit including the cool down, she stretched and trotted to the girls' locker where she changed to running gear. She met Rod up front and they walked to the parking lot.

"Where to?" she asked.

"I don't know. Let's see." He stretched his quads and leaned over to give his hamstrings a slow extension. "What do you think about running down by the River? It will be windy but it is beautiful this time of year on Front Street."

"Great. Three miles?"

"Perfect."

They leaned forward simultaneously and started a slow jog. They jogged out of the parking lot and turned onto the street. It was late and traffic was very light. They ran for about a quarter of a mile without speaking. As they adjusted to the effort, Rod pushed out a little ahead and Randy followed. By the half mile mark Randy had passed him and by the mile she had pushed out ahead by fifty yards. Rod struggled a little but finally caught up.

"Whew. You're feeling good," Rod said somewhat breathlessly.

"Yes, I do. I feel great now that the case is over. And I feel even better that we can be together again." She literally jumped with the excitement.

"Down, girl."

Randy slowed and pretended her feelings were hurt. "Well, aren't you a little glad to see me? Just a little bit?"

Rod grinned at her and replied, "Sure I am. It's been torture to see you every day and not be able to . . ."

"To what?"

"You know." He paused as she still wanted to hear the answer. "To hold you."

Randy smiled and kicked it again. Rod fell in behind and pursued. They ran through the historic district of old houses and beautiful lawns. They turned down by the courthouse and ran by it then climbed a slight hill before going down to the Cape Fear River. When they reached the walkway along the River, Randy slowed and Rod pulled along side. Usually the River walk was covered with tourists but at this hour, they were virtually alone. After a couple of minutes Randy spoke.

"How serious do you think Butch is about prosecuting Ben?"

"Very. That is the most upset I've seen Butch since I started working for him. He can't stand a crooked lawyer. And he thinks Ben just went too far to try to win."

Randy did not say anything but gave Rod a hard look.

"Look. I don't have anything to do with it."

"Ben is under a tremendous amount of pressure."

"Butch is under pressure in this case too. Women's groups have been driving us crazy."

"Yeah, but they wanted you to lighten up on Wanda."

"Well, we tried but she wouldn't take the deal. When it fell through, we had to do all we could to see that she was vigorously prosecuted." Rod stumbled but regained his footing quickly. "And the press. God, they have covered us up in this case. Plus some Senator down in South Carolina knows Butch from the old days. He's been calling Butch and trying to get Butch to settle the case."

"That's strange. What's he got to do with it?"

"He serves the Florence area and the people there were familiar with Ralph from his tobacco days. They're putting pressure on him and he's passing it on to Butch."

"Still. That's strange. This case was not that big."

Randy grew quiet and picked up the pace. They turned and started the slow climb from the River back to the health club. Rod and she stayed quiet as they slowly worked the incline. Finally Randy spoke. "What do you hear about the break-in at our offices?"

"I called Lieutenant Jones at the P.D. They really don't have any solid clues. No fingerprints, nothing stolen. Just rifled through the files. And Ben is no help. Mrs. Skittleran thinks there was a break-in but really Ben is not as organized as Jim or you."

"You gotta admit. It's pretty fishy. I think it has to have something to do with the Stickley case. That's the only thing that ties us all together. Plus the burglar didn't steal anything. Could've gotten thousands in computer equipment. They were looking for something."

"I'll let you know if I learn anything else about it."

They turned onto the street where the health club was located and started slowing down considerably to cool out. By the time they reached the parking lot, they were walking. The lot was almost empty except for a couple of employees' cars and Rod and Randy's vehicles.

Randy said, "We're almost too late to get back in."

"No, we're all right. I've got a twenty-four hour pass key."

Randy walked over to her car and Rod followed. Randy started opening the door with the key she had tied on her shoe. Rod asked, "What are you doin'?"

Randy grinned mischievously, opened the door and got in. "Let's get in and talk for a while."

Rod was a little reluctant. "No, let's go in and get our clothes and bags before the place closes."

"We can do that any time. Come on."

Rod still held back. "You know we have a city ordinance against loitering in motor vehicles."

"Well, how do you define loitering?"

"I don't know. Let's see." Rod grinned a little and scratched his head. "Wandering aimlessly about. Going around without some good purpose."

Randy grabbed him by the arm and pulled him in. "I can guarantee you you will not be loitering about aimlessly."

"Randy, we ought to go to my apartment."

"Don't be ridiculous."

She put her arms around him and pulled him to her. They kissed softly and Randy could feel the warmth of his body as they lingered in the embrace. They broke for a moment and Rod pulled her to him. He kissed her a little harder this time. Randy could feel her body tremble with anticipation as she ran her hands over Rod's body.

"You are trembling," Rod whispered.

"I am melting," Randy replied. "God, I have missed this. I have missed you."

She looked directly into his eyes and continued to let her hands gently slide over his upper body. She felt the muscles hardened from the workout in the gym. They were breathing harder and harder. They kissed again and Rod's tongue feverishly searched her lips. A light fog began to develop on the windshield.

"I can't take it any more," Rod said. "Let's climb over in the back seat."

Randy slid between the seats and Rod nimbly followed. When they reached the seat, Randy lay back and Rod extended himself lightly over her. They kissed hard again. Rod's hand began exploring Randy's chest and Randy pressed her fingernails into the lower part of his back. She playfully nibbled at his ear and then worked her way in a light sucking motion down his neck.

Rod sat up and said, "I'm dying. I've got to get rid of this shirt."

Randy helped him slide it over his head and he tossed it into the floorboard. He pressed against her and kissed her again. She pushed him partially back up. "Fair is fair," she said and started tugging at her tee shirt. Rod helped. When they slipped it up over her hair, she pulled him down on her. The light beard on his chin gently chafed her chest as he kissed her breasts. He took the front part of her breast into his mouth and sucked with some force. Then he did the same with her other breast as he massaged the other breast with his hand.

Randy pulled at his running tights and Rod gave in immediately. He pulled them off and began tugging at Randy's. She finished the effort with her running shorts with a hard pull and let them fall in the floorboard. Rod stretched out and let his body glide gently over her moist body. The car was totally fogged in and a light stream of steam slipped up from the crack in the rear window. He slid down and sucked at her breasts again. Randy's body was on fire.

"I want you, Rod. I want you now," Randy breathlessly whispered.

Rod started to slide back up to position when Randy rolled him over. Randy came forward until she was almost sitting atop Rod as he extended his body in the seat. They joined as one. Randy closed her eyes and slowly began to rock back and forth. Rod joined the motion and soon they were in a rapid rhythm. When it happened, Randy clawed Rod's arms and moaned. Just as soon as it started to subside, it started again and Randy frantically started rocking so hard the car began to shake with the motion. Rod grabbed the running tights and slid them around her buttocks. He started pulling until he had harnessed her movement and began to control it. She let out a murmur, "Oh, oh." She climaxed in long, flowing waves that seemed to transport her. Rod released the tights and let them gently, sensuously slide up and down her back. As he began to rise with her, he pulled the tights around her again and pulled himself deeper. Rod exploded.

After a while when the urgency subsided and they had slowed to a slow rocking motion, Randy whispered, "God, I needed this. This was pure lust."

Rod pulled her down to him and said, "I take it you are not mad at me."

"About what?"

"The case."

"Not on your life. You were a perfect gentleman and a great lawyer. I think we've just proved you can make war in the courtroom and make love in . . ."

Rod finished the sentence. "In the parking lot."

Randy giggled and looked around at the fogged rear window. "Sorry but I couldn't take it any longer. I needed this. I needed you."

Rod pulled her a little closer. "I needed this too. But I need something more."

"What?" Randy asked somewhat puzzled.

"Randy, I'm not a one night stand kinda guy. I want it to mean more. I want . . ."

Randy giggled. "I can't believe it. You must be the only guy in the world who would say that and actually mean it."

"Be serious, Randy."

"I am, Rod. You really are one in a million and a million to one."
She kissed him and whispered, "It does mean more."

*   *   *

Later that night Randy dropped by her office to pick up some files on the Big Burger case when she noticed that the light was on in Ben's office. At first she thought they had been burglarized again but she could smell the pungent odor of cigar smoke wafting down the hallway. She walked to her office then after retrieving her files, decided to drop in on Ben. She opened the door to his office and leaned in. The lights were off except for the lamp by Ben's desk. Ben sat slumped in his seat. Cigar smoke flowed upward in a swirl as the cigar lay in the ashtray. In front of Ben sat a bottle of Jack Daniels. A tall tea glass filled with the Knock'em sat beside it.

"Are you serious?" Randy asked. "Are you going to drink that?"

"With all my heart."

Randy watched him reach forward with a shaky hand, pick up the glass and take a large drink. He smiled a possum smile then looked at Randy as if to say, "How'd you like that?"

"What's wrong with you, Ben?"

"Oh, nothin'," he slurred his words, "Nothin' that a little vacation wouldn't cure. A little trip without leavin' the farm."

"What?"

Ben picked up the glass again and took another drink. He held out the glass to Randy. "You know," he spoke with a slur, "a little trip with my friend Jack." He rubbed the gray hair at the side of his head and added, "Nothing a little Grecian Formula wouldn't cure."

"Do you have a way home?"

"Got a home. Where there's a home, there's a way."

"Well, you had better not drive. Butch would love it. He'd love to have you on a DWI."

"Butch, smutch, he can kiss my red, rosy. That guy has been in power too long. He thinks he can run the world."

Randy watched Ben as he bumped his cigar so that it fell out of the ashtray. The ashes mushroomed up and flew out in a sprinkle over his desk. He picked up the cigar, blew at the ashes, and lay the cigar butt, end first into the ashtray.

"I'm driving you home. You've had enough excitement for one day."

"Huh, I'm not that far along. Just beginning to mellow out this evening. Mellow this evening out. Or one of those." Ben's eyes tried without much success to focus on the mess on his desk.

Randy sat down and Ben offered her a drink from the bottle. She waved it off and decided to stay with him awhile at least until she could convince him to let her take him home.

"Where's Margaret?"

"At home. Not feeling too well so I thought I would give her a little break from the ogre."

"You are not an ogre, Ben. Where do you get this stuff?"

"Well," Ben began to argue and attempted to focus his eyes on Randy. "Let me see if I can sum it all up, counselor. I lost the case, Wanda is in prison, . . . for most of her life. Jeremy is in foster care. A life with Ms. Caroline Markham. Good luck, Jeremy. Butch is mad at me. Going to indict me. I may go to prison myself. I'm going to lose my license to practice law. And you, Randy, who knows? Maybe I got you in trouble over this perjury business."

"No, you didn't."

"Well, at the very least, I didn't help you enough on the Big Burger case. You might get sanctioned. Even get thrown out of court." He shakily threw his hands up in the air demonstrating an explosion. "Poof and it's gone."

"I'll take care of Big Burger. I knew your hands would be full."

"How's about Roddy the Body?" Ben hiccuped. "Oops."

Randy grinned and sighed thinking about him. "Ummm. You mean, Rod. No problem."

"Problems, problems," he mumbled and reached for the glass again.

"Not all is lost."

He took a long drink. "Whatd'ya mean?"

Randy smiled at him and said, "You saved Thor."

Ben grinned back at her. "So I did, so I did. I saved a dog. Tell'em that down at the State Bar. Maybe they will let me practice in Wapner's Animal Court."

"You saved Nora Jean."

"Yeah, I did, didn't I?"

"Seriously, Ben. You are taking all of this too hard."

"You're right," he slurred. "I'm at the bottom. It's all up from here." Ben lifted his glass to toast the moment. "Three cheers. Down is up and up is Down."

"Surely nothing else can go wrong."

Ben sat his glass down with a thud. He looked as serious as a booze hound who has run out of liquor. "Something can always go wrong and it can always get worse. You can quote me on it."

He bumped the cigar again and it fell from the ashtray onto his desk. As he tried somewhat unsuccessfully to maneuver it back in place, the telephone rang. He looked at Randy with a "Would you get that?" look. Randy picked up the phone and took the message. She slammed the phone down and stood up.

"Ben, let's go," she stated excitedly. "That was Skittle. She's at the hospital. They've been looking all over for you. It's Margaret. She's been taken to the ER."

CHAPTER NINETEEN

New Hanover Regional Medical Center was busy for a Friday night. The parking lot was full and the halls were packed with patients, nurses, orderlies, doctors, family, and friends. The facility designed to serve the City of Wilmington was bulging at the seams with the health problems of a quickly expanding urban population. People moved around freely along the corridors and access was freely given to the public to almost every part of the hospital.

One area that was sequestered and strictly secured was the Intensive Care Unit. Referred to as the ICU, the unit occupied the greater part of one floor of the hospital and was cloistered with a parameter coded entry system. The system was designed to keep the great push of humanity that occupied the halls at bay and to provide an area where very high risk patients could receive skilled medical and nursing care 24-7.

Ben punched the buttons at the door to the ICU without much success. He pressed then banged the numerical keyboard. Nothing.

Randy watched as Ben quickly lost his temper. "Are you sober?" she asked.

"Sober as a judge," Ben grumbled and continued to attempt to access the number pad. "We've got to get in here."

"I told you we should have waited until someone brought us up from the ER."

"You don't wait in a time of crisis. You take command." Ben fired back as he continued to punch various combinations of numbers into the coded entry assembly.

Finally an orderly came to the door and started to ask what the problem was. Before he could speak, Ben said, "Margaret Down. Which room is she in?"

"Sir, you can't . . . "

Ben pushed on in followed by Randy. He started to walk on toward the nurse's desk and the orderly rushed forward and stepped in front of them.

"Wait a minute. I'm tellin' ya' you can't come in here without permission."

Ben feigned a move to the right faking out the orderly and marched on to the nurses' station. Randy shook her head in wonder at Ben's persistence. She followed at a distance. When Ben reached the nurses' desk, a little short round lady built like a small Volkswagen dressed in starchy nurse's white stood and put up her hand.

"Stop right there, mister."

Before she could say anymore, Ben informed her, "I'm here to see Margaret Down. Where is she?"

Nurse Volkswagen stared at him and sniffed him. She said, "Sir, have you been drinking? If you do not leave immediately, I will be forced to call security." She looked at the orderly who had a look of uncertainty on his face. "This young man will escort you to the ICU lobby."

"Not a chance," Ben remonstrated. He looked at the orderly who withered up under his glare. "I'm here to see Margaret Down. As soon as I have done that, I will do anything you say. Until then, deal with that." He slapped his State Bar card on the desk as though it were an official pass to go anywhere he chose.

The VW bent over slightly and scrutinized the card. She huffed. "That's a card that says you are a lawyer. Might've expected this kind of conduct from you. And how about you?" Nurse VW asked referring to Randy.

"Oh, I'm one too. And be careful it may be contagious."

Nurse VW picked up the phone and punched in a series of numbers. "Security, we have a problem in ICU. Please come at once."

A middle-aged doctor who had observed the commotion came quickly down the hall and called, "Ben, Ben." When he came closer, he spoke to Nurse VW. "Mary Jean, it's all right. He's okay. I know him well. He's Ben Down, a lawyer here in town and I have his wife here in the ICU."

She looked at the doctor then looked back at Ben. She shook her head as if she were hesitant to obey the doctor's suggestion. Eventually she relented although it was clear that it was against her better judgment. "All right, Doctor Patel, if you say so." She picked up the phone again and punched in the numbers. "But that's not the way we do things here. It's not."

"It's all right," Doctor Patel repeated.

She told the security office the problem had been solved and to cancel the request for security. The doctor directed Ben and Randy to a family conference room between the patients' rooms. When they were seated, Ben asked, "Nori, how is she?"

Doctor Patel had a very concerned look on his face and spoke in even measured tones. "Frankly it's not too good, Ben. I don't want to alarm you but Margaret is a very sick person. She was admitted to the ER after being transported by emergency services and she was complaining of chest pains and shortness of breath. Since I was on rotating duty in the ER, the resident called me for a consult. When I found out who it was, I came on immediately."

As he talked, he began to notice Randy who had followed them to the conference room. Ben said, "Sorry, Nori. This is Randy Bost. She is an attorney here in town and practices in the same building with me."

"I thought I had seen her. Been seeing you on the television in that murder case." He offered by way of explanation. "Ben used to be a prosecutor at the courthouse. I used to have to testify a lot when I was a resident so we become pretty good friends. And his daughters are friends with my daughter. Ben, have Sandy and Mary Lee been notified?"

"No, I don't think so. I was just wrapping up the murder case." Ben gave Randy a hard look to make sure she did not mention the drinking. "I just found out myself so I don't think they have been called. I'll call them myself in just a little bit. How is Margaret now?"

"She is stable but very weak. We suspect a heart attack but we haven't been able to confirm it. We are getting some very strange x-rays for one thing. We're going to have to get a radiologist who can make some sense out of them."

Ben asked, "Can I see her?"

"Yes, but just for a few minutes. Margaret is a strong woman but she needs all of the rest she can get now. She's down the hall, 304, let's see, three doors down on the right."

Ben stood and walked out of the room. As he did, Doctor Patel spoke to Randy. "He is a great lawyer, yes? He was in the courtroom when I was there. He make good points, he win a lot of cases."

Randy looked off in the distance. "He's better than even he knows. Looks like he's in for a hard road with Margaret."

"Yes, she is very sick. I think we will find a heart attack but I cannot be sure. And those places on the x-rays look too big to be benign. Yes, it can be very bad but we will see." He stood and said, "It was very nice to meet you, Ms. Bost. I hope to get to see you in court some day. You be great too?"

Randy stood as well and smiled. Thinking of the Big Burger case which was coming up, she answered, "I hope so."

Ben made his way down the hall and found Room 304. He pushed the door open slightly and peeped in first. He saw Margaret on the bed. Her face was pale and she appeared to be asleep. She was connected to an IV tree and had numerous tubes running to different parts of her body. She had a finger monitor taped in place which gave a digital readout of her blood pressure and pulse on a machine to her side. He listened to the beeps and felt reassured when they pulsed regularly. Ben moved and stood quietly by her bed.

In a few moments Margaret's eyes opened slightly then she drifted back to sleep. Again in just a few moments her eyes opened again and she slowly fixed her gaze on Ben. When she recognized him, she smiled weakly.

Ben reached down and took her free hand. He talked quietly. "How are you?"

"I'm all right. Just some pain every now and then in my chest."

"Has someone let Sandy know? I called and left a message for Mary Lee. I told her I was going to the hospital but it wasn't urgent so she wouldn't hurt herself trying to get here." She looked tired when she finished the statement.

"I'll call Sandy and I'll check on Mary Lee. You just rest and not worry about anything." Ben patted her hand and looked at her carefully.

Margaret's eyes seemed gray and sat deeper in hollow dark sockets. He noticed that the least movement seemed to be drawn out and in slow motion. Maybe it was the medication, Ben hoped. He started getting short of breath himself and he breathed a little harder. A tear formed in his eye and dropped on the sheet.

"Now, now," Margaret comforted. "No need for that. I'm all right. A little time and I will be as good as new. I'm just tired. Just . . . " She drifted back into sleep.

Ben was upset with himself that he had not been stronger. Margaret was everything to him, he thought. He remembered when he married her and how beautiful she was at their wedding on the beach. He remembered her in a picture that was framed into his mind: she was holding Sandy and Mary Lee when they were little on the steps at the back of their house. God, I should have been stronger, he almost spoke out loud. He held on to her hand and thought about his law practice. He never should have spent so many hours on such meaningless cases, he never should have worked at night while Margaret was at home alone. When it came down to it, he thought, the only woman he had ever loved was lying on the bed and who knows, may be dying while he was worrying over some case, a case he had just lost and a case in which he may wind up indicted himself. Margaret was the only one who ever cared, he murmured. Another tear streamed down his face. "I should've been stronger."

He was startled when Margaret spoke. "No, you are strong enough. You are my hero, Ben. Always have and always . . . " She closed her eyes and slipped back into twilight.

*　　　　　　　　*　　　　　　　　*

"Senator Fowler Worrell, at your pleasure, suh," the Senator said and extended his hand. The guest put out his hand and shook the Senator's hand vigorously. Several people still waited to go through the receiving line. "It's wonnerful to see you again. How you doin'? Good. Good."

The Senator stood in the vestibule of the Governor's Mansion with other dignitaries as the crowded line thinned. Most of the guests had located their table and were seated. The Senator stood until he had wrung the last bit of political gain out of the long receiving line.

"Ummm--mmm, smells good. You won't get any bettah eatin' from the Upstate to the Low Country. The Governor's cook is probably the best in South Carolina. Good lawd, that smells like. It is. Collards. Whew. I hadn't had that since I was down at Hilton Head. It's enough to make a Carolina boy wanta take that sandy road back home." The Senator loved a crowd and loved to make sure everyone knew he was South Carolinian born and bred.

Wrenn Davies, the Senator's Chief of Staff, stood within earshot of the Senator so that he could be reached if needed. He talked to the legislators from Orangeburg and Cheraw as he watched the Senator. When the crowd finally dissipated, the Senator motioned at Davies indicating he wanted to take a smoke and pointed toward a side door to a garden. Davies diplomatically begged the pardon of his small group and worked his way over to the door. The Senator hugged the "dahling" wife, as he called her, of State Senator Camden and slipped out the door.

Davies pulled out a cigarette and handed it to the Senator. He lit it for him and then lit one for himself. Worrell took a deep draw on the cigarette and exhaled as though he were letting off a little steam. He savored the smoke and the night air.

"Columbia in the winter," the Senator sighed. "Too hot in the summer but lovely in the winter. One of the finest places I've ever been. You know, Wrenn, I served five terms right heah on this hill in the legislature. I enjoyed it. Times were lean then but they was easy. I always enjoy comin' back heah. I coulda even have been Guv'nah but I was always dreamin' biggah."

Davies enjoyed the cigarette and remarked in agreement, "Yes, Fowler. I like this place too. The players here seemed to be a little more provincial, more down to earth and the game seemed to be a little less hard ball. But I can't complain either. We're doing very well."

The Senator slapped Davies on the back. "Very well? Hell's bells, boy, business is boomin'. The truth is we've never had it so good. I remember when I was pickin' cotton, seven cents an hour. Chilly in the mornin' and hot, steamy swamp in the aftuhnoon. It was killin' me. But now. I don't even have to pick up the telephone and I've made a cool million. In fact if I worried about anything, I'd worry about those IRS boys. Hard to hide this much money comin' in."

"China turned out to be a gold mine."

"Exactly. You can say a lotta things about those Chinese but one thing is for shore. They don't mind spreadin' out the money. We're already rich, Wrenn, but you know if it keeps up we might turn out to be like Howard Hughes or Onassis."

The Chief of Staff flipped his ashes out over the small fence and took another pull at the cigarette. He gazed out over the lights of downtown Columbia. "Fowler, that case in Wilmington wasn't as important as we thought it was. She's convicted, case closed. And Chen went through the defense attorneys' files. They weren't even close. They don't have a clue."

"Now there you go, Wrenn, countin' your chickens before they hatch. There's still a loose end or two. For one thing they've got one of 'em checkin' old Stick's mother. She's dirty as a chimney sweep. If they dig enough, things could unravel from there. I think we bettah get ol' Chen to make a visit to that ol' Southern belle. See if we can get her to sit on that money a little tightah."

"Seriously, Senator," Davies advised, "we ought to let that slide. They've finished the case. It's over. And they won't find out anything about her and I know she won't tell them anything."

The Senator disagreed with the advice. "You underestimate that lawyer Down. He may be a drunk but he's no quitter. When I was havin' him checked out , I heard a story about 'im. One time when he was a DA up thah, a judge came to town and started turnin' evahbody loose. Made ol' Down mad. He stood up, right in court, tol' the judge that's all the cases he was callin' in front of that judge and he walked right out tha door. Boom, out the door he went. Well, the judge sent for 'im. He wouldn't come. The judge sent the Sheriff to get 'im. He wouldn't come. The next time the judge sent the Sheriff back with a message if he didn't come, he was goin' to jail. He still didn't come. So the Sheriff picked him up and took 'im in front of the judge. The judge said, 'Why didn't you come?' 'Cause I'm right and you're wrong' he said bigger than evahthang. His mouth got him put in the jail. His boss threatened to fire him if he didn't apologize. He wouldn't apologize. And you know what happened. After a while they just gave up. He wore 'em out." The Senator spat out into the garden. "He's a hard case, boy. Never underestimate a hard case."

Davies did not respond. He knew the Senator: when his mind was made up, there was no changing it. Davies looked back inside the dining room and saw that most of the people were locating their seat. "Maybe we ought to head back, Fowler."

"In due time, in due time," the Senator commented offhandedly as though he were still in thought. He pulled in another drag off the cigarette and said, "You know the FBI is absolutely stonewalled in China. I would've nevah believed it if I hadn't seen it with my own eyes. Ol' Fries." He laughed out loud. "When I see Fries on television, I can tell he is so mad he could bite through a railroad spike."

"China is a closed society. Closed even to the great power of the United States."

"Yeah, that big ol' wall won't put up theah for nothin'. The thinkin' that built that Great Wall is still thinkin' ovah theah." He flicked the ashes on his cigarette and watched the sparks get lifted up by the breeze.

"They'll never break the assassination over there. If anything happens, it will be right here in the United States."

"What d'ya mean?" The Senator seemed irritated that something could go wrong on this end.

"Chen. He's good but he has no fear. One slip and he's gone. If he's gone, who knows? Maybe we're gone."

The Senator laughed heartily. "Chen. Are you kiddin'? That boy is put togethah tightah than a tick. He won't mess up nothin'. And he will do anything, anything we say. When ol' Gedney was runnin' his mouth down at the prison in Goreville and wantin' this and that for his brother Bobby, and I didn't want to do anything about it, and then he actually threatened us--whew, I coulda killed him myself--well, anyway we sent ol' Chen to work on him. Problem solved. You know what Chen did?"

Davies looked a little surprised. "I do but how'd you find out? I thought he was to report only to me."

"I didn't get it through Chen. I got it from a friend of a friend and put two and two togethah. Anyway. Chen went down to Conway, right to Gedney's house, and talked to 'im. I don't know what he said but it must've scared him pretty badly. Then ol' Chen went to Gedney's mother's. You know how crazy Gedney is about his mothah. Chen broke in and put a rope around her cat's neck right in front of her. Strung the cat up and he and the ol' lady watched it kick and choke 'til it was dead. Told her she was goin' to get to watch the same thing happen to Gedney. No doubt she tol' ol' Gedney about it. She reported it to the police but it was so crazy they didn't even believe she was tellin' the truth. Anyway." The Senator laughed. "Ol' Gedney shut up. I ain't heard nuthin' from 'im, you?"

Davies shook his head. The Senator grew quiet and worked on the remainder of his cigarette. He was in deep thought until a lady tucked her head out of the door of the ballroom and asked, "Senator, you going to avoid us all night? The pretty ladies won't like it." The Senator threw up his hand, smiled at her and indicated he was coming in.

He leaned back on the rail and looked out over the garden. Finally he stood up. He looked at Davies and had that dead earnest look he would get when everything had been said and done and it was time to make a decision.

"Never underestimate a hard case." The Senator flipped his cigarette into the garden and turned to go in.

*   *   *

Joel Rueslo's father was a judge and his father before him was a judge. It was a family tradition that was as deep as the folds in the elder Rueslo's robe. So it came as somewhat of a surprise and disappointment when Joel left college with an eye toward becoming a singer. He sang in theatrical productions off Broadway and regional theater throughout the South but although he was well-received, the career he desperately wanted never took wings. Tired and defeated he returned to the waiting arms of his family who immediately opened doors to the family law school at the University of North Carolina at Chapel Hill.

Upon graduation he joined a firm in the quaint little piedmont town of Lincolnton where he was assigned to collections, research, and second banana to the firm's senior trial lawyer. He worked hard and developed trial skills while he made friends among the Bar by entertaining the attorneys and their families with song at the Christmas party each year. When the county political leaders needed someone to sing the national anthem at the opening of the county convention, he was the natural choice.

He gravitated more toward the business work of the firm and after several years became corporate counsel for the two largest concerns that the firm represented. When the opportunity presented itself, he moved to in-house counsel for Insock Corporation, a textile firm with a regional footprint. In two years he became associate counsel and in five years he was named chief counsel. He made political friends as he fought the North American Free Trade Agreement which threatened textile jobs in North Carolina. By the time he had reached his late fifties, he had grown tired of the travel, the politics, the corporate infighting and the sixty hour weeks.

It was at that time that his father was retiring as judge and without much effort at recruiting support, he was named by the Governor as the replacement. In chambers he was known to break into song but on the bench he gained a reputation of being obstinate, short tempered and grumpy. Well-versed in the law he was intolerant of lawyers who had not done their homework. He was a stickler for courtroom decorum. He was from the old school of lawyers who had not fully accepted women in the courtroom.

Pro big business, gruff and antifeminine. It was this reputation that Randy confronted when she found out which judge had been assigned to hear the Big Burger sanctions motion. Again Skittle and she put the "rolling road show", as they called it, into motion by carrying boxes and carting the files generated by the Big Burger case into the courtroom. Since this was a motions docket dedicated to hearing preliminary matters in cases that were scheduled for trial in the next few weeks, there were numerous lawyers present. The road show had an immediate support staff as the male lawyers helped move the boxes and carts into the courtroom.

Randy was very familiar with Rueslo's tactic of blowing out the first lawyer who had not fully prepared so she had researched, studied, graphed, plotted, and exhibited her presentation. She put two easels against the wall that tracked the course of discovery in the case. She stacked the boxes of documents that had been located, copied in triplicate and alphabetically arranged for ease of access. The array was impressive and visibly demonstrated the work she had done in the case.

The issue itself was rather narrow: had the plaintiff failed to fully respond to the defendant's discovery requests? The result though could be particularly brutal: sanctions entirely in the judge's discretion up to and including dismissal of the case and payment of attorneys fees which could be considerable since two law firms, Diehlinger in Wilmington and Bayready in Atlanta, were running their meters at full throttle. Simple matter but with potentially devastating results, Randy thought, as she sat with Skittle on the first bench behind the tables in the courtroom.

As Randy waited with the other attorneys for the opening of court, she scanned the courtroom to see who was present for the calendar call. All of the big firms were there. Represented by the junior members of the firms who were accompanied by the associates who had done all of the real work on the cases, the attorneys from the largest law firms in town were back at the office generating fees. The silk stocking lawyers, as Randy called them, were visibly absent and the argyle boys, again as Randy called them, were lined up to do the firm's tedious work. In the back of the courtroom she saw through the crowd the flaming red hair of her opponent Diehlinger He was busy pompously regaling the juniors with some war tale.

Skittle asked, "How do you think it will go?"

"Don't know, Skittle," Randy mumbled. "I've heard this judge is a woman hater and since he was a corporate lawyer, has a big business bias. Could be a bad day for the home team."

"You'll do all right," Skittle encouraged. She started singing softly, "Keep your eye on the prize."

Randy grinned at her and said, "I'll do my best."

In a few moments they could hear some noise outside of the courtroom. As the crowd settled down to hear what was going on, the noise cleared to the sound of music. It was the judge singing. His voice was beautiful and full as it carried from the judge's chambers through the hallway into the courtroom. The voice easily moved through the scales and then picked up a recognizable tune.

Suddenly the door popped open and the judge trailed by the bailiff briskly walked into the courtroom. As the bailiff opened court and everyone stood, the judge turned his attention to Randy's display on the side wall of the courtroom. As soon as everyone was seated, the judge picked up his docket to begin the call of cases then laid it down. He turned in his chair and stared directly at the stack of boxes.

"Whose mess is this?" he asked.

Randy felt the palms of her hands turn moist. She stood and spoke somewhat mouselike, "Mine, uh, Your Honor."

"Speak up. You're a lawyer, aren't you?"

"Yes, sir, " Randy said a little louder this time.

"What's this all about?"

Randy had regained her voice and her composure enough to say, "I have a case on Your Honor's docket."

"Well, sure you do, but why all the show?" The judge was curt and peered down over his glasses.

"Uh," Randy began to stumble again. "A motion for sanctions."

"Well, let's get this over with right now. Is the other attorney here?"

From the back of the courtroom Diehlinger stood and began walking proudly toward the front. "I am, Your Honor, and may I say? I particularly enjoyed the melodious rendition this morning."

"Diehlinger. It's you." The judge groaned under his breath. He looked back at Randy and demanded, "Well, young lady, what's this motion all about?"

Diehlinger started to speak and the judge without looking at him said, "I'm not talking to you, sir. I'm talking to the feme counsel." He seemed to spit out the word feme as though it left a bad taste in his mouth.

"This is the case of Barefoot versus Big Burger Corporation," Randy tried to explain. "The defendant has moved for a dismissal of our lawsuit contending that we failed to answer interrogatories."

"Yes, yes, yes, but what are all the boxes and diagrams for?"

"They depict the amount of work we've put into answering defendant's requests for information in this case."

The judge looked at Diehlinger and asked, "Are you the only counsel in this case?"

Diehlinger smiled at the judge. "Oh, no, Your Honor. I'm pleased to be associated with the Bayready firm in Atlanta on this case."

"Huh," the Judge grunted.

"All right, Mr. Diehlinger. What do you say about this motion?"

Diehlinger was a little surprised to be called to make his presentation before the docket call and began to fumble through his briefcase for the brief. The judge gave him about three seconds to fumble then asked, "Aren't you ready in this case, Mr. Diehlinger?"

"Uh, yes, sir, Your Honor," he stated as his face began to pick up a little color.

"You don't need the brief. Tell me what it's about."

"Ah, here it is," Diehlinger announced as he finally dug the motion itself out of the briefcase. "Your Honor, this is a motion for dismissal and attorney's fees."

"We know that," the judge stated matter of factly.

"Yes, sir." Diehlinger flipped through the first couple of pages of the motion and said, "The plaintiff in this case failed to answer interrogatories eight and eleven of the fourth set of interrogatories."

"Fourth set," the judge commented.

"Yes, sir, and failed to give us the information we required on interrogatory seventeen of the fifth set of interrogatories. And the admission on requested admission twelve of the second set of Admissions of Fact was unclear. We are requesting that the plaintiff's case be dismissed for this egregious violation of discovery rules."

Judge Rueslo peered down over his glasses at Randy. "Well, what do you say?"

Randy started to walk over to one of the easels to point to the graph on the chart. Judge Rueslo stopped her and asked, "Why do you need all that? Can't you just answer the question?"

"Well, Your Honor, I thought I could explain why we thought we had complied and do it more clearly with the exhibit."

"No. We don't need that. What we need today are lawyers who speak clearly, who can create a picture with the brilliance of their words. You know an operatic soprano with just the lilt or caress of a tone can express volumes in mood. We spend too much time on useless things rather than trying cases." He looked over at Diehlinger. "Like discovery disputes. Now," he turned his attention again to Randy. "Tell me one sentence at a time what this case is about and paint a picture with each sentence."

"Um, Your Honor," Randy continued to stumble.

"All right, come on. You wanted to be a lawyer. Here's your chance."

"Yes, sir." Randy stood up straighter and thought quickly through the case. "This is a case of Phoebe Barefoot versus Big Burger Corporation. It is a case of David versus Goliath. Big Burger is a multinational corporation with the best lawyers money can buy and Miss Barefoot has had the temerity to hire me. I'm doing the best I can." She looked over at the railroad boxcar full of paperwork.

"Uh-huh." The judge nodded.

"Phoebe was employed at Big Burger. She along with two other female employees was forced to strip and was stripsearched by their employer. There was absolutely no reason for it. She was humiliated, devastated, virtually became a shut in over the nightmare." She looked over at Diehlinger. "Now we have answered every question, provided every document. I've called every governmental agency and obtained the documents they've requested, I thought, until this motion came up. I've gone to the Clerk of Court's office, the Register of Deeds, the tax office, the IRS, previous employers, and . . . "

The judge held up his hand to stop Randy.

"All we want is our day in court," she continued. "We started with three plaintiffs and the defendant through private detectives, lawyers, governmental agencies has browbeat and intimidated us until we are hanging on, barely hanging on, with one plaintiff. And all she wants, all I want, is a chance to have this case heard. Win or lose, just give us a chance." Randy was more frustrated than she thought and was surprised at her speech. She added one more thing. "Your Honor, let us sing the lead one time."

"I get the picture." The judge nodded his head and then swiveled in his chair toward Diehlinger. "Well, Mr. Diehlinger, what do you say about that?"

"Your Honor," he argued putting his hands out in front of him pleading with the judge. "All we want is for them to comply with the rules. Just simply . . ."

The judge interrupted him. "Well, let me give counsel a picture. You are wasting too much time with junk in this case. Get down to the meat of it. Try your case, counsel. Motion dismissed." He turned to the audience and announced, "All right, counsel at the bar. Let's get this docket called."

Out in the hallway Skittle was congratulating Randy as they waited until recess to remove the boxes and carts from the courtroom. As they waited, Diehlinger pushed his way out of the courtroom. His face was scarlet red. He charged over to Randy and Skittle.

"I saw you and Down lost your big murder case," he groused. "And looks like the singing judge is going to let you have a chance to lose this one."

Randy did not respond. Diehlinger's eyebrow twitched from the repressed anger. "You know you can settle this case," he stated. "All you have to do is be reasonable."

Randy replied, "No thank you, sir. I've tried reasonable. It doesn't work with you."

Diehlinger turned even redder. "Well, have it your way. But it won't be so easy after this. Bayready is coming to try the case. I'm the thunder and he's the lightning."

"So you're out and Bayready's in. Hope he's better than you. You've lost everything we've had together."

Diehlinger was so angry he started to stalk off and turned directly into the wall.

"Careful," Randy cautioned.

Diehlinger whirled around and angrily exclaimed, "No, you better be careful."

"I've got the picture."

*   *   *

Ben reeked of whiskey as he took a seat at the table in the conference room. The room was lined with old law books and had a smell of its own. Musty and dark it was hardly ever used unless there was a need for more space. Ben, Randy and James were meeting to discuss the appeal in Wanda's case and needed a large table to spread out James' computer and all of the paperwork contained in their files. When everyone was seated, Randy had a very concerned look on her face.

"Ben, how's Margaret?" she inquired.

"Not very good. She is going to have a heart catherization today. Doctor Patel is almost certain she has had a heart attack but they have to stabilize her before they can do anything for it." His eyes welled up with tears. "She has congestive heart failure and they have been trying to pull the fluid away from her heart. And to complicate matters, they have found a mass in her right breast. That didn't show up until they did an MRI."

"How is Margaret holding up?" James asked.

"Margaret? Better than can be expected. I mean she always was the strong one in our family. Emotionally she seems to be fine." Ben choked up a little bit as he talked about it.

"How's Ben holding up?" Randy wanted to know.

"Not too good. She's . . . she's . . ." He just could not talk about it further and changed the subject. "Let's talk about the case. I've got to get my mind on something else for a while."

Randy reached over and patted his arm. "Ben, if we can help, you know we will."

"Really. It's okay." He cleared his throat. "What about Wanda? Does she still want us on the appeal?"

Randy opened the file in front of her and scanned a note. "I told her if she would rather someone else handle the appeal in view of her feelings about the trial, we would be glad to apply to the court for a replacement attorney for the appeal. I told her we needed something in writing from her."

She pushed the note out on the table and James picked it up. He read out loud. "Randy, do whatever you want to about the appeal. I am not in any frame of mind to think about it. My heart is broken. I will very likely never see Jeremy again. Wanda Stickley."

Ben winced and wiped at his eyes.

Randy said, "I know she's still upset but I think we will have to go forward with the appeal. We're still her attorneys and will be until the court tells us differently. The way I interpret the note we really have no choice."

"Well, I think we could apply to the court to be removed," Ben offered, "but I really don't want to. I think we ought to follow it through to the bitter end."

Randy argued, "That's pretty negative. This case is ripe for appeal. There are numerous errors in the case."

"Such as," Ben inquired.

"Numerous evidentiary rulings are not supported by the law. I mean Butch got away with murder on some things. Judge Godboldt repeatedly overruled our objections to Butch's characterization of Ralph's assault on Wanda as a 'scuffle'. The record is replete with rulings that aren't supported by the law."

"Error but not reversible error," Ben offered.

Randy was a little put out by the assessment and asked impertinently, "Well, what do you think is reversible error in the case, Ben?"

He leaned forward and put his head in his hands as though he were nursing a pretty serious headache. He did not function quite as pleasantly with a hangover and replied just as haughtily, "Well, I'll tell ya' this. This is a murder case. They won't say the rules are different but they are. The DA can get away with evidentiary murder when the stakes get this high. The appellate court will find that the judge's rulings were error but it will never overturn a verdict on evidentiary technicalities." He rubbed his head and squinted as he tried to talk and think at the same time. "There are two places in this case where the judge erred and they are serious enough to warrant a new trial."

Randy looked at him as though she doubted his analysis. Ben noticed and responded, "Really it has to be a major violation of the rules to justify remanding for a new trial."

"Well, let's hear them."

He stretched slightly and his head began to spin a little. His face turned a little white and his palms were clammy. "Sheeeeees," he said and tried to concentrate. "All right, here it is. First. Judge Allgood's ruling admitting Wanda's statement into evidence violates her right to remain silent and her right to counsel. Constitutional violations. Secondly Judge Godboldt's denial of the motion for a mistrial when Butch put in evidence my so-called statement to Jeremy, 'tell them you did it'. Serious hearsay violation, injected my credibility in the case and violates the defendant's right to effective assistance of counsel. If the appeals court is going to give us any relief, it will come right there."

Randy seemed convinced and did not argue the point. She turned to James. "What do you think?"

"I've never taken a case up on appeal. I don't have any idea what will turn the Supremes on."

"Court of Appeals, Jim. They are not the Supremes or even Justices. They are appellate judges." Ben was in a cranky mood.

"See what I mean. I don't even know who will rule on it. I'm willing to help with research and document preparation but someone else will have to do issue development."

Randy looked at Ben. Ben looked at Randy. They were reaching a mental impasse over who would do what in the appeal. Finally Randy caved in. "All right. I'll take the bulk of it. I've already done the research for the motion to suppress on Wanda's statement. I'm going to read the transcript so I'll develop the evidentiary errors. James, you help Ben with research on the so called perjury issue." James nodded and Ben tried to, but his head hurt. "I'm going to trial on the Big Burger case in a few days and we won't get the transcript for another sixty days so we've all got some running room."

Randy looked at Ben and James. "All said and done?"

"No," James said as he happened to think of something. "It's a little late but I finally put together some information on Ralph's mother." He clicked his computer on and ran through several files until he came to the right one. He read from the screen. "Ruth Leslie Stickley. Widow. Formerly married to Walter Garson Stickley. Deceased seven years ago. Resides Wilmington. According to Register of Deeds records. Sold house about five months ago. Tax records say it was worth $85,000. Still had an uncancelled deed of trust. Bought a new house on Oleander. Tax says it's value is $367,000 at purchase. No deed of trust. Credit report indicates she has made purchases all over town. Maxed credit cards."

"Very interesting," Randy commented.

"That's not all. DMV shows she has a brand new Cadillac Seville and convertible BMW Spider."

"Wow, wish my estate looked so good," Randy said.

"Another tidbit. She was a drill instructor in the WACS in World War II. She gets a pension, believe it or not. It' not much, certainly not enough to buy all this. She is one tough lady."

"One recently rich lady," Ben observed suspiciously. "Somebody needs to talk to her."

"Youdaman!" James said.

Ben put up his hands. "Not now. I can't do anything until I know how Margaret is." Ben grew silent and tears welled up in his eyes again. He was a little embarrassed that he was getting teary eyed every few minutes. "Man, I'm sorry but I can't stand it."

Randy walked over to him and put her arm around him. "Ben, we're really sorry for you and for Margaret. We know how close you two are and I know this has to hurt."

A tear trickled down his cheek. He replied, "She's . . . she's been my whole life."

CHAPTER TWENTY

Days slipped into weeks and weeks into months. Azaleas blazed along the streets of Wilmington as it awoke from a cold weather slumber. Color was everywhere. The beautiful warming yellow of forsythia and the whites and pinks of dogwoods were arrayed on a carpet of fresh early green grass. Runners had stripped down to shorts and tees for a race through the festive streets. Dog lovers frolicked with their canine charges and Frisbee athletes effortlessly glided disks above the warming earth. Pick up basketball games featured "shirts" and for the first time in many months, "skins".

Randy stood on the south side of the Judicial Center grabbing the last few rays of sun before the trial was to begin. It was soothing and even relaxing to soak in the sun for a few minutes so she lingered. The effect was transporting, almost transcending the harsh realities: a looming battle that had assumed titan proportions in her own mind. Barefoot versus Big Burger.

She leaned back against the column and let the sun work its magic. A war with opening volleys was set to begin, she imagined, between the Lilliputians and the Gargantuans. She was the gladiator, the lead counsel. This was the first time she was lead counsel in an important case. She shivered at the thought. It was a little unnerving. The intensity of the prospect jarred her back to reality and she opened her eyes involuntarily into the sunshine. The bright light stung. She closed her eyes and slipped back into the battle theater. She thought about Phoebe, fragile Phoebe, victor or vanquished? They would know in a few days. It was all up to Randy. She lifted her sword in an imaginary charge against the great giant, Bayready. Bayready stood up to reveal he was twice as large as she had imagined. He presented two great weapons: gold encrusted sword and a razor sharp scepter. She charged and the great giant laughed heartily.

"Hey, girl," Rod called out. "Ready?"

Randy jumped. "Whoops," Rod apologized. "Didn't mean to startle you."

Randy grinned recognizing Rod and leaned forward to give him a hug. They brushed cheeks and lingered a moment in the embrace. When she let him go, he asked again, "Ready for the big case?"

"I hope so. I've certainly worked long enough on it."

Rod turned around and put his back to the column as well, assuming a position beside Randy. Feeling the sunshine on his face, he tilted his head back and closed his eyes. "Gosh, I've missed that. A warm sun." He peeped over at Randy and seeing that she appeared tense. "Don't worry. You're ready."

"I don't know. Hope so. I wish Ben were here."

"What do you hear out of Ben?"

"He's drowning in alcohol. He spends the day at the nursing facility with Margaret and the nights, he spends with the bottle. He's gotten pretty bad. I went by to see him night before last and he looked awful. Hadn't shaved, pale white, disheveled. Hardly comes to the office. He's taking it awfully hard."

Rod nodded his head. "I'm sorry to hear it. They must be pretty close."

"Sometimes I think too close. He's letting this thing with Margaret consume him."

"How is Margaret?"

Randy adjusted her position and turned a little more toward Rod as she continued to bathe in the sun. "Margaret is not well. She came through the bypass surgery alright but they have had a continuing problem with the congestive heart failure. A lot of swelling. They are trying to use very powerful drugs to remove the fluids from around her heart. And they still have the mass in her breast to deal with. As soon as she is well enough, they will start her on radiation therapy then chemotherapy."

"Is she strong enough for that?"

"I don't know."

"Are they going to have to remove her breast?"

"Probably. They've biopsied and know it's malignant."

"I see why Ben is so shook up. I don't know if I could handle that either if it was someone you loved so much." He opened his eyes enough to squint at Randy.

Randy could feel him staring at her. She opened her eyes slightly and smiled at Rod. He reached out and put his hand over her hand. "Me either," she agreed.

They drifted back into the warmth and glow of the sun, starved for spring's embrace and reassured that the earth was awakening after a cold, blustery winter. In a few moments Rod broke the spell. "Well, you were able to file the Stickley appeal on time. Get any help from Ben on that?"

"Oh, yeah. We met and divided the appeal into several parts. I had already done a lot of the research so it was just getting it put in proper form for the appeal. Ben and James worked on the violation of right to counsel involving Ben's interview with Jeremy. Ben already knew the area quite well and gave the cases to James. James updated it on Westlaw. They actually turned it into me before I was finished."

"Good. You got the notice that the Court of Appeals has waived oral arguments?" Randy nodded slightly. Rod continued, "We should be getting a response from the Court of Appeals any day I think."

"You sound pretty confident."

"I am. We did a good job in that case. There shouldn't be reversible error there."

Randy disagreed but let it go without further comment. Rod leaned forward and watched the jurors filing in from the parking lot. Suddenly he remembered that he had the docket call in the criminal session that morning. He started stretching and Randy felt the movement. She aroused enough to say, "Oh, don't go. We have a lot of time yet."

"Got to. My turn at the arraignment docket."

Rod squeezed her hand and started to walk in the door. Randy called after him. "Oh, I forgot. What's Butch planning on doing about indicting Ben?"

Rod looked around and walked back to Randy. He spoke in a hushed tone. "The indictments have been prepared."

Randy looked surprised. "You're kidding?"

"He's dead serious. They are on Butch's desk. Been there. I don't know why he hasn't presented them to the grand jury. He's not talking to anybody about it."

"This is a major mistake. He will lose a lot of support over this. Even the people who don't like Ben will be upset with him. Besides," Randy continued to argue the point, "this is not the time to do anything. Ben is . . . is sliding down fast. That might be just enough to push him over the brink."

"I agree but you know Butch. He's a hard man sometimes."

Rod walked in the courthouse and Randy leaned back absorbing the sun. Randy's thoughts continued to dwell on Ben and she tried to push them out of her mind. She consciously thought of the imaginary battle that was coming but the spell was broken and the imagery was not right. She couldn't envision anything except the dread of getting beaten by a skilled, seasoned advocate. If Diehlinger was a monster, what would Bayready be like she wondered. The sun started slipping behind a tall building leaving her partially in the shade and she had a choice of moving or going inside. Reluctantly she picked up her briefcase and slowly, grudgingly pushed open the door. She stumbled in.

"Good mawnin', Miss Bost. May I introduce myself? I am Hamilton Bayready. My friends call me Ham." He put out his hand.

Randy shook hands with him and was too stunned to say anything.

"Looks like we're going to be spending some time togethah the next few days. I look fahward to it." He released her hand and bowed his head slightly.

Hamilton Bayready stood about five feet two inches, wore an almost white linen suit and carried a dark black cane encrusted with a gold head and tip. His shirt was a shade whiter than his suit, starched but not stiff and accompanied by a blue silk tie. A watch fob that was connected to a light gold chain and a royal blue handkerchief properly folded and placed in his coat pocket completed his wardrobe. He wore a pleasant smile and exuded the easy, calming manner of a Georgia gentleman. His eyes never blinked and he looked directly into the eyes of the person he was addressing.

"You aren't anything like I expected," Randy stammered.

"Bettah, I hope." He smiled and stepped to the side. "Anything that I can help you with, my dear?"

"No, but thank you just the same." Randy pulled her briefcase up to her and started to walk toward the courtroom.

Bayready walked back to several people who were waiting for him. Randy noticed that they were very well-dressed. Very possibly the entourage, she thought: subordinate lawyers, investigators, research assistants and gophers. They immediately surrounded him and listened to his instructions. As Randy began walking up the steps to the courtroom, she looked back and Bayready gave her a discreet smile and made a small bow toward her.

In the courtroom she walked over to the plaintiff's table where James was already setting up. "Glad you decided to second me on this, Jim," she said and laid her briefcase on the table.

"What do you think?" James asked. "Everything ready to go?"

"I hope so. I just had the strangest experience. I met our opposition, Bayready. He was . . . "

"The monster?"

"No, actually quite the gentleman. It surprised me. I researched him. He's extremely brilliant. University of Georgia, with honors. Harvard, J.D., Law Review. Straight to the top at LaForge and Maynard in Atlanta. Splintered off with the best litigators five years ago. Top of the profession. Gazzillion bucks. Rolls Royce. Supposedly he's the best. But . . . but . . . "

"But what?"

"Nobody said he would be such a gentleman."

"Well, snakes look like a stick until you pick one up. Be careful."

She laughed at James' attempt at humor. "That sounded just like something Ben would say. At least he's here in spirit."

James nodded accepting the intended accolade. He said, "You were right. I saw Judge Allgood getting out of his car this morning. He's been assigned to the civil session."

"I thought so. I called the court director in Raleigh. The assistant director said it would be him or some judge from Mt. Airy. Looks like we are in for a treat. He's a good judge. Straight as an arrow. He'll give us the best shot we can get."

Bayready came into the courtroom. His entourage followed. One of the suits sat beside him and at Bayready's suggestion, the President of Big Burger assumed the chair between the two attorneys. At the direction of Bayready the remainder of the entourage spread out in the courtroom so as not to give the appearance that this small foreign army had invaded. After everyone was positioned, Bayready went around the courtroom shaking the hands of the bailiff and the clerks. He was personable, gregarious and charming.

At the appointed hour Judge Meykus Allgood walked into the courtroom and the bailiff called everyone to attention. As soon as the judge was seated and had arranged his robe, Bayready, already on his feet, asked for permission to approach the bench. The judge nodded approving the request. Bayready beckoned Randy to join him in the bench conference. At the bench Bayready introduced himself and then introduced Randy by making a gentlemanly gesture toward her and by saying, "Your Honor, may I introduce my worthy opponent, Miss Bost?"

Judge Allgood knew Randy from his previous term of court in New Hanover when Rod and she had argued the motion to suppress in Wanda's case. Judge Allgood acknowledged Randy and the attorneys returned to their seats. By the time the preliminary motions in the case had been completed, Bayready had charmed almost everyone in the courtroom with his chivalrous and engaging way. The bailiff was referring to Bayready as Ham during the recesses and Judge Allgood was allowing every motion Bayready made to approach the bench. Randy watched it all somewhat helpless to hold back the flood of good feelings toward the attorney and concomitantly the defendant.

Randy commented to James mimicking Bayready's Georgian drawl, "Yo' Honor, may it puh-lese the court? Pardon me while I charm the pants off of evahbody in this here courtroom."

James was a little put off by her charade and said, "Really Randy, he does seem to be quite a nice fellow."

"You can't be 'a nice fellow' and sick a pit bull like Diehlinger on us the way Bayready has done," Randy fired back. "He's killing us with kindness."

"Well, what are you going to do about it?" James asked.

"Fight fahr with fahr," she answered again mimicking Bayready. "Twiddle-lee-dee, I'm going to be sweetah than a Georgia peach."

By the time jury selection was complete, Randy was convinced that Bayready's personality was going to be a factor in the case. Although the composition of the jury, seven women and five men, was just as Randy had hoped and worked for during jury selection, the male jurors were overly helpful during questioning by volunteering information and a couple of the female jurors were gushing with sweet smiles and diplomatic giggles at Bayready's little asides. During the break the clerk laid a couple of chocolates on his desk and the bailiff was keeping his picture of water filled to the top.

He never let the entourage approach him directly while the jurors were present. They had to present their assistance through the co-

counsel. Even when the judge ruled against him in the bench conferences, Bayready smiled gracefully and nodded toward the jurors. Basking in the glow from the credibility and importance attached to his hanging on the judge's bench, he made sure the jurors were watching by occasionally "accidentally" bumping his goldheaded cane against the bench.

Randy led off opening statements with a long compliment to her opposing counsel telling the jurors what an "honor, privilege and a pleasure" it was to get to try the case with Bayready. After the saccharine sweet introduction, she turned her attention to the case. She graphically dwelt on the horror of the stripseach as Phoebe sobbed softly at the defense table and the rest of the time, she walked though the deposition testimony about the great wealth of Big Burger for purposes of explaining punitive damages.

"The only way to stop this outrageous conduct," she stated, "is to dig into Big Burger's deep pockets and make it pay." She ended with another compliment to her opponent. "I'm sure my esteemed colleague, Ham. Oh, I'm sorry. Mr. Bayready will now keep you entertained with an incisive and perfectly charming opening statement."

Bayready studied her icily and gave her a look of "touche" as she sat. He smiled at the jurors and then stated to the judge, "Oh, I won't bother the jurors with that. I'll waive opening statement until the defendant opens its evidence. But thank you just the same, Miss Bost."

Randy called Bertha Bogwig as her lead off witness. She identified herself as "Bert. That's what most people call me."

She explained that she was the night shift manager for Big Burger and Phoebe and the other two girls, Stella and Louise, had been under her supervision as clerks. It was the policy of Big Burger that all the managers were responsible for the money count on each shift and any discrepancies were taken from the manager's wages. When the twenty dollars were missing, she said she immediately closed the registers and marched the three girls into the stock area.

"I thought one of them surely had took it," she said, "and none of 'em would admit it. So I made them take their clothes off one at a time."

"While all of them were present?"

"Why, yeah. I didn't think nothin' about it."

"Were they completely naked?"

"Buck naked. Just like the Good Lord made 'em." She said and smiled at the jurors.

"How long were they that way?"

"I don't know. Five to ten minutes."

"Did any of them ask to put their clothes back on?"

"Your person, uh, your client did. The others didn't seem to mind too bad though."

"Did she resist the order to remove her clothing?"

"No, none of 'em did."

"Did she have any choice?"

"Naw, I don't think so."

"How did she react to it?"

"She cried." She looked over at Phoebe who had her head down on the table. "Kinda like she's doin' now. But I tell 'ya. It didn't hurt 'em none."

Randy pretended not to hear and put her hand to her ear. "What did you say?"

"Gettin' 'em naked. Didn't hurt 'em none."

Randy gave her a look of disgust. "Well, Ms. Bogwig, it's been almost a year since this happened and she is still crying about it and you don't think that it hurt her?"

She did not answer and Randy then asked her about the Big Burger policy on stripsearches. "They don't have one as far as I know. We're managers and we're supposed to do whatever we need to make the money count work out."

"And did the money work out?"

"Yeah."

"After you stripsearched them, did you find the twenty dollars?"

She laughed. "I went back to the registers and counted again. I guess I had just miscounted. It was all there."

"So there was no missing twenty dollars?"

"Right."

"Did you apologize to my client for stripping her and searching her?"

"No."

"Did anyone at Big Burger?"

"Naw."

"What happened to you for doing this?"

"Nothin'. They didn't fire me or anything."

"And where are you working now?"

"Big Burger," she said and smiled obtusely.

"Same position?"

"Oh, no. They moved me to the bigger Big Burger on College Road. Promoted me too."

"And what happened to Phoebe?"

"She never came back but as far as I knew she was all right."

Randy looked over at Phoebe who was still whimpering audibly. "Let me ask you this, Ms. Bogwig. When you stripsearched her, did you actually see her vagina?"

She smiled like it was a dumb question and looked around at the judge as though she were unsure whether she should answer.

He nodded at her and she said, "Why, sure."

"In other words you and the other women who were there saw her completely, totally, stark naked without her consent?"

"Yeah, I guess."

"And you put your hands on her, didn't you? Put them into her private parts."

She kept the same inane gaze on her face and shook her head in disbelief. "Why, yeah. You can't search anybody if you don't put your hands on 'em."

"And you don't think she was hurt by that?" Randy put her arm around Phoebe who was still crying then looked at the jurors. Before the witness could respond, Randy stated brusquely, "That's all right. I withdraw the question."

Bayready tried desperately to rehabilitate her but found she was so dense she was hurting as much as helping. Randy could tell he was particularly perturbed and probably, she thought, because he had made Big Burger keep her on as an employee to make her a friendly witness and had spent time prepping her as a witness, all to no avail.

Next Randy called Stella Barton who described the stripsearch in complete detail. "She put her hands between my legs, you know, right there." She indicated by pointing at her groin. "Then she did Phoebe. She'd rub all around there to see if we were hidin' anything."

"How'd Phoebe react?"

"She just cried and tried to cover herself up."

"How did you feel about being stripsearched?"

"Huh. I knew it wasn't right but, I don't know. It made me mad and all so I just quit. Couldn't do anything about it anyway. I mean me against them big shots." She pointed at Bayready's table.

"Objection, Yo' Honor," Bayready said, "That characterization hardly seems fair."

"Objection sustained."

Again Bayready tried to lessen the sting of the adverse testimony during his cross examination of the witness but found she was so biased and angry toward Big Burger that she blasted the company in every answer."

"Why, ma'am," he summed up. "You just do not like your formah employer at all, do you?"

"Not worth a dime, Mister. No matter how you dress 'em up, they are still rotten to the core."

When Phoebe took the stand, Randy had a very difficult time trying to get her to express herself. Even though Randy had prepared her by telling her to look directly at the jurors as she testified and to explain her answers in detail, she stared at the table just below the witness stand and mumbled "uh huh" and "huh uh". As Randy led her through her testimony into the store room where the search took place, she turned a shade of scarlet and started to look as though she were going to regurgitate.

"Are you all right?" Randy entreated as she stopped the testimony.

"Uh huh."

The bailiff took her a glass of water and Phoebe sat it in front of her without taking a drink. "All right. Let us know if you need a recess. Will you do that?"

"Uh huh."

Although Randy was dissatisfied with Phoebe's presentation on the witness stand, Randy pushed on with the direct examination. Randy started using very descriptive, adjective filled questions that fleshed out the degrading, debasing acts by the night manager and the abuse and condonation by the corporate management. When Randy mentioned the word, "naked", Phoebe buried her face in her chest and clammed up.

Bayready, the gentleman, reluctantly gnashed his teeth and sat on his objections while Randy in a very ladylike manner eviscerated Big Burger with a depictive, disgusting rendition of the events. With

Phoebe as the puppet and Randy as the puppeteer, Phoebe's sad story took on the hue and sound of a holocaust victim's account of survival during the Nazi reign of terror. When it was Bayready's turn to undo the damage, Phoebe kept her eyes on her feet and came up with alternating grunts, a shorter version of uh-huh, huh-uh.

When it was over and Bayready released her from the stand, Phoebe broke into tears and raced off the stand. Sitting at the table beside Randy, she hid her face in her hands and sobbed uncontrollably. Randy put her arms around her and gave Bayready an indignant look of "How could you?". A few of the jurors reacted to Phoebe's testimony with sympathetic looks and one dug into her pocketbook and offered a Kleenex to the bailiff for Phoebe.

Phoebe's mother, Lila Barefoot, followed Phoebe on the stand. She was a plain woman but her description of Phoebe before and after the stripsearch surprised Randy. It was much better than anticipated: it made the connection between the stripsearch and Phoebe's slide into isolation and seclusion seem real.

"Phoebe's always been a sensitive child," she pointed out. "She's private. She never let me see her without her clothes after she got old enough to put her own clothes on. And after that happened at work, she ain't ever been the same." She looked over at the jurors as comfortably as though she were telling them to watch out for her barking dog at the trailer as she had done Randy. "I really think if Miss Bost hadn't come out there and . . . and made her . . . " She reached in her sweater pocket and pulled out a tissue. "I think she would'a died."

"What do you mean, Mrs. Barefoot?"

She looked at Phoebe and cried lightly as she spoke. "She was so depressed over this. Phoebe would'a taken her own life."

Not wanting to appear insensitive and running the risk of angering the jury, Bayready went lightly on the mother during cross-examination focusing more on Phoebe's physical condition.

"She could still walk, Mrs. Barefoot?"

"Yes, sir."

"She could still talk?"

"Yes, sir."

"So physically, she did all right then, did she not?"

"Well, she wouldn't eat, hardly ever. She talked more here in this courtroom than she did to me. I don't know. I guess so."

Bayready imperceptibly shook his head acknowledging his bad luck and gave up.

Randy's next witness was the psychiatrist who had worked with Phoebe and brought her back to the point she could speak about the incident and could be coaxed into the courtroom. He testified that as a result of the "invasion of her person", she had sunk into a deep, unrelenting depression.

"I have become very close to Phoebe." Phoebe raised her head to look at him and he smiled at her. She smiled back then immediately dropped her gaze back to the table top. "And I am convinced that she would not have come out of that depression and would have died within a matter of months. In my opinion if we had not intervened, she would have terminated her own life."

Bayready could easily spar with the professional witness without any danger of alienating the jury. This was the first witness who was fair game so Bayready seemed to take great delight in elucidating on his knowledge of psychiatry. Being on an even keel with the doctor, he could diminish if not deflate the importance of his opinion testimony.

"Now Doctor," he asked, "psychiatry is not an exact science, is it? I mean in mathematics one can add one and one and it is always two but in psychiatry, one can add all the information we have in this case about Phoebe and different psychiatrists will come up with different results, correct?"

"Yes, sir. That is correct."

Bayready looked at the jury as though he were asking them the question. "So you are giving us your best guess, aren't you?"

"No, my best professional judgment after working with Phoebe these last eight months."

And so it went back and forth until the two battling intellects were finished. Each satisfied that he had won the battle for the minds of the jurors while the jurors collectively scratched their heads at the nebulous   psychiatric-legalistic   thrusts   and   parries.

Bayready had no further questions and tendered him back to Randy. Before she had a chance to speak, Bayready used an old ploy to underscore his final area of inquiry. He asked, "Oh, by the way, Doctor, one more question if you will?"

The doctor nodded suspiciously and Bayready asked, "You're a paid witness, aren't you? In other words your testimony is not free? The plaintiff Miss Barefoot is paying you for the testimony. Right?"

He laughed slightly and said, "Well, she hasn't yet." Some of the jurors smiled at his complaint that he had not been paid and he said good-naturedly completely deflecting the poisoned barb in the question, "Someday maybe I'll be paid. I hope so."

Bayready closed the cross and yielded the witness to Randy's questioning. Randy was quite satisfied with the state of his testimony and asked no further questions. She did use the opportunity to reply to Bayready's offer in a most ladylike manner, "No thank you, Mr. Bayready, but I thank you gentlemen for giving us quite an education in the field of psychiatry. Very informative." Bayready tipped his cane at her accepting the accolade.

Next Randy plowed into the punitive damages issue. In a civil suit Big Burger could not be imprisoned or fined for its bad conduct. The only way Big Burger could be punished for the offensive conduct of its night manager was for the jury to award punitive damages. In other words for the plaintiff Phoebe Barefoot to win, the defendant Big Burger would have to be required to pay Phoebe and pay Phoebe big. So the jurors needed to know how much wealth Big Burger had before they could determine how much money to take away and give to Phoebe.

Randy called several accountants and vice presidents of Big Burger. Then to make sense of it all, she called an accountant that she had hired as an expert in the case. He explained their testimony and supplied evidence of Big Burger's net worth. When he had concluded, Randy surprised everyone by calling the President of Big Burger. He slowly arose from the table between Bayready and the other attorney as though not quite sure whether he should testify. Bayready whispered to him that it was okay and after he was sworn, Randy immediately complimented Big Burger's financial prowess quoting from an article in Restaurant magazine. Her approach completely threw him off. Without much additional prompting he corroborated everything that the witnesses had been saying. On the stand he was so proud of the success of Big Burger that he seemed to forget that he was in a lawsuit.

"Our revenues have been phenomenal this year surpassing anything that we expected," he bragged to Randy as Bayready

inconspicuously attempted to get his attention. Not noticing
Bayready's discomfort, he continued with a forecast of things to
come. "I predict Big Burger will dominate the fast food market
internationally by the end of next year."

Bayready was so unsettled by the unexpected promotion of the
plaintiff's case that he purposely dropped his cane to get the
witness's attention. It made a loud noise as it bumped the table on its
way down and everyone looked. Randy knew what was going on and
seized the moment. She stood immediately, retrieved the cane and
carried it to Bayready.

As she presented it to him, she looked at the gold top and said,
"This one may be dented, Mr. Bayready, but surely your client Big
Burger with its great wealth and success will buy you another."

She smiled politely and released the cane to Bayready who had a
rather sour look on his face. She turned to the judge and said,
"Thank you for Your Honor's patience with us. I have no further
questions of this witness."

Bayready tried valiantly to get the jurors' attention again as he
cross-examined the president. He tried to play down the president's
testimony but most of the jurors seemed more intent on trying to see
the dent in the golden crown of his cane. He noticed their curiosity
and laying the cane behind him then underneath the table out of their
view, he gave up on the futile quest.

Randy announced, "We rest, Your Honor."

Later that afternoon while they were on recess, the bailiff came by
the conference room and said, "Miss Bost, Ham, uh, Mr. Bayready,
would like to see you in his office, uh, the witness interview room?"

Randy followed the bailiff to the room. Bayready waited alone.
This must be pretty important, Randy thought, since he had sent his
small army of support staff away. She walked in; he stood, bowed
politely and offered her a seat. When she sat down, he looked at her
and began applauding quietly. "Well done, Miss Bost. Well done."

She waited. After a few moments Bayready said, "You've done
an excellent job with your case. Now how can we settle this thing?"

Randy knew her case had developed very well and she anticipated
that Bayready would wait until she had put all of her evidence up
before he would react to it. So here it comes, she thought: the offer.
She cut him off before he became too hopeful. "The case is not for
sale, Mr. Bayready."

He put his finger across his lips gently and smiled. He looked at her slyly. "Everything is negotiable in this business, Miss Bost. We are prepared to offer $50,000. and each side pay its own costs."

Randy smiled this time. So it's worth that much, she thought. Although she almost giggled, she remained stolid. She could not believe that she had brought the case forward so well that it was worth that much to the great Hamilton Bayready. She knew as well that if he was offering $50,000, it was worth more. Much more.

Her cavalier manner must have aroused Bayready's ire because she could see some color around his cheeks and his smile turned to a rather stern countenance. He said, "Look. I've tried hundreds of these cases. This case has some merit, not much, but some. Let's be realistic here. This young girl is counting on you. And think what she can do, what you can do with that kind of money."

"Really I appreciate your offer but . . . "

"No buts, Miss Bost, Randy. You don't know what's in front of you in this case. I do. It's . . . "

"I'm sorry," she said firmly, "but the answer is no."

"Here's what I am authorized to do. I can offer $75,000. That offer is firm. Of that you get one third, $25,000. I know you are just starting out as a lawyer and I know your finances, you need this very badly. Take my advice. Take the money and let's go home. Your client is happy, we're happy, you're happy."

"No, Mr. Bayready. My client would not hear of it. I've talked to her about the probability of this and she . . . "

Bayready became extremely angry and rapped his cane on the table. "Take the money, young lady, if you know what's good for you."

"Are you threatening me?"

"No." He was livid and stood up from the table. "But you don't know what's out in front of you. $75,000 is a lot of money and you're stupidly letting it get away from you. Take it or you will pay an awful price."

"I'm sorry but . . ."

"Remember this," he stammered and banged his cane on the table toward Randy. "This day is the day you will remember for the rest of your life. You've just made the biggest mistake of your life and ruined your client's life in the process."

He seemed to catch himself. He was angry, much angrier than he thought he was. As he straightened up, he cleared his throat and pulled his cane back. He said in a more modulated tone, "Sleep on this tonight. If you don't take this, your client will be ruined. If she thought a stripsearch was unbearable, wait until we put on evidence tomorrow morning."

Bayready smiled lightly and rubbed the gold head on the cane. "Besides," he said wryly, "hell hath no fury like a lawyer with a good paying client."

*   *   *

The next morning before court was scheduled to begin, the bailiff saw Randy in the hallway and told her that Judge Allgood was looking for her. She followed the bailiff to the judge's chambers and after being let in, she sat and waited for the judge. She wondered if this conference with the judge had anything to do with Bayready's threat of the previous evening.

After a while the door to chambers opened and Judge Allgood came in carrying a woman's coat. "Hello," he said, "I've been trying to find you. Hope you haven't been waiting too long?"

"No, sir. I had just arrived when you came in." Randy stared at the long winter coat that the judge was holding.

The judge noticed and held the coat up. "This is my wife's coat. Nobody loves dogs like my wife except possibly myself. She's down here with me while I am holding court and last night while we were out for our customary evening walk, she was playing with a dog that another walker had on leash." He brushed the coat and continued, "Must've been shedding. When we got back to the hotel room, she had white fuzzy hair all over her from holding the little mutt. She's put me on a mission: get my coat cleaned or else."

Randy smiled at the thought of someone else telling the judge what to do. The judge, observing her, asked, "What's so funny?"

"Well, most of us never think of the judge having a boss but I guess we all do. Have bosses, I mean."

The judge laughed and replied, "Speaking of bosses, where's your lead counsel in the Stickley case, Ben?"

"He's not doing too well, Your Honor. His wife Margaret has had surgery several months ago and continues to have severe health problems and well, Ben is having a hard time with it."

"I had heard as much. How's he doing now?"

"He spends a lot of time with her. She's in a nursing facility. And he hardly ever comes in to the office. I . . . I'm really worried about him."

The judge did not respond immediately to Randy's statement but said, "Well, I guess you are wondering why I have you here."

"Yes, sir. The bailiff said you had been looking for me."

"Well, this involves Ben too," the judge remarked as he lay the coat over the back of a chair. Randy looked puzzled and the judge continued with the explanation. "You know I was the judge who ruled on the motion to suppress the statement of Wanda Stickley. You and a Mr. Pemberton with the DA's office argued the motion before me before the trial started."

"Yes, sir," Randy responded as she waited with anticipation.

"Well, I just received the opinion in State versus Wanda Stickley back from the Court of Appeals today. Have you received your copy yet?"

"No, sir. How did the Court rule?"

"Your client Wanda Stickley was granted a new trial."

CHAPTER TWENTY-ONE

"You know, I think I'll start exercising," Skittle said as she admired Randy's thin frame. Skittle started exercising her arms and lifted up and down on her toes.

Randy said, "Huh, I wish I could say exercise leaned me out this spring but really I haven't been able to exercise very much. This is worry and stress. No appetite." She patted her stomach. Then looking at her bare arm, she said, "Too thin for me. Between Phoebe's case and worrying about Ben, there hasn't been enough time to do anything. And now we have to gear up for a retrial in Wanda's case."

The office was relatively quiet since the offices had just opened. Skittle had just unlocked the doors. Randy, arriving right after Skittle, had scheduled a meeting with Ben and James concerning the preparation for the retrial of the Stickley case. Randy laid her stack of books on Skittle's desk. "Jim here?" she asked.

"No, I haven't seen him this morning."

"How about Ben? Did he say he was coming for this meeting?"

"Said he would." She looked askance at Randy and said, "But you know Ben. Maybe, maybe not."

"I'm here," Ben called out from his office in a rough, gravely voice.

Skittle gave Randy a look of surprise and called back, "Ben, when did you get here?" They walked back to his office.

He sat at his desk. He was unshaven and his hair was unkempt. He was wearing no tie but had on a dress suit. Having the appearance of one who had just crawled out of a bed in which there was no sleep into a morning which was full of hangover, Ben groused in reply, "Been here all my life . . . it seems like." He studied Randy and Skittle. "You ladies need to gain some weight. Randy, look at you. Skin and bone. And Skittle, you always were too scrawny. Women, always watching their weight, huh."

Before Skittle or Randy could join the argument with what's wrong with men, James called out from the lobby. Skittle called him back to Ben's office and when he arrived in the doorway, Ben said, "Jim, my man, what do you think about this? These pretty ladies wasting away?"

James grinned and said, "Pineing over you, Ben. Heartbroke is my guess."

Skittle hit James playfully on the arm and James pretended to be hurt.

"Well, they're wasting valuable time if that's the problem," Ben mumbled.

Randy who had remained very serious throughout the repartee snapped back very quickly, "Well, let's not waste our time. Let's get on with this conference."

Ben turned his attention to Randy and complained, "Chilly. Hmm, much too serious." He was still grouchy and did not want to give up one of his favorite pastimes: grumbling.

Randy returned the complaint. "You are serious, much too serious yourself."

Ben could tell his attempt at sharp-edged humor was not finding any willing participants so he gave up. "All right, if that's the way it is, let's get down to it."

Skittle said, "I'll bring some coffee." She closed the door behind her and went down the hall to start the coffeemaker. James came in and took a seat. Randy continued to stand and Ben tried to break the ice with a compliment. "I hear you are pinning Bayready's ears to the wall. Killing 'em with kindness, huh?"

She replied, "I'm doing just like you told me to do. I'm on the game plan. And the plan is working so far." Randy sat down and began to warm slightly to the conversation. "Just like you said, Bayready soaked in all of the plaintiff's evidence before he made an offer."

"How much?" Ben asked.

"Start $50,000, end $75,000."

"What does Miss Barefoot say?" Ben asked.

"She doesn't care about the money, she says. Leaving it up to me."

"So what are you going to do?"

"Thinking about it. I don't know. Bayready's threatening. Says we'll be ruined when he puts on evidence."

"What's he got?" Ben asked again.

"I don't know. I've talked to Phoebe and her mother, talked to the psychiatrist. Nobody has a clue what it could be. What do you think we ought to do?"

Ben grinned. "Well, first there will be another offer. See what he puts on the table. This one will probably be his last one. If your client does not take it, hold pat. He made you play your cards. Make him play his. If your case is as good as Skittle says it is . . . "

"So she's your source," Randy blurted out. "I thought you knew too much about what was going on in the case."

Ben grinned again. "I've been keeping up. I wasn't going to let you be out there all by yourself. Like I was saying: if your case is as good as it sounds, he could drop a bomb and you'd still be all right." Ben's head started hurting and he put his hand to his temple, "Oooow, I'm thinking too much. Giving me a headache. Let's hear about Wanda's appeal."

Randy had gotten over her angry spell with Ben and reached into her briefcase. She rifled around and then pulled out three copies of the opinion from the Court of Appeals. She handed a copy to Ben and James then gave them a few moments to review the head notes on the case.

Finally Ben looked up. "The motion to suppress. I knew it. The State couldn't use Wanda's statement in evidence. She had demanded a lawyer when she asked for me and was not given the opportunity to get one before she was questioned. The State should not have been allowed to use her confession and Judge Allgood should have suppressed it. Great."

"One problem," Randy said. "Judge Allgood is the judge trying my civil case with Big Burger. Think there will be any fall out since we got him reversed?"

"Not for a second," Ben came back. "He's one of the most professional judges we have on the bench. He'll probably even brag on you for doing such a good job on the appeal."

"Already has," Randy added. "But still I worried about it."

"Don't. Stay focused on Bayready. He's the problem."

James who had been reading the rest of the opinion stated, "Ben, you'll like this too." He flipped to the page on which the particular ruling he was looking for was located. He scanned the page then began reading, " . . . and the State's use of the statement 'tell them you did it' by the defendant's attorney to the child Jeremy Stickley put the attorney's credibility at issue. This clearly undermines the attorney's effectiveness in representing his client. The defendant's right to the effective assistance of counsel during her trial was abridged." James flipped a few more pages and read again, "Reversed and remanded for a new trial consistent with the rulings in this opinion."

Randy who had already read the opinion and had had some time to think about the effects of the ruling stated, "This is a whole different ballgame. On a retrial the State can't use Wanda's admissions and can't use Caroline Markham's testimony that Ben tried to influence the child to take the blame for the killing."

"If there is a retrial," Ben added. "The DA will offer Wanda something I believe. Probably better than he had offered the first time."

"He already has," Randy said to the surprise of Ben and James.

"Well, that's fast," James remarked.

Randy smiled mischievously. "Not when you have the inside track."

Ben shook his head realizing the source of the information. "What's Rod offering?"

She cut her eyes toward Ben and made the report without commenting on Ben's insinuation. "Plead guilty straight up to voluntary manslaughter. Will even accept a no contest plea without a personal admission of guilt. Sentencing tied to the presumptive range. No danger of a sentence in the aggravated range. It means Wanda could be out in a year."

"I like it," James offered, "but what about Wanda? I thought Wanda was pretty upset with us. What makes you think we will be representing her anyway?"

Ben pulled a crumpled letter out of his pocket and unfolded it. "This is from Wanda. I received it a few days ago. "'Dear Ben," he read, "I have had a long time to think about what happened to me in court. As I look back on it, I know that you tried to help me. You, James and Randy tried hard to help me as much as you could. It was a difficult time for me and I just could not see it then. I am sorry that I did not follow your instructions but truthfully to this day, if I thought for a moment that anything I would do would hurt Jeremy, I could not do it. I am not trying to say that I think it was right to call Jeremy as a witness but in thinking my way through the case, I can

understand why you would think that way. Maybe you've not run
the risk of losing anyone you loved so dearly." Ben cleared his throat
as he thought of Margaret in the nursing home and continued to read.
"I forgive you and I hope that you forgive me. Wanda.'"

Ben folded the letter and put it back in his pocket. He said, "She
mentions several other things that she would like to have done with
her property so that Jeremy could benefit from it while she serves this
prison term. But I think it's clear that she wants us as her attorneys
but . . . "

"But what?" Randy asked.

"But I can't do it," Ben said. "I'm just . . . I'm just not up to it."
Ben looked weak and Randy looked at him harshly. "Seriously
Randy, I've got too much on my mind."

"Ben," she chided, "I never thought I would see the day that this
would happen. You're giving up. That's right. You're quitting,
aren't you?"

"I'm not quitting anything." He looked at James. "Tell her, Jim.
I've got a lot on my mind. I'm losing Margaret and there is nothing I
can do about it."

James stared at him and said nothing. Randy looked very
disappointed. Ben continued to plead, "You don't know what this is
like. Don't judge me unless you have walked a mile in my shoes.
Randy, Jim and you can take this case and run with it. You've seen
everything already. It'll be a rerun with the DA having one arm tied
behind his back. Really."

It was awkwardly still. No one said anything. Finally Ben
whined, "I can't do it. I just can't do it."

Ben pilfered in his drawer where he usually kept his bottle of Jack
Daniels. He found the bottle and without lifting it out so that Randy
and James could see what he was doing, he shook the bottle lightly
and saw that it was empty. His hand shook slightly as he tried to
gently lay the bottle back in the drawer.

Aware of what he was doing, Randy spoke. Her words were
dripping with icicles. "I don't think you'll find any courage in
there."

*   *   *

Later that morning she sat with Phoebe at the plaintiff's table in the courtroom waiting for court to begin. As she sat pouring over her notes from the previous day's testimony, Bayready led his entourage into the courtroom. He sat down and smiled coolly toward Randy. After making a few adjustments in the chair he was sitting in, he stood and walked over to Randy's desk.

He whispered, "Well, what did you finally decide?"

"My client will not accept the offer. It does not admit any wrongdoing on the part of Big Burger and it is woefully deficient."

Bayready stared into her eyes with a cold stare. "You have one more chance. I am authorized to offer $100,000, no admission of fault by Big Burger. We share costs. This is it. Take it or leave it. And by the way if you don't take it, prepare to reap the whirlwind. When the Bar hears that you turned down $100,000 and walked away with nothing, you will be embarrassed for the rest of your life."

Randy swallowed hard but did not blink. She responded, "I'll speak to my client but I wouldn't hold out any hope."

Bayready grimly smiled although there was nothing to smile about. He walked back to his table and started to sit down when Judge Allgood came into the courtroom. After court was convened, Judge Allgood called for the jurors. While they were waiting for the jurors to file in, Randy talked quietly to Phoebe and her mother at the table. With the jurors in place, Judge Allgood recognized Bayready for a presentation of the defendant's evidence.

Bayready stood and said, "Thank you, Yo' Honor." He looked over at Randy for her answer. She swallowed hard again and shook her head indicating that the offer was not accepted. He continued to stare at her with penetrating eyes as he said to the court, "Well, then. As our first witness, we call Robert Deflowers."

A young man relatively well-dressed and clean-shaven stood and approached the witness stand. As he did, Phoebe dropped her head into her hands and started weeping. Randy demanded to know who he was and Phoebe mumbled through her fingers, "He's . . . he was my . . . boyfriend."

"What is he going to say?" Randy quietly but forcefully demanded again.

"I . . . uh . . . I don't know," she murmured between sobs.

Randy braced for the worst and Bayready did not waste time. He had the young man to identify himself and to indicate how he knew the plaintiff Phoebe Barefoot. After a few more preliminary questions, he asked, "So I take it, Mr. Deflowers, that you were the paramour." He looked over at the jurors and decided that he was speaking over their heads. "That is," he stated, "you were Miss Barefoot's boyfriend?"

"Yeah, we dated for a while."

"About how long and when did you date?"

He thought back and decided that they had started dating after Christmas and after more prompting, he concluded they had broke off the relationship about a month before the trial started. "And what kind of a relationship did you have?" Bayready asked.

"Uh, what do you mean?"

Bayready smiled at the jurors letting them know he was being very patient with the witness who was a little slow to understand what was sought by the questions. "Well, let's see. Were you handholding, kissing or more?"

"Oh," he said as though a light had been turned on, "more."

"Well, tell us about that," Bayready directed. Deflowers still did not quite get it again and Bayready amplified the question. "Were you and Miss Barefoot ever alone?"

"Yes, sir."

"In a motel?" Bayready asked leading the witness.

Again a light came on for the witness and he smiled and replied, "Yes, sir. We were at the Starlite."

"And were both of you fully dressed or did you take your clothes off?"

Randy stood and forcefully said, "Well, objection, Your Honor. This is irrelevant and invades my client's privacy."

Bayready smiled. This was exactly the objection he wanted so that he could highlight the testimony and make Randy appear as though she were hiding something from the jury. He looked at the jury and talked to the judge. "Irrelevant? I thought she would say that. This is highly relevant and this jury needs to hear it. The plaintiff is not as lily white as she would have us to believe."

"Objection, objection, Judge Allgood," Randy stated even more forcefully. "He's arguing his case to the jury and he's trying to poison this jury against the plaintiff."

Still watching the jury, Bayready argued, "I knew she didn't want us to know about this. The plaintiff is trying to hide this evidence."

"Now wait a minute," Judge Allgood finally ordered. "Approach the bench."

The argument between counsel at the bench was heated. Bayready tried to justify the testimony of Phoebe's former boyfriend by saying Phoebe "had flaunted herself in the presence of Mr. Deflowers and had even danced around naked as the day she was born." He argued, "That flies in the face of the impression she's given of being embarrassed and humiliated by not having her clothes on."

Randy was just as adamant that the evidence offered nothing the jury needed to know. "Private acts between lovers have nothing to do with being forcefully made to disrobe and parade yourself in front of others. It's irrelevant at most and at the least, its probative value is outweighed by the danger of unfair prejudice to my client. Your Honor, don't let them do this. Don't let this boy kiss and tell."

"They got to tell it all and so should we," Bayready fired back.

Allgood listened patiently to the bickering between counsel and finally ruled that the subject matter was offensive but was also material to the jury's understanding of Phoebe's claim of pain and suffering and the issue of her credibility as a witness.

As they were seated, Bayready picked up the direct examination. "Now, let's see. Where were we? Oh, yes. Our dahlin' little plaintiff was naked as a jaybird in a motel room with you."

"Objection. Object to the characterization and he's testifying again, Your Honor," Randy argued.

"Sustained. Move on, Mr. Bayready."

Bayready stood and bowed slightly to the judge acquiescing to the ruling. He knew that he had accomplished his goal: telling the witness's story through his own words painting his own lurid details. "Yes, Yo' Honor. Now Mr. Deflowers, what did ya'll do while you were in that motel room?"

"A lot of things."

"Kiss?"

"Yeah."

"Touch each othah's body?"

"Yeah."

"Have sex?"

"Yeah."

Bayready looked over at Phoebe who was still hiding her face in her hands and asked, "Did she take her clothes off?"

"Yes, sir."

"Did you make her?"

He smiled a little and replied, "No, I didn't."

"Well, did she get up in front of you and dance around without her clothes on?"

"Yeah."

"Did she seem squeamish, I mean, was she embarrassed at all?"

"No, she was laughing and carryin' on."

"Not cryin', not hiding her face, not afraid, not afraid to talk." Bayready's voice was building in intensity and he stood up and started shaking his own body to demonstrate. "Not doing anything except dancing around naked and seemed to be enjoying it?"

A couple of the jurors were smiling at the spectacle and Randy tried to break up the little show by objecting.

"Objection sustained, Mr. Bayready."

"Sorry, Yo' Honor, but, and I apologize, I just feel some points ought to be made as strongly as I can for my client."

Bayready went on with the examination but the damage had been done. He had expertly drawn a picture of a nude Phoebe dancing for her boyfriend and enjoying it. When Deflowers was turned over to Randy for cross-examination, she was able to diminish the impact of his testimony somewhat by getting him to admit that Phoebe's dance had occurred long after she had started therapy and getting him to testify that they thought they were in love and were going to be married. He admitted that Phoebe and he had broken up but he was not mad at her. "But," he added and looked at Phoebe disdainfully, "he'd never take her back as long as he lived."

Still Randy could not shake the image out of her mind and if she could not, she knew the jurors could not. Randy began to worry that she had been too confident. She had passed $100,000 on her own cocky notion that her case was invincible, she thought. Maybe she should have been more conservative; afterall, $100,000 in the hand was better than a zillion in the bush. One picture, she thought, one picture of a naked Phoebe is worth a thousand words and may have just cost them a $100,000. If she was wrong and Bayready was right, she would be the laughing stock of the Bar.

Randy's palms began to sweat as Bayready went through the next witness, an employee from Big Burger personnel who testified that Phoebe had withheld information on her employment application. The lady was a minor witness on a relatively minor point but enough to keep perspiration on Randy's upper lip.

Bayready enjoyed watching Randy sweat. He seemed to be invigorated by it. He called a store clerk who testified that Phoebe had written two checks that had bounced. Again the witness was a relatively insignificant player in the trial but enough to shake Randy's confidence.

By the time Bayready rested, Randy was a basket case. Each time she would close her eyes she would see Phoebe naked and smiling as she danced, the complete antithesis of Randy's theory in the case. At the end of the testimony, Randy was able to open and close the final arguments. That allowed her to sandwich Bayready between her rendering of the case for the jury. More importantly it allowed her to be active, to do something. She had been sitting while Bayready paraded his witnesses before the jury and the prolonged wait was killing her. As long as she was active, participating, she felt, she could stand the intensity of her rising doubts. When she closed the final argument, it was all a blur. The only thing she remembered was James' remark. "Good job, Randy. It's done. Now it's all up to the jury."

As soon as the judge finished his final charge on the law to the jury, Randy smiled vacantly and walked straight to the bathroom. Her face looked normal as she studied it in the bathroom mirror, she thought, even though she knew she was quaking underneath like the beginning of an earthquake. Although she could feel the tremble, her hands were steady. She felt like she was swimming in sweat but except for a little moisture on her forehead and upper lip, she appeared relatively dry.

She tried to relax as she waited for the jury's verdict but found herself pacing in the hallway. As she counted the blocks in the floor tiles for the umpteenth time, she happened to pass by Bayready's conference room. The door popped open for a second as someone went out and she saw Bayready: dapper, cool, relaxed, and assured. He looked as though he were getting ready to take an afternoon siesta. Finally she returned to the conference room and waited with James, Phoebe, and Phoebe's mother.

At five o'clock the judge called everyone in and declared a recess for the day. That night Randy was just as tormented and second guessed every decision she had made. As soon as she would drift off to sleep, she would see Phoebe again: nude, dancing, swirling, laughing, throwing hundred dollar bills up in the air in bunches. It rained money as she performed. After a restless, sleepless night Randy arrived back at the courthouse exhausted and tense. The jury was returned to the jury room for deliberations and the long wait continued. And Randy paced.

Late in the afternoon of the second day, she settled down enough to nap. Just as she dropped off, James hit the conference room door in a rush. "The jury's knocked. Got a verdict. Let's go."

They filed into the courtroom and the impact of the long wait was quite visible. Bayready was unrumpled, fastidious even, calm and patient. Randy was hollow-eyed, fatigued, nervous and sitting on the edge of her chair, expectant and impatient. She was so absorbed in the wait that she heard only a part of the verdict: One. Did Big Burger through its manager intentionally inflict severe emotional distress on Phoebe Barefoot? Yes Two. What amount of compensatory damages is the plaintiff entitled to recover? $8,256. Her heart was beating so rapidly she never heard the last issue: Issue Number Three. What amount of punitive damages is the plaintiff entitled to recover?

It was James who finally told her. He whispered loudly enough for everyone to hear: "$675,000." She could not believe it and asked him to repeat it.

"$675,000. That's six seven and five followed by three of the biggest fattest zeros we'll ever see."

She relaxed the grip in her hands and leaned back in the chair. She hoped the verdict would be large and prayed it would be more than $100,000 but even she had not dreamed it would be that large. She sat in a blur as the judge released the jurors and directed the plaintiff's attorney to prepare the judgment.

"Miss Bost . . . Miss Bost," he repeated trying to get Randy's attention, "it's your duty to prepare the judgment reflecting the jury's verdict."

Finally tuning into the judge's voice, Randy nodded "Yes" and finally mumbled, "Yes, sir."

The court was adjourned and Randy and the others moved to the conference room where the celebration was almost juvenile if not silly. When it finally sank in, Randy pulled Phoebe from the reverie and explained the judgment to her. Phoebe gave her a hug and Randy told her to wait in the hallway and she would walk her and her mother out to the car.

Bayready spotted Randy as she came out of the conference room and walked over to where she was standing. He said, "Well, done, Miss Bost. You tried a good case."

She acknowledged the compliment somewhat coolly and Bayready added, "You know we are going to have to test this one on appeal."

"Oh, yes, but this case is error free," she argued. "The appellate courts will uphold what we've done here. The trial is clean and the verdict is not excessive. It's fair. And it's . . . "

Bayready held up his hand as if to indicate, "I give. I give." He said, "Let's stop the verbal fisticuffs for a moment. Seriously, Miss Bost. Randy, if I may. You did try an excellent case. You've got what it takes to be in the big leagues. A zeal, second to none and magnificent trial skills. All that hard ball stuff I gave you was just for show. Part of the game. But look. You've got what it takes. I knew it when you left that $75,000 lying on the table. And then when you passed on $100,000. That took nerves of steel."

"But my life is here. I've got friends here."

"I've heard about your friend, Mr. Down. Very unfortunate. He will just . . . "

"No, he is more than a friend. He was a friend when I had no friends in this town. He's . . . "

Bayready held up his hand again. "You win but remember this: if this doesn't work out, there is a place for you at Bayready, Fore, Paine and Destorm in Atlanta. Who knows? Maybe we could open a satellite office here."

Randy shook her head and said, "Thanks but no . . . "

"All right but promise me you'll think about it." He put out his hand and she shook it. "Until next time, counselor."

As Randy walked over to Phoebe and started assembling her briefcase and paperwork, the bailiff walked up to Bayready and said, "Well, Ham, thank you for the box of pecans. My wife will be making pecan pies for a year."

"Think nothing of it, my good man. The pleasure was all mine."

The bailiff said, "Sorry the case didn't quite work out like you wanted it to. I'm going to miss you big boys. One time I saw F. Lee Bailey and Johnny Cochran up in Winston-Salem when they was trying to get a subpoena for somebody in that O.J. Simpson case. Boy, they kept it exciting. Watchin' you boys is like going back in the old days. It's like watchin' a gunfight."

Bayready laughed and playfully bumped the goldheaded cane in his hand. He watched Randy escort Phoebe down the hallway toward the front door of the courthouse. "Nowadays though," he observed, "it's different. Yes, sah. Sometimes the gunslingers wear high heels."

*   *   *

The secretary called into the DA, "Butch, it's the Senator again."

Butch wondered what he could be calling about as he answered the phone, "Good morning, Fowler. Good to hear from you again. Hope all goes well."

"Not too good, Butch," the Senator complained. "I thought everything was sailing along hunky-dory then I picked up the paper this morning. I got it layin' heah right in front of me. That Stickley woman is gettin' a new trial."

"Yes. I read the opinion. It looks like some of the evidence should not have been allowed in by the judge," Butch responded shifting the blame entirely to Judge Allgood who allowed Wanda's statements into evidence.

"Well, what's gonna happen now? The gov'ment gonna appeal from the appellate court ruling?"

"No, Fowler. I talked to the Attorney General and that office is not going to appeal from the Court of Appeals. They were afraid that we might get a reversal all along because, uh, of the judge's ruling. The AG is not going to appeal to the Supreme Court so it looks like we're gonna have to retry the case."

"What?" The Senator sounded angry and Butch heard some noise like a fist pounding on the desk.

"Yes, sir, Fowler. I'm as indignant as you are. I can't believe it but it's just something we are going to have to deal with."

"I thought this thing was ovah. I mean, you tried that woman and the judge salted her away for twenty years. Those appellate court judges must be a buncha lily-livered, knee jerk liberals. Evah now and then, we get one around heah but they don't stay too long."

Worrell seemed to calm down after he had vented. Butch listened hoping that his old friend would relax and not get so upset with him. The Senator continued in a more modulated tone. "Well, what are you going to do?"

"Retry her, Fowler. We don't have any choice. We've offered her everything but the courthouse."

"What did you offer her?"

"Voluntary manslaughter. Sentencing in the mitigated range. My assistant and I calculated the time in prison counting the credit for the time she has already served and if she took the negotiated plea, she would be out in thirteen months and a few days. I am telling you, Fowler, we are trying to work with them but we keep getting nowhere with her lawyers. Their response so far is 'we'll talk to our client and get back to you'."

"It's a sweet deal. Is that fellow Down still her attorney? I thought he got in trouble over that last trial and was out."

"No, he's still in as far as I know."

Butch heard a loud noise again as though the Senator was slapping the table with his hand. The phone went silent for a few moments. "Well, Butch, I heard that he had tried to get some kid to lie in court about the case, take the blame for all of it."

"Yes, he met with the son of the defendant and tried to get him to say that he had killed Ralph Stickley. Fortunately we had a witness, the child's guardian, who overheard the conversation."

The Senator's voice seethed with anger. He spoke between gritted teeth. "Butch, can you imagine the kinda man that would do somethin' like that. He's not worth the salt in his carcass. He oughta be taken out and shot. Can't you do somethin' about it? I mean, that's lyin' in court."

Butch pulled open his desk drawer and looked at the indictments that had been prepared charging Ben with subornation of perjury and influencing and intimidating a trial witness. He laid the two documents on his desk and said, "Yeah, I've been laboring over it. It's a difficult situation. If I indict him, well, you know how the Bar is, they won't like it."

"Yeah, but look here, Butch, won't he be off the case?"

"Well, yes, but . . . "

"But nothin'," the Senator fired back. "You know he's just showboatin'. He's afta the publicity like all of them TV lawyers. Out to make a name for hisself. Look here. You get him off the case and that Stickley woman will have to have a new lawyer. One that's reasonable and one that knows a sweet deal when he sees one."

"Fowler," Butch said calmly as he tried to reason with the Senator. "It's not that simple. There's politics involved in this thing. If I indict Down, the Bar here will chew me up. They might not like Down but they will come together over this. There could be fall out."

The Senator laughed. "Butch, you underestimate yourself. You are the oldest rat in the barn up theah. Nobody's gonna beat you."

"I don't know, Fowler. Time's are changing and I'm not getting any younger. One of these young lawyers might take a shot with that going on."

Worrell was tired of arguing with Butch over the decision and stated emphatically. "Look here, Butch. The public won't stand for it. A lying lawyer and you let 'im get away with it. Get 'im out. Indict him."

CHAPTER TWENTY-TWO

"I quit," Ben declared to himself. He poured a couple of fingers of Knock'em into the only clean glass.

The local television stations had a field day with the news. Indictments always made interesting news and provided great visuals of the indicted defendant being handcuffed or fingerprinted or being processed through any number of degrading things that happen to the person named in the indictment. For Ben it was the ignominy of barking out a "No Comment" as the reporter pushed the microphone into his face when he came out of the Sheriff's office after being served with the indictments.

Ben looked up from the evening news and took a quick drink from the elixir. He waited for that heady feeling that came in a rush after he took the whiskey straight. It came in a sudden rush of heat like a hot flash rising from his chest up the front of his face. Suddenly he was hot and tried to pull up out of the chair to open a window. Staggering to the window and fumbling with the curtains, he finally determined the window was stuck. He jerked the door of the refrigerator open and planted his face in between the milk and the wilted vegetables. He cooled slowly then, satisfied that the heat wave had passed, he grabbed the evening paper from the bar and fell back in the chair.

He read the headlines on the top half of the page then flipped to the lower half. "Former DA Indicted," he read. "Crap," he grumbled and started to throw the paper toward the trash can. He thought better of it and pulled the paper back in. Laying it across his lap, he fumbled for his reading glasses and almost fell out of the chair reaching for them. He was pretty disgusted when he found the pair that only had one ear attachment.

He precariously balanced the one arm glasses on his nose and studied the article about his indictment. ". . . indicted for subornation of perjury and influencing a government witness. Down allegedly influenced the minor child of convicted murder defendant

Wanda Stickley to take the blame for the killing of her former husband Ralph Stickley."

Someone was knocking at the kitchen door but he was too absorbed in the article to attend to it. He continued to read. "Court officials commented on the irony of Down, a former assistant district attorney, being indicted by his former boss, longtime DA Butch Yeager. When questioned, Yeager stated, 'I'm sorry that it had to come to this but we cannot permit this type of egregious conduct by attorneys.'"

"Egregi . . .ous." Ben slurred the word as though he were spitting it out. "Tell them what's really going on, Butchy boy. Gettin' rid of me so I can't try the Stickley case."

Ben reached over to the coffee table and poured some more Jack Daniels in the glass. Before he took a drink, he lifted his glass in toast. "Well, Butch, here's to you. Looks like you finally won this one. Got me." He hoisted the glass and drank until the last drops dripped into his mouth.

The knock became a little louder and he called out. "All right, all right. I'm comin'." The banging continued. "Good Lord, man. Knock the door down, won't ya'?"

Ben opened the door and Randy stood on the deck. She had a rather frustrated look and as she pushed in, she said, "Why didn't you answer the door? I've been to the front door and the back door."

"Randy dandy, come no doubt to give me some advice," he asserted. Ben turned toward the living room and stumbled toward his chair. "Well, I didn't order any and I'm not taking any."

Randy followed him as he stepped unevenly into the living room. It had been a while since she had been to the house. She remembered how airy and beautiful it was when Margaret was at home. The flowers always gave it an outdoorsy, sweet smell. Randy tweaked her nose from the smell of stale cigar smoke, old pizza crusts and whiskey. She noticed an arrangement of flowers that had drawn up into brown, dead clusters. As she picked them up and started with them to the trash can in the kitchen, Ben watched without comment. Randy returned to the living room and started assembling the jumble of old newspapers into an orderly stack.

Ben liked watching her work around the house. It reminded him of Margaret who was a born homemaker. She loved it. He remembered Margaret's old saying, "The earth is big enough for me between the kitchen and the garden." He reached for the bottle and Randy beat him to it. She lifted the bottle up and held it away from him.

"Boy, can you break up a cheery mood." Ben reached for the bottle and Randy pulled it a little further away.

"We need to talk, Ben," she said. "There are some important things that we need to discuss and I need you clear headed."

Ben thought he would try to win her over with a little buttering up. "You're right," he pretended to agree while keeping his eye on the Knock'em. "Oh, by the way, did I tell you what a great job you did with BB1? You're the best."

Randy melted a little and started to set the bottle on the coffee table. Ben grabbed too soon and she snatched it away again. "Good Lord," he grumbled, "this is going to be hard. All right, what is it? The sooner we get this over with, the sooner we . . . uh . . . get this over with or something like that."

Randy noticed that he had the newspaper open to the article about his indictment. She walked the bottle over to the kitchen table, sat it down with a bang as if to emphasize a point and came back to a seat beside of Ben's.

"What are you going to do about counsel?" she asked.

"Gettin' the best."

"And who is that if I might ask?"

"You may. This lawyer is a hot shot, good in trial and good on appeal. She'll get me off at the trial or on the appeal. She's that good." Ben smiled.

"Does this so-called hot shot have a name?"

Ben's eyes blurred a little as he talked and he rocked a little in his chair. "She sure do. Randy Bost, winner and champion. Won Wanda Stickley a new trial on appeal. Pinned that peacock Hamilton Bayready's ears back and sent him packin'."

"I'm flattered but . . . "

"No buts. You're the best. Really. You won the biggest verdict that anybody can remember in a severe emotional distress case. I mean, really, the victim wasn't cut, shot, stabbed, run over. No broken bones, no blood. Hurt feelings. $675,000 punitives. Yeah, you can be my lawyer."

Randy loved talking about the case and had received congratulations from most of the people around the courthouse. She thought she would never tire of it and found she would even tolerate Ben's half drunk observations to revisit the most successful case of her career to date. She smiled at Ben's description and said, "Yeah, it was pretty good, wasn't it? But I just followed the road map that you drew out. Worked like a charm."

"You're too kind," Ben said then winced a little as he looked in the kitchen at the bottle of Jack Daniels. "Well, sometimes." He thought about the compliment and, even though his liquid supplicant had been unmercifully cut off, he began to warm to Randy's overtures. His voice softened and lost its acidic tone. "Yeah, it did. Yeah, it did."

Randy started to speak and Ben interrupted her. "Randy, you know I always wanted Sandy and Mary Lee to go into the law but it never worked out. Sandy went off to Meredith. She always was good at music. And Mary Lee. She always was more like her mother. But you." He looked tenderly toward Randy and his eyes moistened. "You've been like a daughter to me. The daughter who became a lawyer, a stand up, in your face trial lawyer."

She reached out and put her hand on his. Her mixed emotions of warmth generated by the strong bonds between them, the anger that had been brewing within her over his drunkenness, and his perceived weakness when it came to dealing with the prospect of losing Margaret seemed to wither into a heartfelt tenderness. "Ben, Ben, what am I going to do with you?"

Ben smiled at her and both of them sat there in the silence. After a few moments, the hum of the refrigerator motor broke the stillness and Ben looked back toward the kitchen. Spying the bottle of whiskey, he started to get out of his chair and Randy said, "Wait, Ben. I went by to see Margaret this evening and she said they have her scheduled for surgery in the morning. Is she strong enough for that?"

A tear ran down his cheek. He seemed to go numb. He barely replied. "No choice. The doctor says the mass is growing. Got to do it."

"Anything you want me to do? Want me to call Sandy or Mary Lee?"

"They know. They're coming."

"I'll wait with you at the hospital tomorrow."

"No. Work on Wanda's case. You and Jim are her only hope now. I'm out. Butch has seen to that."

"No, you are not," Wanda disagreed very strongly. "You are still lead counsel."

Ben fumbled with a stack of papers under the coffee table and pulled out a letter. He handed it to Randy. She read the letter and the attachments quickly.

"The Bar wants a voluntary surrender of law license until the felonies are resolved. What are you going to do?" she asked.

"Already done it. I signed a consent order providing for a temporary suspension."

She looked back at the papers and saw Ben's signature on a copy of the Consent to Surrender License to Practice Law. Randy was surprised and somewhat angry at Ben's lack of resistance. "Don't you think you should have talked to me about this first?"

"No, they've got me. Got me 'til I deal with this perjury business."

"Well, Jim and I are going to need a lot of help."

"I can't. I . . . "

"And you need to be sober to work on your defense."

"I . . . ," Ben tried to offer an excuse.

"And Margaret needs you. Really, Ben."

"I know that but I'm . . . "

Randy stood up and walked toward the door. "I'm disgusted with you, Ben. I can't believe you. You need help. I mean you really need help. You've got to pull out of this. Margaret is as concerned as I am."

"You leave Margaret out of this."

"Really, Ben." She shook her head in disbelief. "It's all about Margaret."

Ben dropped his head and did not speak. Randy walked to the door and opened it. She looked back and said, "Really, Ben. Come on." Ben did not look up and Randy said as she walked out of the door, "I'll see you at the hospital in the morning. Be there and be sober."

The door slammed and Ben sat without moving. His eyes began to clear and he focused on the papers in front of him. He looked at the headline again: "Former DA Indicted". He struggled to get out of the chair and ambled to the kitchen. Ben grabbed the bottle by the neck and turned to go back to his chair. Before he reached the chair, he turned the bottle up and drank the remainder. As he started to sit the bottle on the coffee table, he noticed the Consent to Suspension of License to Practice Law and picked it up.

"The nerve," he said to no one. He stumbled and turned toward the kitchen table.

Ben looked out over the kitchen and imagined he was appearing before the State Bar. He watched the Grievance Committee who was reviewing his case for permanent disbarment. He held the bottle to the side of his leg to give it less prominence and at the same time waved the Consent to Suspension form before the imaginary board. The committee members looked up from their review and eyed him coldly. The chairman, an old, craggy man, peered over his glasses and pointed a finger at Ben. "Speak, lawyer," he commanded, "while you still are one."

"Ladies and gentlemen," Ben mumbled and straightened his frame. "We lawyers are much maligned but it's a majestic profession. Thomas Jefferson wrote the Declaration of Independence but once. Think of the thrill of that."

He stumbled and caught himself. "But we lawyers," he argued finding his voice, "we get to do it every day for some poor soul. These financial wizards, these technonerds puking up microchips are the gods of the third millennium but we lawyers . . . we get to soar with the eagles. We get to fly to the great vortex of human existence where freedom of the man runs headlong into the constraints of mankind."

He sat the bottle down and let the paper drop. He fell to his knees and raised his arms above him toward the heavens in one final plea and pleaded, "God, I want to be a lawyer."

*   *   *

The wind swirled as it spread yellow dust over the great Tiananmen Square. Beijing was in the midst of spring in early May and with it, came the dust storms of very fine particles of silt from deposits in the northern plateau and the desert. The golden spray was everywhere covering the streets, seeping into houses and dusting those who were braving the chilly air in the Square. A nuisance to the residents, it was remarkable, even surreal and inscrutable to visitors who watched the city bathed in gold.

The trees were beginning to bud with new green and with the great forest of trees in Beijing, there was an expectancy in the air. It had been a dry and cold winter with only a hint of snow. The static electricity, always a problem when the humidity was low and the air was in motion, had almost abated to the great relief of a country of bicycle riders and a particular joy to lovers who had to endure the "zap" when they kissed. Now the rising sap, the shifting winds and the warmth of spring offered hope and possibility and a cessation of the rigors of winter.

Tiananmen Square standing in the heart of the old Forbidden City was stark and beautiful. Standing on almost one hundred acres, its vast openness was a scene in contrasts of great political theater with over a million people who had come to pay homage to Mao at his death and to the thousands who had come to find their freedom and instead found "Dong Xiaoping, the butcher of Beijing". Though heavily guarded and protected, its large open space provided an excellent place to meet and visit without fear of intrusion or interference.

FBI Director Fries had just come from the temporary office on Chan An Boulevard and had begun to walk by the beautiful Qian Men Gate. Followed by two other agents who were providing security, he watched as several tourists gathered to take a picture beneath the scenic Gate. The photographers waited for several strollers dressed in Mao suits to move then grouped for the picture. Fries followed the walkers with his eyes and marveled at the simplicity and the sameness of the suits. Blue or gray and always well appointed, they were symbols of something larger, he thought.

"Sir," Bays Covington called as he approached, "my apologies for being late but we were in traffic and . . . "

"No problem, Bays," Fries responded. "Beijing is a traffic snarl. It has to be the bicycle capital of the world."

They joined each other and walked ahead of the agents who were with them. Fries had desperately wanted to avoid any possibility that they would be overheard. He was sure that they would be followed but the Square gave them an opportunity to walk and talk without fear of discovery. He held his hand to his mouth as he spoke so that his words could not be monitored at long distance and he waited until the ringing of bicycle bells and background traffic noise muffled their conversation. Fries gravitated toward a larger group of tourists who were being quite noisy.

"Bays," he said as they approached the knot of people, "I'm sure we are under surveillance so I'll be as brief as I can. HQ at Chan An Boulevard is bugged so we'll meet like this when we have to. Otherwise Newman will be the go-between."

"Where is Mike, sir? I thought he would be joining us."

Fries developed a look of disgust and reported, "Mike's en route to Shanghai. He's following another lead that the river bed along the Huangpu River contains sand similar to that found at the assassination site."

"Again? How many of these have we had to pursue?"

Fries did not answer directly but continued to look disappointed. "Too many. You know, looking back on it, it was a mistake to share our research on the sand particles with the Chinese. Back then it seemed important to impress on them the reason for our interest in Tientsin and we thought, incorrectly it seems, that we would encourage their co-operation. But they've used the research to find additional sites. Every single sample we have looked at from the sites they have offered has not been close to the original seizure at Figure Eight."

"You're right, sir," Bays agreed. "Mike will find it's another wild goose chase."

The crowd began to disperse and walk by them. The Director moved them toward a park bench at some distance from the crowd. When they arrived, he made a sweeping motion with his hand toward the yellow silt that had collected on the back of the bench. As he did, the wind picked up the dust and it flew into nothing.

"Right, Bays, as much as the Chinese have to have been aggravated by all of this dust, they have to know every particle of sand on the continent and where it comes from." He sat and invited Bays to sit. "What did they find with the sweep in your offices at Tientsin?"

"We're contaminated. Every room is bugged so we've been moving to the streets when we have anything important to move through."

"Well, State knows. We'll apprise them of your situation as well. We're hesitant to make a complaint. It will just provide another opportunity for the Chinese to claim we are being arrogant and unco-operative. I think they are just looking for something to send us packing."

"Yes, sir. Secretary Baker's complaint was felt all the way to the Chinese guards at our office. We were getting to know them a little. They'd even smile when we pass. It's as cool as Mao's tomb since she petitioned."

"Right, Bays. Let's continue to work around it. We can't improve it so let's just step lightly around it."

They were getting chilled sitting in one place so the Director stood and strolled toward the Monument to the People's Heroes. The Monument, constructed of granite and prominently placed, usually attracted a lot of attention from tourists due to its marbled terraces and from the Chinese who came to read Mao's inscription in his own calligraphy: "The People's Heroes Are Immortal".

When they approached the noise around the base of the monument, Fries inquired, "What do we have now?"

"Possible contact."

"Mafia or underground?"

"Underground." Bays looked around as though he were uncomfortable talking about it. He stepped a little closer to Fries and spoke in a hushed voice. "This is a dissident. Pure line to Tiananmen as far as we can determine. Picked up by police, detained. We're not sure about the length but he was in detention for several months. Never tried but still as far as our people can place him, he's legitimate."

"I hope so," Fries commented. "The mafia have been packing our ears full of possible scenarios and suspects. I'm sick of dealing with these guys. I can't tell whether the government is sending them to us or whether the underbelly is just that rotten. Either way we go, they have been as helpful as the Ministry of Public Security."

Bays started to continue with the report and Fries interrupted him. "Another thing," he complained, "makes my skin crawl. We have meetings twice a week with the Minister of Public Security. He walks out and tells us what he is doing for us this week. Assigning fifty top investigators, making the police labs available, providing security at any facility we want to investigate. He never smiles, he never frowns. Just makes his report like a company manager talking to his employees. All of us know it's a bunch of Chinese checkers but what really galls me is when he asks for an update of the investigation. As if he doesn't know more about it than we do."

"We're as frustrated down the line, sir. We're getting the same old: 'we're doing everything we can'."

"Then when we provide a pro forma report," Fries continued as though Bays had not even spoken. "He suggests that we are not making any progress because the assassins may be elsewhere. God, the nerve of that guy."

"Yes, sir," Bays stated and waited patiently to continue with his report.

"And the President. President Daniels is extremely frustrated with the 'slow crawl', as he put it, of the investigation. I'm getting signals that he may call me back for a report at the end of this week. We need something badly." He slipped into deep thought for a moment about how to frame a report that did not sound like the same report he had made on fifteen other occasions. When he noticed Bays waiting, he said, "Well, you see what we are up against, Bays. What does the informant say?"

"Sir, he has a contact in Tientsin. She is a doctor. She works at the hospital and is a consultant to a local import facility."

"How does it tie in?"

"Well, our lab was able to give us the make and brand of the shoes worn by the assassins. They were manufactured by Chiang Mai in Thailand and shipped by Macao International in Hong Kong. Although they were pretty much generic and their allocation was widespread, we did learn that they were shipped to China through Shanghai and Tientsin. Not all of them but the great bulk of them was imported by an import company by the name of Shang Chou International located in Tientsin."

"Right. So we've traced the sand on the shoes to Tientsin and now we have traced the type of shoe to Shang Chou International in Tientsin. What does your informant have to offer by way of the doctor?"

"It's a little complicated. The informant is Liu Bang. He says that the doctor works at the hospital in Tientsin. She is trained in orthopedics although as many physicians do there, she performs many services including general surgery. She is quite respected and has developed some expertise in medical supply particularly in the field of orthopedics. Shang Chou International is a conglomerate. It's very powerful and has its hands in many areas but one of its primary businesses is the importation into China of medical supplies and technology. The doctor serves as a medical technology consultant to the business. She is pretty high up."

"All right, but why would she want to help us?"

"Her brother is Wu Han."

"I've heard that name somewhere before," the Director mused.

"Correct, sir. His picture went out on the wire and appeared in newspapers across the nation. He was the one holding the poster in Tiananmen Square during the uprising. He was one of the heroes of Tiananmen and Chinese authorities wanted him pretty badly. Word was that he fled to Guangzhou. He was captured there and disappeared. Most people believe he is still being held by the Chinese but if he is, they aren't talking. His sister, the doctor, has tried several times to find his whereabouts but even as important as she is, they won't tell her. She wants us to help her find him. She's willing to trade what she knows about Shang Chou. We've set up a meeting today." Bays looked at his watch. "In fact, they should be getting together about now. I wanted to meet personally with you to see how far we should go with this."

"What's the down side?"

"Well, it's always high risk. If they found out, she might be killed. And if they got to her, they might get to our agent who is here undercover."

"Who's our agent?"

Bays covered his mouth with his hand. "Jimmy Tang from Seattle. He is half Chinese on his mother's side. He knows the language and he's been very helpful to us. We could put him at high risk. And if the Chinese get him, you know they will make the charge espionage and will suspend the investigation into the assassination."

Fries looked concerned. "Have you talked to him? Does he know if he's caught, we cut him loose?"

"Yes, sir."

Fries thought for a few moments. "All right. It's a go but talk to Jimmy again. Tell him how serious it is. We don't want an international incident. And find out all you can about the doctor. Could be a set up."

"Yes, sir. We've checked and so far, she looks legitimate but I can't vouch. She's too far removed from us."

"All right. What is her name?"

Before Bays had a chance to speak, Fries noticed a young Chinese man in a gray Mao suit who was standing closer to them than the others at the Monument. The man appeared to be straining to listen to the conversation. Fries put up his hand to stop Bays from answering but he was too late.

"She is Dr. Su Ling."

*   *   *

In Tientsin the streets were crowded as Jimmy Tang dashed across the street. He weaved between cyclists and making the sidewalk, briskly walked the short distance to the restaurant. He went in and saw his contact who waved at him to join him. Tang hung his coat and joined Liu Bang at the table.

"Good to see you, my friend," Liu commented and stood as Tang took a seat. "Cold?"

"You know how it is in spring. Cold mornings and warm afternoons. Our guest arriving on time?"

"As far as I know. All is well. And with you, Jimmy?"

"It's very well. We thank you for helping. This is important. More important than anything else that we could be doing for our countries."

"Yes, it's true."

Tang looked at the menu and Liu reached for his. As they spoke, a pretty young woman entered the restaurant and removed her coat. She was wearing a dark blue Mao suit with a striking red scarf. As the receptionist helped her with her coat, she turned toward the dining area of the restaurant to look for the people she was to meet. Liu, upon seeing her, jumped to his feet and hurried to her. He accompanied her back to the table and when they approached, he said, "Mr. Tang, may I introduce Dr. Su Ling?"

Tang stood and bowed slightly. "It is so nice to meet you, Dr. Su. I have heard so much about you. It is quite an honor."

Liu said, "Dr. Su, this is our friend, Jimmy Tang. He comes to us from America. He is very interested in meeting you."

Su Ling studied Tang very carefully. She was not completely convinced that the Americans could provide any help in finding her brother and was not sure that she should expose herself and her family to the risk of contacting an American even if he did look and act Chinese.

"It is so nice to meet you, Mr. Tang," she said politely but still wary.

When Liu offered her a chair, she sat and Liu and Tang followed. Seated, Tang noticed how lovely she was and could not imagine how she had accomplished so much at such a young age. He commented, "You, you are not as I imagined."

"I hope I did not disappoint," she said with a smile.

They continued to look at each other as the tea was served. They waited quietly until the waitress had left.

"Not in the least," he returned as he smiled with his eyes, "but you are so young, so young to be a physician of such high standing."

"Looks can be deceiving," she remarked. Liu laughed and Tang, reminded that all of them were involved in a charade in some way, joined the laughter.

Liu spoke first. "Well, it looks like we will get along famously." He picked up his tea and said, "Here's to us, here's to all of our friends who depend on us."

Tang and Su Ling joined in the toast. Then Tang looked around the tables to see who might be listening or looking. Satisfied that they had the corner table to themselves, he said, "We need help, Dr. Su. We have reason to believe that the assassination of our Vice President is directly connected to Shang Chou International. We frankly do not know the full depth of the involvement of Shang Chou but we are convinced the assassins are connected in some way to the corporation. We need your assistance."

Su Ling watched Tang's eyes as he talked. She felt his statement was heartfelt and he was being truthful with her but still she planned to be very cautious. "This is dangerous talk," she commented and glanced around the room. "It's possible I can help but I too come with a great need. My brother Wu Han is missing. He is a patriot who has paid dearly. I believe he is in the hands of the government."

Tang looked very serious. "Su Ling, I am very sorry about your loss. I knew from my discussions with Liu Bang that this was a source of great sorrow for you. I am committed to helping you find your brother. We have one of the greatest investigative resources known to the world. If there is a way, we will find him for you."

Tang put his hand out and touched Su Ling's hand and she withdrew it. Immediately sensing that he had gone too far, he said, "I am sorry. Uh, I did not mean to be discourteous but your words touched me. I am sorry."

She smiled slightly and said, "There was no offense taken." She started to get up. Liu and Tang stood immediately. As she stood, she noticed a man outside the window of the restaurant who appeared to be peering in at them. She thought she recognized him as he turned away quickly. She turned a shade of pale.

"Everything all right?" Tang asked.

She continued to watch the window as she spoke, "It's all right. It's just . . . . Well, let me give some thought to what you have said. We will meet again. Liu will contact you. We'll meet . . . but not here."

She turned to walk away then turned back. "I can help you."

"How?" Tang asked.

"I know the assassin."

＊　　　　　　　　　　＊　　　　　　　　　　＊

The hospital was quiet. It was late and most of the visitors had gone. Randy and James had stayed for several hours then departed several hours before, when the doctor reported that Margaret's surgery was completed and she had been transferred to the ICU. Sandy and Mary Lee waited for several more hours then at Ben's insistent urging, went to Ben and Margaret's where Ben would call them if needed. Ben waited alone.

He had shown up sober and it was beginning to show. He had been as nervous as a death row inmate at two minutes before midnight on execution day and now was exhausted from the waiting and worrying. He lay on the worn couch and mindlessly looked at the television screen. As he lifted his watch to see what time it was, he noticed that his hand was trembling. He squinted at the watch: 2:30 in the morning, then let his hand drop. As he turned to get around an uncomfortable bump in the couch, he almost slipped off of the front of the couch. The sudden lurch surprised him. Fully awake he sat up.

Ben studied the lump in the couch and wondered how much misery the bump represented as he imagined family member after family member twisting and turning on the couch as a loved one lay nearby in the ICU between life and death. He started to stand but felt a thud in his head as though it had been pressed in a vice. He leaned back on the couch and glanced at the TV again.

Suddenly a nurse appeared in the doorway and spoke just above a whisper, "Mrs. Down is awake and is asking for you."

Ben stood up quickly and asked, "How is she?"

"Well, I'll let the doctor speak to you about that," she responded quietly. "If you will follow me."

Ben was a little nauseated from jumping to his feet so quickly but fell in line behind her. They walked the long hall to Margaret's room. The nurse stepped to the side and invited Ben into the room. She whispered, "Just a few minutes if you will, please."

Ben stepped in quietly and approached the bed. Margaret lay very still and appeared to be asleep. He watched her and waited patiently for her to awaken. She appeared to be resting and Ben focused on her breathing. It was even and deep. As she lay, he noticed her hair, usually long and shiny, was somewhat tangled and appeared lifeless and dull. He remembered the sun glistening through her hair as she worked in her garden during the past summer. She seemed so vibrant, so strong then as she pulled and struggled with the weeds that were choking the vegetables and flowers. He thought of the cancer that was slowly eating away at Margaret. He bit his lip and attempted to hold back his tears.

Margaret moved slightly beginning to rouse. Ben reached out and took her hand. As he did, her eyes opened slightly but did not focus. She closed her eyes again and slipped back into a slumber. In a few moments she awoke somewhat and tried to look at Ben. She spoke haltingly and asked, "Ben, Ben, is that you?"

"Margaret," he replied and squeezed her hand softly.

"Is Mary Lee with you?" she asked still in a haze.

"No, she and Sandy are at our house. I'll call them and they will come a little later. How do you feel?"

She groaned a little and tried to pull herself out of the daze. She muttered, "How about Sandy? Is she coming?"

Realizing that she was not fully awake, Ben smiled at her and repeated what he had just said. She tried to stretch as she became more aware but the movement was painful. She grimaced.

"How do you feel?" Ben asked.

She did not respond but asked, "Where's Randy?"

"She's been here, Margaret, but I told her to go home. Jim was here too but he's gone too. It's very early in the morning and all of them have been here since yesterday morning."

She tried to move again and could not. "What day is this?"

"Thursday."

Finally her eyes honed in on Ben and she smiled at seeing him and recognizing who he was. "It's you, Ben."

Ben smiled back and pretended to be hurt. "Who were you expecting?"

Again she did not reply but lay there watching him. She was quiet for a long time and listened to the sound of nurses and orderlies moving up and down the hall. Ben felt a surge of strength in her hand and gave a gentle squeeze in return. "Are you all right?" he asked.

"Uh, huh," she groaned and felt a sharp pain. She was still somewhat groggy but groaned a little more distinctly when she felt the pain. When the discomfort subsided, she spoke. "Ben, I know what you've been doing. You've been drinking . . . heavily."

Ben patted her hand. "Now, now. You don't need to be concerned about that."

She responded. "And I know about the suspension . . . and the indictments."

"Has Randy talked to you?"

"No," Margaret protested weakly. "I heard the nurses. They were talking about it in the hall." She paused to regain her strength and tried to move again without success. "But I talked to Randy. I had the nurse to call her for me. We talked."

Ben was crestfallen. He had desperately wanted to shield her from all of the bad news. He could barely stand the shame and embarrassment himself and he did not want Margaret to be concerned with anything except her recovery. The news was devastating and although he knew she would eventually find out, he hoped that it would be well after her mastectomy.

He dropped his eyes and stared at the floor. "Margaret, you don't need to be concerned with that. You are the one . . . "

She pushed his hand trying to get him to look at her. Ben would not look up. Tears started flowing freely down his cheeks. "God, Margaret, I blew it," he said.

"Ben, I know you are hurt. You, Sandy, Mary Lee, home have been my life. But you always had the law. You love it. You are the greatest lawyer I ever knew. I can't believe you would let them take that away from you . . . without a fight."

"But . . . "

"It's not like you. And your drinking. I never said anything but I always disapproved. You were a great husband and a great father. I knew it was bad for you but it was your only fault."

She grew quiet and tried to take a deep breath. She strained against the pressure in her lungs and exhaled slowly. When she spoke again, she was more reserved as the effort of speaking had exhausted her. "Ben," she murmured and shook his hand again to get him to look at her. He finally looked up. "I may not make it through this."

"No, you . . . "

"I've thought about it. I just have too much wrong with me. I'm trying but . . . ," She inhaled again slowly. "I'm not sure I can do this."

Ben took her hand in both of his hands and stared at the floor again. He could not bear the thought that he might lose Margaret. She had been the center, the strength of his life and now she was slipping away from him.

"No matter what happens," she said feebly, "you have to pull things together. You've got to stop drinking. It's killing you and it's killing me. I can't bear it. If you won't stop for yourself, stop for me."

She took another long pause and Ben started to speak. She pushed his hand again signaling that she did not want him to speak. When she regained her strength for the moment, she continued with her thoughts. "It's Wanda's case. You know she's innocent and it has driven you . . . . You are her only hope and I believe she may be your only hope. You've got to fight for you and you've got to fight for Wanda." After another long pause, she stammered, "Don't let them take your dream away. You were meant to be a lawyer."

Her eyes closed and Ben's eyes were blinded by tears again. In a few moments he felt the slightest stirring of strength in her hand again and her eyes opened slightly. She tried to speak but the words would not form.

Ben leaned over and put his ear next to her lips. She spoke in a fading whisper. "Promise me . . . promise me, Ben, that . . . you will save Wanda. It's the only way you will save yourself."

CHAPTER TWENTY-THREE

"I'm back," Ben stated, "Simply back. It's no big deal."

Randy, James and Skittle stood in the doorway to Ben's office and were speechless. Ben was different, really different: clean shaven, hair neatly parted, air blown and brushed, bright eyed, freshly pressed blue striped suit, white starched shirt, burgundy tie, leather belt with silver buckle aligned perfectly with his shirt buttons and his pant zipper line, neatly pressed and creased pants, shoes blacked and shined. Penultimately GQ.

The office smelled of men's cologne, conservative yet stirring. No repugnant stale smoke, no odoriferous aged whiskey, no cigar wrappers encircling his chair, no Styrofoam coffee stained cups at his feet, no semimasticated cinnamon buns, no dog-eared court advance sheets littering the office. Even the General Statutes of North Carolina, usually misplaced or missing, were in a bookcase at the side of his desk right side up, numerically arranged and indexed.

The only thing that was not different was the rest of his desk. It was stacked with legal files, papers, copies of cases, prosecution summaries, motions, briefs, evidence lists, transcripts, depositions, and newspaper clippings. The pictures of Margaret, Sandy and Mary Lee on the credenza behind his desk were upright and turned to be visible to the client and the client's family or friends. All of it was, in a word, different.

"What gives?" James asked as he scratched his head in bewilderment.

"Nothing," Ben responded as if it were just another day at the office.

"Nothing." Randy smiled wryly and looked at Skittle as though she knew what it was all about.

Ben looked at them as though they were from another planet. "What?" he asked nonchalantly. "What?"

Skittle shook her head in disbelief as well, commenting, "Well, I thought I would see the moon and the sun bump into each other before I would've seen this."

"Seriously, what gives?" Randy demanded. "What's the meeting about?"

Ben stepped to the side of his desk and pressed his hair back at the side of his head. "All right. I'll tell you. I have called you here to witness an event that has profound meaning in my life. You are my friends, my very good friends, and I want to share this moment with you."

James and Skittle looked at each other with a look of uncertainty as Ben scrambled around in the right bottom drawer of his desk. They heard the sound of glass bumping as the bottles and the used cups fell over each other. It took two hands to clear the mess. Ben set out an empty bottle of Jack Daniels then followed it by another. By the time he had cleaned out the drawer, there was a small calvary of empty bottles accompanied by a small infantry of stained coffee cups. Finally Ben pulled out a bottle of Jack that was three-fourths full. He sat it on the desk with great ceremony.

He looked at the mess and quickly disbanded the army of debris into the trash can behind his desk. He picked up the bottle, put it under his arm, and gave a nod to the three of them to follow him. Ben had a devilish twinkle in his eye as he paraded the four of them down the hall to the break room. He went over to the sink, held the bottle up to the light and then ceremoniously twisted off the cap. James, Skittle and Randy, still somewhat stunned, continued to watch the show without comment.

A streak of morning sunlight beamed across the room from the window. Ben tossed the cap into the waste basket as though it was part of a ritual and held the bottle up in the ray of light. The Jack gleamed in the sunlight and took on the appearance of a brown crystal. It seemed more than it was with the reflected rays twisting in different directions as the liquid splashed inside the bottle.

Ben spoke to the bottle at the ceremony in a dark, commanding voice. "Tis sad sorrow that we part. I thought ye a friend. But alas, I have seen ye in yer true light. A beguiling friend that wraps his hand in merriment around yer brain and the other sinister hand that secretly robs yer heart."

Ben held the bottle up high over the sink and let the Knock'em splash vigorously into its basin. He watched the whiskey slide down the drain and concluded the ceremony with an epitaph: "Drown,

drown in your own tears. I'll not join ye'. Down has enough of his own."

He turned around to the applause of his audience. James called, "Here, here. Here, here." Randy called for congratulations, "Hip, hip." The others joined the "hooray".

Ben enjoyed the moment and continued the production. He announced in his best theatrical voice. "Time has been divided according to B.C. and A.D. Let the word go forth that henceforth Down shall be known as Down O.K. and Down A.K. To those not familiar with the exact science of division, be it known that that stands for Down On Knock'em and Down After Knock'em."

They stood and gave him a standing ovation. In a few moments after the merriment had died down, Ben turned very serious for a moment. "I know," he waxed rather genuinely, "that I have not been the easiest to get along with and I know that I have not been as helpful as I should have been." He looked down at his feet and continued to talk. "I apologize. I want to say thank you for all that you have done for Margaret and for me. And I want to apologize for being . . . " He fell silent.

Randy finished the sentence for him. "A jerk," she said with a slight mist in her eyes.

"Exactly," he agreed. "I can always count on Randy to find just the right sentiment."

Everyone laughed and Randy stepped up and hugged Ben. Skittle followed and James put out his hand and said, "Give me five, bro'."

Ben gave him a high five then stepped back. He announced, "There's more."

"Oh, great," Randy exclaimed. "Cigars out the back door. Let me help."

Ben looked at her with exaggerated disappointment. "One vice at a time, please. No, this is much more serious than that."

"Are you sure you can do this? Cold turkey?" Randy asked.

"Got to. It's killing me. It's killing Mar . . . " He stopped. "I'll do it."

Ben cleared his throat and stated quite seriously, "One more thing. I want to tell you I have come to a conclusion." He waited until everyone had grown quiet in order to give the announcement the solemnity and importance it required. "I . . . I will not rest until I solve Wanda Stickley's case."

Ben's face assumed a countenance of firm resolution. "The more I have thought about this case, the more I think we have missed the boat. We've always reacted and rightfully so because we have been defending Wanda. That's the problem though. We have never tried to solve this case."

The telephone rang at the receptionist's desk and Mrs. Skittleran raced up the hall. James continued to look puzzled at Ben's reasoning and Ben, sensing the confusion, particularly directed his remarks to him. "Really, Jim. Every time we received some information or piece of evidence, we thought: how does this affect Wanda's case? We then spent our time trying to refute it, deny it or defend against it. We didn't look at it and ask: what does this tell us about who killed Ralph Stickley?"

"So?" James said expressing his doubts.

"So," Ben emphasized, "so we take the case apart piece by piece down to infinitesimal form and measure it against the issue and the issue is . . . "

"Who killed Ralph Stickley?" Randy finished the thesis. "I see. So that's what all of that is on your desk."

"Exactly." Ben announced as though he had just found the cure for the HIV virus. "Exactly." He paused and then opened the floor for debate. "Well, what do you say?"

Randy replied first. "Well, I say it looks like we are back in business. Jim, what do you say?"

Jim grinned and pretended to be one of the three musketeers. He put his hand out, fist down and announced, "It's all for one and one for all." Ben put his fist up against James' fist and bumped knuckles. Randy put her fist on top.

"All right, that's settled then," Ben proclaimed. "Here it is. I can't represent Wanda but I can lead . . . if you will have me?"

Turning to James, Randy asserted, "Have you? Are you kidding?" James nodded as well.

"All right, Randy, here's what we need from you. " Ben started to hand out the assignments.

"I knew this was coming," Randy feigned a complaint.

"Randy," Ben continued matter of factly with the directions as he laid out the game plan, "Why was Ralph transferred to South Carolina? We need a thorough inquiry into his business connections, his political connections, his associates before he went to prison, his pals in prison, his connections in the South Carolina prison department. I believe the North Carolina Department of Correction would be a dead end. After all, if South Carolina wants a prisoner, DOC is going to give him to South Carolina."

Randy said, "I see your point but I'm not sure I agree with your premise. I'll check North Carolina DOC anyway."

"That's the spirit. And one more thing. How could Ralph have gotten out of prison the night Wanda was raped? I didn't find anything in any record I saw that he was disciplined for it. He must've had an important contact in Goretown. Who?"

Ben turned toward James. "Ralph's finances. If we can follow the money, we can find out who his connections were. And his mother. There is still something fishy about a mother that won't weep for her son. Keep working on that. And one more thing for you, Jim. South Carolina Senator A. Fowler Worrell. He called me right before the trial trying to encourage a plea, claimed his constituents were concerned about the DA mistreating Wanda. What South Carolina Senator has the time to deal with some small trial up in North Carolina? There's something wrong there."

Randy interjected, "Worrell's calling Butch too. He apparently knew Butch from the old days. From school or something like that. I agree: something is wrong with that."

Ben nodded his head in agreement. As Ben reached into his pocket and pulled out a letter, Randy tried to count up everything that needed to be done. She noticed that everybody was doing the leg work except Ben. "Hey, wait a minute. What about you? What are you doing?"

"Plenty," Ben defended himself. "First, I'm going to get a plenary polygraph of Wanda. I know we are convinced she did not kill Ralph but I want to be careful about it. I want her pinned down on every aspect, every detail. And secondly, I would like a polygraph of Jeremy?"

"Good luck," Randy stated.

"Still. We need it. Work on it, Randy."

"I'll try but don't get your shorts in a knot. Won't happen."

"None of us believe Jeremy could have done it but it would be nice to have him on the record on the sequence of events. We'll see," Ben said as he opened the letter. "One more thing. I received this letter this morning from Nora Jean Lyerly." He looked at Randy and James to see if they recognized the name.

Randy did and immediately interjected with a sly grin, "Found a pen pal, huh?"

Ben was too bent on getting to the bottom of Ralph's murder to take time out to joust with Randy about Nora Jean. He pressed the letter so it would stay open. "Let me read this part to you and you tell me what you think it means. 'Dear Babycakes,'. Ben turned a little pink in the cheeks and cleared his throat. He continued to read, "I found someone who has information concerning the murder trial of Mrs. Wanda Stickley. If you would like to find out who it is, please go to Bird Island. In the mail box marked Kindred Spirit, you will find a green notebook. Turn to the twenty-ninth page for a message that will tell you how to contact him. Told you I'd help, Sugar Pie. Love ya', mean it, Nora Jean.'"

Ben looked up with an expression of wonder on his face. "What's this all about? Hoax? Do they know something?"

Randy answered, "Umm, I don't know what this person knows but I know about Bird Island and Kindred Spirit. Rod and I cycled down to Bird Island. It's the last island along the North Carolina coast. It's undeveloped and isolated. Years ago some man put a mailbox up and put notebooks and pencils in it so that the people who go there can write messages in it. Kindred Spirit is the name on the mailbox. So people--lovers, beachcombers, and others--write all kinds of things to each other and to Kindred Spirit. Usually they write about the beauty of the beach or some important event in their lives."

"Can I drive to it?" Ben inquired.

"No, you can drive to Sunset Beach then walk to it. Just a couple of miles."

"Walk two miles?" Ben was a little exasperated.

"Be good for you," Randy stated. "You ought to go. We need to know what this is about. Besides, you might find you would enjoy a little exercise."

"I'll do it but I won't like it." The grumpy old Ben began to surface.

Randy was still concerned about how the work load was being divided. "And what else are you going to do?" she demanded.

"I'm . . . I'm going out to visit Thor, the leashed dog," he said with a smile. "That's one thing I did right."

"And?" Randy insisted.

"I'm going to correct something I did wrong."

"What?"

"You'll know."

Later that day Ben went to the courthouse. He walked down the long hall to the DA's office and locating the office he was looking for, he knocked. Receiving a brusque "Come in", he stepped in. The person behind the desk did not look up for a few moments and Ben waited. Finally when he did look up, there was an immediate chill in the air.

"Down," Jack Krait grunted with a look of disapproval, "What do you want?"

"I came to see you. I came to . . . "

Krait grabbed his nose and said, "Good God, what's that smell?"

Ben had not noticed any strong odor but then remembered that he had just returned from visiting his thankful canine client Thor. In his exuberance Thor had jumped up on him and planted two big paws squarely in his chest. He thought that he had brushed off his foot prints but the dog had apparently left a distinct doggy odor. Ben, having smoked his way through forty years of smelly cigars, had not noticed anything.

Ben brushed his lapels and apologized. "Sorry. I had no idea that there was an odor."

Krait fanned himself with sheet a of paper to drive the smell away from him and demanded, "All right, get on with it. What's this about?"

"I . . . I came to apologize," Ben stammered.

Krait put up his hand as if to ward Ben off. "Look, Down, if you've come for some help on that perjury indictment, you are barking up the wrong tree. I can't help you. You got yourself into it and you can get yourself out."

"It's not that."

"I shouldn't even be talking to you. My God, you aren't even a lawyer any more." He stood up and walked toward the door to usher Ben out. Krait peeped out of the door to see if anyone was around and said, "You'll get me in trouble coming up here."

"Wait a minute," Ben urged. "Hear me out. I'm sorry. I'm . . . "

Krait pointed toward the door indicating Ben should leave and Ben said, "It will only take a minute."

Krait did not want to cause a scene which might bring the other assistant district attorneys or even Butch himself out into the hallway. He slumped his shoulders resigned to the fact that he was going to have to listen to Ben's apology. He walked back to his chair and dropped in the seat.

"Let's hear it," he said.

"All right. Krait, uh, Jack, I am sorry, truly sorry for the way I acted. Somehow our chemistry just did not work, er, I mean I just did not let it work the way it should have. I did some things. Uh, that thing with the dog was way out of bounds."

Krait squirmed a little in his seat as he remembered sitting in the chair slimed with dog drool.

"And I should never have gotten Rod to have you in court that day so that I could pull that stunt on you with Nora Jean. It was rotten. I'm sorry."

Krait did not budge or indicate any conciliatory feeling whatsoever. "Is that it?"

"No," Ben stated. "I was arrogant. It was my fault. I should have never done anything like that to you or anyone else. My mother did not raise me that way and I am ordinarily not that way. Sometimes the pressure . . . . Well, that aside. I am sorry for what I have done and if I can make it right with you, I will."

Krait remained silent. Ben dropped his eyes and looked at the floor. The sound of the copying machine at the end of the hall was the only thing breaking the stillness between the two of them. A few seconds passed although it seemed an eternity to Ben.

Finally Krait spoke. He seemed to soften a little. "You could have ruined me, Down. Butch could've canned me but he didn't."

"I'm sorry. It was totally out of character for me and I regret that I caused you any harm. It was devious and childish."

"Right."

Krait walked to the door way again and waited for Ben to leave. Ben took the hint this time and stepped out into the hall. Krait walked back to his chair and sat as Ben left. Krait picked up the paper and started fanning the odor away from him again.

*   *   *

Dr. Su Ling had given much thought to the meeting that she had had with Liu Bang and Jimmy Tang. She was extremely torn between the desire to help her brother Wu Han, who was very likely imprisoned because of his involvement in the Tiananmen Square uprising, and the need to protect the rest of her family. Any careless movement whatsoever would place all of them in danger.

As she stood in the operating room supervising a resident's surgical procedure to replace a hip joint, she had great difficulty concentrating. Still wary, she had postponed meeting further with Liu and Tang. The intervening time had tormented her as she sought to analyze everything she knew about them and everything that was said at the meeting with them.

"Doctor," the resident said then waited patiently. When she did not respond, the resident timidly repeated himself. "Doctor Su Ling."

She finally heard him and realizing his difficulty, she responded, "Yes, the retractor stays positioned there. Wait until you are certain it is retaining its position before you insert the suture."

She watched the resident, who having been reassured by the chief surgeon, skillfully move the retractor into position. He waited until the blood flow ceased and then continued with the suture. "Very well done," she added.

She checked the anesthesiologist's instruments and satisfied that the patient was stable and the procedure was proceeding successfully, she drifted off again into her troubled thoughts. Wu Han, her younger brother, had been an excellent student at the university and very likely would have followed in her footsteps if he had not gotten into trouble. An intellectual and academically gifted, Wu Han and she had been very close, much closer than with her other brother. They shared not only family but a great love for knowledge.

That thirst for knowledge, she thought as she let the glare from the bright lights of the OR mesmerize her, was the beginning of the end for Wu Han. At the university he always pushed the envelope challenging his professors and leading his fellow students. His forays into forbidden areas attracted attention and he became the subject of closer scrutiny by university officials. Disciplined and occasionally publicly humiliated by the authorities, he became the focal point for the quest for freedom at the university and finally out into the Square.

She shook her head, then caught herself. She glanced around to see if anyone had noticed that her concentration was elsewhere. No one had seen her break in attention and she thought back to the visit she had with her brother while he was holding forth with his fellow students in the Square. She had warned him of the great danger he was in and asked him to think of their parents if not himself. He was not to be reasoned with. He was wild with excitement as he told her of the great era coming in which they could freely associate, could read, write and communicate as they chose. Then the army, the tanks, the blood ran on the Square as the barriers were bulldozed.

Momentarily the resident's hesitation caught her attention. "Clamp, clamp," she stated to the nurse. She spoke again reassuringly to the resident. "It's small. No need to worry but close it quickly." She could see him smile slightly in appreciation over the top of his face mask.

The clamp was placed and the anesthesiologist nodded at her indicating the patient was fine. She looked at the site of the procedure and stated, "All right. Well done." She looked at the assisting surgeon and directed him to close. He nodded understanding the direction to take control of the procedure. He stepped up as the resident stepped back. She smiled again at the resident and stated, "This is your second hip, Yong. Quite well done." He nodded respectfully in thanks for the praise.

She walked to the cleansing room and pulled off her face mask and her cap. Peeling off her gloves, she shook out her long black hair over her scrubs. Checking her scrubs carefully for blood and surgical debris, she stepped to the sink and began the process of washing thoroughly. As the water ran over her hands, she thought back to the last time she saw Wu Han. He had raced to their home after the soldiers had broken through the barricades onto the Square. She remembered the bloody shirt he was wearing. At first she had thought he was injured but he said he had pulled an injured friend from the road out of the way of the tanks. As he packed a small duffel bag for his escape to Guangzhou, she tried to find out where the family could contact him. He charged around the house furiously trying to locate everything he would need. As he left, he hugged her and said, "Don't try to contact me. I will contact you. Be careful. All is lost now." She saw his face as he smiled at her. It was the last time in many years and she wondered how he would look now.

The water, never very reliable, suddenly turned hot and Su Ling jerked her hands back. It broke the spell and she adjusted the spigot and finished washing. As she dried her hands, a hospital administrator came into the sterilizing room and said, "Doctor, Doctor Guofeng asks that you assist in the north wing operating room."

She knew that that was the operating room that was used for harvesting organs for transplantation. Although her expertise was in orthopedics, she had provided assistance when the work load was very heavy. "Please tell Doctor Guofeng that I have just finished supervising a resident and I am not in a position to assist at the moment."

The administrator gave her a hard look. "I must remind you that Doctor Guofeng is your senior. He has told me not to take 'no' for an answer. A cadaver has been delivered to the north wing. There is no one to remove the kidneys which are needed for immediate transplantation. He said to make sure you are aware that time is of the essence and you must come."

Su Ling was tired, bordering on exhaustion. She had worked two shifts already back to back to cover for an ailing assisting surgeon. Shaking her head in disagreement, she caved in and followed the administrator to the north wing. When they arrived, she found that there would not be an assisting surgeon and only one attending nurse who would be responsible for transporting the kidneys to the waiting recipient. The work would be intense without assistance and she complained to the administrator.

"We can't continue to work like this. We must have help. I cannot perform this procedure alone with any degree of certainty that the organs will not be damaged," she said as she changed scrubs and started the work up for the surgery required.

The administrator replied, "I will report this to Doctor Guofeng immediately. If anyone is available, he will have them report to provide assistance."

Reading between the lines of bureaucratic mumbo jumbo as she usually had to do, she knew that there would be no help. She finished final arrangements and entered the operating room where the attending nurse was waiting. The nurse helped her put on the latex gloves.

Su Ling looked at the body as it lay under a sheet on the gurney. While adjusting her gloves, she asked, "How long has the body been deceased?"

"We were told by ambulance operators that the automobile accident occurred within the last forty-five minutes," the nurse replied as she arranged the surgical instruments in a tray.

"How did we get it so fast?"

"Sorry, Doctor Su, I do not know."

Su Ling lifted the sheet to begin work and noticed that the body was that of a relatively young male. As she studied the contour of the abdomen to begin opening the body, she was surprised to find that the head was missing.

"What?" she said. She lifted the sheet and looked along the body. Then walked to the bag in which the body had been presented. Without touching it, she observed that it was flat and contained nothing. "Where is the head to this cadaver?"

"I'm sorry, Doctor Su. I do not know. We have it as it was delivered," the nurse said rather apologetically and deferentially.

Su Ling studied the laceration along the neck that had severed the head. It was clean and even, too even she thought to have been in an accident. She saw no marks on the body and no road grit typical of a severely damaged body from an automobile accident.

The nurse scrubbed the body and covered it in an antibacterial antiseptic. When the body was ready for removal of the kidney, Su Ling decided, since there was no help to move the body, to proceed with a long abdominal incision. She worked for approximately fifteen minutes to make sure that access to the kidneys was uneventful. She was particularly concerned that without sufficient suction of surgical debris and blood removal that she would interfere with the integrity of the organs. As she worked she noted that the cadaver appeared to be that of a male in declining physical health. Possibly around thirty years of age she thought. There was virtually no fat on the body and the organs appeared to be deteriorated considerably. She wondered why this body would be chosen for a transplant. After she had concluded her work, the kidneys were removed and delivered to the assisting nurse. She iced them and carried them out immediately to the waiting operating room for transplantation.

Su Ling pulled her mask and sighed with fatigue. As she turned to go back to cleansing, she saw another person coming toward the operating room. He carried a box which partially concealed his face. She saw that he was going to enter the operating room without being properly dressed or sterilized. She called to him.

"Stop. You cannot come in here. Stop immediately." As she spoke, he lowered the box and she recognized him. "Chen Sheng. What are you doing here? You know you cannot come into the operating room like this."

She knew Chen quite well through Shang Chou International where she served as a consultant and Chen worked in security. He had absolutely no business in the operating room she thought and she was ready to give him a stern warning.

He laughed out loud and sat the box on the table. He quickly turned quite serious. "Dr. Su, you are in great danger."

Always fearful of the strange Chen, she was somewhat frightened by his statement. They were alone in the operating room and she looked toward the door.

Chen stared at her. "You have been talking to the Americans, Su Ling. That could jeopardize your position here. You are an important person, too important to Shang Chou International to let yourself be caught up in this."

She did not speak but was chilled at Chen's brazenness. She was sure he knew that she had met with the dissident Liu and the American Jimmy Tang. Her eyes widened and she started to breathe harder as she realized the danger she was in.

"I have done nothing. I . . . "

Chen stepped closer and continued to stare in her eyes. "Do not lie, Doctor. You will only make things worse."

She was not sure what he had in mind. She started to walk toward the door and he blocked her.

"Out of my way, Chen," she demanded.

"If you will not think of yourself, think of your family. Your mother, your father."

She listened, terrified. She did not speak. Chen walked back to the operating table and said, "Think of your brother."

"What do you know of my brother?" Her voice trembled as she asked.

Chen smiled again. His casualness chilled her until she could feel a hollowness in the pit of her stomach. He opened the box and lifted a human head out of the box. He held it up in front of her and then tossed it on the table by the headless corpse.

Su Ling screamed, "Wu Han," and fainted.

CHAPTER TWENTY-FOUR

Seagulls flew up and hovered as Ben pulled into the parking lot of the Jolly Crab's Restaurant. He exited and started toward the front when a greasy character appeared at the back door and motioned for him to come over. When Ben walked a little closer, the man stepped out of the kitchen wiping his hands on a dirty towel.

Ben watched the man carefully as he approached and said, "I'm trying to find Kindred Spirit."

"I know who you are," the man replied.

The man looked around furtively and indicated for Ben to follow him. They walked a short distance to an old pier that provided tie downs for the restaurant's shrimp boats. Served by a finger canal that spilled into the Intracoastal Waterway, the vacant pier was somewhat hidden from the front of the restaurant and offered a concealed location for a meeting.

The man obviously a dishwasher at the restaurant kept drying his hands and checking over his shoulder as they went to the end of the pier. The rickety old pier looked out over a huge stretch of marsh that was teeming with egrets, gulls and brown pelicans. Satisfied that they were far enough from the restaurant and the parking lot so that they could not be heard, Ben asked, "What's this all about?"

"Sorry I had to be so careful but this is dangerous business." He laid the towel on the hand rail of the pier and felt in his pocket for a cigarette.

"What's dangerous business?"

"This. This meeting," he explained as he checked the parking lot and the restaurant. "I didn't want to contact you directly. Too dangerous. Had to use that Kindred Spirit mailbox down on Bird Island. You gotta cigarette?"

Ben pulled out a cigar and offered it to him. The man looked at it and waved it off. "Cigarettes are my thang."

Too interested in the clandestine meeting and the strangeness of the dishwasher to smoke himself, Ben tucked the cigar back in his pocket and asked, "How do you know Nora Jean?"

"He's wild, man," he said. He shook his head and laughed somewhat tensely. "I had just got out of a sentence down in Goretown. I came back to Leland where I'm from and they picked me up on some old bad checks. Ain't right but it was good enough for three hots and a cot for ninety days in county. A piece a crap ratted me out over a little marijuana in my jail cell and they sent me to prison. Met Noah in there. Any way we got to talkin' and pretty soon, we made the connection."

"How's Nora Jean doing?" Ben asked.

The man hit his shirt pocket absentmindedly searching for a cigarette again. "Noah. Are you kiddin'? He owns the place. Party never stops when he's on deck. Look, Noah said you could be trusted. He ain't tellin' me wrong, is he?"

"No, you can rely on what Nora Jean tells you." Ben paused and looked carefully at the man. "I've seen you somewhere. Who are you?"

"Skids. I mean Bobby Reynolds. Skids is what most people call me though. Yeah, I saw you too. When you came down to Goretown to Superintendent Howell's office. I was sweepin' out the hallway."

The light came on for Ben. "Right. I remember you. I walked right by you and you acted as though you wanted to tell me something."

"Couldn't. Woulda got me killed."

Ben let it drop since he seemed uncomfortable talking about it and asked, "What do you know about Wanda Stickley?"

"Lots." There were some vacant spaces in Skids, times when he would become silent. Ben did not speak but waited for him to continue. "I knew Ralph Stickley. I was in stir with 'im down in Goretown."

Ben was immediately interested. "What do you know about him?"

"I know he was a piece a crap. He had it made and blew it, man." Ben waited again for him to speak. "Ralph was connected, man. Bigger than anybody woulda ever dreamed. But he wouldn't share it, man. Ralph was for Ralph. Looks like it got 'im killed."

Skids' eyes searched the parking lot and then looked out over the marsh. "Anybody see you down at Bird Island?" he asked nervously.

"No, it's pretty deserted down there. Just some young guy jogging by."

"What did he look like?"

"I don't know. Young guy, Asian, good runner, friendly."

"He speak?"

"Yeah, he came over and asked how far it was to the end of the island. Seemed pretty nice, great shape."

"That's it?"

Ben looked a little puzzled. "That's it."

Skids seemed to relax a little and Ben asked, "How did Ralph get into Goretown?"

"I don't know about that. He just said he was covered, had some big people lookin' out for 'im."

"Who were they?"

Skids turned and looked at Ben rather hard. "That information is let out on a need to know basis only. I'll tell you that when the time is right."

A seagull looking for a handout flew down and gently landed next to them. Skids picked up the towel and waved it toward the bird to shoo it away. The bird bounced up in the air and hovered for a couple of seconds then settled further along the hand rail. The horn of a distant shrimp boat suddenly blasted and Skids jumped. He looked at Ben and shrugged his shoulders. Ben let the subject drop about Ralph's contacts and told Skids about the night Wanda was raped. He asked how Ralph obtained his release from prison that night.

"Ralph was let out on a couple of occasions I know of. Guard would show up and say, 'got to see you, Ralph' and they'd leave. I remember he came back real late that same night you're talkin' about. Excited, couldn't sleep. Sweatin', pacin', talkin'. I knew he had done somethin' big. Whatever it was he got cocaine for it."

"Did he tell you what it was all about?"

"Naw, not exactly. He said he'd be rich when he got out. They was gonna parole him early, he said. He started actin' like a big shot. Blowin' off his big mouth. He blew his big mouth off one time too many though 'cause they were comin' to kill 'im. That was the rumor I kept hearin'. They put up a big fuss over a ballgame out in the yard as a set up. Three of 'em, I heard, got Ralph back in a bathroom. Fought it out. Ralph killed Jimmy Bob."

"What's Jimmy Bob's real name?"

"Tuslow. I think it's uh, James Robert Tuslow but nobody called him that. Too afraid."

"What happened after Jimmy Bob was killed?"

"Ralph escaped. They cleaned the mess up and made it look like Jimmy Bob was killed in an accident at the garage. The next thing I heard was Ralph got hisself killed at his wife's house. I'll bet she didn't kill him. They killed him."

"Who's they?"

Skids smiled. "You're fulla questions. Due time. I don't know if I can trust you yet, man."

Ben was disappointed and tried to get the information he wanted from another direction. "Well, did Ralph ever say anything about his former wife, Wanda?"

"Yeah." Skids smiled. "Yeah, he's pretty mad at her. He raised hell about her every few days. He'd get on a jag about it. Man, he had woman trouble. Thought his own mama was tryin' to cheat him out of a fortune."

"What was that all about?"

"Who knows? He said his wife's the one that got him the time, you know, for rape. That really made him mad. I can still hear him railing about that. 'Rape. You can't rape your wife, man,' he'd say. 'Get that any time you want it.' That's what he'd say. Make him crazy."

"Did he ever say why he would go back to her house?"

"Oh, yeah, he's gonna kill her when he got out, he said. Bragged about it. Besides, he always told me, that's where he could get money and a car if he ever needed to run for it."

"Two questions, Skids. These are important. Your answers may mean saving Wanda Stickley from spending most of her life in prison. One. What was Ralph into? And two. Who was in it with him?"

Skids blew air out of his lips as if he were releasing a load of frustration. "Man, you don't know what you're askin'. This could get me killed. Hey, man, this could get you killed." Skids thought about it for a minute. "Look. I'll give you one thing. You check it out and see if I ain't tellin you fair and square. And in the meantime we'll see if anything happens, see if I can trust you."

"All right."

"You check on the report where Jimmy Bob was killed. An investigation was done. It was all a pack of lies of course but you see whose name is on that official report. That name is where it begins."

"Where what begins?"

Skids looked at him with a quizzical look. "You really don't have a clue, do you? This is big. Biggest conspiracy the world has ever known. You check out that report. You see who's involved. Then if I don't have any trouble and I'm convinced I can trust you, I'll tell you the rest."

"When do you want me to contact you?"

"Don't. I'll contact you." He ran his fingers down in his pocket for a cigarette again and finding nothing, nervously bumped his fingers on the rail of the pier. "When I do, I'll tell you what Ralph told me. It will blow the top off of the whole world."

*   *   *

Wanda sat patiently in the inmate interview room at the detention center while Ben reviewed the results of the polygraph. She had changed a lot since it had happened. The scars were gone from her face and the regimen at Central Prison had caused her to gain a few pounds. If adversity tests character, she had passed but at a cost. She had been the repeated victim of an abusive husband. Almost murdered herself, she had survived to be charged with, tried, and convicted of murder. In one night of madness she lost her freedom, her son and her home. All she had left was character.

She looked around at the interview room. It had been months since she had been there, months since she had been in Wilmington. She tried to imagine the salt breeze as it lifted up from the brine of the Cape Fear along the waterfront. The picture would not form and she thought harder. Nothing. She studied Ben who worked feverishly through the lie detector's report. He was older, she thought, but somehow younger. He looked healthy even robust.

Ben looked up and saw her staring at him. He asked, "Everything all right?"

"Fine," she said without shifting her eyes from the stare. "You look good, Ben. You look really good."

Ben grinned a little at the compliment. No one had told him he looked good in . . . . He could not remember the last time anyone said that to him. He said, "Thanks, Wanda. You are looking pretty good yourself." She smiled back at him and he said, "Give me just a moment. I'm about finished."

She waited. She had learned to wait. In fact, she thought, there was little to do but wait. Her mind wandered back to Jeremy as she waited for him at school. The typical soccer mom, she read the newspaper and glanced at the school door waiting for him to come out. He popped out suddenly and she caught just a glance of him. She lay the newspaper down and looked back up. Jeremy was a middle age man. The same age he would be when she finished serving her sentence. He had two children with him that she did not recognize. The vision was so startling she immediately returned to reality. She noticeably started at the thought and Ben looked up again.

"Sure you're all right?"

"Fine. Where's Randy?"

"She's coming. Said she'd join us later. James will be here too."

Ben looked back at the paper he had been busily studying and counted off, "78. No deception indicated, 79. No deception indicated and 80. No deception." He flipped the report onto his desk and looked at Wanda who was still watching him. "You're innocent," he announced.

"I know."

"I mean you are innocent of everything. It was totally self defense. And more, you didn't cause the wounds to Ralph's neck. The polygraph tech says you told the truth about everything. You didn't kill Ralph."

"And Jeremy didn't kill Ralph," she added.

"Exactly. It leaves one conclusion. The same conclusion we wrestled with at the trial. Who? The phantom?"

Wanda was quiet. She did not respond to Ben's questions. Randy came in and laid her briefcase on the table. She spoke to Wanda and Ben then joined them at the table.

Ben pushed the polygraph results over to Randy and she picked them up. She turned to the last page of the summary. "The candidate indicates no deception in any response," she read outloud.

"I waited until Randy was here to bring this up, Wanda," Ben stated, "but we, you, need to make a final decision about the plea. Butch is chomping at the bit. We will be ready for trial next week. As you know the DA is offering to allow you to plead guilty to voluntary manslaughter, no admission of personal guilt, sentence in the mitigated ranger. If we proceed next week with a plea, you will be out in thirteen months and a week. I know you have told us repeatedly that you want a trial and you do not want to plead guilty but we are down to the wire."

"What do you recommend, Ben?"

Ben's face betrayed his feelings about the hard decision she would have to make. "First and foremost, you are innocent. You are not guilty of anything. As a friend I would advise you to plead not guilty. But as your lawyer, I have to recognize the realities. The evidence, even without your statement to the police, is still strong against you. Although we have a witness, this Skids, who can testify that Ralph was coming home to kill you, we do not have the puzzle solved. I have been painstakingly going over this case piece by piece and I still cannot tell you who killed Ralph. So we are stuck with the phantom theory as weak as that is. So." Ben stared directly into her eyes. "As your attorney I have to recommend that you take the plea. You are out in a little over a year."

Randy added, "There's one other factor that Ben is too nice to mention but I will. Ben is still under the suspension by the Bar and he will not be the lead attorney. I will."

"That part won't make any difference," Ben reassured Wanda and encouraged Randy. "Randy is as good as they come. She will represent you vigorously and zealously."

Wanda already knew her answer before she had been asked. She wanted to know what her lawyers thought about the plea. After all she had had a lot of time to think about it. This time the choice was actually easier. She had seen the worst and she knew she could survive it. Having been tortured by the loss of her son, by the humiliation of being convicted of a murder she did not commit and by enduring the numberless days of mind numbing imprisonment, she had reached a plateau that few people see or even know of. It is an area in the mind that lets one endure the unendurable, that lets one overcome the impossible.

As she turned to Ben, her face firmed into a resolution and conviction that was deeply felt and genuinely expressed. She spoke evenly with no anger but with great resolve. "I would not plead guilty to a crime I did not commit even if I could walk out of this jail today. Not now, not ever."

Ben was taken aback for a moment by the intensity of her statement. When he spoke, he started somewhat haltingly. "Well, uh-hum," he said to Randy, "we've got our work cut out for us. Tell Rod we are ready to go."

Randy said, "It's done." She then spent the next few minutes covering the format of the trial with Wanda. She stated that the DA would probably lead off with Ralph's mother again, then proceed with the first officer who arrived on the scene. The detectives who investigated the case would be called next. They would describe the scene and the location of the physical evidence including the screwdriver, the knife, and the gun. This time the lead detective would not be able to offer Wanda's statement into evidence. This would force the State to try to tie Wanda to the crime by circumstantial evidence, a weaker but, as Randy indicated, still an effective method.

"By this stage of the case, no one has stated that you have done anything to Ralph. They've got you standing over him. Along with other incriminating circumstances, that may be enough though," Randy explained.

Ben interjected, "We still need to evaluate whether we will put Jeremy on."

"No, we don't," Wanda said. "Jeremy is still out."

"All right," Ben said, "but even if he is out for us, the State can still use him."

Wanda had been through it all before and this time she did not show the same emotion that she had with previous decisions. She did not comment on the DA's possible use of her son to testify against her. Instead she asked, "What is the most they can do to me this time?"

Randy answered, "Second degree murder. No more than the sentence you are already serving."

Wanda nodded dispassionately and Ben stated, "Let's talk about tactics later. Randy, I want to get the report from the prison department of South Carolina. What about it? Able to check out Skids' story?"

Randy opened her briefcase and pulled out a raft of papers. As she turned through the stack of papers, she said, "I checked Ralph's transfer from North Carolina to South Carolina. North Carolina Department of Correction has a letter from the DA in Florence, South Carolina requesting the transfer. That's all I could get."

She kept turning until she pulled out a white sheet of paper. "Here's what I was looking for. This is the judgment from the court in South Carolina sentencing him to prison in South Carolina." She handed the judgment to Ben. "His lawyer's name is on there. I checked on him and he's a courthouse flunky. Just takes what the court hands out. So if there was a deal, all he would probably know is the sentence and not the details of how it was all arranged. Ben, you'll notice there's nothing unusual about the judgment."

Randy scrambled through the paperwork until she found the next sheet she was looking for. She pulled it out and said as she handed it to Ben, "Now this gets a little more interesting. I went to law school with a staff attorney at the South Carolina Supreme Court. I wanted to get into the South Carolina Department of Correction without arousing any suspicion so I asked her to get the info for me. This form you are looking at is a consent form between North Carolina DOC and the South Carolina prison department agreeing to the transfer of Ralph to South Carolina. Nothing unusual about the form but look down at the right hand corner."

Randy pointed at the particular location on the consent form and said, "See that. Approved: G. Howell, Superintendent." She looked again through the stack of papers and pulled out a blue sheet and handed it to Ben. "The plot thickens. This is a request for assignment form. It is basically a request from a particular prison for an inmate to be assigned to that specific prison. Look at the top. Stickley, Ralph. Now look down at the bottom. This one has a signature. Gedney Howell, Superintendent, Goretown. Looks like Howell asked for Ralph to be assigned to Goretown."

Ben studied the blue form and Randy handed him another set of pages stapled together. She said, "This one is entitled Report on the Death of Inmate # 2504088 James Robert Tuslow."

This was the form he was most interested in. He dropped the other sheets he was holding and turned through the pages until he found the summary at the end. He read out loud, "The investigation was thorough and plenary and reached several conclusions. In pertinent part I found that Inmate # 2504088 James Robert Tuslow died of a wound he received from a fall at the bus garage on the premises of the correctional center. The immediate cause of death was massive internal bleeding as a result of an accidental penetration by a long metal object located in the floor of the bus garage during horse play by the inmate. CAUSE: Accidental. RECOMMENDATIONS: No criminal charges warranted and no disciplinary action necessary. Respectfully submitted, Gedney Howell, Superintendent, South Carolina Department of Correction, Goretown Unit # 30."

Ben looked up at Randy who had been following along on the report and stated, "It's just like Skids said. Gedney Howell signed the report. It's a whitewash no doubt."

"Gedney Howell's name is all over everything," Randy said. "The transfer, the consent, the approval, the report. He's the next step in solving Ralph's murder but how do we get through to him? He wouldn't even talk to you when you went down there."

James walked in after overhearing the statement about how to get to Gedney and commented, "Maybe we ought to look in his wallet, so to speak. We can follow the cash flow and that may lead us to his accomplices if he has any."

"Good idea, Jim," Ben offered. "I'm going back to Skids to see what else he'll tell us. I need to talk to him anyway to see if he will voluntarily come in and testify for Wanda about Ralph's threat to kill her when he got out of prison."

Ben let out a sigh of relief and commented, "Finally some good news."

James pulled the newspaper out of his briefcase and threw it on the table in front of Randy, Wanda and Ben. "Have you read today's paper? It's not all good news."

Ben picked up the paper and turned it around so he could read the lead story. The headline read, "Local Woman Killed in Hit and Run".

Ben looked at James with a look of uncertainty. "What does that have to do with us?" he asked.

"Read a little further," James directed. "Check the name of the victim."

Ben started reading the article and when he came to the name, he blurted it out. "Ruth Leslie Stickley."

CHAPTER TWENTY-FIVE

"Please rise," the bailiff announced. With those words the second trial of Wanda Stickley began in the New Hanover County Courthouse. The retrial was not getting the attention the first trial did. The protesters, indignant and angry, who had filled the sidewalks at the first trial had gone on to other issues and places. The television media gave the trial a brief mention burying it in a round up of old news. The local newspaper was a little more interested and gave it first page coverage although it was below the fold line.

It was almost a year since Ralph had been killed but in the courtroom the trial had the same look and feel of the first trial. Butch was there for the opening and Rod was carrying most of the trial load again. There were some noticeable differences. Butch crafted his opening statement around circumstantial evidence. "We're going to paint a picture for you," he pointed out. Randy on the other hand focused more heavily on self defense. "We will prove to you that Ralph Stickley came to her house with murderous intent. He was in a killing state of mind," she argued.

Another difference was that Ralph's mother had been replaced as the State's first witness by an aunt who, fresh from the funeral of Ralph's mother, was much more emotional and teary in her testimony about Ralph than his mother had ever been.

Another noticeable difference was the presiding judge. Judge Seth Thomas Thorogood had been assigned to the retrial. From the old port town of Elizabeth City, he brought an air of erudition and dignity to the courtroom although in chambers he loved to be called Tommy T, his frat name at N.C. State, and he loved to be the one telling the jokes. His lead off joke set the tone for chambers hearings: What do you call an attorney with an IQ of 50? Answer: Your Honor. And he loved lawyer jokes. His favorite was the old saw: You know we lawyers are disliked so much there are skidmarks in front of a snake that has been run over and no skidmarks in front of a lawyer who has been run over." His courtroom demeanor was just the opposite, for example, he hardly ever smiled but treated everyone with great courtesy. His pleasant demeanor and courteous manner was a breath of fresh air after the prickly Judge Godboldt.

The most notable absentee at the trial was Ben. He stayed at the office and continued to pour over the mountain of documents that the case had generated. He was available immediately by telephone to Randy and James and he was present for the evening conferences with Wanda and the recap with Randy and James. Without Ben though, the case lacked the sizzle that the verbal pugilistics of Ben and Butch brought.

Wanda sat between Randy and James at the defense table. Randy enjoyed the position of lead counsel but she missed Ben. She missed being able to lean over and make some cogent remark about some aspect of the trial and getting his seasoned assessment. And she missed making some flippant observation about Rod's anatomy to break the tension of the trial and being able to watch Ben's reaction. On the other hand she was quite pleased with James. He brought a scholarly approach and could put his hand on the right case within minutes if not seconds. What he lacked in experience, he brought in zeal. They worked well as a team and brought not only a youthful exuberance to the defense but a skilled, professional approach.

Even with the skilled maneuvering of defendant's counsel though, the noose began to tighten and Butch's picture with Rod as the skilled painter started taking on a shape and dimension that pointed directly toward Wanda as the killer. By the middle of the first week of evidence, Randy lamented to Ben on a telephone call at a recess, "Wanda should've taken your advice. That plea might not have represented the truth but it was the best way to save her."

Ben asked, "It's going that badly?"

"Let's see. Butch likes to paint a picture. Let me see if I can. We've circled the wagons, the Indians are picking us off one at a time and are closing in. We have one hope left. A drunk dishwasher named Skids who might not show up."

"That's bad. How's Wanda doing today?"

"She's a trooper. One of the best clients I've ever worked with. She's tough." Randy thought of something she had planned on telling Ben when she had called earlier but had forgotten. "Oh, you'll never believe what's going on."

"What?"

"The lawyers are circulating a petition asserting that the evidence does not warrant a prosecution of you for the felonies charged. They are recommending that the prosecution be dismissed. I haven't talked to him about it but I'm hearing that Butch is livid.":

"I can't believe it."

"They admire you Ben even if they don't go along with you on some things. And there is obviously some self serving as well. A lot of them can see themselves in your situation. Oh, and here's something that will blow your socks off. Guess who has signed the petition. It's the last person you would ever expect."

Ben thought for a moment. "I don't know. Who? Butch?"

"Get real. All right, the second last person you would ever expect."

"I don't know."

"You're no fun. Nobody has a good sense of humor anymore."

"Who? Come on. You're driving me crazy."

"Better take a seat. It's . . . Jack Krait."

"Well, that's awfully nice of him."

"And brave too. Butch may send him out the door over that. I can't imagine him of all people doing such a thing. Strange."

Ben smiled to himself and said, "Underneath he's probably a pretty decent guy."

"Huh?" Randy thumped on the phone. "Am I speaking to Ben Down? Hello?"

"Come on, Randy. He's probably turning over a new leaf. At any rate I'll have to thank everyone who ventured Butch's wrath by signing the petition. Get me a copy if you can. And this. James wants us to get together for a few minutes this evening. He developed some information about Ralph's mother. Got time?"

"Yeah, I'll come by after court. Hey, gotta go. Bailiff is giving me the look."

Later that evening Ben, Randy and James gathered in the coffee room at their offices at the Rice Building. James turned on his computer and ran the files up on Ruth Leslie Stickley. He printed out a single copy on his computer then made a copy on the copying machine for Ben and Randy. Ben served the coffee that Skittle had made for them before she left for the day.

Randy tried to read the faded copy and complained, "I must be losing my sight. I can't make this out."

Ben handed out the coffee cups and started pouring. "Black, right, Randy?"

"Right."

"Jim, one cream, one sugar, right?"

"Yeah." James took the cream and sugar and stirred as he scrolled down though the screens of information on the computer.

"Tired, Randy," Ben commented. Randy looked at him as though she did not understand what he meant. "You're tired. That's the reason you can't see well. Look."

Ben started reading her copy of the faded report. "Executrix Report. I certify that the following is a complete and accurate list of the assets of the deceased Ruth Leslie Stickley at the time of her death. How did you get this so soon, Jim?"

"Her sister qualified as the personal representative of her estate and filed the will in the Clerk's office today. I'll have a copy of her application to be appointed executrix of the estate, the certification of assets and liabilities, and the last will and testament of Mrs. Stickley." James sipped the coffee. "Ummm, just right," he said. "Ben, look at the list of real estate."

Ben read from the copy, "Real property: One house and lot, Wilmington, North Carolina, fair market value, $385,000. Personal property: Residential furnishings, fair market value, $38,000; one Cadillac Seville, fair market value, $27,000 (predamaged value) Note: working with insurance to settle damage claim; one Lexus, fair market value, $39,000; Certificate of deposit, National Coastal Bank, $50,000; Savings, National Coastal, $2,367. Liabilities: Erline's Dresses, $3, 562.11; Premier Jewelry, $1,400.89. Total estimated net estate: $500,000."

"Wow," Randy yawned and commented. "I thought the Stickley family went bust with Ralph's shenanigans."

"They did," James stated. "I checked with her sister and she was pretty straightforward about it. She showed me a copy of a $500,000 check to Ruth Leslie Stickley from American Corporation. Mrs. Stickley received it about a year ago and deposited it at Coastal National Bank. Before that she had a small house and was just making it on social security. Her sister didn't know anything about why she got the check."

"I knew it. Something's wrong with this lady," Ben said. "What do you know about American Corporation?"

"Nothing yet but I'm working on it."

"Well, keep digging, Jim. This could be critical."

James pointed to another sheet of paper in Ben's hand. "There is something else. Look at the list of beneficiaries."

Ben looked at the list and saw it contained one name, the name of Mrs. Stickley's sister. "Well, I'll be. I saw that her will did not leave anything to Jeremy. And she did not even list him as an heir. Completely disowned him."

"Ruth Leslie Stickley was a mean old woman," Randy commented.

Ben did not respond but lay the estate papers on the table. He sipped at his coffee in silence. "Well, I checked with Ed Jones at the Wilmington Police Department," Ben noted. "He's in charge of the investigation of the hit and run involving Mrs. Stickley. They don't have very much. No witness. Just a paint scraping on her left front fender. The hit and run driver hit her on the driver's side as they went over the Cape Fear bridge. Ran her into the Cape Fear at high tide. She couldn't escape and drowned. Pretty gruesome. Bloody scratch marks inside the vehicle and torn fingernails. Must've been awful."

Randy shook her head without commenting. Suddenly the telephone rang. Randy looked at Ben, Ben looked at James. Nobody moved. Ben said, "Let it ring. Everybody's tired. If it's important, they'll call back."

After a couple of more rings, Randy said, "I can't take it." She struggled to get up and picked up the phone. She listened then held the phone. She looked at Ben with a bit a mischief. "It's for you."

"God, Randy," Ben whined and took the phone. He listened for a moment or two and then said, "And you are who? Oh, Leland Police Department. I see. Who? He did what?" Ben listened for a long time then said, "You ought to suspect murder. Sure. Yes, sir. I'll be here tonight. I'll wait."

Ben hung up the phone. He turned toward Randy and James with a rather stunned look on his face. "That was the Leland Police Department. You won't believe it. Skids is dead."

"What!" Randy exclaimed as the news woke her up.

"They think it's a suicide. Gunshot wound to the head, gun in his hand. They found my name in his wallet and they want to talk to me.

There are some strange things about it. I told them they should suspect murder."

"Why is that?" Randy asked.

"The officer said he had scratch marks on his chest that looked like an R."

*   *   *

Later the next morning the telephone rang at Randy's apartment. "Randy," the voice said as she struggled to pick up the phone and answer it.

"Huh?" she responded still asleep.

"Randy, wake up."

"Ben . . . Ben, is that you?" she responded weakly and turned over the bedside clock as she tried to check the time.

"Yeah, listen . . . "

"Do you know what time it is?"

"Yes, do you?" Ben replied in a cheery tone.

"Well, no, but it's . . . ." She finally sat the clock up and said, "It's . . . it's five thirty in the morning. Have you lost your mind?"

"No, I've found it." Ben was still very excited.

"Huh?" Randy yawned into the phone. "Found it. Found what? Have you gone crazy?"

Ben paused a couple of seconds to give her head a chance to clear from the sleep. He said, "I know why Ralph was out of prison the night he raped Wanda."

"Okay but couldn't that wait until later this morning? Say around 9:00 o'clock."

"No." Ben waited awhile to let the news sink in. "I also know why Ralph came back to Wanda's the night he was murdered."

"Well? Why?"

"Are you awake?"

"All right, I'm awake. Tell me."

"All in due time. There's bigger news."

Randy groaned and sat up in bed. "No more games, Ben. What's going on?"

"I believe I know who killed Vice President Anderson."

"Ben, you've gone absolutely crazy. What's this all about?"

"Not over the phone. Get dressed and meet me down at the evidence room at the Sheriff's Department in forty-five minutes. Understand?"

"Well, yes, but . . . ," she said and Ben hung up.

Earlier that same morning all of the lights were out in the Rice building except for a lamp on the desk in the office of Ben Down. Under the umbrella of dim light, Ben sat hunched down in his chair with his head in his hands. His suit coat lay crumpled in a chair to the side of the desk. His shoes were tossed in the corner and Ben was barefoot. The detective from the Leland Police Department had left hours earlier and after reviewing the files on his desk for the umpteenth time, Ben drifted off into an uneasy sleep.

His desk was ground zero for the effort to solve the Ralph Stickley murder. The stacks of files and documents had been read, reviewed, combed, and studied in their minutiae for a solution, a clue, anything that would break the case. The search for the clue had been as committed and dedicated as anything Ben had ever done. The hunt for the phantom had taken on an additional meaning for him. It was a mission, his mission not just for Wanda but for Margaret and for himself. It was the lifeline that would pull him out of the doldrums of mid-life. It was the avenue he must use to resolve the issue around his ethics, the ticket to his salvation as a lawyer. It was Ben's obsession.

As he slept, he slipped into another world. He smiled as he dreamed he was at the coast walking toward Kindred Spirit again on Bird Island. As he strolled easily along the beach, the light wind kicked up suds and spray from the surf. It was a magical time as he felt the sun in his face and the sand at his feet. He splashed childlike in the ankle deep water. It was a beautiful day and he had a sense that all was well. Suddenly it changed. A great sea eagle fell from the sky in a tremendous explosion of the sun. The clouds moved landward in a swirl and a rush. The wind tossed the sand so that it beat against his face and hands and the waves that had just been gently falling over each other began to crash in a noisy, cacophonous pounding on the sand. Skids appeared and stared at him in fear. He raced past Ben toward land. Ben was nauseated by the motion of the sea, the air, and the land and started following Skids to the high shore. Wanda stood helplessly between the thin line of sand dunes and reached out to Ben for help. He raced toward her to help but his movement was slowed to a creep as he struggled intensely to reach her. Unexpectedly a huge wave crashed over both of them.

Ben awoke tired and stiff. He found himself slumped and semicurled up in his chair. He tried to move but found that his legs were leaden. He looked at the mound of paperwork on his desk and groaned audibly. He became aware of a wet feeling having perspired heavily from the troubled sleep. Finally he was able to stretch lightly and put his arms up over his head to extend the muscles in his back that were still asleep. When he put his feet out, he felt his bare feet touch the floor. Instead of feeling the warm texture of the carpet as he expected, Ben was a little surprised to feel sand beneath his feet. He pushed his chair back slightly and attempted to see how much sand was on the floor under his desk. Unable to see in the dim light, he put his feet down and slid them around lightly over the sand. As he did, it seemed to electrify him. It was the electricity generated when a small fact powers up into a great theory.

"Sand," he said out loud as though it needed to be recorded somewhere lest it be lost. He leaned forward and quickly started turning through the stacks and stacks of papers. "Where did I put it?" he spoke to himself angrily. He looked like the mad scientist who had misplaced the secret formula.

After a few moments of frantically searching, the pile became so disorganized it had disintegrated into a dump like an area serving a garbage landfill. Finally he found it. He pulled the sheet of paper out and held it up. He could not read it in the light from the lamp so he raced over to the light switch by the door and turned on the overhead. He studied the paper and talked to himself as though he were trying to convince himself of what he already believed.

"Evidence," he read. "Alleged Rape, Wanda Stickley. Notes. ID Tech Sweeny. New Hanover SD." He scanned down the page. "Here it is. One white linen sheet: located bedroom, scene of alleged crime, possible semen stains, recommend submit for DNA, large areas were very wet hours after alleged attack, torn in lower right corner, hard rubbery substances (approx. eight, pea shaped), sand all over sheet."

Ben looked up. "Sand. That's it. Sand and rubber."

Ben took the paper and walked back toward the coffee room. When he reached the broom closet, he opened the door and switched on the light. In the back of the closet sized room was a stack of old newspapers that Skittle kept for recycling. Ben pulled out one stack and carried them to the table in the coffee room. He clicked on the light and started sorting through the stack. Reading the headlines on the front page, he searched vigorously for a particular article that he had read several months before. Unsuccessful he walked back to the closet and pulled out another bundle of old newspapers and continued the same feverish search.

When he found the article he was looking for, he sat down and started scanning the paragraphs. He let his thumb run down through the article until he found the lines he had been searching for. "Ah, here it is," he exclaimed. "Summary of the investigation of the assassination of the Vice President." He pulled out his pen and circled the language and raced back to his office. He grabbed his coat and started out the door when he thought to himself: Randy needs to know this. He checked his watch: 5:30. He went back to Skittle's telephone and called her.

Forty-five minutes later Randy and he were standing at the desk of the evidence room custodian on duty at the New Hanover Sheriff's Department. Randy still had a sleepy yawn every few moments as they waited. She was a little perturbed with Ben who had put her off when she asked for an explanation. He told her to wait until they saw the evidence and it would make more sense. The custodian said he would have to show the evidence only to Randy since she was listed as the attorney and since Ben's name had been removed from the list of permitted examiners. After a little squabbling, the custodian relented and finally agreed to let Ben be a witness.

Randy signed the form and the custodian walked back into the locked area of the evidence room. He returned in a few moments with a plastic bag containing a white sheet. The custodian indicated only he could handle the sheet and asked how they wanted it displayed. At their direction he opened the bag and carefully spread the sheet out on a table. Ben and Randy watched.

When the sheet was fully spread out, Ben approached and started examining the sheet in the bright light of the evidence room. Randy held back a little and asked, "What are we looking for?"

Ben replied without looking up from his search, "Sand and rubber."

Randy walked to the other side of the table and said rather nonchalantly, "The search is over. There is sand all over this sheet."

"Right," Ben agreed facetiously. He handed the copy of ID Tech Sweeny's notes to Randy and pointed. "Read here."

Randy read the note and looked back at the sheet. "This is it," she said referring to the sheet. She pointed at one corner of the sheet. "There's the tear in the lower right corner."

Ben nodded and continued to examine the sheet. The custodian was interested in the reason for the examination of the sheet and nosily looked over Randy's shoulder as she continued to study the report.

"Oh, yeah. Here's one." Ben pointed to a glob of rubbery substance about the size of a pencil eraser. He pulled out his reading glasses and studied the rubber without touching it. He stared at it intently for a long time. Finally he scanned the area around it and announced, "Here's another one."

Randy still did not know what it meant but looked back at the ID Tech's notes as the evidence room custodian continued to try to sneak a peek at the notes. While he was distracted, Ben slipped a glob of the glue in his pocket.

"There should be eight or so," Randy reported.

With better eyes than Ben's, she easily found four more while Ben found the next one. As Ben scrutinized the fabric in the sheet, he began to notice small nettles that were embedded in the cloth. He recognized them as the same kind that covered his pants when he fished in the marsh off Wrightsville Beach. He let a couple of them attach inconspicuously to his shirt sleeve. After thoroughly examining the sheet, Ben instructed the custodian in charge to carefully wrap the sheet back up being particularly careful not to lose any of the sand or the rubber on the sheet.

Randy and Ben walked out into the lobby without speaking. Out in the parking lot, Randy could not take the suspense any more and stopped Ben as he started to open his car door. In exasperation she demanded, "What's this all about, Ben? Come on."

Ben reached in his pocket and handed her the page of the newspaper he had retained from the stack in the broom closet. He pointed her toward the circled language in the article. She read it slowly trying to absorb what it meant. "The investigation into the Vice President's assassination got a boost when glue found at the scene of the bombing was traced to China. The glue, a nondescript rubbery substance, was not of particular importance but small granules of sand contained in the glue led investigators to China."

Randy looked up from the article and realizing what Ben was thinking, she said, "You've got to be kidding."

"Not for a second, not over this."

"You think the rubber on that sheet came from Ralph. You think that rubber is glue and contains grains of sand that will tie Ralph to the assassination of . . . "

"Correct. Wanda Stickley was raped on the same night the Vice President was killed." Ben stepped a little closer and pointed to the article. "Ralph Stickley was involved in the murder of Vice President Anderson and I think we can prove it."

CHAPTER TWENTY-SIX

Skittle appeared suddenly in Ben's office door. She looked somewhat pale and frightened.

"What's going on, Skittle?" Ben asked trying to imagine what could have upset her.

She announced, "FBI. They want to see you, Ben."

Ben got up from his desk and followed Skittle into the reception area. There were four men and one woman dressed in dark suits. They stood somewhat at attention and had arrayed themselves behind one older man in a dark gray suit.

Ben recognized one of the FBI agents, Steven Teague, as the agent assigned to the Wilmington field office. Ben had worked with him on several drug trafficking cases in the old days when Ben was still a prosecutor. Teague was the FBI agent to whom he had given the glob of glue for lab analysis. He nodded his head at him in acknowledgment and the agent smiled slightly in return.

"Yes, sir. What may I do for you lady and gentlemen?" Ben asked speaking to the senior member of the group.

The older man stepped forward and said, "Bays Covington, Mr. Down. I am a Special Agent with the Federal Bureau of Investigation. I think we need to talk to you."

Ben smiled knowingly and looked at Skittle with a wink. He replied, "Certainly. Come to my office." As Ben walked past Skittle, she whispered, "What have you gotten yourself into now?" Ben did not comment but led the way back to his office.

When they were seated, Covington introduced the other agents and commented about Ben being an attorney at law.

Ben looked a little chagrined and said, "Well, I guess you ought to know that I am not presently an attorney. I was but my privilege to practice law has been suspended and I am under indictment involving allegations of subornation of perjury."

Covington smiled slightly and said, "Yes, we probably know more about you at this point than you may know about yourself."

"Such as?" Ben asked inquisitively.

"Well, I know you are a Wake Forest man, undergraduate and law school, and consequently those alleged ethics violations are probably bogus."

Ben warmed up to Covington immediately.   Ben smiled congenially and responded, "Correct on all points, sir. You must be a Wake Forest graduate yourself."

"No, I was a West Point graduate but my father was. I am very familiar with *pro humanitate*," he referred to the University slogan. "And I know the quality of the students they produce. Several of my cohorts are from Wake."

"You have done your homework very well."   Ben smiled again. "Now how may I help you?"

"Let me be a little more forthcoming in my identification of myself," Covington responded and adjusted his seat. He sat up a little straighter in the chair. "I have been assigned by the Director of the Bureau as the agent in charge of the investigation into the assassination of Vice President William Keynard Anderson and I suppose we can begin by finding out where you obtained the smear of glue that you gave to Agent Teague to be analyzed."

For the next hour and a half, Ben described chronologically how things had developed to the point that he had taken the glue from the evidence room at the Sheriff's Department and had given it to Agent Teague for lab analysis. Ben explained that he had not wanted to reveal the source of the glue to anyone except the FBI for fear that there was a larger conspiracy and there was no certainty about who was involved in the conspiracy. Ben also mentioned that the nettles he had seen on the sheet were the same kind that he had seen when he was fishing in the inlet between Wrightsville Beach and Figure Eight Island, scene of the assassination. As Ben talked, the subordinate agents took notes feverishly and Covington absorbed all of it with great interest but without much comment.

When Covington did speak, he was just as frank and revealed that the lab analysis of the sand particles in the glue that Ben had given to the FBI was consistent with the sand particles in the glue found in the tracks of the assassins at Figure Eight Island. Ben's hunch was right on point: Ralph Stickley was up to his neck in the assassination plot.

"My best guess," Ben said, "is that Ralph Stickley is the one called Big Foot as the taller of the two assassins has been called in the press. I'll bet he was present at the assassination and was killed by his co-conspirators when he would not keep quiet about it."

"That's our assessment as well," Covington agreed. "But proving it is another thing. We need to work our way up the chain of conspirators until one breaks under the pressure. That's the only way we can make the case. These guys will be too smart to leave a paper trail."

"What about China?" Ben asked. "From what I have read in the papers, it is very likely the source of the conspiracy. Can't you develop anything there?"

For the first time Covington showed some emotion: a look of disappointment. "I've just returned from Beijing after being there for seven of the last eight months," he reported dejectedly. "The bamboo curtain is harder to penetrate than anything I have ever done. Harder than the Cosa Nostra, harder than the violent right wing. Even harder than the Russians at the height of the Cold War. Initially we thought we were going to get full Chinese government support but we were stonewalled at every turn. When we turned to the underground, we developed some significant leads, for example, we had a doctor who worked at Shang Chou International in Tientsin, China where we had traced the assassins, but that dried up. We heard that her family was terrorized and she clammed up."

Covington shook his head in amazement and lamented, "Strange. After all that work in China, we are sitting here today in Wilmington, North Carolina, the scene of the crime. That's basic police science, almost too simple. I can still remember our instructor at the Academy saying, 'The killer will return to the scene of the crime. If you are going to solve the crime, you will probably solve it right on the scene.'"

"We've sat with this thing for a year ourselves," Ben commiserated. "I know how frustrating it can be. We've had the possibility hanging over us that an innocent woman would be convicted of a crime she did not commit." Ben thought for a moment. "She was and may be again."

"How do you know Stickley's wife was not in the conspiracy?" Covington asked.

"That's a fair question," Ben replied. He knew this would be an issue after he had determined that Ralph was involved in the Vice President's murder and he had thought about this for some time.

"First, I've known her for many years. She is a devoted mother. She'd never do anything to jeopardize her son Jeremy. And secondly, the relationship between Wanda and Ralph was too strained to permit a conspiracy. They were like fire and gas. Explosive. And third, and more objectively reasoned, Wanda passed a lie detector. She was completely truthful when she denied she was involved in any wrongdoing with Ralph. Fourth, she has an ironclad alibi. There's more but the truth is Wanda is a victim of this conspiracy not a participant."

"We would still like to interview her."

"Sure. I'll arrange it whenever you would like. She'll co-operate fully."

"Who do you think is involved?" Covington prodded.

"Well, that's not so easy, is it? I suspect without knowing that Ralph's mother was involved in some way. She received the half million dollars just before the assassination. She has just been killed. Possibly to silence her. Although I don't think this poor soul, Skids, was involved, I think he knew too much and he paid for it with his life. He definitely knew Gedney Howell, the warden at Goretown, was involved. The paperwork on Ralph's transfer from North Carolina to South Carolina will demonstrate that. So far the trail stops cold there and I don't know what it would take to move Howell. He's a pretty cold fish. Wouldn't budge when I was there to talk to him."

"Don't worry about Howell," Covington said. "We'll take Mr. Howell from here. There is one more conspirator we know of."

"Who's that?" Ben inquired not quite sure what he meant.

"Littlefoot. The assassin out there in the marsh on Figure Eight Island with Ralph Stickley. He or she is pretty bloodthirsty and may be the hit man who took out Ralph, his mother and Skids."

"Yeah, the phantom," Ben said.

"Who?"

"That's what we've been calling the killer who murdered Ralph: the phantom. When we started the trial, I would've never guessed in a million years it was Littlefoot."

Covington asked, "Who else knows about this?"

"Randy Bost," Ben said as Covington nodded at one of the agents to make sure he got her name down. Ben continued, "She practices in the same building with me and presently represents Wanda

Stickley. We decided not to tell anyone else for several reasons. First, it was speculation until you filled in the blanks. And two, the information can be dangerous. There's still a killer or killers out there."

"Good, Ben," Covington offered. "Look, we will get the sheet and run tests on the remainder of the glue droppings and the nettles. We'll pick up the investigation on Mrs. Stickley and Skids. Silence is critical. And let's keep it that way until we can develop Gedney Howell into a government witness."

"Yeah, but we've got to bring this to a conclusion before Wanda Stickley's trial is over. This may be the FBI's only solid lead but this is her life. We've got to find the real killer or she will pay the price: innocent and convicted. Again."

*   *   *

Randy watched as Rod led another expert through his testimony. She admired the way he transformed the ordinary, a small spot on the kitchen floor or a fiber obtained from the table in Wanda's basement, into an evidentiary point of utmost significance in the trial. He was adept at the nuance and the innuendo and, she thought, he looked pretty good while he was doing it too. So good she almost hated to deflate the effort but she took the self-described expert in hand and soon had him to admit he had no knowledge about the case except his examination of some minute aspect of the physical evidence, his opinion that he had developed from the examination, and no, he did not know who killed Ralph Stickley. As the wounded expert figuratively limped from the stand, Randy glanced over and smiled at Rod as if to say "touche". Rod nodded accepting the defeat in the skirmish. He could be quite gracious since he knew she had won the battle, but he was winning the war for the hearts and minds of the jurors.

The State's case against Wanda was strong, maybe even stronger than the first trial. Even though there was less evidence, the evidence that was presented was straightforward and dedicated to the issue of guilt. There were no conflicting statements in Wanda's confession for the State to contend with, no side issue of the credibility of

Jeremy, and no Ben to muck up the State's case. This time the State had the gun and with that, no loose ends. The evidence was circumstantial but it was clearly pointing toward Wanda's guilt. Butch's picture that he promised in his opening statement was filling in quite colorfully and only needed a few brush strokes to finish the work.

At a conference with Judge Thorogood during a recess on Friday of the second week, Butch casually mentioned that the State had one more witness and would rest its case. The judge whimsically commented, "Why? What more do you need?" Although not appreciating the judge's sense of humor on the subject, Randy assessed it the same way. She felt as though she were standing in front of a fast moving train with no way to get off of the tracks.

Once court reconvened again the State called its last witness, the same closing witness from the first trial, Itzak Vari Dundail. He was a surprise witness the first time he testified but this time Randy knew what to expect or so she thought. She could already hear his testimony providing circumstantial evidence that put the knife in Wanda's hand at the time of the murder and she could hear Butch's closing argument telling the jurors he had painted the picture just as he had promised and "Wanda Stickley was caught red-handed".

Butch was in again for the final kill and was closing the case by calling Dundail. After a few preliminary questions in which Dundail identified himself and told what he was doing the night of the murder, Butch asked, "At some point were you attracted to the residence of Wanda Stickley?"

"I was, sir. I heard a car backfire or possibly it was gunfire from that direction. I stepped out into my yard and looked up toward Mrs. Stickley's. I saw a man run out of the house and fall. I saw another person run out behind him and stand over him."

"What was the person doing, that is, the person who was standing over the other person?" Butch asked routinely.

"The person was cutting and slashing with a knife at the person on the ground."

"Could you identify the person who was cutting the person on the ground?" Butch asked the question expecting to hear the answer given at the first trial, that is, that Dundail could not identify the person at that point but after Dundail had gone inside and made the 911 call, he came back out and could identify the person then as

Wanda Stickley. It was strong circumstantial evidence but still not quite completely making Wanda the killer. It had left some room for a reasonable doubt argument by the defense at the first trial.

"I can, sir."

"Uh, what?" Butch said expressing his surprise.

"I can identify the person who was slashing at the person on the ground."

"Well, then, uh, who was it?" Butch asked still surprised. He looked over at Rod who was shaking his head as though he were surprised as well.

Dundail stood and pointed directly at Wanda. "It was her. Wanda Stickley. She slashed at his throat until his hands stopped flailing."

Butch had no idea why the testimony changed but he ran with it just the same. It was much stronger than at the first trial. Now the State had painted the picture. The picture was painted with Ralph Stickley's blood and featured a bloodthirsty, knife wielding Wanda Stickley as the killer.

On cross examination Randy had to scramble. She tried desperately to discredit his testimony. She asked him point blank why he changed his testimony from the first trial. He denied it. She showed him his testimony in the transcript from the first trial in which he said he could not identify Wanda until he had made the 911 call and had come out to find Wanda standing over Ralph. He said he was sorry but his memory had improved.

"He had thought about it and thought about it," he testified. "He had a distinct recollection of Wanda stabbing and slicing Ralph Stickley as he lay on the ground."

When it was over, his credibility had been attacked but he had done the job on Wanda even better than Butch and Rod had hoped for. Randy could sense the elation in Butch's voice as he announced, "The State rests, Your Honor."

With court adjourned for the weekend, Randy, bone tired and dejected, crawled back to her office. It was the first time she not only felt the case was hopeless but that she was powerless to stop the inevitable: a verdict of second degree murder with another sentence of twenty years for Wanda.

As she walked in, she noticed that Skittle had gone home. She checked the clock in the lobby and noticing it was past 5:30 Friday, she did not expect to find anyone in. She walked past Ben's door. It was closed and she walked on to her office. She threw her files on the table and started to walk back to the coffee room for a soft drink. Finding that she was too tired to move, she flopped in the chair and pushed the files and books on her desk out from her to make a space to lay her head down. She slowly slid down into a crumpled heap and laid her head on her hands.

"Still want to be a lawyer?"

She looked up and saw Ben standing in her doorway. "Ohhhh," she moaned and raised up from the desk. "I'm tired. I never thought I could work so hard. Eighty hour weeks. Am I crazy or what?"

"You love it. You know you do." Ben stated as he pushed the door open a little further and came in. He took a seat across the desk from her.

She looked at him bleary eyed and grinned a little. "Well, yeah, kinda," she admitted reluctantly.

She stretched a little and Ben pulled her favorite soft drink out from behind him. "Just for you, counselor," he said and handed it to her.

She took a drink and began to wake up a bit as the caffeine started circulating. "Whew," she creaked, "we took a whipping today. The State finally rested the case. Oh, you'll never believe it. Dundail, Butch's big surprise the last time we tried the case, changed his testimony. Put the knife in Wanda's hand and cut Ralph's throat with it. Said he saw it this time. Chris', he lied through his teeth. I tried but I couldn't shake him."

"Don't worry about it. Witnesses will do that. I know you did the best you could do." Ben tried to comfort her. "How do you assess it?"

She looked at Ben and shook her head. "We're dead in the water. They've got us. And what have we got? Wanda? I don't think so. There are too many lies she'll have to answer for if we call her. Jeremy? The State wouldn't take a chance on him and call him. Too afraid he will try to exonerate Wanda. And we can't call him. Wanda won't let that happen. And our star witness Skids who could've made out a perfect case of self defense for Wanda? Dead. Just like our case is."

"Now come on, Randy. It's not that bad. They haven't heard your brilliant closing argument yet."

Randy tried to force a smile but it just would not happen. "Right," she said with a smirk. She took a sip of the soft drink again and thought of the news she had heard during the afternoon recess. "Skittle said the place was crawling with FBI agents. What's going on?"

"The FBI confirmed what we suspected. The sand in the glue on the sheet matched the sand in the footprints out at Figure Eight. Ralph was one of the conspirators who killed the Vice President."

Randy brightened and sat up a little straighter. She popped the soft drink can down on the table with a bang. "I sense a defense here. Supports our theory of a phantom killer, besides it is so riveting, maybe the jury will get distracted. Let's go with it. It's better than nothing."

"It's not that simple," Ben explained. "Covington, the lead FBI agent, says that the information is sensitive. Affects national security and revealing it may jeopardize the assassination investigation."

"No, that's not right. We've got a right. We've got a duty to protect this client. And right now we have nothing. Nothing, Ben." Randy was angry and Ben thought, unreasonable.

"Wait a minute, Randy. This is bigger than we imagined. We've got to be careful. This could affect a lot of people, this whole country. We've got to work our way through it."

Randy stood up and was clearly angry. "I'm a lawyer and I've got a duty to save my client. What's more important than that?"

Ben saw he was getting nowhere and tried to assuage the situation. "Hold on. Hold on. Look, you're tired. You need a rest."

"I need a defense. We are dying up there."

"I know that. Look, go home. Get some rest. Give me a chance to work on it."

Randy slowly sat in her chair. She did not speak but picked up the soft drink and took another drink. She let the fluid slowly slide down her throat as she thought. Her voice was forced when she spoke again. "Ben, we've got to do something. We've got to."

"I know. Let me work on it, okay?"

Still quite upset she did not respond and Ben was anxious to move her on to another subject. "One more thing. This information is dangerous. Do not tell anyone what we know yet. Not even Jim. It could get you killed. It could get all of us killed. There are killers at work as we speak."

*   *   *

A small convoy of law enforcement vehicles drove hurriedly through the tall pines of the South Carolina low country. Led by the Sheriff of Horry County the dark colored Caprices of the federal agents and the gray van of the IRS agent followed by a bevy of cargo vans blew swirls of dust along the sandy roads. A small boy on a bicycle waved at the Sheriff then felt compelled to wave at each of the vehicles until the convoy passed.

Upon reaching a small rise in the sandy tidewater, the Sheriff wheeled into the parking lot of the Goretown prison unit and pulled up to the administration building. In hurried succession the entourage followed and filled the small lot. The Sheriff exited and waited for the agents to unload and follow. When the last gray suit rolled out of the gray van, they marched into the lobby to the terror of the receptionist. While one remained in the lobby, the rest followed the Sheriff down the corridor to the superintendent's office.

The Sheriff opened the door without notice and caught Gedney stuffing some files into a briefcase. "Gedney," the Sheriff said, "Sorry 'bout all of this mess, but these federal boys got some serious business with you."

One of the gray suits stepped forward and produced an identification badge. "Mr. Howell, my name is Bill Walker. I am a special agent with the Federal Bureau of Investigation. We are here to serve you with a search warrant." He produced a copy of the search warrant and handed it to Gedney. "On behalf of the government of the United States of America, I am serving you with a search warrant for the premises of South Carolina Department of Correction, Goretown Correctional Center. We are now taking control of these premises and we will be taking all records."

Another agent stepped forward and seized the briefcase and files directly from Gedney. "What's the meaning of this?" Gedney demanded. "Am I under arrest?"

"No, sir, Mr. Howell, but we will need your presence to receipt you for the items of evidence seized. And we would like your assistance if you are willing to offer it. We particularly are looking for the files maintained on the following inmates: Ralph Stickley, James Robert Tuslow aka Jimmy Bob and Robert Reynolds aka Bobby, aka Skids."

Gedney stepped to the side and agents started going through his desk and through the file cabinets. Gedney recognized one of the people in the group as being the assistant director of the prison department. Gedney pretended he did not know what the search was about and asked him, "What are you doing here, sir?"

"Gedney, I regret to inform you the Director has sent me here to inform you that you are being placed on administrative leave until all of this is worked out." He had known Gedney since their days together as joint committee members on the conference of correction personnel and looked at him somewhat apologetically. Sheepishly he handed Gedney a package of documents. "He wants these filled out in triplicate."

Gedney looked at the assistant director indignantly and pitched the package on the desk. They waited impatiently until the officers had searched the office. Unsuccessful in finding the files they were looking for, one agent moved Gedney to an employee snack room while another called the secretary in to help with the search. After a couple of hours, Agent Walker and another FBI agent walked into the room where Gedney was waiting. They closed the door behind them and sat down across the table from him. Gedney was sweating and had stained his shirt heavily under both arms.

"Mr. Howell, we need to talk to you for a moment," Walker said. "This is Special Agent Ron Teeter with the FBI."

Teeter smiled at Gedney while Walker maintained a grim countenance. "Before we begin," he continued, "I must advise you that you have the right to remain silent. Anything you say, can and will be used against you in a court of law. You have the right to . . .
"

"Am I under arrest?" Gedney asked again.

"No, sir, you are not but you are named in the search warrant we are executing. And you have a right to have an attorney present."

"I don't want an attorney."

Walker pushed on with reading his Miranda rights. "Well, if you can't afford one, the court will appoint one to represent you."

"Not even if they appoint one for me," Gedney said.

"Now do you understand your rights?" Walker asked firmly.

"Yes, but I have nothing to say."

"All right," Walker griped rather angrily. "But I have to tell you we have not found anything that we are looking for in the search. Every file is in place as far as we can determine except . . ." He gave Gedney a hard look and raised his voice. "Except for the very files named in the search warrant."

Gedney remained silent and Walker continued putting pressure on him. "I tell you what I think, Mr. Howell. I think you have concealed those documents and I'll tell you what else. I think you are obstructing this investigation."

Walker turned very red in the face. He was visibly angry and appeared as though he might strike Gedney. "I've got enough to charge you right now with obstruction of justice. Right now. Do you hear me? We can take you straight to jail right now." He stopped and seemed to calm for a moment. "But you know what? We have bigger fish to fry. Mr. Howell, you are a suspect in the assassination of the Vice President of the United States. You, mister, are up to your neck in a situation that may result in your execution. So . . ." He checked his watch and stood up. He walked to the door and slammed it as he walked out.

It was extremely quiet after Walker's shouting. Finally Teeter smiled at Gedney again and broke the silence. "Agent Walker can be a little intense sometimes. He gets a little aggressive, sometimes violent but that's not the way to go. It's just not. He's got to have the information and he'll do anything, anything to get it."

Gedney started perspiring very heavily on his forehead and bathed himself with a paper towel. "What's his problem?" Gedney asked. "That guy is crazy."

Agent Teeter grinned and put his hand on Gedney's hand. "Don't worry about him. As soon as he gets what he wants, he'll calm down."

Gedney seemed to relax a little and Teeter sat back in his chair and assumed a more relaxed attitude. "Look, Mr. Howell, uh, Gedney, if I may? Just between you and me. The agency has information that you are involved in a conspiracy. In other words there are bigger fish to fry in this thing. You have an opportunity, right now, and I mean, right now only, to pull yourself out of this thing. But before we can help you, we need your help. We need to know who is involved, uh, we need to know who got you involved in this." Teeter leaned forward and put his hand on Gedney's shoulder. "Help us, help you," he begged.

Gedney sat silently and did not speak. Teeter said, "I know it's hard. It's got to be hard but it's not your fault. The big guys are going down. Don't let them take you with them."

Gedney was stonefaced. He still did not speak. "This could be your only chance to save . . . "

"Do you think I'm a fool? I wouldn't tell you anything if my life depended on it."

Walker burst in the door. He had obviously been eavesdropping. "Well, it does, mister."

While the agents searched the offices in the administration building and the office complex in the garage, Walker and Teeter grilled Gedney with the bad guy-good guy routine. This went on for a long period until one of the agents involved in the search came in and reported that they were through. Walker and Teeter got up and walked out of the room. In a few minutes Gedney stepped out of the snack room and asked if he was going to be arrested.

Walker never would give him a straight answer but indicated it all depended on the chain of command. Gedney retreated to the snack room and waited. He peeped out of the window of the snack room and saw the agents loading entire file cabinets into the vans. He saw his desk, his chair and the carpet from his office being loaded. When the agents finished, they assembled at Walker's vehicle for a conference then got in the vans. Walker walked back into the building and went to the snack room.

"Looks like you are free for the moment, Mr. Howell," Walker grumbled. "I would suggest to you that you not try to leave. That will force our hands and we'll have to pick you up."

Walker slammed the door and left. The convoy pulled out of the parking lot and lined up for the trip back through the tall pines. As the last van left the parking lot, Gedney walked up the corridor. As he walked, he checked each office and found each one ransacked. Files and cabinets were gone. Desks were standing with drawers open and chairs were pushed into the corners. When he reached his office, he saw an empty room except for the assistant director's package of documents to be completed in triplicate and a telephone. He sat in the floor and cried.

He calmed down enough to reach for the telephone and grabbing its cord, pulled it to him. He dialed a number and waited for the answer.

"This is Fowler, speakin'," the Senator said from his home phone. "Who is callin?"

"Senator," Gedney cried, "they've got us."

"Who is this?"

"Gedney, sir."

"My God, I've told you not to call me here. Nevah."

"But Senator," Gedney begged, "the FBI was just here. They searched and took everything except the telephone. They just left."

"Jesus Chris', son, don't you know this is an old FBI trick. They wanted to see who you'd call. You've killed us, boy."

CHAPTER TWENTY-SEVEN

"How's Margaret, Ben?" the Sheriff's records custodian asked as Ben reviewed the jail log at the Detention Center to see if any of Randy's court appointed clients had not made bail. "I heard she was in bad health."

Ben laid the list down and responded, "She's doing all right as far as the doctor can tell. She went through two major surgeries and is recovering. To me she seems to be in good spirits after having gone through so much but I don't know. She's in Evergreen Care facility across the river. I know she would love for you to come by and see her."

"I should have already. You know, we worked together for three years before she became your secretary. Wonderful times."

"Yeah, the good ol' days," Ben agreed. "Back when I was a young lawyer." Ben thought for a moment and said, "Huh, back when I was a lawyer."

The records custodian looked up from his work and checked to see if anyone was listening. He said, "I'm sorry about that, Ben. Everybody knows it was just a put up job by the DA. If I can help, you know I will."

"Thanks."

"Besides," he added, "my son got in some trouble in Southport. Heavy foot, you know. We need our family lawyer back."

Ben gave him a warm smile and said, "It's people like you that make this world a better place. A lawyer without a client is like a day without sunshine."

The records custodian grinned and continued to load info into his computer from officers' reports. In a few moments he looked up and asked, "Oh, what's all this FBI business about? I heard that a truck load of FBI agents showed up at your office yesterday. Heard you knew something about the Vice President's assassination. Anything to that?"

Ben feigned a grim expression and replied, "FBI stuff. If I told you, I'd have to kill you. Seriously I can't talk about it yet even though it looks like everybody else is."

"Small town. You know how it is," he said and returned to work at the computer.

Ben stayed busy turning the pages in the set of documents. Before the custodian could continue the conversation about the FBI, Detective Gerald Stanton came into the booking area and saw Ben.

As he went to his office, he called to Ben. "Got a minute?"

"Sure." Ben followed him to his office and when he went in, Stanton took a seat and pointed to the other seat.

When Ben sat down, Stanton asked, "What's this all about? The FBI came in here last night and seized the evidence in the Wanda Stickley rape case. They took everything. Then I heard that they had been at your office earlier. Then I heard that the FBI raided the prison down in South Carolina at Goretown. Everybody's saying that you know something about Vice President Anderson's murder out at Figure Eight. What gives?"

"Gerald, I'd tell you if I could but I can't."

Stanton looked hard at him to add a little pressure. "Really I can't," Ben repeated firmly. "If I could, I would. Especially after all you've done for Wanda and for me in the Stickley case."

Stanton gave up and said, "Well, it's a strange business. And I just received information that the police department down in Conway, South Carolina has just found the body of the warden of that prison unit down there at his mother's."

"What?" Ben rose up out of his seat. He could not believe it was possible since the FBI was involved in the investigation.

"Yeah, the computer information system indicated it was the warden, a man named Howell." He shuffled through the papers on his desk and handed Ben the computer printout.

"Gedney," Ben added somewhat numb from the news.

"Yeah, that's right. Know 'im?"

"No, no, . . . but I had met him once."

Stanton pointed to the lower part of the report. "Well, the report indicates he and his mother were found dead about two hours ago at the mother's home in Conway. Gunshot wound to the back of the head. Both of 'em. Execution style. Conway PD put out a request for assistance to area law enforcement for anything suspicious."

Ben sat there in a haze. First Ralph, then Ralph's mother, then Skids, now Gedney, he thought. The conspirators were shoring up the conspiracy. Every time some perceived weakness arose, the remedy was simple: cut off the cancer before it spread. Then his thoughts turned to Wanda. He had hoped the FBI would turn Gedney into a government informant who could testify who killed Ralph. With Gedney dead, Randy did not have a chance. Wanda's defense had just been killed, execution style. He laid the printout on the desk.

"Ben . . . Ben," Stanton repeated himself trying to get Ben's attention. When Ben began to listen to him, Stanton asked, "All of this has something to do with the assassination, doesn't it?"

"I, uh, I can't . . . "

The records custodian barged in the door and said, "There's a call for you up at the front desk, Ben."

Ben stood and still absorbed in the news that Gedney Howell had been murdered, he walked zombie like to the desk. He picked up the phone.

"Ben?" the voice inquired.

"Bays, is that you?" Ben stammered as he recognized the voice of FBI Agent Bays Covington.

"Right, Ben. I'm sorry I had to track you down but something has come up. The South Carolina DOC Superintendent Gedney Howell has been murdered."

"I know."

"What?"

"The news travels like wildfire in a small community. I've just heard that both Gedney Howell and his mother were found murdered."

"J. Edgar Hoover would roll over. I can't believe it. I told those guys to go in low key and deal with it but it looks like we've got some overzealous John Wayne types." The phone went silent for a moment. When Covington spoke again, his voice was more modulated. "Ben, there's more to this. Listen, when we searched the prison, we were able to intercept Howell's telephone calls. He called his mother and he called a very important person in Washington."

"Who is it?" Ben asked.

"I'm sorry, Ben, but we cannot reveal any names. After that debacle with Richard Jewel concerning the bombing in Atlanta, we are under specific restrictions not to identify a suspect until we have enough evidence. We feel sure that we have the kingfish in the conspiracy but we can't move on him. Not enough evidence yet but we are working on it. We've been intercepting calls from his home, his office and his car hoping to find out who else is involved and how the Chinese are tied in. Here's what we are getting. You are in extreme danger. They think you know who is involved. So take extreme precautions until we can get an agent down there to protect you."

"I don't want a . . ."

"No buts, Ben. Don't do anything until we can get you secured."

After the report from Covington, Ben begged off Stanton's attempts to get more information about the FBI's involvement. Concerned about Randy who knew as much as he did and was probably in as much danger as he was, he returned to his office to try to contact Randy. While he was phoning around trying to locate her, James saw Ben's vehicle in the parking lot at the Rice Building and dropped in.

James came to Ben's door and Ben waved him off until he could see if there would be an answer on the telephone. Giving up, Ben motioned for James to come in.

"Thought you would be worn out like Randy," Ben commented.

"No, as lead counsel she's worked twice as hard as I have. Look, Skittle said the FBI was here," James stated.

"Good Lord, is there anyone in this town who does not know about that?" Ben responded with some disgust and anger in his voice. He stood up and started pacing.

"Yo, hold back, bro. No need to get so upset."

"Sorry, Jim, but this thing is getting out of hand." He fumbled in his pocket for a cigar and took one out.

While he fumbled for some matches in his coat pocket, James looked on the desk to help him locate a light. "What did the FBI want?" James asked.

Ben sat and looked directly at James. He laid the cigar in the ashtray and leaned forward in the chair. "Jim, we've been friends for a long time. I trust you and you trust me. right?"

"Yes, certainly."

"Trust me when I tell you I can't tell you what it was about. The contact with the FBI had nothing to do with any wrongdoing on my part. It . . . "

"I know that. I heard it was the assassination."

Ben did not respond directly to James' speculation. "I will tell you as soon as I can. Really. It's a dangerous situation and it's for your own safety. I . . . I just can't."

James looked disappointed. "I'm sorry," Ben apologized. "I just can't."

James did not pursue the point further but opened his briefcase and pulled out a manila envelope containing some records. "I struck pay dirt on Ralph's mother. It was easier than I thought. The check for a half million dollars to her was from American Corporation. I was able to pull American off the Internet and I found it was a subsidiary of a large conglomerate. Shang Chou International. Shang Chou is a Chinese firm trading on medical technology and equipment. American is the facilitator for the U.S. end of the operation."

"Where is Shang Chou International headquartered?" Ben inquired.

James checked the record and replied, "Tientsin, China."

"Bingo." Ben said remembering that the FBI's investigation had been centered in Tientsin.

"Here is the juicy part though," James added. "American is part of a blind trust. I was able to penetrate the corporate veil and found that the major shareholder is, and get this, United States Senator A. Fowler Worrell, your friend from the telephone call. The Chairman of the Board of Directors is Worrell's Chief of Staff Wrenn Davies." He laughed and continued, "So I would say it's not too blind."

Ben was silent. Finally he knew how it worked. He did not know what it was about or what the motivating factor was but he knew that Senator Worrell and his Chief of Staff Davies were key players in the assassination. Most importantly he knew that Davies and Worrell, in that order, were the next links in the chain of the conspiracy.

"Well," James asked, "what do you think?"

Ben tried to play down the importance of the information so that he would not have to involve James. It was dangerous enough, he thought, with Randy at jeopardy and out of pocket at the moment.

He was not going to add James to the possible victims of the conspiracy, a list that was growing by the hour.

Ben tried to appear to be more interested in finding another telephone number for Randy on his rolodex. "That's good, Jim. Hopefully we can tie it all together."

"That's good. That's it?" James asked somewhat nonplused at the restrained response.

"Right. Now do you know where Randy is?" Ben spun his rolodex indicating his frustration at not being able to locate Randy.

James was a little chagrined at Ben's subdued response to the information. He felt the information tied Ralph, his mother and Senator Worrell together in some way, at least enough, to explore further. He was a little put out with Ben's lack of enthusiasm.

"No, I don't know where she is," he said in a curt way as he put the records back in the folder. "She was tired yesterday. Probably sleeping in and won't answer her phone. Anything else you need from me?"

"No," Ben said nonchalantly. "We'll talk tomorrow evening about court on Monday. Randy is desperately searching for a way to go forward with the defense but it looks pretty dim at this point."

"All right. Tomorrow then." James was not very talkative. He put his files back in his briefcase and left.

When James left, Ben called Detective Gerald Stanton at the Sheriff's Department. When the Sheriff's dispatcher got Stanton on the line, Ben said, "Sorry to bother you Gerald but I need your help with one more thing. I was hoping you might be able to go through your law enforcement contacts to get some information. Do you know how I can get in touch with a man by the name of Wrenn Davies? He is the Chief of Staff to South Carolina Senator A. Fowler Worrell in Washington."

*   *   *

The moonlight stretched out across the Cape Fear River as Ben drove across the bridge from Wilmington toward the Evergreen Care nursing facility. It was Saturday night and Ben had been delayed in his regular visit with Margaret. He had looked feverishly for Randy much of the evening without any success. Except for an occasional wave from a tugboat that was working its way up river, the river was calm and reflected the lights of the City. A light fog rolled slowly along the river's edge and began to rise up to the bridge.

Ben always enjoyed the view from the heights of the bridge, one of the highest points along the coast of North Carolina. Built to serve one of the main arteries into Wilmington and to allow the huge ships to pass under it, it was a marvel when it was built and remained as one of the grand monuments of Wilmington.

Ben turned off the main road after he left the bridge and was soon at Evergreen Care. He parked near the entrance since few people were there to visit at the late hour. No one was at the desk by the entrance nor at the nursing station. Ben, disappointed that he was not able to speak to one of the nurses to get an update on Margaret, strolled back to Margaret's room. Her door was closed and he pushed it lightly so as not to make any noise.

As he gently pushed the door further, he was able to see Margaret as she lay sleeping on the hospital bed. Opening it wide enough to slip in, he was surprised to see an orderly by her bed. The orderly turned to Ben and smiled as if he knew Ben.

"How is she doing?" Ben said quietly. Feeling that things were not quite as they should be, he studied the orderly carefully. There was something about him that Ben could not quite put his finger on.

"No need whisper, Mr. Down," he said in broken English and held up a syringe.

Ben was alarmed at what he was seeing and moved to get a better view of the orderly. "I know you," Ben blurted out. Ben was immediately suspicious and finally recognized the orderly. "You're the jogger I saw at Bird Island. What're you doing here?"

The orderly laid the syringe on the table by the bed and turned directly toward Ben. Ben noticed he was Chinese and small of stature. The man continued to smile as if nothing was wrong. "I know you too, Mr. Ben Down. You a man who knows too much."

Realizing that both Margaret and he were in great danger, Ben started to charge him but as soon as Ben took a step toward him, he wheeled around and held up a small black transmitter.

"I have a bomb," he stated coldly.

Ben stopped almost as soon as he had lurched forward. He was face to face with the small device. It was black with a red blinking light indicating, he thought, that it was activated. A silver metallic antenna extended approximately seven inches from the top of the metallic case. Ben's eyes focused on a bright orange trigger which was in the firm grip of the man. Ben's palms started to sweat as he began to fully realize the terror of the situation. If it were a bomb, he thought, he was most likely looking directly at the detonator.

"Let me introduce myself, Mr. Down." The man spoke but Ben's eyes remained planted on the orange trigger. "My name is Chen Sheng. I represent some important people. My job is fix problems and you become quite a problem."

Chen noticed that Ben never looked at him directly but stayed transfixed on the transmitter. "If you wondering if it's real, Mr. Down, I assure you, quite real. And it is quite effective. This same type bomb kill your Vice President of United States."

Ben shuddered at the thought: the man standing in front of him was Littlefoot, the assassin. He had been the target of one of the most powerful investigative organizations in the world and had evaded them. He had stalked and killed at will. No one had been able to stop him. Sweat formed in little beads on Ben's temples and began to join into a slight trickle. Ben could feel his hands tremble.

Chen enjoyed the perceived weakness and said, "Would you like to see rest of it?"

Ben did not speak but continued to watch Chen's hand. Holding the transmitter between himself and Ben, Chen bent slightly and pulled back the sheet on Margaret's bed. Beneath the bed a large liquid container was attached to a black box. Both were taped to the steel tubing of the bed. Ben was horrified at the bomb. It looked crude but he remembered the massive destruction he had seen at the house on Figure Eight Island where the Vice President was killed.

He mustered enough courage to speak and said, "She has nothing to do with this. Leave her out of it. I'll do anything you ask."

Chen laughed eerily as he let the sheet drop. He stared at Ben with eyes like tombstones. "She everything to do with it. And yes, you will do anything I ask you." Chen playfully flicked at the trigger with his finger. "Anything, Mr. Down."

"What do you want?" Ben stammered.

"Some entertainment." Chen's reply was almost nonchalant as he reached in his pocket and pulled out a 9 mm Glock semiautomatic pistol. As he pointed the gun toward Ben, he lowered the hand with the transmitter down by his side. "Let's go for a ride."

Chen motioned with the gun toward the door. He said, "Walk out. Don't do anything stupid. We're going to the parking lot."

Ben refused to move and Chen immediately became angry. "I told you. Nothing stupid. Come with me and I will let your wife live. She know nothing. But you." He laughed again to try to conceal his anger. "I have plan for you."

Ben looked back at Margaret and thought about his options: charge Chen and possibly blow all of them up or obey and buy some time, but to do what? He slowly walked to the door. When he stepped out of the room, he looked back to see Margaret. Chen bumped him with the gun to continue. Concealing the gun and the transmitter in his green scrubs, Chen followed and motioned for Ben to go to a gray Honda Accord in the parking lot.

Chen directed, "Reach into the rear seat and get the flak jacket. Put it on."

Ben did as directed. He reached in and strained to lift the jacket out of the rear seat. It weighed fifty pounds or more and Ben needed both hands to pull it out. He struggled with it but was finally able to remove it from the car.

"Put it on."

Ben strained again to lift the jacket. Too afraid to resist and run the risk of Chen exploding the bomb under Margaret's bed, he tried to comply. He failed in his first effort. On the second try he slipped it rather sloppily over his shoulders and hoisted it in place.

Chen indicated to him to secure the front of it with a lock in the right front pocket. Ben did as instructed and located the lock. He locked himself in the weighted jacket then waited to see what was next. Chen motioned for Ben to go back around to the driver's side of Chen's car. Ben labored under the weight of the jacket and trudged in the direction Chen indicated. When Ben arrived at the driver's door, Chen barked an order. "Now, go for ride. You drive."

As they exited the parking lot, Chen began to give instructions. Ben drove the short distance and turned onto the road to Wilmington. As they approached the bridge through the fog, there was no traffic at the late hour. Chen turned toward Ben and holding the gun in his right hand and the transmitter in his left hand, he said, "Now, Mr. Down, you want your wife Margaret to live. She can if you do as told. You have two choices. When we reach top of bridge, exit immediately. Step up on railing and jump. If fall doesn't kill you, you will drown. Either way you will probably die. Who knows? Maybe you live. This way you have chance. If you die, it will be suicide and right now, I need a suicide. What's one more depressed dead lawyer anyway?" He grinned at his joke.

"This is madness," Ben cried out.

Chen was high with the excitement. The sheer terror and the power combined to titillate Chen. He actually shivered with the thrill. "No, it is only choice you have if you want Margaret to live."

Ben's voice cracked as he asked, "What's the second choice?"

Chen laughed. "I will shoot you and throw you over bridge. It's messier but you definitely die that way."

"And if I don't do it?"

Chen held up the transmitter and barked emphatically, "Margaret dies and then you die."

Ben drove to the center of the bridge and at its pinnacle, Chen put the gun into Ben's face and commanded, "Now, Mr. Down. Live or die. You decide."

Ben stopped the car and pulled himself out of the car. His body visibly shook with fear as he attempted to climb the railing. He looked at the swirling water far below the bridge. The cool night breeze rising up from the river chilled his face and the noise of a distant ship's horn startled him. He was frozen in fear as he attempted to balance on the rail. He wobbled as he looked back at Chen who was so charged with energy he seemed to bound into the driver's seat.

"Now, " Chen screamed. "Now."

Ben turned and leaned forward. He closed his eyes and thought of Margaret sleeping. As he turned loose of his grip on the railing, a car appeared out of the fog and raced toward them. The car instead of slowing continued at speed. Chen's attention was diverted to the car and as he turned to see it, the car plunged into the rear of the Accord knocking it forward.

At the same moment Ben lost his balance and fell from the railing toward the river. Ben caught with one hand and fought to hold on. He clung to the railing and finally managed to grab the railing with his free hand. Slowly he pulled himself up and flopped over the railing onto the pavement. Regaining his feet he lumbered toward

Chen's car. When he reached the driver's side, Chen appeared to be unconscious. Ben searched frantically with his eyes to locate the transmitter. Quickly scanning the front seat and floor board, he could not find it. He opened the door and leaned in over Chen. The flashing red light of the transmitter caught his attention as it lay partially hidden under Chen's pant leg. Ben reached for the transmitter and as he did, Chen grabbed his wrist. They struggled for the transmitter and finally Ben pushed it away from them into the floorboard.

When Chen lunged for the transmitter, Ben wrapped his arms around Chen and using the weight of the jacket, leaned backwards to pull Chen from the driver's seat. Neither had the transmitter when Chen fell out of the car on top of Ben. Chen slammed Ben in the face with his fist and Ben retaliated by holding Chen by the collar of his scrubs. Ben pummeled Chen with a right to the side of his face and Chen seemed to lose strength momentarily.

Taking advantage of Chen's hesitation, Ben pulled him down and started to get up. As he did, Chen tried to punch Ben and missed. Ben brought a right down squarely on Chen's face and Chen fell back on the pavement. He was unconscious and did not move. Ben turned toward the car once again to search for the transmitter. He walked a few steps. With Chen down, the surge of fear began to subside and combined with the weight of the jacket, Ben stumbled and fell. Almost unconscious himself, he sat in a daze.

As he sat there trying to regain his strength, Chen roused and sat up behind Ben. Ben did not see him and Chen slid his hand furtively into his boot. He produced a pointed dagger. As he stood and stumbled toward Ben, he lifted the knife and put himself in position to cut Ben's throat from behind.

He reached for the back of Ben's head. At that moment an arm with a large tire iron connected with the back of Chen's head and he fell in a thud on the pavement. Ben heard the commotion and looked around to see what had happened.

"Jim," he said breathlessly and managed a weak smile, "I had him."

James, who was still dazed from the car crash, dropped down and sat beside of Ben. "Sure you did. One more punch and he would've been out."

Ben reached out and punched James weakly on the arm. He smiled wearily and asked, "How did you know?"

James laid the tire iron down and leaned back against the Accord. "Huh, I been following you all night. When I gave you that information about American Corporation and Senator Worrell, I knew something was up. I've been studying that poker face of yours for the last year and believe me, you can't fool me. I know when you are holding a full house. I knew you had it all figured out. And when you wouldn't tell me, I knew it had to be dangerous. Too dangerous to go it by yourself."

As they sat there, traffic began to come up to them on the bridge. In five minutes there was a traffic jam and in ten minutes a New Hanover Deputy Sheriff and a State Highway Patrolman were on the scene. As the deputy took Chen into custody and called for an ambulance for all three of them, the patrolman directed traffic which had locked up in both directions. Several ambulances arrived and with the swirl of red and blue lights from the emergency vehicles, the scene was congested and almost chaotic.

In thirty minutes FBI Agent Steven Teague maneuvered through the snarl of traffic and arrived on the scene. He trotted directly to Ben who was in the back of the patrol car with James.

"Hey," Teague said to Ben, "I'm supposed to be protecting you."

Ben pointed at Chen who was being loaded into the ambulance. "Well, get busy. He's all yours."

CHAPTER TWENTY-EIGHT

Chen Sheng lay in the New Hanover Regional Medical Center under the protective custody of the FBI. Having sustained a serious injury to the head, he also was under the watchful supervision of the medical personnel. Officers waiting for him to regain consciousness guarded him both inside and outside his room.

Slowly, quietly Chen slid his hand under the sheet and removed the IV that was taped to the back of his hand. He held the end with the needle in one hand while he pulled the other end of the tube until it separated from the fluid bag on the IV tree. As easily as he had surreptitiously crawled across the yard of the Feinstein house on the night of the assassination, he imperceptibly snaked the tube under the sheet, millimeter by millimeter.

He thumped the interior of his arm at the elbow to bring an artery to the surface. Without blinking or wincing or moving, he placed the sharp point of the needle against his skin until it slid across the bump created by the aroused artery. The needle separated the outer layer of skin then tore through the artery wall and lining until it was embedded into the flow of blood.

Chen allowed a sliver of light to penetrate into his eyes until they had adjusted to the fluorescent glare in the room. Moving his eyes as slowly as he had obtained the tubing, he spotted the FBI agent in the chair beside of the bed. As his eyes acclimatized to the distance, he was able to make out another guard just outside the door to the room. And finally he pinpointed the shape of a nurse at the end of the bed writing on the chart.

When the nurse completed her entries, she turned and walked toward the door. As the agent's eyes followed her as she exited, Chen brought the end of the tube to his mouth and sucked quietly. As his heart pushed and his lungs pulled, he brought the scarlet fluid to his lips. The taste of his blood assured him that the siphon was functioning as he had planned.

Again with the stealth of a snake on a silent hunt, he slid the hose down his chest and to the side of his body until it uncoiled and slithered down the far side of the bed from the agent. He listened for the telltale sign of the drops of his blood tapping against the tiled floor. He strained to hear over the electronic drone of the heart monitor and the noise from the hall. Nothing.

He held his breath to force his heart to beat harder. Through the slit in his eyes, he watched the flicker of the pulse rate monitor. It began to reflect more quickly off the porcelain in the bed pan sitting on the adjustable table. His heart rate quickened and the arteries raced with plasma. As he slowly released his breath, he focused every sense toward the end of the tube for the tapping, lapping of his life blood against the floor. Hearing nothing, feeling nothing, smelling nothing, he turned ever so slightly to see. He almost lost control of his face as he tried to conceal the smile upon seeing the stream of blood running in a rivulet toward the back wall and beneath the curtain. He watched until it formed a puddle.

Underneath the fasade of lost consciousness, the killer was ebullient. Always efficient, always clandestine, and always masterful, he was achieving his final victory proving once again that he was more adept, more powerful and more capable than his opponents. He was even disappointed that it was so painless, so unremarkable. He lay back in his last moments of glory and breathed deeply enjoying the last surge of power as his mind and body overcame the enemy. He drifted into a dream of his homeland. Mother China beckoned him to come, run and splash through the fields of rice and swim with the other children in the Yellow River. He dove from the junk deep into the muddy water. By the time the alarm went off and the nurses and guards had raced to his bedside, he never heard it. He had slipped away. The killer had become victor. He had killed the killer.

In another part of the hospital, Ben, unaware that his nemesis had made his final exit, waited impatiently along with James for the x-rays to return. Ben had been treated and released under the watchful eye of Agent Teague but James had significant abrasions and chest pains that required a closer examination.

As they waited, they watched through the doorway as several nurses and interns raced to an emergency down the hall. Thirty minutes later the same personnel walked slowly back down the hallway. They had a look of disappointment and Ben assumed that whatever the emergency was, they had not been successful. Over the next hour several law enforcement officers and FBI agents arrived and passed by the door traveling in the same direction. Ben caught a glimpse of Bays Covington as he was escorted down the hall in the presence of several FBI agents.

Ben tried to get up from his chair but found the effort too great. He was stiff and sore. Teague offered to help but Ben waved him off and sat back down. After a short while, Covington appeared in the door and told Teague to wait for him in the hall. When Teague stepped out, Covington came in and had a seat beside of Ben. He had a look of dejection as he studied Ben and James.

"How are you two doing?" he asked.

Ben replied first, "I'm all right. Bruised and battered but I've been released. I'm waiting to see how James is."

James said, "I slammed the steering wheel pretty hard when I crashed into Chen but I'm okay. They are going to keep me under observation for awhile."

"Good," Covington stated. "Glad you fellows are all right."

"I've been trying to find Randy and I can't find her anywhere," Ben said. "Can you get somebody out to locate her?"

"We've been trying to find her since I talked to you. She's in as much danger as you are and we tried to get to her. We can't find her but we are still looking."

"God, hopefully Randy is all right," Ben said. "It's not like her to be out of pocket like this."

"We'll do our best." Covington bit his lip as though he had an unpleasant task before him. " We've got some bad news down the hall though. The man that tried to kill you . . . is dead."

Ben was astonished at the news. "He wasn't hurt that bad. What's going on?"

"Suicide. We've known of this guy for some time. Chen Sheng. He's a Chinese national. Pretty well connected with the Chinese political hierarchy. CIA knew him as a covert operative in the People's Liberation Army several years ago then the file died. No one knows why. We had picked him up through Interpol with corporate espionage in the field of medical technology. He always hovered in the background and no case was made. Teague filled me in on your debriefing. Ben, our best assessment is that you're right. He's Littlefoot. The bomb generally fits the description of the one that killed Vice President Anderson. By the way how is your wife?"

"Margaret is fine. A little groggy when I talked to her. She didn't even know anything was going on. And she didn't even wake up when the bomb squad was there to remove the bomb," Ben replied.

"It's just as well," Bays said. "Chen Sheng was a desperate evil man."

"I'm sure he was connected to Skids' murder," Ben added. "Skids had contacted me to tell me about Ralph Stickley's involvement with the assassination. He was afraid to contact me directly so he had me to go to Bird Island to get his location."

"Yeah, Ben. I was told that you had mentioned seeing Chen Sheng there. It seems logical that he followed you, got the same information you did and then located Skids and killed him. We will follow up on it."

Ben tried to stretch a little as he sat in the seat. Although his arms and legs were stiff, he was able to extend them with some difficulty. Covington noticed the effort and asked, "You sure you are all right?"

"No problem." Ben extended his arms fully out in front of him and brought his legs under him. He stood slowly with Covington's help. "Look. Where does the investigation go from here?" Ben asked. "You have Ralph Stickley and you have Chen Sheng. Gedney is dead. Where to?"

Covington's face darkened and he said, "We have one more source. A powerful figure in Washington is part of and maybe the leader in the conspiracy. We had planned to use Chen to work our way up the ladder to the leadership. That's gone. And now our suspect in Washington has clammed up. We are getting nothing by visual surveillance or telephonic interception at this point. We are dead in the water until we can break the few leads we have."

"Wanda Stickley sits in front of a jury of twelve people on Monday morning. In a little over twenty four hours. You know and I know she did not kill Ralph Stickley. Very likely this Chen Sheng or some other member of the conspiracy killed Ralph. Where does this leave her?" Ben demanded.

Bays shook his head. "We'd like to help, Ben, but we can't. We can't go public yet with what we have. It will jeopardize the investigation."

Ben became angry and said, "That's not right. An innocent woman is about to be convicted of a murder she did not commit and you can't or won't help. That's not right, Bays."

"I'm sorry. Really."

"It's not right."

Both of them became quiet upon reaching an impasse. Ben sat down and Covington walked over to the door. "Two things, Ben. And I'm quite serious about this. All of you, Randy, James and you, are still at risk. Co-operate with the protection we are giving you until we can sort this out. And second thing. I'm going to have to ask that you keep a lid on what you know." Covington noticed that Ben was not looking at him and kept his eyes firmly on the floor. "Ben, don't do anything stupid and jeopardize this investigation."

Covington stared at Ben and Ben did not look up or speak. Covington looked over at James who had listened to the discussion and gave him a smile. "James," he said, "don't let him get himself killed. We don't know how many other Chen Shengs there are out there."

"He's a hard case when he gets his mind set on something," James responded.

Covington stepped out of the door and said as he left. "We'll keep working on Randy."

James continued to lay on the gurney as Ben tried to stand again. Stiff from the altercation, Ben had some difficulty with the effort although it was lessening with each attempt. Covington walked down the hall and Ben watched as he gave Teague instructions. Instructions no doubt, Ben thought, that would keep Teague covering him like the fog covers the low country. James pulled up slightly and leaned back on his elbows. He watched Ben limp as he paced back and forth.

"What's going on this time?" he asked.

Ben looked toward the door and put his finger to his lips. He stepped over to James' bed and replied in a whisper. "How are you doing?"

James groaned slightly. "I'm all right. Just sore but you know they're going to be careful. X-rays, physical examination, the whole nine yards. What are you so nervous about?"

"I've got to get out of here. We've got one more chance and time is critical. As soon as we find out how you are, I have got to give the FBI the slip."

"What are you talking about?"

"Wrenn Davies," Ben whispered. "I could tell from the way Bays was talking that the FBI doesn't know about him. They are working on the Senator, hoping that he will slip up and that could take forever."

"Don't do anything, Ben. Let the FBI handle it," James pleaded.

Ben watched the door for Teague to reenter as he continued the whispered conversation with James. "I let the FBI handle Gedney and look what happened. And it looks like the FBI handled Chen Sheng. Not a chance, Jim. I'm going after this one myself. Besides I've got some leverage: Davies probably doesn't know that Chen Sheng is in FBI custody and I would bet a double cheeseburger he doesn't know Chen Sheng is dead. Chen Sheng can serve a valuable purpose yet."

James sensed there was no use to argue with Ben and asked, "What do you want me to do?"

Ben checked over his shoulder again and seeing that Covington was still giving Teague the drill, he replied, "Two things. First, as soon as we get the doctor's report and if everything is all right, get Teague's attention so that I can slip out. Secondly, find Randy at all costs. If everything is all right, tell her we need to meet Sunday night at ten o'clock at the office."

James nodded in agreement to their own little conspiracy. "And one more thing," Ben said. "Thanks. Thanks for saving my life out there." Ben put his hand out and placed it on James' arm. James raised his hand to give Ben a high five. As Ben lifted his hand to do the same, both of them groaned audibly and gave up the effort. They laughed slightly and James said, "No problem. Glad to be of service."

Ben kept walking to try to work out the soreness. After a few minutes Teague, somewhat red-faced from the lecture, returned to the room and resumed his chair. They waited and finally the doctor came in and said James' x-rays revealed no broken bones, his blood pressure had remained normal and steady, and his chest showed no evidence of any abnormal swelling. The doctor was ordering that he be released to bed rest and Tylenol for discomfort. As soon as the doctor left the room, James winked at Ben and suddenly reached for his chest. He pretended to be strangling and strained to get out the word "help".

Teague who had had enough misfortune on his watch jumped immediately from his chair and went to James. As soon as Teague's back was turned, Ben gave James a thumb's up. He slipped out of the room, down the hall and out into the early morning darkness.

*   *   *

The US Airways jet turned on the final leg for the landing at Ronald Reagan National Airport. Skipping its tires along the tarmac and reversing its powerful jet engines, the plane slowed quickly and reached the taxi way in short order. At the airport, Ben arranged a rental vehicle and pulled out into the early Sunday morning traffic of Alexandria, Virginia.

Ben drove the short distance to the Potomac and skirted the Virginia side around the Pentagon. As he pulled along the four lane by Arlington National Cemetery, he thought of Vice President Anderson who had been buried there only months before. Ben thought that any hope for a resolution of the great mystery surrounding the Vice President's death and any chance at justice lay in his hands as he drove toward McLean, Virginia, an upscale affluent suburb of Washington, D.C.

When Ben reached Dolly Madison Boulevard, he started looking for the road that led into the residential areas of McLean. Finding his turnoff, he drove the rental into the development he was looking for and started watching the street names. At Manassas Court, Ben slowed to a crawl as he tried to locate house numbers. He stopped at 1407 Manassas Court, the address Detective Stanton had obtained for him.

The house was an expansive English Tudor with a beautifully landscaped front yard. When he rang the doorbell, no one answered. He rang again and heard footsteps.

The door opened and the man looked at him rather suspiciously. Ben asked, "Sir, I'm looking for Wrenn Davies."

"I'm Wrenn Davies. Who are you?"

"I am Ben Down, an attor . . . uh, a former attorney from North Carolina and I would like to speak to you."

Davies started to close the door without responding to the request. Ben interjected, "This is important. I want to talk to you about Gedney Howell, sir."

Davies continued to shut the door. Ben inserted his foot in the doorway and blocked the door momentarily. He looked directly into Davies's eyes. "Chen Sheng is in FBI custody."

Ben felt the pressure on the door release slightly. At the same moment a woman appeared behind Davies and asked, "Who is it, dear?"

"Uh, an attorney, Sarah. It's business, won't take but a few minutes."

Davies stepped out of the door and closed it behind him. He said, "Follow me."

He led Ben around the house into the back of the flower garden. Ben admired the well manicured lawn and the well cared for shrubbery. He was reminded of Margaret's hard work and passion for her lawn and garden.

At the back of the house, Davies looked around to make sure no one was within hearing distance. He said curtly, "What do you want, Mr. Down?"

"I want . . . ," Ben started to say. He looked at Davies and realized how far things had come. He felt as though he should be demanding, demanding the truth, plain and simple, but it was never so simple and never so plain. As with anything worth doing, it would take great care and effort. Ben restrained himself. "I want," he enunciated between gritted teeth, "the truth, Mr. Davies."

Davies stared at Ben as though he did not understand what he meant. The pause helped Ben to let some of the anger abate and some of the disgust diminish. He repeated, "The truth. I have a client, Wanda Stickley, who for the last year has been serving time in a stinking prison cell because of a lie. I think you can change all of that. I think you know the truth."

Davies continued to play dumb. "I have no idea what you are talking about, Mr. Down. Now if you will excuse me, I have important matters that I need to attend to this morning."

Davies started to walk Ben back toward the front of the house. Ben did not move. He said, "Nothing is more important than Chen Sheng."

Davies stopped cold in his tracks and turned around to face Ben. "What do you know about this person, Chen Sheng, Mr. Down?"

Ben was seething but concealed it very well. "Chen Sheng, sir, is a Chinese operative who is presently in the custody of the FBI. And you, sir, are in so much trouble it will take a courtroom full of lawyers to get you out."

Davies blinked. He was nervous but he had enough fortitude to continue the charade. "And what does any of this have to do with me?"

"The assassination," Ben replied as he watched Davies's eyes. They looked straight ahead without acknowledging Ben's accusation. "The assassination of Vice President William Keynard Anderson."

"So?"

"So," Ben continued, "at this point the FBI does not know about you."

Davies smiled slightly. When Ben said, "But they will soon.", Davies countenance turned dark and he firmed his jaw.

"How do you know so much, Mr. Down?" he tried to ask coolly.

"It's not how I know, Mr. Davies, but what I know."

"And what might that be?"

"Ralph Stickley was one of the assassins who killed the Vice President. Chen Sheng was the other. Ralph Stickley's mother knew about it and she was murdered to silence her. Ralph's fellow inmate Skids knew too much and was murdered to keep him quiet. Gedney Howell was instrumental in getting Ralph Stickley released from prison so that he could help perpetrate the assassination. But you know the most important thing I know, Mr. Davies?"

"No," Davies said as nonchalantly as he could with a throat that was locked tight.

"Ralph Stickley was not killed by Wanda Stickley."

"And who, pray tell, was the killer then, Mr. Down?"

Ben stared directly into the eyes of the devil. "Chen Sheng. And you know that, Mr. Davies. And if you had half the courage that you ought to have, you could tell the world that."

Davies attempted a laugh but it caught in his throat. "Now why in the world would anyone want to come forward and admit that they were involved in an assassination that would result in their own destruction?"

"Let me explain it to you if you don't understand it, Mr. Davies," Ben said. "First, the FBI knows about Senator Worrell. He is down for the count. The FBI is investigating him as hard as they can. They know he is the ring leader. The FBI also knows that Ralph Stickley and Chen Sheng are the assassins. Chen Sheng is in FBI custody after attempting to kill me last night on the Cape Fear River bridge in Wilmington. Who knows what he has told them?"

"I don't get your point, Mr. Down."

"Let me be as clear as I can be. You are going to die, Mr. Davies. Senator Worrell will be caught. He will try to save himself by implicating you. Who knows where Chen Sheng will lay the blame? Even if the FBI cannot nail you, and don't get me wrong, I'm sure they can, the Chinese will. You are up to your neck in a world of quicksand. The Chinese will have you murdered to protect themselves. Maybe not today, maybe not tomorrow, but soon. You know they will."

For the first time Davies stared at the ground bumping his foot against a stubborn weed. He was considering the options and the options offered death at every turn. He sought refuge in some way. He asked, "But you are suggesting that there is some way out?"

"There is," Ben replied smugly.

"What is that?"

Ben handed him a piece of paper. Davies looked at it and began reading it. When he recognized what it was, he said, "A subpoena?"

"Exactly. Respond to this subpoena. That is your only hope. Your only hope of salvation."

"How so?"

"Come to North Carolina tomorrow morning and tell the truth in the case of the State of North Carolina versus Wanda Stickley. At this point the FBI does not even know who you are. At this point the Chinese are probably just becoming aware that Chen Sheng is in custody. Come forward and put your statement on the record under oath in a public courtroom."

"I don't understand," Davies said.

"If you have put your statement on the record in a public forum, the FBI will want you to testify against Worrell. You will have come forward when you are not under investigation and your credibility will be high. That's the only way the government will not seek to have you executed. If you are the government's witness that solves the assassination, you will be helped. Now the Chinese have no reason to kill you if you have already told what you know in a way that the world will know. There will be no need to silence you. You have already made your statement."

Ben waited awhile to let it soak in. He knew that the conspirators had reached the end of the conspiracy but he was not so sure if Davies had reached the same conclusion. "What do you say?" he asked.

Davies looked at him and smiled. There was no warmth in the smile. Ben tried to read the enigmatic smile but he could not. Davies walked away leaving him in the back yard.

*   *   *

Ben was bone tired as he dragged himself into his office late Sunday night. He checked his watch and saw that it was 9:30 p.m. He had caught a taxi directly from the airport to his office and had not given much thought to the time. He knew that he had an important meeting with James and Randy, if Randy was all right, he thought. As he had gotten out of the taxi, he picked up a liquor bottle that some litterer had dropped on the sidewalk in front of the office in the Rice Building.

He flopped into his chair in his office, laid the bottle on the desk and laid his head in his hands as they propped on the desk. He wondered how long he had been awake. So long, he thought, that he could not count the hours. He had gotten some sleep at the airport while he waited for his flight but it was not enough. As the warmth of the office and the comfort of his old chair conspired against him, he slipped into a deep sleep.

It seemed as though he had been asleep less than a minute when he received a tug from someone. He resisted the effort to awaken and shrugged off the intruder to his well deserved sleep. He felt another push and this time he decided to awaken long enough to give the person a piece of his mind. "What in the world do you think you are doing?" he said.

"Trying to 'rouse another drunk," Randy stated.

Ben recognizing the voice said, 'Randy. . . Randy, it's you."

"And who else were you expecting at this ungodly hour?"

Ben slowly opened his eyes and began to make out the silhouette of Randy standing over him at the desk. She reached out and took the liquor bottle from the desk. She threw it into the trash can with such force that the sound made Ben's head hurt. He reached for his head and found that his arms were still stiff from the confrontation with Chen Sheng. He bumped himself in the eye with his thumb.

"Owww," he complained as he tried to find his eye again with his hand. "What in the love of god is all this? Owww."

"This," Randy replied betraying her irritation at Ben's supposed drunkenness, "is the way the homeless drunk stumble bum wakes up to breakfast every morning."

Ben rubbed his eyes and finally began to reach a semblance of cognition. He was awake but barely. At the same time he began to recognize that the intruder was Randy and that she was all right, he picked up on her anger at his lack of sobriety. He laughed and immediately held his head from the headache.

"You think I'm drinking. That's funny, Randy."

She gave him a deadpan look. "There's nothing funny about it. You told us you had quit. You promised."

Ben reached over in the trash can and took out the bottle. "Look," he said pointing at the label. "This is not Jack. This is some rot gut whiskey. I'm not drinking anything. I found this on the sidewalk on the way into the office. I'm just sleepy."

Seeing that Ben was waking up and that he was certainly not inebriated, Randy realized her error and apologized. "Ben, I'm so sorry. I just saw the bottle and you, and I put two and two together and came up with about ten. Sorry."

Ben was so happy to see that Randy was all right, he said, "Don't worry about it. It's okay. No harm, no foul." At the same moment he became a little incensed that she had not been where he could find her as he had searched over the weekend. "Where in the world have you been? I've been looking. Jim has been looking. My God, even the FBI has been trying to find you."

Randy grinned. "A girl has to have a little time to herself. Really, Ben. I was worn out. I needed some rest so I took a place down at Carolina Beach for the weekend. Sorry I caused so much trouble. Looks like I missed a lot. Jim told me what happened. How are you doing?"

Ben tried to stretch out a sleepy arm and said, "I'm all right. Just sore, I guess."

"I want to hear the play by play of the battle with Chen Sheng up on the bridge. Jim said it was unbelievable."

Ben had already been through it in some detail with the FBI briefing and said, "Later. We've got a lot of ground to cover." Randy looked disappointed. "I promise. Every detail, later." Ben was anxious to change the subject and asked, "What's going on with you?"

"Bayready called the office. Wants to settle BB1. What do you think?"

"His appellate attorneys have looked at the case and they are telling him its appeal proof. What's he offering?"

"Half."

"Hold out. He'll pay a lot more."

"I have my own FBI agent," Randy said as she looked out Ben's door toward the parking lot. "He's just outside the door. They say we are in a lot of trouble. By the way they are furious with you. They want to know where you've been."

Ben grinned sheepishly. "I've been doing their job for them."

They heard the front door open and in a moment James came in. He moved relatively well considering he was wearing an upper body brace. He asked, "How did everything go, Ben?"

"I don't know. Time will tell."

"What's going on?" Randy asked.

James sat down and the three of them leaned onto the desk. Ben answered, "All right. Here it is. Let me lay it out for you."

CHAPTER TWENTY-NINE

Ben sat in the back of the courtroom and waited as Wanda's trial was to resume. Randy came in from the side door followed by Wanda, James and the bailiff. In a few minutes Butch and Rod came in another door carrying files and a stack of law books. While everyone waited for the judge, Ben's attention dwelt on a reporter seated on the front bench. He was a young man, a rookie, Ben thought, assigned to cover the trial while all of the other senior reporters and media journalists were out covering the bigger story at the bridge, at the hospital and at the local FBI headquarters. Ben smiled to himself as he thought the rookie was about to get the biggest scoop of his life, that is, if everything went according to the plan.

Randy turned around in her chair and looked directly toward Ben asking a question with her eyes. Ben looked around the courtroom at the smattering of people who had collected there then threw his hands up slightly, indicating the answer was "no". She gave him a look of disappointment, turned and started going over her notes for her final argument.

Another bailiff came in the courtroom from the judge's chambers followed by Judge Thorogood. Everyone stood on cue for the opening of court then returned to their seats.

"Good morning," Judge Thorogood announced, "I hope everyone is doing well this morning and we are ready to proceed."

Both the District Attorney and Randy indicated they were ready. Judge Thorogood called for the jurors and as soon as they were located in the jury box, the judge said, "All right, ladies and gentlemen, at this time I recognize counsel for the defendant for a presentation of the defendant's evidence."

Randy turned and looked at Ben again. He shook his head "no" joining her in the disappointment. As Randy turned to tell the judge that the defendant rested the case and that the defendant was ready to proceed with final arguments, a man walked into the back of the courtroom and stood for a moment as he tried to locate a seat or someone.

Ben stood immediately and walked to the rail. He leaned over and pulled at Randy's suit jacket.

"Mr. Down," the Judge said, "What's the meaning of this?"

"Sorry, Your Honor, but there is an important development in the case and I had to let Miss Bost be made aware of it."

Judge Thorogood ordered, "Have a seat. We are trying to have a trial here. Be seated. Let's proceed Miss Bost."

Ben looked at Randy and nodded his head. Ben responded to the judge courteously, "Yes, sir, I'm sorry for the disturbance, Your Honor." He secretly winked at Wanda and returned to his seat.

Randy turned to the judge and announced, "The defendant calls Wrenn Davies, Your Honor."

Butch looked at Rod and Rod looked at Butch. They had no idea who the witness was. Butch stood, "Your Honor, we would like to interpose an objection. This is highly irregular. This witness is not on any of our witness lists."

Judge Thorogood sent the jurors out and conducted a brief hearing. Davies sat beside of Ben and watched the proceedings unfold. He sat stone still and remained expressionless. After a lot of wrangling in which the State took the position that the witness could not testify because of two things, one, he was not on the witness list, and two, the State was totally surprised by the tactic, Randy promised Judge Thorogood that the witness is "crucial, critical and imperative".

Thorogood smiled at the adjective heavy description. He turned his attention to Butch though and said, "I believe this case is full of surprises, Mr. Yeager. It seems one of the State's witnesses surprised all of us with a much improved memory." He referred to Dundail who remembered much more in the second trial than he had in the first trial. "What's good for the goose is good for the gander. Let's hear the witness. Call for the jury, Mr. Bailiff."

When the jurors were seated again, Randy called for Davies. Distinguished looking in a gray pinstriped suit, he walked casually to the witness stand and stood erect as he was administered the oath. Ben watched the rookie reporter writing in his notebook. Ben surmised he was trying to figure out the spelling of the witness's last name, a name that would be on every television station and in every newspaper in the nation before the week was out.

As Davies was seated, Randy turned and smiled at Ben. He nodded accepting her thanks and she turned to address the witness. "Sir, please state your name for us."

"Wrenn Davies," he answered in a modulated, even tone.

"Where do you live and what do you do for a living, sir?"

"I reside in McLean, Virginia and I am the Chief of Staff to the United States Senator from South Carolina, A. Fowler Worrell."

As he was answering, Bays Covington accompanied by four other FBI agents entered the courtroom quietly and walked down to the row of seats where Ben was located. Bays sat beside Ben and the other four agents took seats behind them. Ben looked at Bays and whispered, "How did you know we were here?"

"We were alerted when you filed the copy of the subpoena for Davies. We knew something was afoot," Bays whispered back.

Randy continued with the direct examination as Davies sat comfortably belying the emotional context out of which the testimony arose. "Do you know if the Senator knew the deceased in this case, Ralph Stickley?"

"I do," Davies responded and looked at Randy to see if he should continue. She nodded slightly and he said, "Senator Worrell met Ralph Stickley many years ago. At that time Senator Worrell was a legislator representing people from the Florence area in the South Carolina state legislature. Ralph Stickley was a businessman from this area who was opening a tobacco warehouse in Florence. The Senator went by there on opening day and eventually he and Stickley became relatively close political associates. Later they became business partners. They had a joint venture in which they were going to develop some land on Figure Eight Island. Stickley had grown up here and was very familiar with the Island. He knew of a large tract of land for sale there. The plan fizzled though when most of the land turned out to be swampland or wetlands as they are called. They never did get the development off the ground so to speak."

"What happened to their relationship?"

"Well, after the wetlands fiasco, other things started going south for Stickley and he lost his business in Florence. He dropped out of the political scene there in Florence and the relationship between Senator Worrell and Stickley became distant. I think Stickley may have contacted the Senator a time or two for some help when he was in trouble but otherwise there was no contact for a long period of time. Stickley went to prison here in North Carolina so that was pretty much the end of it at the time."

"What happened to change that?" Randy asked.

"Well, it's a long story but to make it as succinct as possible," Davies continued. He was slow and methodical as though he were recounting the history of the local civic club rather than a story of murder and international intrigue. "Let's see. As Stickley's fortunes decreased, Senator Worrell's increased. A vacancy occurred in the United States Senate and Worrell was able to obtain the appointment. He was then elected to the seat and developed a strong incumbency. On a trade mission to China, he met a Chinese business man named Wen Zheng Ming who was interested in securing technologically state of the art medicines and equipment for China. Worrell was able to assist with that plan in many ways, some legal, some not so legal. To protect Worrell's interest, American Corporation was created. It was placed in a blind trust so that ostensibly at least Worrell had no involvement. Profits, that is, Worrell's profits were diverted to American from Wen Zheng Ming's business, Shang Chou International."

Davies reached for the glass of water that was made available to witnesses as they testified. He took a rather large drink and continued with the explanation. "They soon learned that there was a fortune to be made in transplanting, that is, the harvesting and selling of human body parts to Americans. Shang Chou was very well connected to the government and to the medical community so it was able to provide a virtually unlimited supply of harvested parts, kidneys, hearts, livers and so forth, from Chinese prisoners."

Judge Thorogood who had kept a firm countenance during the testimony was astounded at what he was hearing and dropped his jaw. He turned in his seat to face Davies and joined everyone else in being mesmerized by the story that was being told. Ben watched the cub reporter whose head was buried in his note pad. He was trying to take everything down as though he were a court reporter and failing in that, he gave up and actually started to listen.

Davies again looked at Randy and she nodded for him to continue the testimony. "This," he said, "continued for many years and became extremely profitable. In fact the profits were beyond anyone's imagination. Unfortunately with the increase in knowledge and skill in transplant surgery and with so many Americans involved as recipients, the American public began to become aware of the trade. Some were angered that the transplanted organs came from prisoners. One of the first American politicians to give it lip service was Vice President William Keynard Anderson. He was at first rather moderate but as time went on, his position hardened and he became very vocal about human rights violations by the Chinese. Then to the horror of the Chinese and to Senator Worrell, he succeeded into a position of dominance that very likely would make him the next President of the United States."

Ben leaned forward in his seat to hear all of the testimony. Much of what he was hearing was as much news to him as it was to everyone else. Although he knew the schematic of the conspiracy and many of those involved, he did not know the motivation or the monetary basis for it.

"We knew," Davies continued, "that as soon as Anderson became President, this country would move into an unprecedented reversal of our Chinese policy. Diplomatic ties would be cut, Americans would be barred from travel to China. In other words the business which had become outrageously lucrative would be destroyed. It was decided that the only way out was to terminate the source of the trouble."

"And by terminate you mean what, sir?" Randy asked.

"To kill."

"To kill whom?"

"Anderson." When he spoke, the silence in the courtroom was so thick it could not have been interrupted with a bomb.

"And who made that decision?"

"Senator Worrell and Shang Chou President Wen Zheng Ming."

"What does any of this have to do with Ralph Stickley?" Randy asked bringing the testimony to the relevant point.

"Well," Davies said and reached for the cup of water. He held it in his hand balancing it carefully as he related the rest of the story. "The Senator received the report, a typical report that congressmen receive about the agenda of the President and Vice President, that Anderson was going on vacation just before the coming election. He was to vacation at Figure Eight Island here in North Carolina. The Senator was familiar with the island since he and Stickley had planned on going into business together there. The decision was made to obtain a hit man from China who would have the skills to surreptitiously enter the island and kill the Vice President. Although Worrell knew the island, he did not know it as well as Stickley who had hunted and fished there as a boy. So with a little work, we found Stickley imprisoned in North Carolina and with a little help from a friend of the Senator's, Gedney Howell, a superintendent at a prison in South Carolina, we were able to have Stickley transferred to a South Carolina prison. That way we could get him in and get him out of prison as needed."

"And what happened then?"

"Wen Zheng Ming sent us Chen Sheng. He was former army and trained for assassination. We brought in Stickley. He knew the island well and even knew the inside of the house where Anderson was staying."

"How much did Stickley get?"

"He was very expensive. Five hundred thousand dollars paid to his mother and a promise of early release. He and Chen planned it and carried it out. Unfortunately Stickley was much more of a loose cannon than we had thought. And so was his mother."

"What happened then?"

"His mother started blowing his money. New house, new cars. And Stickley went off the deep end. Also we found out that he had gone by his wife's house on the night of the assassination and had raped her."

Randy said, "And by his wife, you are referring to my client Wanda Stickley. Is that correct?"

"Yes. And even worse he had a horrible cocaine habit and when he got high, he was quite talkative. He was telling too much."

"What was done about his 'talkativeness' as you put it?"

"Again the decision was made by the same people to shut Ralph up. They tried to have him killed in prison but he escaped. Chen was sent to find him and kill him. Chen located him at his wife's house, uh, Wanda Stickley's house shortly after his escape from prison, and killed him in the driveway."

This was the truth, the truth that they had wanted from the very beginning. To hear it was such an event that Randy almost missed it. She asked, "I'm sorry. Repeat what you just said, please."

"I said that Chen killed Ralph Stickley."

"Chen killed Ralph Stickley?" Randy repeated to emphasize the point.

"Yes. Chen reported back to me that he had killed him by cutting his throat. He was confident that he had made it appear as though it were done by Stickley's wife, Wanda Stickley. He said that he had carved an R in his chest to mark him as a rat, that is, a person who tells something they should not. He, Chen, was quite amused that the authorities thought it stood for rapist. Since he hadn't planned that part, he thought it was quite gratuitous." Davies attempted a brief smile but it was not contagious. Everyone even Butch and Rod sat in stunned silence.

"This man, Chen Sheng," Randy asked, "was a cold-blooded killer, was he not?"

"Yes," Davies answered and finally took a drink of the water. Ben marveled at how steady his hand was as he talked of such ghoulish things. "Chen later killed Stickley's mother and made it appear as an auto accident, a hit and run accident. He also killed a man who was Stickley's cellmate in prison because he knew too much. When Gedney Howell became a liability, Chen murdered both him and his mother. He is a dangerous man but I understand he is in the custody of the FBI."

Covington looked over at Ben and smiled. "I wonder where he got that idea."

Ben grinned sheepishly and Randy asked the witness, "Are you afraid of him, Mr. Davies?"

"Extremely."

Randy stood and addressed the court. "Your Honor, if you will give me a moment?"

"Granted," Judge Thorogood announced.

Randy turned and stepped back to Ben. She spoke in a low tone of voice. "Ben, what do you think? Anything else?"

Ben smiled at her. He was joyous that the truth had finally surfaced. He looked over at Butch and saw that the color had drained from his face. He said, "No, Randy, I think you've done quite enough."

Randy turned back to the judge and announced, "That's all, Your Honor."

Judge Thorogood asked, "Questions, Mr. Yeager?"

It was time for Butch to scramble. He stood slowly while he was trying to think. When he reached his feet, he asked, "Your Honor, may we have a brief recess?"

"Granted," the judge said and sent the jurors out with the admonition not to discuss the case among themselves or with anyone else.

As soon as the bailiff announced the recess, the rookie reporter jumped to his feet and raced out of the back of the courtroom. He carried with him the biggest story of his career. Davies stood and calmly stepped down from the witness stand into the custody of two of the FBI agents who waited for him. As they walked Davies past Ben toward an interview room, Davies stared at Ben without emotion, without speaking. Bays Covington introduced himself to the DA and he and the two remaining agents followed Butch and Rod to the DA's office.

Ben stepped up to the huddle between Randy, James and Wanda. Randy said, "It went down just like you said, Ben, but I believe Davies soft-pedalled his part. What do you think?"

"Oh, yeah," Ben agreed, "one of the advantages for Davies in coming out of the cold early is to put this horror story in his own words. Yeah, he's heavy on Worrell and light on Davies for sure. It will sort out down the road. The main thing at the moment is how it will play in the DA's office."

They waited for fifteen minutes then received word that the DA would like a longer recess. An hour and a half went by while Covington and the other agents briefed Butch about their investigation and how it corroborated Wrenn Davies. It was a long, slow wait for the defense team. They retreated to the prisoner interview room. Randy called Bayready about settling BB1, James worked at his computer and Ben, although exhausted, could not sit down. He paced. And paced.

The bailiff appeared and notified them to return to the courtroom. They filed in and sat down. Ben studied Butch's face. It was just as white as it had been two hours before. The news had spread like wildfire. There were a half dozen reporters in the courtroom this time and people had filed in from the adjoining courthouse offices and the streets. Soon the judge appeared and the court was reconvened.

"All right," Thorogood announced. "Everybody ready?"

Butch stood and cleared his throat. He was still having a hard time digesting the bad news about his case. He stuttered, "Your . . . uh . . . Honor, . . . uh . . . after hearing the testimony we have just heard and . . . after reviewing this matter thoroughly with the representatives of the Federal Bureau of Investigation who are here, we . . . uh . . . I have decided to take a voluntary dismissal."

Judge Thorogood turned to the jurors and said, "You are dismissed." He turned to Wanda and said, "You are dismissed as well, Ms. Stickley. Adjourn court, Mr. Bailiff."

Everyone stood and Wanda turned toward Ben. She gave him a look of uncertainty as if she did not understand quite what it all meant.

He leaned over the rail and said, "It's over, Wanda. It's finally over. Let's go home."

CHAPTER THIRTY

Azaleas at full blossom lit Wilmington as though it were on fire. Seagulls raced up and down the Cape Fear River in search of the next fishing boat while the brown pelican solemnly guarded the waterfront. All of the brown and gray of the trees, shrubs and grass had turned to varying shades of green and the great old houses took on that hue of brilliant white that gave Wilmington its old Southern charm. Summer had arrived at last and with it, the streets were teeming with droves of tourists and summer college students.

The Rice Building was dressed in all of its glorious foliage and displayed its ancient heritage as the fiery azalea bordered the facade nearest the parking lot. Vines of ivy climbed the walls and intertwined with the magnolias that stood as sentinels to the old structure. Adding to the decor of the old Georgian style architecture was the iron ornamental post for displaying the names of the business concerns that were housed within. The post having served many generations of lawyers was being adorned once again as a part of the celebration of a new summer.

Ben hooked the last chain in place on the shingle and started down the ladder as Skittle and Wanda Stickley looked on. "There," he said as he admired the old English lettering on the sign, "'Ben Down, Attorney at Law. All seems right with the world again. Indictments dismissed, bar suspension lifted. Ah, yes, the lawyer in his lair."

Skittle remarked with a cutting tone, "The king in his castle is more like it."

Wanda laughed and Ben winced a little. He commented, "Skittle, you always did have a sharp tongue."

Before she could bring its rapier edge to bear on Ben's comment, James pulled into the driveway of the parking lot in such a hurry that all of them watched. He got out of his car, grabbed his briefcase and a newspaper, and walked hurriedly to where they were standing.

Admiring the shingle, he said, "Glad to see you got your license back, Ben. Always nice to know a celebrity."

Ben, who was puzzled by the comment, asked, "What do you mean, 'celebrity'?"

James held out the newspaper so that all of them could read it. In a banner headline, it read: Assassination Solved. And in smaller print beneath the headline were the words: Local Attorney Ben Down Instrumental.

James commented, "Youdaman!" and bumped fists with Ben in celebration of the moment. As Skittle shook her head in mocking disapproval, they walked back inside into the reception area. James asked Ben, "Is today the day?"

Ben said, "It is. Margaret will be released this afternoon. It will be wonderful to have her home again."

James nodded his head in agreement. He asked, "Is Randy here yet?"

"No, we're waiting for her now," Skittle replied. "Should be here any minute."

As they watched out of the window in the reception room, Ben walked back to his office to get a cigar from his coat pocket. When he reached across his desk to get his coat, he noticed an old rusty fish bucket partially covered in dirt and spiderwebs. He picked up the bucket and tried to pry off the top. After several attempts it yielded begrudgingly. When he peeped inside, he was amazed to see several rolls of hundred dollar bills.

He was so astonished, he spoke out loud to himself, "What in the . . . ?"

"Looks like a fee," Wanda said as she appeared in the doorway.

Ben jumped when she spoke. "What is this?"

Wanda smiled and said, "Well, you always said if I ever found Ralph's money, you would get your fee from that. I'm not saying I did and I'm not saying I didn't find it but I had a long time to think about it in prison. I knew that our cat Esmeralda was too skittish to go in that crawl space the night Ralph was there in the basement. She would only have done it if she had followed Ralph under there. So it didn't take an Einstein to figure out that Ralph wanted something from that crawl space."

"But . . . but . . . " Ben was still exasperated. "How much is it?"

"Fifty thousand dollars in that can and its all yours." She looked around. "At least I don't see anybody else claiming it. Besides you deserve it."

"What about Randy and James?" Ben stammered as he asked the question.

"There's more than one can," she replied and gave him a devious smile.

"Well, for the first time in my life, I don't know what to say?"

Wanda smiled mischievously again and said, "I do. Let's just say the cat drug it in."

Before Ben could respond further, Skittle, who had continued watching out of the window for Randy, called out, "They're here. Come on."

Wanda raced out of the door and Ben followed. Out in the parking lot, Randy was pulling her Jeep in beside of James' car. Seated next to her was Jeremy. When he saw Wanda, his face lit up. Beaming from ear to ear, he jumped from Randy's vehicle and ran toward his mother. As they embraced, tears streamed down Wanda's face. Wanda told him how much she had missed him and Jeremy started crying too.

Ben looked over at Skittle and she was getting teary eyed. He said, "Well, I'll be. You too, Skittle." She shook her head without speaking and wiped the tears.

After everyone had dried out a little, Ben said, "Well, Randy. What are you going to do with all of that BB1 money?"

"A vacation," she replied. "Rod and I are off to the Virgin Islands for a well deserved vacation. After that we'll see."

"When are you coming back? Business is piling up," Ben asked seriously.

"You mean if we come back, " she said with a devil-may-care look on her face.

Everyone laughed and Ben retorted, "Seriously, Randy, we are going to need you."

"Well, if you have to know. We will be gone for two weeks then you can find us out by the Cape Fear River. We've bought a little place that is special to both of us."

They started to go back inside when James called out, "What's that?"

They turned and looked off in the distance at a large object coming along the street toward them. As it got closer, Ben recognized it. "Why it's Thor?" he said.

Ben bent down as Thor came running to him. The big fur ball moving in ten directions at once started stopping about ten feet too late and plowed into Ben knocking him over. Thor started licking his face and thumping him with his paws as he tried to get back up.

Randy remarked, "Looks like another case for Ben Down."

Get

CONVICTED

. BY

CASH MARTIN

In CONVICTED, Ben Down is a lawyer whose world comes crumbling down around him. He must fight to save his client who has been charged with a murder she did not commit. Moreover, as he becomes entangled with the powerful forces who have assassinated the Vice President of the United States, he must wage a war of his own. He must confront the demons in his own life that threaten to destroy him. Finally his efforts to save his client become a battle to save himself.

Use this page to order

Send to

American Publishing
761 Blue Hollow Road
Mt. Airy, North Carolina 27030

Please send me the following copies of Convicted by Cash Martin at $19.95 per copy. Send check or money order, no cash or C.O.D's. Please add $3.95 for the first copy and $1.95 for each additional copy to cover postage and handling.

Number of copies _____
Amount enclosed   _____
Ms./Mr./Mrs. _____
Address   _____
              _____
City/State   _____Zip_____
Prices and availability subject to change without notice

Look for

Accused by Cash Martin

Fall, 2000